Readers love Kim

Good Bon

"I truly enjoyed every moment of reading it."

—Smitten with Reading

"…the story-telling aspects made the story come to life in a funny, tender way."

—Between the Covers

"…action and romance and a surprising amount of heart."

—Red Hot Books

"I can't really find anything negative to say about this one. It was romantic but not sappy and just an all around great read. I enjoyed every minute of it."

—Amethyst Daydreams

"The sex scenes are many, varied and hot, all the more so for the men's desperate need to connect with another person. You will not be left unsatisfied."

—A Rogue Librarian's Reading List

"…an impressive and enjoyable saga."

—Literary Nymphs Reviews

By KIM FIELDING

NOVELS
Brute
Good Bones

FEATURED IN THESE ANTHOLOGIES
Animal Magnetism
Don't Try This at Home
Men of Steel

NOVELLAS
Speechless

COMING IN 2013
Venetian Masks
Night Shift

Published by DREAMSPINNER PRESS
http://www.dreamspinnerpress.com

BRUTE
Kim Fielding

Dreamspinner Press

Published by
Dreamspinner Press
5032 Capital Circle SW
Ste 2, PMB# 279
Tallahassee, FL 32305-7886
USA
http://www.dreamspinnerpress.com/

Brute

Cover Art by Paul Richmond
http://www.paulrichmondstudio.com

ISBN: 978-1-62380-226-4

Printed in the United States of America
First Edition
December 2012

eBook edition available
eBook ISBN: 978-1-62380-227-1

 # CHAPTER
One

MUSIC was his companion.

Brute sang about a love lost at sea as he settled the stone slab more comfortably on his massive shoulders and began to trudge uphill on the narrow path. He sang quietly, because with his very deep voice and inability to carry a tune, he knew he sounded terrible and the other men would glare if he became too loud. Nobody was close enough to hear him if he kept his voice low, and the music made his burdens seem a little lighter, made the pathway a little less treacherous under his feet. He sang the bawdy songs that rumbled in the tavern under his room and the wistful ballads the women sang when they gathered around the well at dawn, and sometimes he even hummed the lullabies he half remembered someone crooning to him.

It had rained the night before, and although the sky was now clear, the ground was slick. So he set each foot carefully before taking the next step. His bare toes sank into the mud, giving him a little more traction. He'd once saved up enough money to have a pair of boots made—none of the shoemaker's ready-made goods were large enough—but even though they were well crafted, the boots didn't last long, and now he knew better than to waste his few coins.

"Hurry up!" came an impatient shout from the top of the ridge, but he ignored it. He had no wish to tumble off the path and onto the sharp rocks below. He kept on setting one foot in front of the other and singing about a storm and a shipwreck, until finally the slope leveled out. Then he grunted and let the stone slide to the ground, where it landed with a soft *squelch*.

Without even stopping to unkink his muscles, he turned to head down the path again for the next stone. But the foreman grabbed his arm. Darius was a lean man, his hard, weathered face set into a perpetual scowl. "You're slow today. The prince himself is arriving tomorrow to inspect our progress, and we better fucking well have some progress to show him."

"The path's slippery."

"I don't fucking care, and the prince won't fucking care either. Haul ass."

The harsh words were nothing unusual and didn't hurt. Didn't hasten him either. As much pressure as Darius was under to finish the bridge quickly, he could hardly afford to lose a worker. Especially someone who was capable of carrying twice the weight that any other man could bear and who managed the tricky narrow bits of the pathway better than horses or mules. Brute's immense size and strength were his job security, so long as his back held out.

Three more journeys down the hill, where the brothers Osred and Osric paused in their chiseling to heft another block of granite into the rudimentary back sling, and three more journeys back up, with the mud warm on his feet and a lullaby on his lips.

Just as he neared the crest of the hill, he heard a crash and a volley of swearing. "Don't fucking touch it!" Darius yelled at someone. "Wait for Brute."

Wait they did while he eased the stone off his back, two dozen men glaring at him as if he were somehow the cause of the current calamity. "Move this," Darius ordered, pointing.

One of the structural timbers—an enormous tree that had grown in the forests to the north before being felled, stripped, and arduously hauled—had fallen from a cart and rolled, so that nearly half of it was hanging off the cliff. If the timber were to fall into the river below, it would be swept away, an expensive loss.

"Don't stand there like an idiot, Brute. Move the damn thing."

"The horses could move it."

"I'm not going to waste time unharnessing them from the wagon and then hooking them back up again."

Brute eyed the log for a moment, debating whether he could move it by himself and considering the likelihood that he'd go tumbling off the cliff if he tried.

Darius stepped forward, his hands clenched into fists. "It's not that hard. Even *you* ought to be able to figure it out. You pick the fucking thing up and you move it back where it belongs."

Brute thought about refusing, but his confidence in job security went only so far. If Darius decided that he was too difficult, the foreman wouldn't waste any more time on him. He'd sack Brute and make sure none of the other foremen hired him. Brute had no skills beyond the simplest manual labor. Sometimes Darius called him an ox with hands. And without a job, well, Brute had enough coins saved to last him six weeks, perhaps two months if he ate very little. Once winter came, he'd either freeze or starve.

The other workers stood and stared, maybe hoping that Brute would create some kind of fuss. From the looks they gave him sometimes, he could tell they assumed that violence came as easily to him as to a bad-tempered bear. In truth, he hadn't raised a hand to anyone since he was a boy, but he supposed he looked frightening enough. And Darius wasn't popular—the men wouldn't mind seeing him pounded and Brute fired. Or maybe they just wanted a diverting break from their labors.

Whatever the other men wanted, Brute didn't give it to them. He nodded slightly at Darius and walked to the fallen timber. He looked at it for a few moments. He might possibly be able to drag it the few yards to the cart, but his arms—despite their length—wouldn't fit around the broad trunk. "You'll need to tie it to me," he said to nobody in particular.

Sensing a new form of entertainment, several men scrambled forward. With some difficulty, they managed to tie a thick rope around the log, then handed the end of the rope to Brute, who improvised a sort of harness for himself. He took a few deep breaths, bent his knees a little, and began to pull.

At first nothing happened, except for the rope digging painfully into his chest and shoulders. He worried a little that his shirt might rip. He wasn't certain it would survive another mending, and he owned only one other. Perhaps he should have taken it off before tying the rope around himself. Then it would have been his skin that tore, but that was nothing new. He'd heal. In any case, it was too late for that. He inhaled again, and as he exhaled he heaved with all his might.

The timber shifted a little. Unfortunately, it also began to roll and, slowly, more of the log shifted off the edge of the cliff. Only a few more feet and the entire timber would go over the edge, dragging him with it. He was apt to survive the fall less successfully than the log would. Panic began to nibble at the edges of his mind as he was tugged backward a few inches, his feet sliding in the mud as he fought desperately to retain his footing. "Help me!" he shouted, but nobody moved. They just watched his struggle, morbid interest sharp on their faces. If they'd had more time, they probably would have placed wagers on his success. He wondered what the odds would have been.

The rope hurt his chest and back. But it was less painful than crashing down the cliff and smashing into the jagged rocks, he reminded himself. He roared and lurched forward again, and this time the timber moved with him.

His audience responded, some men cheering and others hissing with disappointment. He ignored them, grunting as he set one foot in front of the other. His burden was a little easier now that momentum was in his favor, but it was still very heavy. His heart felt like a beast trying to escape the cage of his chest, and his lungs rasped painfully. Sweat dripped down his face, stinging the tiny cuts and scrapes he'd accumulated throughout the day. But he bent his body forward and continued to move.

He didn't even notice that his eyes were closed until he bumped into the cart. Only then did he allow his legs to give out, and he collapsed to the soft ground where he lay on his back, fighting for oxygen and enjoying the bliss of being free of his burden.

"Shift your lazy asses!" Darius growled. "Get the goddamn log back on the wagon."

Brute remained on his back as the other men untied the rope from the timber. It took the whole lot of them to lift it up. Someone trod on Brute's hand, but the soft ground saved him from too much injury. The log echoed loudly when it thudded back onto the others. Brute was still there when the horses led the cart away.

"Get up," Darius said, kicking lightly at Brute's leg.

As he slowly rose to his feet, Brute felt every inch of his seven and a half feet, every one of his three hundred pounds. Not for the first time, he wished he were an ordinary-sized man who was given ordinary-sized duties to perform. But he'd learned a very long time ago—before he even had the words to express the idea—that wishing was useless.

"Back to work," said Darius.

"I'm done for today."

Darius glanced up at the sky. "We've another hour of sunlight."

Brute shook his head. "I'm done."

"I'll dock you half a day's pay."

It wasn't fair; they both knew that. Brute had already accomplished more than any of the other men, and that wasn't even counting his rescue of the timber. But Darius was stubborn, and Brute knew that fairness was of no consequence to the foreman. So he shrugged, turned, and descended the path.

People stared as he plodded down the road to the village but, as usual, passersby didn't meet his eyes. He'd gone through a period a few years earlier when he tried smiling and greeting people, but nobody ever smiled back or bade him good day, so he gave it up. At least today no old people made warding signs as he walked by, and no children jeered or called him an ogre. But it was still a long walk, and his back itched as the accumulated mud dried and flaked.

The landlord of the White Dragon—a squat man named Cecil— was Darius's cousin, but then so was a good percentage of the village. Those who weren't directly related were generally indebted to the Gedding family in some way. Darius's father had been sheriff for years, and now the post was held by Darius's older brother. The priest at the small temple was another brother, and the local healer was his aunt. So if the landlord overcharged for room and board, there was little Brute could do about it. The other workers had families and lived in little huts near the edge of town—rented from the Geddings, of course—but Brute had a tiny room above the White Dragon with a too-small bed and mice in the walls.

There was a well in the courtyard behind the inn. Horses snorted softly in the stables as Brute peeled off his shirt and upended a bucket of water over his head. The little lean-to behind the tavern contained a battered metal tub, but it was a tight fit for Brute. Cecil charged him two coppers for each use, so Brute splurged only infrequently, usually in the depths of winter when he couldn't quite face another dunking in frigid well water. Today, though, the well water felt good. He used his shirt as a makeshift towel to wipe away the worst of the grime, promising himself he'd wash the shirt before he went to bed. For now, though, he looked down at his torso, where bands of bruises were already forming, red and purple lines over his bulky muscles. He'd be sore by morning.

He rinsed his feet and drank two cupfuls of water before climbing the stairs to his room.

Because he usually worked from shortly after dawn until dusk, it was rare to see his room in the daylight, and the mellow glow of the late afternoon sun certainly didn't improve things. The floorboards were bare and splintery, the walls streaked with decades of grime, the bed and tiny table rickety. His bedding was more patches than blanket; the curtains were hardly more than rags. The entire place reeked of smoke and grease and sour ale. And when he lifted the lid of the chest where he kept his few belongings, the hinges squealed in protest.

In the midst of all this was his one other shirt, clean and neatly folded. It had originally been made for a much smaller man, and the tailor had added wide strips of fabric at the side seams and along the bottom so it would fit Brute. Not exactly stylish, but there was really no use trying to make himself look passable. He pulled on the shirt, ran fingers through his damp hair—which had grown too long again—and trudged downstairs.

Cecil gave him a sour look as Brute entered the tavern's main room. "'S early," he grumbled.

Brute didn't bother to answer. He crossed the room with his head down, ignoring the stares of the other patrons, and sat on a bench in the far corner. It was the darkest corner of the tavern, even now when the last of the sun's rays stole through the open front doors. On the very first day that Brute had moved into the White Dragon, back when he was still a half-grown boy, Cecil had ordered him to sit there. "Don't want to upset anyone's appetite," he'd said back then, and Brute hadn't dared to retort that the Dragon's food could do that all by itself.

As soon as Brute was settled, Cecil brought him a tankard of sour watered ale and a tin plate heaped high with... something. Most of the time, Brute was thankful that his dark corner made identification of his meals an impossibility. Whatever was on the plate, it always tasted the same: bland but slightly gamey, with pockets of grease and bits of squishy stuff that might have once been vegetables. There was always a stale hunk of bread to sop up the drippings, which Brute always did, because a body like his demanded as much food as he could shovel into it.

He ate quickly, washing away the taste with generous gulps of ale, and it wasn't long before his plate was clean and his cup empty. And gods, he was tired. He wasn't quite sure of his age—twenty-seven or twenty-eight was his best guess—but right now he felt eighty, every joint and muscle protesting as he stood and walked the length of the tavern floor. Neither Cecil, his wife, nor his son wished Brute a good night. They never did.

Luckily, he'd remembered to bring the dirty shirt down with him, so he didn't have to climb the stairs to fetch it. He washed it as best as he could in the trough beside the well, hoping the caustic hunk of soap would cleanse away the grime without actually eating through the thinning fabric. But when he held the shirt up, he saw a few new tears and he sighed. His attempts at mending were clumsy at best, and they would have to wait for another day. Right now he was too exhausted to see straight.

Yffi, the stableboy, limped by just before Brute headed upstairs. He spared a half smile for Brute, and Brute grinned back. Born with a twisted foot and a badly malformed upper lip, Yffi was only a little luckier in life than he. Yffi was a Gedding—or his mother was—and so he'd been granted a job he could manage. He slept in the stable on bales of hay that were probably more comfortable than Brute's bed, and he saved his wages so that someday he might marry the shy girl who worked in the sheriff's scullery. Yffi never teased Brute and occasionally even found a spare moment to exchange a few pleasant words, and Brute tried not to envy him.

The stairs seemed especially steep and creaky tonight, and the noise from the tavern filtered through the floorboards of his room: shouting and bursts of laughter, the clanking of tin plates and tankards, and the pounding of booted feet. Nobody was singing tonight, which was a shame, because Brute was too tired to hum to himself. He hung the wet shirt on his single chair, stripped off his trousers, shirt, and breechclout, and set them aside for the morning. Naked, he climbed into bed. He had to curl on his side so that his feet didn't hang over the edge, and then he had to position himself exactly right to avoid the worst of the lumps in the mattress, but he was long used to such maneuverings, and it took him only moments to fall into a dreamless sleep.

THE roosters began to crow well before the sun rose, and soon morning noises echoed in the courtyard. Gods, he was sore. He stood—carefully—and stretched, hoping to work out a few kinks from his frame. He prodded gently at the bruises from the rope, then scratched at the dark thatch of hair on his chest. Unbidden, his hand traveled south to grasp his cock, which was as uselessly perky as it always was in the morning. It was the only optimistic part of him, and sometimes he wondered when it would give up too.

Once a year, during the Festival of the Harvest Moon—when even Darius was forced to give his men the day off—Brute gathered most of his hoarded coppers into a cloth purse and made the three-hour trek to the royal city of Tellomer. With head held high, he endured the stares and jeers that were always worse than in his home village, where at least the residents were used to him. The dingy little corner with the molly houses and brothels was mostly deserted on the afternoon of the festival, when people spent time with their families and only the most desperate of men and women would be selling themselves. Brute always went to the darkest, most dismal house, the one that didn't even bother with a sign or a name, where the scowling keeper charged him double the usual rates and the whores squabbled over who would be forced to take him.

Brute would stand in the filthy little entry hall and pretend to retain the shreds of his dignity.

Finally, some poor boy would be appointed, often the oldest and the most well-used, and he'd gesture impatiently for Brute to follow him into a tiny back room. Brute always wished that he could caress soft skin, could linger over tender spots. But if he tried that, the boy— the man really; these whores were often older than Brute—would grimace with distaste. So in the end, neither of them would even undress. Brute would loosen his trousers and the boy would loosen his, there would be a perfunctory application of lips and wet tongue to Brute's cock, and then the boy would turn around and present his backside for Brute's use.

Every year as Brute walked home, he'd promise himself that he wouldn't return to that house in Tellomer, but when the next festival came around, he always did. It was the only time anyone ever touched him, and, as meaningless as those touches were, he suspected that he'd shrivel up and die without them. Or worse yet, that he'd lose his humanity altogether and become the monster everyone assumed he was.

The festival was months away, and he had no time this morning for the only other touch he experienced—his own right hand. He gave his cock a warning glare before pulling on his breechclout, trousers, and the now-dry shirt that still needed mending.

His morning routine varied little. He used the outhouse that was in one corner of the courtyard, washed and roughly shaved at the trough, then entered the tavern, where Cecil wordlessly handed him a bowl of lumpy porridge and gristly meat. Sometimes Brute was fortunate—if Cecil was in a good mood and the hens were laying well, he would receive an egg or two. This was not one of those mornings. He ate his breakfast and grabbed the metal bucket that had been left on the counter. The bucket contained his lunch, which was generous in portion but no more tasty than the White Dragon's other fare.

As Brute neared the river, his long strides overtook a few of the other men on their way to work. They seemed a little nervous, and he remembered, belatedly, that the prince would be inspecting the bridge today. The only noblemen Brute had ever seen had been passing through the village on fine horses. He was uncertain how to behave in the royal presence. He supposed that his best bet was to keep his head down and his feet moving, to act the stupid beast.

The prince had not yet arrived at the worksite, and Darius had worked himself into a minor frenzy. Several members of his family were standing impatiently at the bottom of the hill—the sheriff and his wife, the priest and three of his acolytes, the former sheriff and other elder members of the Gedding clan, and a half dozen of the village's wealthier merchants. Aside from the priest and acolytes, who wore white robes, everyone was dressed in bright finery. The hems of the women's skirts were dragging in the dirt.

"Stop goggling!" Darius shouted at nobody in particular. "You're paid to work, not to stand about like fucking fools." Some of the women laughed, and the workers ran to their places. Osred and Osric began to chisel at a hunk of stone, shaping it into a rough cube. Their task was nearly complete. Within a week or so they would have produced enough of the stones to construct the bridge's foundations. Other men scurried up the slope to assemble the bridge components that were waiting for them. Brute found the rope and canvas harness that he'd discarded the previous afternoon and tied it around his shoulders and back. It hurt a little, but at least the straps were too wide to dig very deeply into the narrow bruises.

Osric and Osred hoisted a stone into the harness, and Brute began his first uphill trek of the day.

It was midmorning when the prince and his retinue arrived. Brute was on his way down the hill at the time and heard the clop-clop of their horses before he actually saw them. He was relieved they had finally shown up, because the waiting crowd was getting very restless and Darius was growing ever more ferocious with his tongue. The foreman had picked up one of the switches used to hurry the cart horses along, and it was clear that he wished he could use it on his men.

Brute didn't pause in his work when the prince arrived. He simply waited for the next block of stone to be lifted onto his back and listened as the crowd shouted greetings to their royal visitor. Brute was already on his way up the hill again before the prince had dismounted.

But when Brute descended once more, the prince was still standing there, chatting loudly with the sheriff about transportation costs. Brute snuck a look at him while waiting for Osric and Osred. Prince Aldfrid was a tall man in his midthirties. He was handsome, with a thick mane of yellow hair and a small, pointed beard. But if it weren't for the deferential way the other people stood around him, Brute never would have guessed that the man was the son of the king. He wore plain traveling clothes—no doubt well made, but free of decoration or frivolity. They contrasted markedly with the costumes of the villagers, making the locals seem gaudy and maybe even a little silly.

Brute had just allowed himself a small smile at this notion when Prince Aldfrid turned his head and caught sight of him. "What is *that*?" the prince asked in a booming voice.

Darius frowned. "Nobody. Just one of the workers."

Prince Aldfrid laughed. "He looks more like several of the workers." As the Geddings and their lot looked on askance, the prince strode over until he was standing a few feet in front of Brute, looking him up—and up—and down again.

Brute didn't know what to do. Was he supposed to bow? Should he say something? He felt twice as huge as usual, and three times as ugly. He ended up just standing there like a dimwitted statue.

"Who are you?" the prince asked, his head cocked slightly.

"I-I-I'm—"

"Brute," Darius finished for him. "He's nobody important, Your Highness. He carries things. Now, if you'd care to speak with one of our masons—"

"I'd like to speak with Brute," the prince interrupted. "I'm assuming he is capable of human speech." His words were teasing, but Brute saw only good humor in the pale blue eyes, not cruelty.

"I can talk. Your Highness." Brute hoped that was the proper way to address him.

"Speaking and carrying things. A man of many talents indeed. And on hot days you can provide shade for all the mere mortals around you."

Prince Aldfrid was smiling, and Brute couldn't help but grin back. "And shelter when it storms, Your Highness."

He had a nice laugh, Brute thought. Loud, as if he was used to having an audience, but it seemed genuine. And it was by no means a jeer. He laughed at Brute's small joke the way friends laughed together in the tavern, the way Osred laughed when Osric did his imitation of

Darius. He even clapped Brute familiarly on the arm. "Have you ever given thought to joining the Royal Guard?" he asked.

"The Royal Guard?"

"We'd hardly need to train you. Just stick a battle-axe in your hands and post you by the palace entrance. Nobody nefarious would even think about trying to get by you."

Brute had a brief image of himself, resplendent in uniform and shield, proudly guarding his prince. He would probably even have boots, black ones that shone. "I, um—"

"He's just a beast of burden, Your Highness," Darius interrupted. "Doesn't have the brains for anything else. Besides, he's not the type you'd want guarding anything. His father was hung as a thief, and his mother was a poxy whore. It's why he turned out looking like that."

"She wasn't," Brute said in a near whisper.

The prince rolled his eyes at Darius before turning back to Brute. "We'll speak some more when my tour is finished, all right?" He didn't look disgusted at what the foreman had said.

"Of course, Your Highness," Brute murmured. Prince Aldfrid touched his arm again before allowing himself to be led away.

The brightly dressed crowd followed the prince and his men up the path, chattering loudly the whole way like a flock of excited chickens. Brute stood as a large stone was placed in his back sling. He could almost forget the complaints of his muscles and the lingering ache in his chest, so long as he pictured the friendly way the prince had spoken to him, the kindness in the prince's eyes. Prince Aldfrid saw him as a wonder, as a potential asset, not as a freak. Brute smiled and hummed as he began to climb the hill.

The bridge didn't seem like such an engineering marvel to him, but then, what did he know? It certainly seemed to capture the prince's attention for a long time. Brute made a half dozen trips up and down the hill as Prince Aldfrid inspected the supports, which were nearly complete. Soon the construction of the wooden deck would begin, but Brute would not be part of that enterprise. Instead, he and the rest of the crew would turn the narrow pathway into a proper road, and when the bridge was complete, they would construct the road on the other side of the river. According to gossip in the White Dragon, once the project was finished, travel time between coastal Tellomer and the inland city of Harfaire would be reduced by nearly a day. Not only that, but many more travelers would pass through the little village. The Geddings family was doubtless already counting the money they would earn.

As he completed his seventh trip up the hill, Brute saw that the prince had abandoned the bridge itself and now stood at the edge of the cliff, gazing out over the river. He looked very regal, Brute thought. He looked like a man who could handily conquer the world.

The villagers stood a short distance away, talking to the men who'd accompanied the prince—the royal financiers, perhaps. The men had the shrewd-eyed look of people who counted coins for a living. Brute had a vague idea that the crown had funded most of the costs of the construction, and he wondered how the Geddings had convinced the king to have the bridge built here, instead of at one of the villages downriver, closer to Tellomer.

Maybe Prince Aldfrid didn't care about financial matters. He seemed to be ignoring the conversation, anyway, taking a few steps farther from his companions until his toes hung over the edge of the cliff.

And then the soil crumbled.

Thinking about that morning much later, Brute concluded that the ground had been softened by the rains, and that the runaway timber had weakened the edges even more. Probably somebody should have thought of those things while the prince was standing there. Darius should have warned him to stand back a little more. But Darius didn't, and the earth gave way. Prince Aldfrid shouted with alarm and disappeared from sight.

For what seemed like hours, the Geddings and the prince's men and the workers and Brute all just stood there, mouths hanging open in shock. And then somehow, Brute was the first to move. His long legs covered the ground very quickly, and although other people were closer when the prince fell, Brute reached the edge before they did. Heedless of whether the ground would hold his weight, he peered over the edge.

Prince Aldfrid had fallen about forty feet and was sprawled facedown and motionless on a small outcropping of rock, one of his legs twisted at an unnatural angle. The rock was small enough that one of his arms hung over the edge. If the prince rolled only a few inches to the side, he would fall again, probably landing on the sharp rocks in the river below.

Brute mumbled a few words to the gods—he didn't know any real prayers—and clambered over the side of the cliff.

He'd been an ordinary-sized child until he was nine or ten, maybe even a bit on the small side. He'd still been ugly, however, still the orphaned son of a thief, and the other boys had hounded him mercilessly. He'd taken more than a few beatings, just because the other children knew nobody would protect him. He spent most of his days running errands and mucking out the stables where his great-uncle worked, but when he had a little free time, he would escape to the river, climb up some rocks, and hide in a small cave. Sometimes he even spent the night in the cave, when the weather was warm and his great-uncle had been drinking enough to start reaching for his cane. The great-uncle had died just about when Brute began his freakish growth spurt, so Brute had stopped climbing the rocks and visiting the cave and had begun earning his keep for real.

He was much taller now and many times heavier. But his hands and bare feet remembered how to grip into the smallest cracks and fissures, and he was much, much stronger, so his arms could easily hold his weight when he couldn't find a foothold. He made his way down the bluff, only glancing up once to see the alarmed faces staring down at him.

It took very little time to reach the small outcropping, but he had to be careful not to jostle the prince, not to send them both tumbling over the edge. He knelt beside the prone body and was enormously relieved when the prince shifted a bit and moaned.

"He's alive!" Brute called to the people above. And then, more quietly, he said, "Don't move, Your Highness. Please don't move."

Prince Aldfrid moaned again and rolled his head a little. His eyes fluttered open. "Brute?" he rasped.

Brute was strangely pleased that the prince had remembered him. "You've fallen, sir. I'll… I'll help you back up."

The prince moved, just a little, and groaned as Brute grabbed his shoulders. "Don't!" Brute said. "You're… really close to the edge."

"I'm… oh. I think my leg's broken."

Only then did Brute notice that dark blood was staining the rock beneath them. A lot of dark blood. "Uh, Your Highness?"

"For the gods' sake, stop calling me that, at least until you're done rescuing me."

"Um, okay." Brute glanced up again, but none of the bystanders were offering any assistance. "If we can get you into my back sling, do you think you can hold on while I get us back up?"

"I'll damned well try."

The prince's voice sounded a little stronger, which gave Brute more hope. He shifted the prince very cautiously, still eliciting a choked cry from the stricken man as the injured leg was moved. "Such a damned fool," the prince mumbled.

"Sorry!"

"Not you! Me."

Brute really couldn't argue with that—the prince should have been more careful. So without saying anything, he continued to maneuver Aldfrid as gently as possible, all the while very aware of the closeness of the precipice. The prince assisted as best as he could, and soon he was seated in the back sling, his arms wrapped around Brute's neck.

"Don't strangle me," Brute warned.

"That would be counterproductive."

Climbing up was a lot more difficult than climbing down. The prince's weight on Brute's back not only added to the strain on his arms but also altered his center of gravity. Prince Aldfrid's rasping, hot breath on the back of his neck would have been a terrible distraction if Brute wasn't so worried about losing his grip, sending both of them to their deaths.

As they reached the halfway mark, Darius belatedly decided to shout directions. "Grab that rock over there! No, not that one, idiot! Watch where you're putting your feet!"

Brute ignored him until the prince mumbled, "What an ass." Under other circumstances, Brute would have laughed in response. But the prince's voice was thready and his grip was weakening. If he lost consciousness, he'd fall, most likely dragging Brute with him.

"Almost there," Brute lied. His arms and shoulders burned, his back was one huge cramp, and his legs felt like Cecil's over-boiled noodles. The bruises he'd acquired the day before were like sharp blades digging between his ribs. If he survived the climb, he was going to have to take the afternoon off again, and Darius had damned well better pay him for the full day this time.

He was perhaps fifteen feet from the top when his left hand slipped. His body began to slide down the rock, Prince Aldfrid groaned in pain, and the audience gasped. For an endless moment Brute was positive he was going to fall. But his right hand gripped its hold just a little more tightly and his feet jammed deeply into a crack, and his left hand was able to regain contact with the cliff.

Brute let out a long breath and kept on climbing, foot by agonizing foot.

He couldn't feel his fingers and toes anymore. He couldn't see anything but gray stone in front of his nose, and all he heard was the prince's ragged breathing. He tasted salty sweat on his lips and longed for a tankard of cool ale. "Almost there," he repeated, but this time it was the truth. And just moments later, when he'd risen another arm's length, hands reached down and grasped him. Brute scrabbled against the rock with his feet as he and the prince were hauled up and over the edge.

He lay there with his face in the trampled grass, his lower legs still hanging over the edge. It seemed to him that the prince continued to try to hang on, even as the bystanders pulled him off Brute's back. The sudden removal of the extra weight wasn't as much of a relief as he had expected. He wanted to know how badly injured the prince was, but was too weak to make his throat work to say the words. Likely nobody would have answered him anyway: all the Geddings and workers and members of the prince's retinue seemed to be jabbering away at once, all of them nearly hysterical over the prince's plight. None of them were paying attention to Brute.

Which was perhaps just as well, because when the ground crumbled again, nobody but Brute was close enough to the edge to fall.

For one single moment, he felt as if he were suspended in air, floating over the river like a cloud on a windless day. He felt as if, with only a bit of effort, he would fly—away from the cliff, away from the village. Just away. But instead he fell, the breath stolen from his lungs as he plummeted. His shoulders banged against the stones, then his lower back. Something cracked, but there was no pain. His head thudded against something hard and sharp, and his world went black.

 # CHAPTER  *Two*

HE DIDN'T know whether his mother really had been a whore, but he knew she had loved his father. And his father loved her. They lived in one of the tiny stone and timber huts near the edge of the village, and his parents would sing together. They probably drank a good deal as well—Brute remembered the scent of ale and spilled wine—but they were happy. They laughed all the time. And when Brute was very, very small, so small that the entire world seemed enormous and out of his reach, they would sometimes let him sleep between them on their warm, soft bed, and they would tickle him and tell him that someday he'd amount to something wonderful. Possibly they believed that. Probably they were drunken fools.

Then one day there was lots of shouting and screaming and crying—his mother collapsed on the floor, sobbing into her hands, and nothing he could do would console her. He saw his father one more time after that, in the village's main square. His father had looked very pale and frightened atop the makeshift wooden structure, with his hands tied behind his back and the sheriff scowling at his side, but Brute's father had managed a last weak smile at Brute and his mother. There was a terrible *crack* after that, and Brute's father was dancing in midair.

The men had come that afternoon and taken everything away. Their chickens and goat, their pots and dishes. They'd taken the cunningly carved set of wooden animals Brute's father had given him during the previous Festival of the Harvest Moon, and his mother's soft and beautiful shawl and pretty rings, and even his father's spare pair of boots. Then they'd taken the table and chairs and chest of drawers and the small cot where Brute usually slept, and finally they'd taken the big, comfortable bed. He'd never again slept in such a wonderful bed.

Not long afterward—maybe even that same day—Brute's mother hugged him tight and kissed the top of his head and told him he was a good boy and she loved him. And then she drank something bitter-scented from a flask. He remembered wondering why the men hadn't taken the flask as well. Minutes later, she collapsed to the ground, twitching and frothing at the mouth.

His great-uncle had grudgingly taken him in, and Brute had spent his nights curled in the corner of another small hut—this one filthy—wrapped in two scratchy blankets. When the great-uncle had died, Brute moved into the stables, and that was actually an improvement of sorts. There was hay to cushion him, and the horses gave warmth and a bit of companionship. They smelled better than the great-uncle had too. Then Brute began to grow at a pace that alarmed even him. He'd often trip on his own feet or knock things over when he forgot how large his body had become. Darius hired him to quarry stones for the bridge, a project which had just begun. Brute had moved out of the stables, into the little room above the White Dragon, with the bugs and the mice and the lumpy, short bed.

And this meant he must be dead, he concluded, because he could feel the softness of a real mattress beneath him, a pillow cradling his head, and warm, smooth sheets above him. Everything smelled clean, like a meadow after a spring rain. The afterlife, then.

But no. Because his body was wracked with pain: a throbbing leg, a pounding head, hips that felt screwed on too tight, and a left hand that was clenched agonizingly and wouldn't relax. There wouldn't be such pain in the afterlife, would there?

He tried to open his eyes, but his lids were too heavy. He almost could have laughed. Here he was, the great beast of burden, and he couldn't manage to lift even his eyelids. The puzzle of his whereabouts was too much for his pounding head, and he gave up.

Time twisted strangely after that. Sometimes he'd be awake, filled with pain and struggling to make sense of blurry shapes and colors, of broken bits of sound. Then it was as if reality jumped somehow, and the light would be different, or someone would be urging bitter liquid between his lips. He floated in and out of awareness, never quite able to grasp reality strongly enough to stay put, let alone to pull himself out of his fuzzy confusion.

And then, gradually, his eyes were able to focus, and he realized he was looking up at dark ceiling beams against pale plaster. Most of his pain had receded to a thudding ache, although his hand still wouldn't unclench. "Drink," said a crisp, slightly familiar voice.

Brute turned his head a little and, with some effort, refocused his eyes. Ah. Hilma Gedding, the village healer. She was an angular woman who seemed to have been born middle-aged and then apparently stopped growing older. She kept her gray hair tucked under a gray cap and wore plain gray dresses; even her eyes were gray. She was holding a tin cup in one of her overlarge hands. "Drink," she repeated.

Brute craned his neck a little, and she brought the cup to his mouth. It wasn't water, as he'd hoped, but something grassy and sour tasting. He swallowed it anyway, figuring it was meant to help him get better. Hilma nodded and set the cup aside, then pulled the blankets down to his waist and settled her palms on his chest. Once when he was still small, Hilma healed him after his great-uncle had broken Brute's arm—Brute was instructed to tell Hilma that he'd fallen from the hayloft. If she doubted his story, she never said so. As an adult, he had injured himself badly enough on two or three occasions to be willing to spare the coppers she charged. So he had some idea what to expect: a slight tingling sensation that radiated from his chest throughout his body, the pleasant warmth that accompanied it, the tuneless chanting of the healer. When she took her hands away, his pain had lessened just a little bit more.

"Sleep now," she said.

"But—"

"Sleep."

He didn't know whether her command carried magical authority, but as soon as she said it, his eyes fell closed and unconsciousness washed over him like a warm wave.

The next time he woke up, she gave him tea and then broth, and when she was done with him, he could move his legs without too much discomfort. Later, she washed his body. He was slightly embarrassed, but he was not strong enough to do anything about it. Besides, the cloth was soft and the water was warm, and the soap smelled like the lavender wands his mother used to tuck into her clean laundry.

It might have been that same day or maybe the next when he heard voices in the adjoining room and realized that his head was finally clear enough to understand them.

"—wagon ready tomorrow, Your Highness," said a voice Brute recognized as the sheriff's. Brute smiled a little to learn that the prince was alive and nearby.

"I'd rather ride on horseback."

"Your leg's not quite healed enough for that," said Hilma. "Unless you want to stay here another week."

"Gods, no. I appreciate your hospitality, but I want to get home."

"Of course."

The three of them chatted a while longer about the prince's travel arrangements, and Brute began to doze off again. But then Prince Aldfrid asked, "And what about him?"

"He's healing," replied Hilma. "He'll be walking again soon."

Brute smiled again because the prince had asked after him. He couldn't remember anyone caring about his well-being since he was a child.

"But what'll become of him?" the prince asked, turning Brute's grin into a frown.

The sheriff sounded impatient. "You needn't worry about him, Your Highness. I'm sure you have much more important—"

"He saved my life. The rest of you just stood there, and he risked himself to rescue me. That makes him very important." There was a pause and a dull thunk, as of a tankard being set on a table. "Does he have anyone to look after him?"

"His father was—" began the sheriff.

"Hanged. I know. Anyone else?"

"He's always looked after himself."

The sheriff's statement was true enough, Brute knew, and yet it made his chest ache. He was good enough at taking care of himself, and he reminded himself often that he didn't need anyone else. He could manage. He was strong.

But the prince's next words tore him apart: "He won't be able to return to his job."

There was probably more discussion after that, but Brute couldn't hear it over the rushing in his ears. He closed his eyes and wished himself back into the state of wooly incomprehension where he'd been spending so much time lately. But it didn't work, and he couldn't unknow the truth he'd been refusing to acknowledge for some time. He opened his eyes and, very slowly, pulled his arms out from under the blankets.

His right hand was fine. It had a few pale scars—and a new wound or two—but his long, broad fingers curled and uncurled as cleverly as always, his thumb and forefinger came together perfectly.

He looked to his left.

It wasn't shocking, not really. His arm, thick with muscle, and a clean white bandage, and then... nothing. Nothing horrible to see except the absence of his hand.

He made a choking sound and tried to scramble out of bed, as if he could somehow escape his own mutilation. But his feet caught in the blankets, and his legs, unused to standing, wouldn't hold him. He fell to the floor with a loud crash.

Hilma and the sheriff came running in. The sheriff frowned, but the healer only shook her head, and then the two of them hauled him back onto the mattress, grunting with effort. Hilma smoothed the covers back over his naked legs and hips, but his arms remained free.

"What...?" he began, but was unable to finish, not even when he swallowed twice.

"It was too badly shattered. I couldn't fix it. It had to come off or it would have rotted away."

"But... my hand...."

"You're lucky to have your life," said the sheriff. "You washed up on that little beach north of the bridge, and it took most of Darius's crew to bring you here."

Funny. Brute didn't feel very thankful. One-handed, he had no means of livelihood. His few saved coppers wouldn't last long, and then... well, he might as well have died in the river. Quicker that way.

He turned his head away and closed his eyes.

HE WAS awake the next morning when the mattress dipped beside him, but he didn't open his eyes until a warm hand gave his shoulder a squeeze. "I'm sorry," said Prince Aldfrid. "If I'd been more careful, this wouldn't have happened to you."

Brute was so surprised at the royal apology that his despair momentarily slipped away. "I'm glad you're all right, Your Highness."

"I'll be limping for a while yet, but I can live with that." He smiled a little, and gods, he was handsome! "My head's not as thick as yours, I think. I wouldn't have survived if I'd fallen off the rock. Thank you."

"It's... it's an honor." Which was true. Brute might be an ugly beast—now a crippled one at that—but he'd saved a prince's life. His mother was right after all.

Prince Aldfrid squeezed his shoulder again. "You're quite a man. Look now. When you're up to traveling, I'd like you to come to the palace."

"To... to Tellomer?"

"Yes. You're a hero, and you deserve a reward."

Brute tried to think of what sort of reward he would get. A medal? A parchment listing his brave deeds? A... fancy hat, maybe? All very pretty, but not of much use to a one-handed laborer.

The prince must have sensed his thoughts because he laughed softly. "A job. A good job, with living quarters more comfortable than anywhere in this village and without that damnable foreman."

"But I can't...." Brute waved his mangled arm, as if the prince might have forgotten he was maimed.

"There's still more to you than most men. We'll find something for you to do, I promise you." He reached into his cloak and pulled out a folded sheet of paper, which he set on the table beside the bed. "Bring that with you. It'll get you past the guards and into the palace."

To Brute's horror, his eyes filled with tears. He hadn't cried since his mother died—not once, not even when his great-uncle beat him—and now he dug the fingernails of his remaining hand into his palm and tried to maintain his composure. "Thank you," he rasped.

The prince stood, a bit awkwardly, and smiled down at him. "I hope to see you soon, Brute." Then he limped slowly out of the room.

Brute's recovery continued steadily after that. Hilma didn't speak to him other than to issue terse commands, and she made him drink gallons of that awful tea, but she fed him—much better than Cecil at the White Dragon ever did—and sang her healing chants. She allowed him out of bed, first just long enough to use the chamber pot, but soon he was wobbling around the room. She produced his spare shirt and a pair of trousers that had obviously been hastily altered to fit him. The clothes he'd been wearing when he fell off the cliff must have been ruined. He learned to care for himself one-handed. Clumsily, but he managed.

Finally, she unwrapped the bandage from his stump for the final time and nodded in satisfaction. He steeled himself for a good look, but it wasn't as horrible as he'd imagined. The hand was gone, cut cleanly at the wrist, and the scars at the end were still pinkish and new looking. But the wound was closed, and there were no signs of infection. He just wished he didn't feel like his hand was still attached, still balled in a tight fist.

"You can't... can't grow it back?" he asked her, knowing he wouldn't have enough coppers to pay even if she were capable.

"I'm a healer, not a witch."

He nodded. "How much must I pay you for...?" He waved his good arm vaguely toward the rumpled bed.

"The prince paid already."

"Oh."

She sniffed and tapped a foot impatiently. "Leave now. I've done all for you that I can."

He took the folded sheet of paper and tucked it carefully into his pocket. He desperately wished to know what it said, but he couldn't read, and in any case, it was sealed by a blob of red wax bearing what he assumed was the prince's signet.

It was midmorning, and the village was bustling as men and women went to the market and back, or fetched water from wells. Children rushed about everywhere, playing with balls and hoops or doing their parents' errands. Everyone stared at him, at his arm. But he kept his head up and worked to hide the remaining limp, even though his hips ached with the effort.

Cecil was standing behind the bar when Brute entered the White Dragon. "Not running a charity house," the landlord snarled.

"I don't need charity," Brute said as he walked past the bar. Ascending the stairs was painful. He would never make it up the pathway at the bridge site, not even without a heavy stone on his back. Even more important, he couldn't lift the stones anymore, couldn't adjust his own harness, couldn't tug on ropes or dig holes or do any of the other tasks Darius expected. It gave him a tiny thrill of satisfaction to know that the last burden he carried in that damned sling had been Prince Aldfrid.

His room looked especially small and squalid after the healer's pleasant house. And his bed.... He sighed, already missing her wonderful mattress, which had been almost long enough to fit him. His own lumpy mattress didn't look the least bit inviting, even though he was tired after the walk across the village.

Opening the chest at the foot of his bed proved tricky: it had latches on each side. He struggled with it for several minutes before he finally swore and gave it a mighty kick. He hurt his bare foot in the process, but at least the old wood caved beneath the pressure. He stuck his remaining hand into the wreckage and retrieved his few belongings: a razor, a short knife, and a scented handkerchief he'd stolen three festivals earlier from a whore in Tellomer who'd smiled at him instead of grimacing. Not much for a lifetime, but most of his salary went to Cecil. After placing the other items on the table beside the letter, Brute used the knife to pry up a loose floorboard near the edge of the bed. In a small cavity underneath was a tin box that contained all the coppers he had saved. He tucked the box under his left arm and twisted off the lid with his right, then tallied the small stash—a pittance, really. He replaced the lid and set the box on the table with his other possessions.

And then he sat on the edge of his terrible bed, looked at the table, and thought. He couldn't imagine what sort of job the prince would find for him in Tellomer. Brute didn't know how to do anything but use his strength. If his hips healed, maybe they could hook him up to a cart and use him like a mule, he thought sourly. Maybe he could stand in the corner and help hold up the ceiling.

He didn't want to be a very large and useless lump, an object of pity acquired by the prince out of a sense of obligation. But he had few other choices, unless he intended to throw himself over the cliff again and hope that this time the rocks finished what they'd begun.

Maybe he should go just to see what the prince had in mind. Brute could simply thank him and walk away if the job proved too demeaning. The river would always be waiting. Besides, this way he'd get to see the inside of the palace. He smiled to himself. He'd be willing to bet that Darius and Cecil and most of the other Geddings had never managed that feat.

 # CHAPTER
Three

BRUTE felt no unhappiness as he turned his back on his home village for the last time. In fact, he felt wonderfully free. It had been weighing him down like a stone all these years, and he hadn't even realized it. He'd paid off his debt to Cecil and bought himself a secondhand cloak that was in decent shape. It had a wide pocket in which he could jam the stump of his left arm. He was still huge and ugly, and people would still stare, but he felt almost whole that way.

The sky was a clear blue, the sun almost bright enough to hurt his eyes, the dusty road soft beneath his feet. He had worried a little about his legs and hips, but he'd allowed himself a few more days to recover before setting out, and even after walking a while, he experienced only a faint ache—not so different from how he would feel after a hard day's work. It made him smile to know that he wasn't at work now. No matter his fate, he no longer had to listen to Darius's abuse, eat Cecil's terrible food, or endure the villagers' contemptuous looks. Other travelers and the citizens of Tellomer might think him a monster, but at least none of them would call him the spawn of a thief and a whore.

Cecil hadn't offered to give him a meal for his journey, and Brute hadn't asked for one, so around the midway point his stomach began to rumble. He was passing through a hamlet by then, a collection of stone houses and shops smaller than his own village but more prosperous. When he'd come this way before, it had always been festival day and everything had been closed up tight, but today shopkeepers were displaying shining pots and lengths of fabric and brightly painted wooden toys. In a little yard beside the inn, a boy was cooking skewers of meat over a fire. It smelled wonderful. After a brief hesitation, Brute entered the yard.

"How much?" he asked the boy, who was gaping up at him.

"Ten pence each."

Brute didn't know how to do more than the most basic sums. He fumbled in his right hand pocket and produced a single copper. "How many will this buy me?"

The boy sneered a little, and in a loud, slow voice, as if Brute were a simpleton, he said, "One copper gets you seven sticks."

"And if I want ale to drink?"

"Five and a tankard."

Brute set the coin on the edge of the brick fire pit.

He didn't bother to sit down on the chairs that looked too spindly to hold him, nor did he remove his small bag of belongings from his shoulder. The ale came in a large tin tankard and was hardly better than the White Dragon's, but it did quench his thirst. The meat, on the other hand, was the most delicious thing he'd ever eaten: hot and crispy on the outside, still slightly bloody at the center, with none of the gristle he was used to. The boy watched with something akin to admiration as Brute quickly cleared all five skewers. "Bet you could eat the whole lot of these," he said, gesturing at his remaining sticks of meat.

"Only if I can have them for another copper. That's all I have."

The boy had a crooked smile. "My da would skin me alive over it. Sorry."

"Maybe another time." Brute walked away with his belly full and his lips tasting pleasantly of grease. He hummed under his breath as he continued on his way.

He wasn't used to Tellomer being so crowded and bustling. It was a wonder to him that there could be so many people, and all of them with such important business to conduct. Some of them led mules or horses, some had carts loaded with sacks and baskets, some simply wove through the chaos with their arms full of packages. Merchants and street vendors called out their wares. Beggars slumped against buildings, palms held out. Babies cried and children laughed, men and women talked and argued, and the mingled scents of food and animals and emptied chamber pots and unwashed bodies permeated the air as if they were entities in themselves. Brute saw three men with dark skin and long, flowing robes—visitors from far away, he presumed. He saw a lithe woman performing gymnastic feats as passersby stopped, watched for a few moments, and tossed her a few coins. He saw a beautiful black-haired man in an expensive suit walking arm in arm with an equally beautiful and equally well-attired brunet.

Brute's legs wanted to turn left at the fountain with the spitting fish of carved stone, which would take him underneath a stone archway and down a narrow, crooked alley. At the end of that alley he'd descend a cobblestoned hill lined with soap-scented launderers, and then he'd find himself in a confusing maze of buildings, most of which promised a few minutes of pleasure in exchange for a handful of coppers. But he had only one copper, and anyway, that wasn't why he was here. He ordered his legs to continue forward past the fountain and down the wide street that rose steeply to the palace.

He'd walked by the palace once before out of curiosity, but hadn't seen much aside from imposing stone walls. He'd never imagined he might actually go inside, and today those walls looked slightly frightening, like a gray dragon waiting to devour him. He silently chided himself for his stupidity and walked to the gate, which was guarded by a half dozen men in scarlet and cream uniforms. The middle-aged one with the graying beard seemed to be in charge. The look he gave Brute wasn't so much hostile as deeply skeptical. "What do *you* want?"

"The... Prince Aldfrid told me to come here."

The guard's bushy eyebrows rose. "Did he now? And since when is His Highness in the practice of parleying with giants? Giants in rags, no less."

Brute glanced self-consciously at his clothing. "He... he was in my village a few weeks ago and—"

"And I'm sure he had a delightful visit. Now, go away."

After a calming breath, Brute removed the letter from an inside pocket. "He gave me this. Said I was to show it and I'd be let inside."

That made the guard frown and hold out a hand. "Let's see."

Brute didn't want to give up the letter; it was his only hope of a future. But the guard was waiting expectantly, and his colleagues were all watching—as were two men waiting to be let into the palace with their donkey and a cart full of sacks of grain. Brute handed the paper over.

The guard peered carefully at the seal. He held the folded paper up to the light, as if he were trying to see the ink, and then poked at the seal with one finger. "I guess this looks genuine," he finally said, clearly regretting the admission.

"It is."

The guard shrugged and turned to one of the others, this one a much younger man with a long, skinny neck and a nose like a beak. "Take him to Lord Maudit." He returned the letter to Brute.

The younger guard didn't look very pleased with his orders, but he barked, "Follow me," and led Brute through the gate.

Brute had assumed that the palace was a single monumental building, but he quickly discovered that it was actually a complex of structures of varying size. Between them were paved passageways and courtyards and small swathes of green, with people and wagons and horses moving to and fro. It was really a small city in itself. There were stables, of course, but he also smelled a bakery and saw steam rising from a laundry. A smith was examining a horse's hoof, a crew of several dozen men was erecting a new stone building, and a scholar of some sort was intoning a lecture at a group of youths who scribbled notes on papers.

Brute quickly grew disoriented, but his guide was confident enough. They entered an ancient-looking building via a side door, walked up several flights of stairs and down long corridors, and finally entered a wide hallway where people rushed back and forth with only a quick glance Brute's way. The guard stopped in front of a pair of large doors that were flanked by two men in uniform. "He's for Lord Maudit," the bird-faced guard said before turning and marching away.

The man to Brute's right sighed audibly and opened his door. It was tall enough that Brute didn't have to duck to enter. He was led to a large room with worn stone floors, lots of wooden chairs arranged against the walls, and several smaller doors leading who knew where.

Following like a very large but obedient puppy, Brute was taken to a bored-looking old man who sat at a desk. The man didn't even bother to gawp at him. He peered at Brute's paper without opening it, handed it back, and waved vaguely at a stone bench under a large window. "Wait there. Don't break anything."

Brute hadn't intended to break a thing, but didn't say so. He sat on the bench and took a closer look around. The ceiling was very high and had a complicated painting involving naked men with beards, winged gods, and sailing ships. Also horses, fluffy clouds, and a lot of words he couldn't read. He'd never seen anything quite like it, and he spent a long time staring, tilting his head this way and that until his neck grew sore. Then he looked at the room's other occupants instead. They were seated on the wooden chairs or pacing the room. Most of them carried sheaves of paper. They were dressed in very fine clothes, and they stared disapprovingly at Brute's makeshift clothing and dirty bare feet.

Time passed achingly slowly. Sometimes someone would pop out from one of the little doors and take one or more of the waiting people back in with them, but nobody ever came for Brute. New people came through the large entry doors, did a double take when they saw him, and sat far away. They were eventually escorted through doorways too. His ass grew sore from sitting on the hard bench, his stomach gurgled and growled, and worst of all, his bladder began to complain quite insistently. He knew it was impossible for the giant with the ugly face to have been forgotten, and yet none of the people who worked there even glanced his way. Maybe they thought he was a new and especially unbecoming statue.

Just as he was about to give in to desperation and ask where he might find a place to relieve himself, a round woman with a feathered hat and the widest skirts he'd ever seen appeared from the far left door and sailed in his direction. "This way," she commanded.

His hips and legs had cramped a little as he sat, and he limped very badly as he followed her.

The far left door led to an office smelling of tea and crammed with books and papers. The woman went away and shut the door behind her, leaving Brute alone with a man who was a few years older than him. The man was dressed in rather plain clothes and was tiny—

barely five feet tall and probably one-third Brute's weight—but he managed to project an aura of such powerful authority that he was almost terrifying. He stood several feet away and looked Brute up and down slowly. "You have a letter?" he finally said.

"Um, yes sir." Brute produced the paper from the folds of his cloak and held it out, but the man didn't take it.

"You will address me as Lord Maudit. You may call me milord or Your Excellency as well, for variety's sake."

"Yes, Lord Maudit."

Lord Maudit rolled his eyes and snatched the paper out of Brute's hand. He tore open the seal without ceremony and scanned the contents. When he was finished, he considered Brute again, this time appraisingly. It reminded Brute of the way Darius would look over a mule he was considering buying. "So you're a hero?" he said at last.

"I—no. I mean, the prince, he—"

"Needed to be rescued from his own foolishness. Again. And rather dramatically, I understand."

Brute didn't know how to answer that. He licked his lips nervously and fought the urge to shift his feet. His bladder was full to bursting, and the glimpses of the sea he could catch through Lord Maudit's window weren't helping.

"Not very chatty, are you?" the lord said. "Good." He folded the paper and slapped it against his thigh before tossing it onto his desk. "Wait here."

"Please!"

Lord Maudit was nearly to the door when Brute blurted out his plea. The little man turned, eyebrow raised. "Yes?"

"I need to—is there an outhouse? Milord," Brute added hastily.

"Garderobe's through there," the lord said, waving at a narrow door in the corner. Brute made what he hoped was a dignified dash for it while the other man left through the main door.

To reach the garderobe he had to climb a set of very narrow, winding stairs. The stairs dead-ended in a rounded little chamber with tiny slits for windows. The room contained a wooden seat with a hole in it and a small table bearing an earthen pitcher of water. Fumbling his laces open one-handed seemed to take forever, but eventually he managed to get his trousers undone. He emptied himself with a long groan of relief. At least he hadn't lost his good hand, he reminded himself for the thousandth time. The gods only knew how he would have managed to get himself undressed then.

Lacing back up again was even more troublesome, but at least his need was no longer quite so urgent. He just wished he could have managed to find a way to pour the water in the pitcher over his hand to cleanse it.

Lord Maudit's office was empty when Brute descended the stairs. Brute resisted the temptation to poke around—he had an eerie feeling that the man would somehow *know*—and instead admired the view from the windows and then a large painting of a hunting party chasing a stag.

"Hideous painting, isn't it?"

Brute jumped at the voice and whirled around. Lord Maudit had returned, but it was his companion who had spoken: Prince Aldfrid, attired in riding clothes and smiling broadly. The prince showed no sign of limping as he crossed the room. "I'm glad you've recovered enough to make the journey," he said to Brute. "How are you managing?" He seemed genuinely concerned.

Brute pulled his stump out of his cloak pocket, which made Lord Maudit's eyes widen. Apparently the prince's letter hadn't mentioned that Brute was maimed. "Your Highness, are you certain—" the lord began.

"Yes," the prince interrupted sharply. "Completely. He's the man for the job."

"The job, Your Highness?" Brute asked.

"That's why you're here, isn't it? I could just give you a sack of gold and send you on your way—you've earned it—but I'm guessing you're not that kind of man. You want to be... useful." His laugh sounded a little sad. "More useful than a king's fourth son."

Brute took a moment to consider the prince's words. A sack of gold. He'd never have to worry about his livelihood again. He could buy a little cottage somewhere, have some clothing made that actually fit. He could eat decent food every day. And then... what? Sit by himself and wait to grow old and die? "I would like to be useful," he confirmed. "But I don't know what I can do for you, sir, not like this. I'm sorry."

"Have you any skills at all?" Lord Maudit asked. "I suppose it's too much to ask that you know how to write."

Brute hung his head, ashamed. "I wanted to. Had no money to pay the schoolmaster." After his parents were dead, when his great-uncle would send him scurrying around the village to fetch this and carry that, Brute used to pass the little schoolhouse now and then, and he'd pause long enough to gaze at it enviously. Once he'd even dared to ask his great-uncle to send him—Brute had promised to work twice as much to pay for it—but his great-uncle had cuffed him hard enough to send him sprawling, then growled that Brute was too stupid to learn.

"Doesn't matter," said Prince Aldfrid, pulling Brute out of the bad memory. "I have something perfect for you."

"Aldfrid, you're taking an enormous risk." Lord Maudit sounded irritated with the prince, but in a resigned sort of way, as if he was used to conversations like this.

"He's the one, Maud."

"But the king—"

"My father, if he notices at all, will see that a very large and not especially bright man—sorry, Brute; I know you're no idiot—has been put in place. That's all."

Brute stood there mutely, slightly surprised at the obvious familiarity between the men and not having the vaguest clue what they were talking about. But then the prince clapped him on the arm and grinned. "It'll all work out. You won't be seeing much of me, Brute, but if you need anything, just get word to Maud here and he'll take care of it." He smirked at Lord Maudit and sped out of the room.

Maudit briefly closed his eyes, as if he were in pain. "Scrambled your brains a bit more on those rocks, didn't you, Friddy?" he muttered. Then he glared at Brute. "Follow me."

It seemed that everyone was saying that to him today. But Brute shrugged and did as he was told.

He was led through another dizzying arrangement of corridors and stairways. Once he caught a glimpse of an enormous room—by far the largest he had ever seen—with a polished marble floor, gilded pillars, and a ceiling fresco considerably more elaborate than the one he'd been admiring while he waited. But he didn't get a chance to enjoy it, because Maudit dragged him along at a pace surprising for a man with such short legs. Guards saluted when Lord Maudit passed, and various well-dressed functionaries and servants all tried to look more industrious. Maudit ignored them.

They eventually left the building—through a different door than the one by which Brute and the guard had entered—crossed an oblong grassy area where several women in colorful gowns sat and embroidered, and entered a narrow passageway between two buildings. The passageway dead-ended at a grim little building of dirty stone. The windows in the building were simply narrow vertical slits, and even those were covered by iron bars. The door was iron as well—arched and sporting a heavy bolt—with a bored-looking guard stationed outside. The guard snapped to attention when he saw them coming.

"Has everything been readied?" Lord Maudit snapped.

The guard nodded sharply. "Yes, milord. The maids just left."

"Good. This is… well, Brute. Obviously. You've been told of his duties?"

"Yes, milord."

"If he needs anything, make sure he gets it. I'll be checking on him."

The guard looked slightly horrified at the prospect but nodded again. Then he unlocked the door and waited for Maudit and Brute to enter.

This time, Brute found himself in a small hallway with a ceiling so low he almost had to bend his head. The walls were rough plaster, dirty and cracked, interrupted now and then by doors made of thick dark timbers. The building smelled of damp and age, with a faint sickly sweet undertone, as if something had rotted long ago.

"What—" Brute began.

"In here." Lord Maudit pressed the latch on one of the doors; the hinges squealed in protest. Brute stepped inside and saw, to his astonishment, a somewhat dim but comfortable-looking apartment. The ceiling was higher than that of the hallway, although he could still have brushed it with his fingertips. The room contained an oversized bed piled with quilts, a chest of drawers with an actual mirror on top, a solid table with two equally solid chairs, and a matching wardrobe and bookshelf. The window was tiny, of course, but the walls were hung with colorful tapestries that depicted scenes of beasts in the forest and creatures under the sea. A small stove with dark green tiles was tucked in one corner, but not lit today because the weather was far too warm.

And in one wall, over near another corner, was a door constructed of heavy iron bars, with only darkness visible behind it.

"Welcome to your new home," said Lord Maudit from the doorway.

"But… what?"

"His Highness has decided that you will be a very specialized sort of guard, with only a single prisoner to watch over."

"Prisoner?" Brute's eyes strayed back to the barred door.

Maudit twitched one shoulder. "See for yourself."

With some degree of trepidation, Brute crossed the room.

The bars separated the apartment from a small cell. He had to squint to see inside—there was no window slit in the prisoner's space—but there wasn't much to see. Bare walls, bare floor, and in the corner, a dirty pile of rags. But as Brute stared, the rags shifted slightly and chains clanked, and a matted mass of hair appeared from under the edge of the fabric. A man, Brute realized. He was looking at a man huddled under a blanket. Chains sounded again, and Brute noted the metal collar around the man's neck, manacles on his wrists, and shackled ankles fastened by chains to bolts in the floor. It was impossible to make out any details of the man past his rat's nest of hair and tangled beard until the prisoner lifted his head slightly. Brute gasped at the man's obvious blindness: eyelids closed over sunken, empty sockets.

Lord Maudit sighed. He still hadn't actually entered the room. "Brute, meet Gray Leynham."

CHAPTER
Four

"AM I a prisoner here?" Brute asked.

Lord Maudit was pacing the hallway outside the small apartment, clearly eager to be somewhere else. "No. You can leave whenever you want. Just knock on the main door and the guard will let you out. In fact, you'll have to leave to fetch meals, your own and his." He jerked a thumb in the direction of the dark cell. "And you're free to roam the palace grounds, even wander the city if you like. We'll give you a pass so you can get in through the gates, although I expect you'll be recognized by everyone soon enough. You just have to make sure you're here to give the prisoner proper care during the day. And you must always be here at night."

Brute frowned, thinking about the chains and iron bars and guarded doors that stood between Gray Leynham and freedom. "I'm not here to keep him from escaping."

Maudit barked a laugh. "Hardly. Make sure he eats. Empty his waste pail now and then."

"And that requires me to actually live next to him?"

For the first time, Lord Maudit gave him a small smile. "You're smarter than you look, aren't you? No, those small chores should take only a little time." He sighed. "Your most important task will come at night, actually."

Brute frowned uneasily, shifting his eyes quickly toward the barred door. "Night?"

"It's quite simple. If he calls out anything in his sleep—and you'll know he's sleeping because the words will actually be intelligible— take note of it, then hurry off and repeat it to the guard at the door. It'd be better if you could write it down, but I suppose there's no chance of that."

"Why do I have to do this?" Brute asked, not feeling at all comforted by these instructions.

"It doesn't matter to you. Just do as you're told. You'll be paid outrageously well for your services, by the way. Room and board, of course, plus you'll be kept outfitted in something more… suitable. And you'll receive a silver coin each month, and an extra for the Festival of the Harvest Moon."

Brute's jaw dropped. As best as he could figure, a silver coin was nearly the equivalent of all the coppers he'd earn in a year of toiling for Darius. And not having to pay for his meals and the roof over his head! What would he do with such wealth?

Maybe Maudit didn't notice his astonishment, because he continued speaking. "You won't actually be given the coins. Too inconvenient. But you'll be added to the exchequer's books, and he'll keep track of your earnings. You simply ask him if you wish to receive some of it in hand. I'd suggest keeping very little. It's always easier to spend it when it's jingling in your purse."

"I… all right."

"Fine then. Come along. I've real work to attend to today, you know. I'll find someone to show you where to get food and such, and I suppose you'll have to be taken to the tailor and the shoemaker." He wrinkled his nose slightly. "Someone will show you the baths as well. And maybe… maybe a haircut would help. Or maybe not."

Without looking at the prisoner or even acknowledging his existence, Lord Maudit led Brute from the apartment, down the hall, and to the front door.

"What did he do?" Brute asked quietly as he ducked to avoid an especially low beam. "Why's he being kept here?"

"It's no business of yours."

BRUTE was handed off to a half-grown boy with a shock of fiery hair. Once the boy decided that Brute wasn't going to tear him limb from limb, he attacked his role with enthusiasm, preening as passersby watched him giving the monster the grand tour. They went to the kitchens first but didn't eat anything, much to the dismay of Brute's empty stomach. He'd never imagined such an enormous place for cooking, or such vast quantities of food. "You'll fetch your meals from here," said the boy, whose name was Warin. "Three times each day. Just ask one of the scullery maids or pot boys and they'll fill plates for you and… him."

They left the kitchens through a side door, out into a courtyard that contained several brick ovens. Boys were carrying armfuls of wood and placing them under the bricks, presumably so the dinnertime breads could be baked. There didn't seem to be much reason to tarry in this courtyard, but Warin walked slowly, and Brute realized his guide was enjoying the other youths' gaping admiration. "Who is he?" Brute asked when they finally exited the courtyard and walked down a path of well-worn cobbles.

"Who?"

"Gray Leynham."

Warin glanced quickly from side to side, as if to check that nobody was listening, and whispered loudly, "He's a witch."

Brute's empty stomach gave an unhappy lurch. "A *witch*? But then can't he use his magic to escape?"

"He's lost his powers."

Brute had no idea how such a thing might happen. Were magical abilities like a small coin, something that might slip through a hole in one's pocket and disappear? Or were they more like a dog or a goat that might stray from home? He'd never met a witch before—just Hilma, who could speed healing with her chanting and herbs—and as a child, the stories he'd overhead of witches had scared him. He didn't much fancy actually living with one, even if this witch was chained behind bars. "Why is he kept prisoner?" he asked as they turned down a wider street.

Warin's answer was fierce. "He's a dirty traitor, that's why!"

"What did he do?"

"I don't know."

"If he's a traitor, why didn't they burn him?" Because that was the punishment for treason, at least in the tales he'd heard.

"I don't *know*." Warin huffed at him impatiently. "It don't matter to us anyway, does it? You just do as you're told. Long as you can, anyhow. The last man that watched over him, he only lasted three weeks. Think you'll do better?"

With another sickening clench of his belly, Brute said, "What happened to him?"

"Nothing awful. He just said he wasn't gonna stay in there no more. I hear he quit the guard and became a sailor instead."

The boy's answer did little to ease Brute's misgivings, so he remained distracted as they ducked down yet another little alley and into a shop of sorts, where a man was measuring a length of fabric. The shelves were stocked with bolts of cloth in many colors—scarlet, cream, and black predominant. There were also racks containing spools of thread, and tables with chalk and string and scissors atop them. "I suppose I'm meant to make a uniform for that," the tailor said to Warin, scowling at Brute.

"Not a uniform, says Lord Maudit. Just decent trousers—three pairs—and a half dozen shirts, and a cloak. Underclothes as well." As Warin rattled off the list, Brute had to fight to keep his face neutral. He'd never before owned half that much. Was it possible that the boy was mistaken? But the tailor didn't seem to think so, because he immediately began to poke and prod at Brute, turning him this way and that so every bit of him might be measured.

The tailor paused when he saw the condition of Brute's left arm. "How do you manage to dress yourself?" His curiosity seemed to be honestly professional.

"Not very well," Brute admitted. "It's hard to tie things."

The tailor nodded thoughtfully and chewed at his lip. "I'll see what I can do."

After the tailor, they visited the shoemaker, who seemed actually eager to make a pair of boots in Brute's size. "Give me two days," he said.

"Deliver them to the Brown Tower when they're ready," Warin ordered, a bit grandly.

"The Brown Tow— Oh. So he's the new— Ah."

Brute was getting tired of people talking about him as if he weren't there, or at least as if he were too stupid to understand. But he didn't say anything, not even to ask whether the shoemaker thought he could make boots that a one-handed man could get on.

The next stop was a barber, who waved his blade around a little too freely for Brute's taste. The barber made him sit on a stool, and then, as an assortment of children watched and giggled, he chopped Brute's thick black hair so short that hardly more than bristles were left. Brute didn't mind—easier to care for this way, and he certainly wasn't vain about his looks. The barber shaved him as well, washing Brute's face afterward with tepid water scented with astringent herbs.

Their final visit was to a low wooden building. The heat and dampness hit Brute as soon as they entered a small entryway, and Warin smiled. "Usually we gotta pay three coppers if we wanna use the baths, but His Excellency says you get in for free this time." He explained Brute's presence—at some length—to the matronly woman who appeared from the back. She looked intrigued but simply handed Brute a stack of towels.

"Wait here," she said.

Brute and Warin waited, both of them sitting on the foyer's lone wooden bench. Brute would have liked to ask more about his new charge, but Warin instead droned on about the palace's various rules and schedules, and the names of who was in charge of what, until Brute's head was spinning and he felt as stupid as he looked. Fortunately, the woman reappeared. "The one on the left," she said.

The door on the left led to a small chamber, in the center of which was a round copper tub filled nearly to the brim with steaming water. The room was floored in smooth stone. "Well?" said Warin. "I don't got all day."

Brute had rarely bathed before, at least not like this. Usually he made do by overturning a bucket or two of well water on his head or, if the weather was cold, wiping at his body with damp rags. He almost never had the coins to spare for the White Dragon's tin tub. On the infrequent occasions when the weather was fine and he had a few hours to himself, he would make his way to the secluded bit of river near his hidden cave and wade in as far as he dared. The idea of immersing himself in a giant bowl, as if he were an ingredient in an exotic soup, seemed strange and a bit decadent.

"Hurry *up*," Warin whined.

Brute hesitated a moment longer before he drew off his cloak and pulled his shirt over his head. Warin took the discarded clothing. "You always been that strong?" he asked.

Brute glanced down at himself. He didn't feel especially strong. He'd lost weight and muscle tone since the accident, but his chest still bulged impressively enough beneath its coating of dark hair. "I used to be small," he said. "Until I was about your age. Then I grew."

"Is your father that big?"

Brute's father had *seemed* very large indeed, when Brute was a boy. At least until the day Brute watched him hanging from a rope. That day his father looked very small. "Not like this," Brute answered.

"Huh." Warin shrugged, and then gestured for Brute to hurry things along. But when Brute managed to unlace his trousers and unwrap his breechclout, Warin whistled long and loud. "I guess all of you grew," he said, clearly impressed.

Brute blushed and climbed hurriedly into the tub, splashing a good bit of water over the sides as he did so. His sex organs were proportionate to the rest of him. It wasn't only his ugly face that made the whores demand double their usual price. The boys complained that, even if he took care with them, they'd be sore afterward, and their master claimed they'd be useless for at least a day.

The water felt unimaginably wonderful. It was lightly scented with something minty and astringent, and just hot enough to make his skin tingle. The tub would have been roomy for most men but was a bit of a tight fit for him. Still, he felt buoyant and light. He would have sung if he hadn't had an audience. Instead, he hunched down and submerged himself completely, staying underneath for as long as he could hold his breath, wondering as he did so how he'd managed not to drown when he fell off the cliff and into the river.

When he stuck his head out of the tub again, Warin was standing there and looking amused. "You look awfully happy to be getting clean," the boy observed. "My ma used to have to just about throw me into the water when she wanted me to bathe."

"She doesn't anymore?"

Warin's face tightened. "She's dead. Two years back. Childbed fever."

"I'm sorry," said Brute, although really he envied Warin a bit. The boy's mother might be gone, but by the looks of things, he wasn't faring too badly. Not like Brute, who'd been stuck with a mean drunkard of a relative, a man who'd resented the child with which he'd been saddled.

"Here," Warin said, and handed Brute a hunk of soap. It wasn't coarse and lumpy like the stuff Cecil supplied at the White Dragon. Brute had always half suspected that Cecil's soap took off more skin than dirt. But this soap was smooth and almond scented, and it produced a rich and creamy lather. There were definite benefits to living in a palace, Brute decided.

Brute scrubbed and then soaked, but eventually Warin grew impatient again, right around the time the water began to cool. Brute's stomach was clamoring louder than ever for dinner, so he climbed out of the tub and took the towel—large and thick—that Warin handed him. Drying off one-handed was a little awkward, and he was forced to put on his old, travel-smirched clothes again, which he regretted.

To Brute's considerable relief, the next bit of their journey took them back to the kitchens. He was still hopelessly lost, and vowed to note the route more carefully when they left. But in the meantime, Warin dragged him to a young woman with rosy, dimpled cheeks, her red hair arranged in a thick braid. "What's this then, brat?" she asked Warin, and Brute realized that they must be siblings. Fond ones, judging by the way she rumpled his hair.

"Brute."

"Uh-huh. And what am I supposed to do with him?"

"Feed him, of course."

She grinned, revealing a chipped front tooth. "Looks like he's apt to eat the cupboards bare."

"Lord Maudit says Brute'll be staying in the Brown Tower now."

Her eyes widened slightly. "Oh. I guess His Excellency's run out of volunteers here, and now he's having to hire one-pawed trolls instead."

"I am *not* a troll!" Brute said indignantly.

"Course not. Trolls are better dressed." Her smile was too warm for Brute to take offense, and he found the corners of his mouth twitching.

"Wait here. No—you're in the way." She pointed at the wall. "Wait there instead."

Brute pressed himself against the smooth stone, and Warin joined him. "That's Alys. Try to find her when it's mealtimes. She's bossy, but she'll set you up real good."

"Do you have other brothers and sisters too?"

"Yep. Four sisters and two brothers. Alys is the oldest."

Brute wondered what it would be like to grow up surrounded by so many other people. Crowded. Noisy. Never any privacy.

Alys returned a short time afterward with two tin buckets. She passed them to Brute, who was able to hold them in his one hand. "See you in the morning," she said before hurrying away.

On the way back to the Brown Tower, they took a brief detour and stopped at a well. Warin filled an earthen jug and hoisted it onto his skinny hip. "This oughta be enough to last you until tomorrow. If you need more, just tell the guard at the door and he can send someone."

Brute nodded and followed the boy again.

Warin stopped several paces from the tower's entrance. As the guard watched them curiously, Warin helped Brute steady the jug in the crook of his left arm. "So it's pretty easy for you from now on. If you need something, let me know."

"Where can I find you?"

"I'm always around somewhere. Just ask someone."

Brute felt an odd sense of abandonment as Warin waved and then scampered away into the growing dusk. The guard unlocked the front door, not quite looking Brute in the eye as he passed. It occurred to Brute that he had no idea whether there were other prisoners here as well, other caretakers. Maybe the place was full of treacherous witches and maimed giants. If so, they were all silent. The only sound Brute heard was the padding of his own bare feet and the slight sloshing of the water in the jug.

The door to his new quarters stood open.

He placed the buckets and the jug on the table. Someone had lit a pair of fat candles that were affixed to shelves on the wall, and a third one just outside the cell. The flames should have cast a cheery glow—the candles were much larger and nicer than any Brute had used before—but instead they only emphasized the darkness of the cell in the corner. The shadows seemed to dance and caper like demons.

"Um… hello?" Brute said, and when the words came out hoarser than he'd intended, he cleared his throat. "I've brought dinner."

There may have been a soft clanking of chains in response, but he wasn't sure. He moved the jug to one side and began to unpack the larger of the tin buckets. He was very pleased with what he found: a loaf of bread still warm from the ovens, a lidded pottery bowl full of a fragrant meat stew, a large hunk of cheese, and two small apples. There was even a jar of ale and a double handful of walnuts. The smaller bucket was less promising—it contained only a bowl of some sort of mush and a crust of dry bread. Was poor food part of the prisoner's punishment?

Brute planned to feed his charge first, but then his stomach complained again, and he decided he just couldn't face the man quite yet. He sat at his table and dove into the meal. It was delicious—the best he'd ever had. The stew was full of succulent meat and tender vegetables and spices he couldn't identify; the bread was crusty and wonderfully soft inside. Even the ale was better than he was used to. Alys had been so generous in her portions that he felt quite full by the time the food was gone.

He placed his empty dishes in the bucket, then fetched a tin cup he'd spied on a shelf. After filling it with water from the jug, he held the cup in the crook of his left arm and balanced the prisoner's meal awkwardly on top. That kept his hand free to unfasten the bolt on the barred door.

"Are you hungry?" Brute asked.

The blanket shifted a bit, and the matted hair appeared, but the prisoner didn't answer. With a sigh, Brute entered the cell.

The space wasn't very big, and he crossed it in only a few paces. He stood uncertainly over Gray Leynham for a moment before dropping inelegantly to his knees. "Here's your dinner."

The prisoner moved again, finally positioning his face in such a way that Brute could see it well. Leynham's beard was as long and matted as his hair, all of it too filthy for the original color to be distinguished. His cheeks were nearly as sunken as his empty eyes, his skin moon-white where it wasn't caked with grime. His skinny neck looked red and inflamed at the edges of the iron collar. Brute couldn't get any sense of his age, and he couldn't tell whether the fetid smell came from the prisoner, his ragged blanket, or the waste bucket in the corner. Maybe all three.

Brute was beginning to wonder what he should do if his charge refused to eat, but then from under the blanket a hand appeared, skeletal and shaking. Leynham still hadn't said anything, so Brute first handed him the tin cup. The prisoner tried to bring the cup to his mouth, but his palsy was so severe that a good portion of the water sloshed out. Brute placed the food on the floor and helped steady the cup as Leynham drank deeply.

"I can get you more if you want," Brute said when the water was gone. "After you eat."

"Th-th-th-thank y-y-you."

Abruptly, Brute was taken back to when he was a boy. The sheriff had decided to emulate Tellomer's wealthy citizens and had craftsmen install a sheet of glass in the front window of his house. It was a wonder indeed, and for days everyone in the village had paused to look, to touch reverently with their fingertips, to gaze at their reflection. Brute had liked the way the light sparkled off the glass in the mornings. And then one afternoon some miscreant with a grudge had thrown a stone, shattering the window. Brute and the other villagers had gathered around to stare at the shards of glass.

That's what Gray Leynham's voice was like: jagged fragments of delicate glass.

"I have a bowl here for you," Brute said.

Leynham's other hand emerged, this one equally thin and trembling, and like the other it sported a wide iron band around the wrist. A heavy chain trailed away from the manacle, no doubt connecting eventually with the bolts set into the floor. Brute settled the bowl in Leynham's palms and watched as the prisoner brought the bowl to his mouth and slurped at the contents. He licked the bowl clean, which made Brute feel guilty about the generous size of his own meal. As Leynham gnawed on the hunk of bread, Brute heaved himself to his feet and left the cell just long enough to put the empty bowl into the bucket and to refill the mug. Leynham took it gratefully when he returned, drinking every drop.

"More?" asked Brute.

Leynham shook his head.

"Can I— Is there anything else you need? I'll empty the waste bucket in the morning."

This time Leynham sighed like the wind whistling through treetops, and shook his head again. He let his head fall back then, so that it was propped against the wall. He looked exhausted, as if eating that simple meal had taken all his energy. Brute wondered what punishment he'd face if the prisoner died on his watch.

It took only a few moments to bolt the cell door, to tidy up the small mess he'd made, to piss in his chamber pot and wash up a little with the water from the jug. He briefly considered taking a fuller inventory of his room: there were items on the shelves, perhaps more in the drawers, and the tapestries were worthy of a long and careful examination. But then he yawned so widely that his jaw cracked. It was early yet, but he'd had an eventful day. After a final hesitation and a glance into the darkness of the cell, he stripped off his clothes, doused the candles, and climbed into the most comfortable bed he'd ever experienced. He had to curl his legs only a little to fit. He'd been having trouble sleeping—his missing hand was clenched so painfully tight—but tonight it took him only minutes to fall asleep.

 # CHAPTER *Five*

"NO! MERCIFUL gods, no! Please!"

Brute was out of bed and on his feet before he realized where he was. A bar of bright moonlight stole in through the room's slitted window, giving him barely enough illumination to make out the details of the room. A piercing scream rang out, and his sluggish brain stirred enough to note that he was in his new chambers in the Brown Tower at Tellomer Palace—and his prisoner was shrieking as if he were being torn to pieces.

Stumbling over his own big feet, Brute made his way to the cell. Gray Leynham continued to shout as Brute fumbled with the cell's latch. And then, just as the bars swung open, Leynham went suddenly and eerily quiet. As Brute yanked the filthy blanket off the prisoner's huddled form, he expected to find a mangled corpse. Instead, he jerked backward as Leynham sat up. In a clear, deep voice, Leynham said, "Gigo Blackwater will die in a fire." Then he collapsed bonelessly onto his side with a rattle of chains.

Brute's heart was racing and his breath came in short gasps as Leynham continued to lie there like a corpse. After Brute had calmed down a little, he cautiously put out his hand and touched the man's bare shoulder.

Leynham jerked and cried out, which made Brute startle so badly he fell back on his ass.

"Wh-wh-wh-what?" Leynham rasped in that broken-glass voice, slowly rising to a seated position.

"Are you hurt?"

Leynham seemed to consider the question for a moment before shaking his head. "Dr-dr-dream." He sighed wearily and held out a hand. "B-b-b-blanket, p-p-p-p—" He gave up with a frustrated growl.

Brute handed him the blanket, and Leynham wrapped it tightly around himself. He looked small and frail, his head hanging wearily. As Brute remained sitting next to him, unsure what he should do, Leynham lifted his head and turned, unseeing, in Brute's direction. "T-t-tell g-g-g-guard," he said quietly.

At first Brute didn't understand what he was talking about, and then he remembered his instructions from Lord Maudit: he was to report anything Leynham said while asleep. Given the nature of this particular dream, Brute decided he didn't want to know why. He rose to his feet and watched as the prisoner scooted backward against the wall. The stone floor would be much less comfortable than even Brute's lumpy old bed at the White Dragon, especially on bare skin stretched over meatless bones. "Do you want some water?" he asked.

Leynham appeared startled by the question, then nodded. So Brute filled the tin cup from the jar and held it to the other man's lips. "Th-th-th-thanks," Leynham rasped when he was through.

Brute relocked the cell door and pulled on his trousers and shirt. He didn't bother lacing up the trousers—too much trouble—instead he clutched the waistband in his fist so the trousers wouldn't fall down. The tower corridor was completely dark. He kept his elbow against the wall to help him find his way. At the very end, he used his stump to bang against the door. The stump was good for that much, at least.

After a moment, the door inched open. "What?" demanded the guard. He was backlit by bright moonlight. Brute couldn't make out his features, but he thought it was a different man than the guard he'd encountered earlier.

"The, um, prisoner. He had a dream."

The guard hissed with displeasure. "Fuck. All right. What did he say?"

Brute repeated the morbid statement about Gigo Blackwater, whoever that was. If the guard knew the meaning of the message, he gave no indication. He only swore again, more softly, and then nodded.

"Fine." Then he slammed the door in Brute's face, and the lock thunked into place.

That left Brute to return to his chambers in the darkness. Leynham was silent, perhaps sleeping again, and Brute was tired. He removed his clothing for the second time that night and again climbed into bed. The sheets were soft against his skin and smelled slightly of lavender; the quilts were old but clean and warm. Nothing whatsoever like a cold stone floor. He tossed and turned for a long time, his missing hand aching fiercely. Finally, when he couldn't stand it any longer, he stood and yanked one of the blankets off the bed. He crossed the room, unlocked the cell door, and tossed the quilt onto the prisoner's legs. He locked the door again before returning to bed, where sleep came swiftly.

IT WAS Brute's full bladder and empty stomach that finally woke him, the bright sun shining through the slitted window and revealing that he'd slept much later than usual. He stretched luxuriously—that mattress truly was a wonder—and glanced inside the cell. He smiled to himself when he saw that Leynham had spread his old blanket on the floor to provide a bit of padding. He was covered so completely by the quilt Brute had given him that only the top of his matted hair was showing. Perhaps Brute would get in trouble for granting that small mercy, but nobody had specifically ordered him *not* to share his bedding with the prisoner, and he might use ignorance as an excuse. People always assumed he was stupid anyway.

After using his chamber pot and putting his clothing back on, he unlocked the cell. "I'm going to empty your bucket. Do you need to use it first?"

Leynham sat up and, using the wall as support, slowly stood. He let the quilt fall to the floor and trailed his fingers along the wall as he hobbled the few steps to the bucket. He was naked, his body emaciated and dirty. Brute supposed he should turn his back and give the man a little privacy, but Leynham couldn't see him anyway, and Brute was shocked at the condition of the prisoner's body: bruised and scraped, covered in dried blood and other filth he didn't want to identify. The iron bands around Leynham's neck, wrists, and ankles seemed to weigh him down. Brute guessed he would have been a fairly tall man if he stood upright. Not as tall as Brute, of course—not even close—but taller than average.

Despite the nightmare and the bits of information Warin had divulged, there seemed to be nothing sinister about the prisoner. He was wretched, pitiable. It could be a ploy, Brute reminded himself. An effort to make the new jailer relax his guard so that the traitorous witch could—what? Cast evil spells? That didn't seem very likely.

After the cell was locked up again and Brute had emptied his own chamber pot into Leynham's bucket, he ventured back down the corridor. He didn't recognize the guard who blinked at him when the door was opened.

"What do I do with this?" Brute asked, indicating the stinking bucket.

The guard made a face and pointed at a tiny building nearby. "Dump it in there."

There turned out to be a latrine, a plank of wood with a hole, set over a wide pipe. Once the bucket was emptied, Brute put it near the entrance to the tower and set out in search of the kitchens. As he walked, he realized that he'd forgotten to bring the dishes from the previous night's dinner; he'd promise to fetch them later.

Along the way, he goggled at the bustle of activity and was goggled at in turn. Alys had a quick smile for him, though, and a little squeeze of his good arm before she hurried off to help another woman pile dishes on trays. He got lost three times on the way to the kitchens but only once on the way back.

Maybe Leynham was waiting for him, because he was sitting up when Brute returned, and his head was cocked as if he were concentrating on the sounds of Brute's movements. Brute gave him back the waste bucket, rinsed his hand with the jug water, and brought Leynham his breakfast—which proved to be more mush. Brute got salted fish and a doughy bread that was slightly sweet and, to his surprise and pleasure, slathered thickly with butter and strawberry jam. He hadn't tasted jam since he was a boy. His mother used to keep a pot of it in the house, and when she wasn't looking, he'd sneak over and dip his finger inside, enjoying the treat all the more because it was illicit.

When was the last time the prisoner had tasted something sweet?

Brute didn't try to speak with Leynham as they ate. Instead, he finished his own breakfast and wandered about the room a little, finally examining the contents in detail. The bookshelf was scuffed and slightly warped, but still sturdy. Its shelves were mostly bare, but a few items sat there: an extra tin cup, an empty glass jar, a neat pile of folded cloths that proved to be handkerchiefs, a knife, a piece of slate and hunk of chalk, three extra blankets, and a few crude wooden carvings of women and beasts. The drawers in the chest were empty, save for a few dried and crumbly sprigs of wormwood. Brute set his pathetically few belongings inside the top drawer.

And then, as he was turning away, he caught his reflection in the mirror.

His mother had owned a hand mirror. The glass was set into a silver frame with vines and flowers worked into the design. It was much too fine a thing for the likes of their little family; most likely his father had stolen it from someone. But his mother loved it, and every day she spent time sitting and looking at herself in the glass, checking to make sure her hair was arranged correctly and that her skin was still unlined. But Brute himself had never looked in her mirror, never ever, not even when he was very small. He knew what he looked like. Still, as he got older he couldn't avoid catching an occasional glimpse of his face reflected in the still water of the White Dragon's trough or even in an occasional puddle. He always turned away as quickly as he could.

Now, though, he drew closer to the mirror, as if he were bewitched by some sort of spell. He saw his dark hair shorn close to his skull, his broad, tanned cheeks stubbled by his morning's beard. He saw the eyes so many people found unsettling—one brown, one hazel—each crowned by a bushy black brow on a protruding forehead. His large nose was canted to one side and had a bump in the center, results of one of the beatings he'd received as a child. He had scars as well: a long one that diagonally traversed his chin, another near the right-hand corner of his lip, and a roundish one on his forehead. His teeth seemed too small for his long, broad jaw, and his chin jutted out like the prow of a ship. Even his ears were grotesque, huge fleshy saucers stuck at right angles to his head. Had he been the size of a normal man, he would have been simply ugly. But with his towering height and overgrown body, his features turned him into something else: a freak.

He frowned at his own self-indulgence and turned away from the mirror—but only after he'd twisted it around so that all he could see was its plain wooden back.

He tidied his bed and stacked the dirty dishes in the largest of the dinner pails and then was left with little to do. He wasn't used to sitting idle. He decided that perhaps he would wander the palace grounds for a while and get a better sense of the layout. If nothing else, he'd be entertained: constant activity buzzed everywhere.

He unlocked the cell and hunched beside Leynham, a tin cup in his hand. "Here's some water. You might want to drink it now because I'm going out for a while."

Leynham paused for a moment before nodding and then pulled the cup to his lips. When he was finished, he lifted the quilt Brute had given him. "H-h-h-here."

"Don't you want it?" The stone walls kept the room cool despite the warm sun outside, and the prisoner had no clothing to protect him from the chill.

Leynham turned his face to Brute, his brows drawn together in confusion. "M-m-mine?"

"If you like. I have more."

"B-b-b-but... wh-why?"

If Brute's hand had been free, he would have scratched his head. He didn't really have a good answer. Instead, he shrugged—which he knew the other man couldn't see—and repeated, "I have more."

After he locked the cell, he wandered around outside, garnering fewer stares than he had on his previous excursions. The palace locals were becoming accustomed to him. That was good. Although he doubted he would ever fade into the background, at least he didn't have to be the center of attention.

A crew of men was constructing a stone building, and Brute wished he could join them. They seemed happy, and their foreman yelled less and worked more than Darius ever had. He wandered to the kitchens, where it was too early for lunch but Alys gave him an apple and a piece of cheese anyway. Outside one particularly grand building, a garden had been planted with a riot of colorful flowers. He stood nearby for a while as two men and a woman pulled weeds and heaped them into a green and brown pile. He prowled around the walls of the palace, staring up at the guards who paced the ramparts, wondering if they got tired of that duty after a few years with no invasions. He found the stables and gave his apple core to a sorrel gelding with a white blaze on its nose. The horse nuzzled at his arm. He liked animals. They didn't care what he looked like.

He came upon a yard where soldiers were exercising, bare-chested and sweaty. He watched them for a very long time, until he finally sighed and wandered away. Maybe when he'd earned his first month's pay he'd visit the bawdy houses. The Harvest Moon Festival was months away, but there wasn't any particular reason why he had to wait that long. Hell, he could afford to fuck monthly now if he chose to. But somehow that thought didn't bring much cheer.

He found the armory and the kennels. He waved at the tailor, who promised him new clothing by the next day. He discovered a pleasant promontory where he could look out at the endless blue-green sea and the boats bobbing at the piers and the gulls wheeling overhead.

And then a tolling bell announced that it was lunchtime, and he made his way back to the kitchens without getting lost. He searched for Alys amongst the frantic activity, but she saw him first, shoving a bucket into his hand. "Bread, cheese, meat, pickles," she said cheerily. "And ale, of course."

He stood there for a moment, waiting, until she gave him a shove. "Away with you. You're too much of an obstacle in here."

"But… the prisoner's food?"

The corners of her mouth turned down. "He gets two meals a day."

Brute took his lunch to a stone bench tucked under the overhang of a building. He should have enjoyed sitting there, eating good food and watching people pass to and fro, but he kept thinking of Leynham, chained in a dark cell and long since deprived of such simple pleasures.

He knew he was being ridiculous. Leynham was a traitor. Once a dangerous man, it seemed. He probably deserved his fate.

A trio of little brown birds appeared from nowhere and landed at Brute's feet. They hopped around, eyeing him demandingly until he tossed a few bits of bread onto the pavement. The birds pecked and squabbled, one of them bold enough to poke at Brute's bare toes, which made him laugh.

But then he ran out of bread and the birds flew away, and his thoughts returned to his prisoner. It seemed to him that, no matter what evils a man had committed, making him suffer purely for the sake of suffering was pointless. It didn't undo the harm he had wrought; it didn't please anyone or improve anyone's life. His father's fate had been less cruel, really. Those last moments of terror, when even young Brute could tell that his father was struggling to keep his back straight and his mouth firm, a horrible drop... and then death. Followed by the afterlife—if it really existed—or simply nothing at all.

By early evening, Brute had concluded that he needed to find some way to occupy his time. Sitting and observing palace life would soon lose its charm. He could venture out into the city itself, of course, and undoubtedly he would soon do so. But even that activity would wear at him eventually. He realized that the wooden figures on his shelves must have been carved by a previous resident of his chambers, some man trying to pass the time. But Brute had never had a knack for carving, even when he possessed two hands. Surely there must be *something* he could do with himself besides eating, feeding Leynham, and emptying chamber pots.

At dinnertime he collected his tin pails from Alys. Two again, although a quick glance inside the smaller one confirmed his suspicion that it contained the usual mush and dry bread.

He lit the fat candles back in his room. In their flickering light, Leynham seemed to be waiting for him, propped against the wall with his knees drawn up against his chest and the quilt wrapped around him. "Hello," Brute said, because it would have felt rude not to.

"B-b-b-b-b—" Leynham made a garbled sound of frustration. "B-b-brute?"

"Yes." Brute set the tins onto the table and, after a brief hesitation, dug out the bowl of mush. "Are you hungry?"

Leynham sighed and shrugged one shoulder. Brute took this as an affirmative and filled the tin cup, noting that he would need to visit the well in the morning. And then, without consciously deciding to do so, he snagged a chunk of tender roasted beef from his own meal—which was accompanied by green beans, carrots, and tiny potatoes—and dropped a few slivers of the meat into the unappetizing bowl of mush.

He decided it would be easiest if he sat beside Leynham on the cell floor. Leynham flinched at first, but then relaxed and cocked his head. "F-f-food?"

"More or less." Brute helped him hold the small bowl.

But when Leynham tasted his first mouthful, he hissed sharply. "Wh-wh-wh-what?" he demanded.

"Just a few pieces of beef. I was afraid you might get sick with more. I can take them out if you don't want them."

Leynham definitely *did* want them, judging by the speed and enthusiasm with which he ate his dinner. He licked the bowl again, then nibbled on his bread until Brute gave him some water to wash it down.

"Wh-wh-who *are* y-y-y-you?"

"Nobody."

"G-g-g-guard?"

"No. I'm—I *was* a laborer. I'm from a village a few hours away." Brute's answer seemed to puzzle the other man, and when Leynham spent a few moments struggling to get his mouth to obey him, Brute decided it probably wouldn't hurt to divulge more details. "The prince had an accident and I saved him, but I was hurt. He gave me this job to thank me, I guess."

"Wh-wh-wh-which p-p-p-prince?" Leynham demanded.

"Prince Aldfrid."

Leynham recoiled slightly. "F-f-f-friddy," he whispered.

"I certainly wouldn't call him that, but yes." Brute sat back, trying to better gauge the other man's expression. That was a difficult task in the dim light, and Leynham's missing eyes masked much of his emotion.

Leynham's shoulders slumped, and he ran a shaking hand over his forehead. He opened his mouth, closed it again, and shook his head slowly. The conversation seemed to be over, and Brute's meal awaited, so he made as if to stand. But before he could rise completely, Leynham reached over and grabbed his knee. "W-w-w-wait. Wh-wh-wh-wh— Fuck!" He took a deep breath and let it out. "Wh-why so k-k-kind?"

Nobody had ever called Brute kind before, and he'd never thought of himself that way. Really, he had done very little for this man. But that little was apparently more than the previous guardian had managed. "I don't know. It doesn't... it doesn't cost me anything to do these things, does it? And I've never really had the chance before to— well, I don't know." He twitched nervously. He wasn't used to having to explain himself. People didn't generally ask him many questions, least of all about himself.

He recognized the expression on Leynham's face then: desperation. "St-st-stay awhile. D-d-d-don't g-g-g-go back to y-y-your v-v-v-village yet. P-p-p-p-please." Every word was a painful effort, and he seemed to hold his breath as he waited for an answer.

"I've nothing to go back to. I'll stay."

Leynham let go of Brute's knee and slumped back against the wall in relief. Brute gathered the empty bowl and cup and crossed to the cell door. But even as he locked it again, the prisoner sat up straight and made a slight noise, like a clearing of his throat. "B-b-brute?" he said.

"Yes?"

"P-p-please. I'm G-g-gray."

"Good night, Gray," Brute replied. He thought maybe he sensed the shadow of a smile cross the other man's lips.

 # CHAPTER
Six

BRUTE'S new clothing arrived on the second day. Although clearly intended to be serviceable rather than fashionable, it was finer than anything he had owned before and fit him perfectly. He spent a long time running his hand gently over the fabric. The tailor had taken care with the design so Brute could dress easily: the shirts simply slipped over his head, and instead of laces, the underclothes and trousers fastened with large buttons made of polished shell. He had even been given a heavy cloak of charcoal-colored wool with a bit of scarlet trim. The cloak would keep him very warm when the weather grew cold. When he wore his new clothing, Brute stood a little straighter and felt slightly less like a monster.

But it was the boots that truly astounded him. Along with the wool socks that had been delivered, the boots fit him perfectly. The dun-colored leather was soft and supple, and the boots fastened with clever metal toggles that he could easily manage one-handed. It was far better footwear than anything he could have obtained in the village. In fact, he was reasonably sure that none of the Geddings possessed finer shoes. He was slightly regretful that Darius couldn't see him now; the foreman would squirm with envy.

Brute wasn't sure what to do with his old clothing. Nobody in the palace would want it, and it wouldn't fit anyone anyway. But he couldn't quite bring himself to throw it away because, aside from his knife and razor, those rags were all that he had owned when he arrived. He ended up washing his old clothes next to the nearby well—

passersby rolling their eyes at him—and when the trousers and shirt were dry, he folded them neatly and placed them in the bottom drawer.

When he wasn't doing laundry or managing mealtimes, Brute had little to occupy himself. He wandered the grounds of the palace so thoroughly that soon he knew the open areas as well as those of his old village—although he didn't enter any of the buildings, aside from the kitchens. Some of the people began to smile and greet him as they passed. One afternoon he walked by the half-built structure just as the men were taking a break, and a few of them chatted amiably with him for a few minutes. They were constructing an observatory, which was apparently going to be used by one of the princes—not Aldfrid—to watch the stars. Neither the workers nor Brute had any idea why the prince would wish to do so, but they all concluded that the whims of royalty were beyond the ken of ordinary folk.

In the evenings, Brute and Gray spoke very little. Brute wasn't used to companionship of any kind, and speech was an enormous struggle for Gray. But sometimes Brute caught himself singing, and Gray didn't seem to mind. In fact, when Brute sang a bawdy ditty about a farmer and his randy wife, Gray made a dry rustling sound that Brute realized was actually a chuckle. Brute continued to mix little bits from his own meals in with Gray's mush, which always earned him a stuttered thanks.

The men had three nights of uninterrupted sleep before Gray woke Brute again in the middle of the night. This time Gray wasn't screaming; instead, he was sobbing, sounding for all the world like a forlorn child. As Brute stumbled his way to the cell, he decided that the shrieking was preferable. When he got to Gray's side, the man continued to weep. Brute simply sat there for several moments, unsure what to do, until he couldn't stand it any longer. Then he wrapped his arms around the huddled figure and patted the quilt-covered back. The crying decreased a little, and Gray leaned against Brute's chest. That's when Brute began to hum one of the lullabies he dimly remembered his mother using when he was very small and needed comforting.

Gray's body was frail and bony against Brute's, with only the quilt between them. Brute hummed and rocked a little and tried not to think about how good it felt to hold someone in his arms, to have a few minutes of human contact.

After a time, Gray pulled away. He sniffled twice. In a little-boy voice with a hint of a lisp but not a trace of stammer, he said, "Sebbi Jonzac. He's going to catch a terrible fever, so very fast. He's going to die from it."

Then he slumped to the floor.

This time, Brute didn't try to wake him. Instead, he left the cell, bolted it shut, and pulled on a shirt and trousers. By the time he was fully dressed, Gray was sitting up again, shivering slightly under his blanket. "B-b-b-brute?"

"I'm going to give your message to the guard. Do you want some water first?"

Gray shook his head, so Brute padded down the hall and pounded on the door. The guard swore viciously when Brute told him what Gray had said. "Do you know— Who's Sebbi Jonzac?" Brute asked.

"Coenred Jonzac is a member of the guard. Sebbi's his only son. He's six or seven years old."

Brute's stomach knotted uncomfortably. "What Gr—what the prisoner said. Is it true? Is the boy dying?"

"Maybe. I don't know. Fuck." The guard sighed noisily. "Get back in. I have to get word to my captain."

Although he wanted to ask more questions, Brute obeyed. He was slightly relieved when he returned to his chambers and saw that Gray had fallen asleep again. But it took a long time for Brute to follow suit, and when he did, he dreamed of dying children.

GRAY was more withdrawn than usual the following morning, turning away to face the wall as soon as he'd finished his breakfast. Brute honestly didn't mind that much. He wondered whether the other man was aware that Brute had held him as he'd cried the night before.

Brute gathered the dirty dishes and brought them to the kitchens, where pot boys were busily scrubbing and most of the bakers and cooks rested before beginning the preparations for lunch. It took a small army of people to feed the palace's population, and they all toiled very hard, with excellent results. Brute had already gained back some of the weight he lost while recovering from his injury. It helped that Alys seemed to have enlisted some coworkers in her endeavors to keep Brute well fed. Whenever he showed up at the kitchens, even if it wasn't mealtime, people would hand him little tidbits of this and that. He suspected that some of what he was given was meant for the tables of the royal family, since he'd never dreamed of the existence of so many delicious things.

"You're not hungry again already?" Alys asked him with a smile as she walked by, lugging a huge basket full of potatoes.

Brute scooped the basket away from her, cradling it in his arms and earning a grin. He followed her over to an enormous table, where several girls were chopping vegetables. "I was just stopping by," he said, grinning back at her as he set the basket down and grabbed a bit of carrot to shove into his mouth.

"And what are you doing with yourself today? Aside from eating our cupboards bare."

The answer was out of his mouth before he even realized he'd made a decision. "I thought maybe I'd walk around the city for a while."

She tilted her head and gave him a long, considering look. "Sounds like a good idea," she finally said. "Do you mind if Warin tags along? He knows his way around well enough, but I don't like him out of the palace by himself."

Slightly bemused at the idea of having company, Brute shrugged. "Sure."

He didn't know how Alys managed to get word to her brother—perhaps she used special magic, because the boy seemed to appear from nowhere almost immediately, bouncing up and down with excitement. "Hurry up, Brute! I have three coppers that are all my own, and there's this sweet shop that has the best stuff in the world. I'll take you there!"

Alys cuffed him gently on the head. "Brute might not want to visit sweet shops, brat."

"A sweet shop sounds perfect," said Brute, who'd never been to one.

Warin took Brute's hand and tugged him impatiently out of the kitchens and to the palace's front gates. A part of Brute still feared he might be a captive here—for what, he wasn't sure; but then, did royalty really need a reason?—so he was pleasantly relieved when the guards at the gate simply scowled as he passed.

He and Warin were almost immediately thrust into the bustling crowds. Warin was very good at worming his way through clots of people, which Brute was far too large to do. He could have used his bulk to simply shove his way forward, but he didn't want to cause offense. Several times he lost sight of the boy altogether, but fortunately, Warin had no troubles at all finding the towering Brute and always made his way back to pull at Brute's hand and urge him on.

They were soon in a section of Tellomer that Brute had never visited. Men and women in fancy clothing strolled down clean pavement, stopping to eye the goods arrayed in shop windows. And what goods they were! Dishes painted in fanciful patterns, jewelry in gleaming silver and gold, rugs that must have taken someone a lifetime to weave, dresses and shirts of beaded and embroidered silk. One shopkeeper with an oiled mustache stood proudly before an array of little glass jars that filled the entire street with the scents of flowers and spices and musk. A short couple were rearranging their display of wooden musical instruments, most of which Brute had never seen before and couldn't identify. One place sold yarns in a rainbow of colors, one was a stationer's with beautiful papers, and another seemed to have nothing but beads and miniature figures made of blown glass.

It was a large shop on a corner that stopped Brute in his tracks, however, much to the annoyance of the women walking behind him. "Glorious gods," he breathed.

Warin had continued walking, not noticing that Brute had stopped, and now he doubled back. "They're just books," he said when he saw what Brute was staring at.

"I didn't think there were that many books in the whole world," said Brute, who had caught glimpses of volumes now and then, usually in the hands of travelers who stopped at the White Dragon.

Warin waved his hands dismissively. "There are more books than that in the palace library."

"You've been there?"

"Only about a thousand times. It's not so great. Dusty. And you have to be quiet and sit still."

"Why would *you* be sitting in a library?"

"Lessons, of course!" Warin huffed melodramatically. "I used to have them five mornings a week, and the schoolmaster would whack my head with his stick if I didn't pay attention, but it was so boring! I don't have to go anymore, though. I'm old enough."

"So… you can read?"

"Of course I can read!" Warin squinted his eyes and looked up at him. "You can't?"

"No," Brute answered shortly, and resumed walking.

The sweet shop was only a block away. There were a few dainty tables outside, populated by women sipping tiny glasses of tea. The inside had a long wooden counter, behind which shelves of glass jars held candies of yellow, red, brown, black, and green. Tables were set off to the side, where two women with pink scarves over their hair poured drinks for the customers and set out delicate little plates of pastries. Warin wasn't the only child in the shop. Several other boys and girls stood in a line along the counter, gazing up at the sweets avariciously. But they turned and gasped when Brute entered the shop. Warin puffed up his narrow chest and walked confidently forward.

The shopkeeper was an old man, not much bigger than Warin. "Yes?" he asked the boy, giving Brute a wary glance.

"One copper each of lemon, mint, and peach," Warin immediately responded. Likely he'd been planning this purchase for some time.

The man nodded and scooped the brightly colored little balls and twists into a paper cone. Brute thought they'd leave the shop then, but instead Warin hurried across the floor and plopped himself into one of the chairs. Brute followed, eyeing the chair suspiciously before sitting down, relieved when it didn't collapse beneath him. He felt ridiculous, though, perched on such a tiny seat.

Warin crunched happily for a few minutes before holding his cone toward Brute. "Have some."

"I haven't any money."

"So? I already paid for them. C'mon. Alys'll tan my hide if she thinks I ate this much on my own."

The boy's casual generosity stunned Brute more than anything he'd experienced since he came to the palace. "Thank you," he said hoarsely and took a couple of candies between his fingers. He popped them in his mouth and sucked at them, savoring their sweetness.

"You're here to keep tabs on me, aren't you?" Brute said after a while.

Warin shrugged. "Sort of. But I really wanted to go. I hardly ever get out of the palace. Everyone's too busy to take me, and Alys says I'm too young to go on my own. Which is *not* true, but there's no use arguing with her."

"Why do I need a minder?"

"'Cause they want to make sure you come back." The boy looked suddenly concerned. "You *are* planning on going back, right?"

"Of course. But the other… the other people who've stayed in the Brown Tower, they haven't?"

"Some of 'em stuck around for a few weeks. One guy was there for three or four months. But one man left after his first night!"

"Because of the dreams?"

Warin used a finger to dig compressed candy from his teeth. "Yeah. They got scared. He only dreams about people who are nearby, and I guess they were afraid he'd dream of them next."

"Do his dreams always come true?"

"Nah. Sometimes they can be stopped. That's how come you have to listen, to tell what he says."

Brute was slightly relieved to learn that Gray's prophesies weren't infallible. "Warin, the things he dreams of… is he just seeing the future, or is he making those things happen?"

"Dunno."

And that must have settled the matter in Warin's mind, because he poured three candies onto the table in front of Brute, shoved the rest into his own mouth, and stood. "Let's go. There's lots more to see. Sometimes there's jugglers over by the green market."

So Brute slipped the candies into his pocket and followed the boy out into the street.

Brute was fairly certain that Warin's chosen route was not the most direct one, but it was certainly interesting, at least from a child's point of view. Brute didn't mind; it wasn't as if he had a particular destination in mind. After several blocks of posh houses, followed by more modest homes where dogs barked at them from front doors, they passed into a tradesmen's district. Warin stopped to watch men hammering metal or cutting leather into various shapes. Even Brute was fascinated by the glassblowers sweating in front of their furnaces, and he enjoyed the scents of the breweries and distilleries. Then a terrible smell filled their noses as they reached the tanneries with their enormous vats of colored dyes. They didn't stay there long, instead twisting and turning down narrow streets where the people looked tired and hungry and where some begged pleadingly with passersby. Brute saw a man—a young man, not much older than himself—who was slumped against a wall, a cracked bowl placed in front of him to receive coins. Both arms ended in angry-looking stumps at the elbows, and for the first time, Brute was thankful for his own misfortune.

Ramshackle hovels gave way to tiny shops and then to taverns that were raucous even at midday. On a street smelling of sour ale and urine, a man stumbled out of an inn and collided with Brute. Despite being two heads shorter, the man blocked Brute's way, swaying slightly and staring blearily. "Not so tough," he said. He drew out all the vowels as if the consonants were sticking on his tongue.

"Excuse me," muttered Brute and tried to move around him.

But the man sidestepped too—clumsily—and wobbled closer. They were almost touching, and Brute could smell his foul breath. "Not so tough," the man repeated.

A small crowd materialized, drunken men and women who were eager for a bit of entertainment, small boys who jeered and clapped. "I won't fight you," Brute said, as mildly as he could. He pulled the stump of his maimed arm out of his pocket, producing gasps and catcalls from his audience. "See? I can't."

His assailant poked him in the chest. "Coward."

"I'm not. But you're rat-assed and I'm damaged, and I haven't any quarrel with you."

Maybe the man would have come to his senses and stepped away, but Warin chose that particular moment to butt in, announcing grandly, "We're the king's men. Now stand aside!"

The crowd erupted in laughter and the man snorted. "King's men, eh? Guttersnipe and his pet monster, more like. King wouldn't have nothing to do with the likes of you."

Warin's face turned almost as red as his hair, and he kicked the man's shin. The audience roared with laughter, but the man growled and backhanded Warin in the face. Warin went flying as blood spurted thickly from his nose. To the boy's credit, he didn't back down. He growled and lowered his head, butting into the man's ample belly hard enough to make him grunt and stagger back a step. The man grabbed a fistful of Warin's hair.

Brute didn't know what the man had in mind to do next, and he didn't wait to find out. He snarled, stepped forward, and brought his fist down directly on top of the man's skull. The man crumpled like a puppet with its strings cut and lay motionless on the cobbles. Warin gave him a vicious kick in the side.

"Is he dead?" called an ancient crone with messy gray hair.

Warin dragged a sleeve under his nose. "Nah."

Brute thought the crowd seemed disappointed at that. "Let's go," Brute said quietly to him, even as the bystanders surged forward with offers to buy them both drinks. Warin seemed slightly hesitant to leave the excitement, but he allowed himself to be hauled off.

By the time they were only a few blocks away, Warin was nearly giddy with enthusiasm. He retold their brief confrontation over and over, embroidering the details a little more each time, until it sounded as if the two of them had taken on a legion of enemies and Brute had slaughtered the lot of them with barely lifting a finger.

"Let's go to the market, Brute," Warin wheedled as he danced back and forth. "The jugglers and the acrobats and— Or maybe the docks? I bet we can get on one of the ships and—"

"We're going back to the palace."

"But it's hardly even lunchtime! I haven't shown you the fish market yet or the weavers or—"

"Another time. I think we've had enough adventures for one day."

Warin pouted but followed along, and it didn't take long before his mood brightened again. He poked tenderly at his swollen nose. "Do you think it's broken? Do you think maybe I'll end up with a bump like yours?"

"I'm sure it'll be fine and straight."

"Oh." Warin sounded disappointed. "Maybe if I sort of whack at it...."

"Why would you want to ruin your face with a nose like mine?"

"Because you... you're amazing! You're like Fenris. In the story, you know? Big as a mountain and brave as a bull and he saves a whole town from the monsters of the chasm."

"I'm only a man, Warin. And not much of one." But Brute couldn't hide the pleased grin on his face, and it stayed there the whole way back to the palace.

CHAPTER
Seven

WHEN they returned to the palace, Brute had to face Alys, who was not at all pleased to have her brother returned to her with his nose swollen and his shirt hopelessly bloodstained. But then Warin began telling her what had happened, complete with reenactments and embellishments that Brute kept trying to correct. All of the kitchen staff who weren't otherwise employed gathered around to listen and watch, and Brute felt his face go scarlet with embarrassment over the attention.

"You really saved Warin with a single punch?" Alys finally asked.

"It was… I suppose. The man was really drunk. A tap on the shoulder probably would have made him pass out."

"You must be a good fighter."

Brute's blush intensified. "Not really." In truth, the first and last time he'd fought anyone was just after his remarkable growth spurt began. Until then he'd been bullied unmercifully by other children— and by his great-uncle. The village boys liked to waylay him while he ran his errands, and he'd curl into a pathetic ball as they kicked and punched and spat at him, knowing that when he got home he'd face another beating from his great-uncle for being late. But then, seemingly overnight, Brute grew. The next time he was attacked, he fought back, earning success more from sheer size than adept technique. The boys had limited their harassment to verbal taunting after that, which he tried to ignore. His great-uncle had continued to thrash him, however, literally until the day the old man died.

Alys reached up and stroked Brute's bicep. "Thank you for protecting my brother."

Brute hung his head and mumbled something inchoate.

A large man in a stained apron appeared and yelled at everyone to get back to work. They scrambled to obey, but not before quite a few of them clapped Brute on the back. Alys shooed Warin away to clean himself up, but she told Brute to wait where he was. She returned a few minutes later with Gray's dinner pail and a large basket covered with a linen napkin. "These are special," she said, nodding her chin at the basket. "They were made for the king and his guests tonight. But we can spare a few, and you've earned them." She smiled and then hurried away.

Whatever was in the basket smelled wonderful, and Brute was famished. He hadn't eaten since breakfast. But as he walked back to the Brown Tower, it occurred to him that Gray hadn't eaten since breakfast either, that he never got more than two meals a day, and that those meals were small and bland.

Gray was awake when Brute entered his chamber, turning his face in the direction of the table, where Brute set the food. "B-b-b-brute?"

"It's me," Brute answered, and couldn't help but notice that Gray sighed with relief. "Sorry I was gone so long. I brought dinner, though. Just give me a minute."

Gray nodded. "D-d-didn't th-th-th-th—fuck!—th-think you'd c-c-c-come b-b-b-back."

"I guess I'm too stupid to stay away," said Brute. "Nowhere else to go anyway." He lifted the fabric from the basket and discovered a half dozen golden rounds of dough, each with poppy seeds sprinkled on top. Alys had put some grapes in the basket too—large red ones—and a bottle of wine. He wondered what the king would think he if he knew that his ogreish new employee was consuming his fine food and drink. Then he shrugged philosophically and took a large bite of one of the rolls, moaning as he tasted the filling of extremely tender and delightfully spiced meat. He gobbled it down quickly before grabbing a second roll and Gray's bowl of mush, then made his way to the cell.

Gray almost yelped with surprise when Brute handed him the roll. "Fuck!" He never seemed to have any problem with that word, Brute noticed and smiled. Gray nibbled at the roll slowly, pleased little sounds coming from his throat the entire time. He ate his mush as well, although with considerably less enthusiasm. He could hold the bowl by himself now, Brute noticed, and without any shaking of his hands.

"N-n-not m-m-m-meant to f-f-feed me like th-th-th-that," Gray said when he was done.

"I know. But you're not going to tell anyone, are you?"

Gray snorted. "N-n-no."

"Then nobody will know." Brute stood and gathered the empty bowl.

He had considerable difficulty getting the cork out of the wine bottle. It wasn't something he'd practiced often even when he had two hands. But eventually he propped the bottle between this thighs and dug at the cork with the tip of his knife, and he was able to get at the liquid inside. Little bits of cork floated in it, but he didn't care. The wine was lovely. He drank it all while he ate his food, and he was left feeling warm and comfortable and content.

He was sleepy too, so he decided to wash up and get ready for bed. He removed his shirt first, but as he was unbuttoning his trousers, he remembered the candies. He pulled them out of his pocket and gazed at his palm: three slightly linty balls, one yellow and two green. He popped one of the green ones in his mouth and looked speculatively toward the cell. What was the point of being happy if you couldn't share it, at least a little, he thought.

Gray startled a bit when Brute opened the cell, and seemed to tense under his quilt. But Brute simply crouched beside him and held out his hand. "Here. This is for you." When Gray didn't react—aside from deepening his frown—Brute gently fished Gray's left arm out from under the blanket and transferred the candies to Gray's slightly clenched hand.

Gray sniffed at the candies, then poked them with a fingertip. "Wh-wh-wh-what?"

"Just sweets. I was given them as a gift today, and I suppose they're mine to give away if I want to."

Gray put the candies in his mouth and spent a long time sucking on them. He had a strange expression on his face, one that Brute couldn't place. But then it was hard to read him anyway, between the dim light and his mass of beard and hair, and the nothingness where his eyes should be. But when Brute stood up, Gray reached out and tentatively touched his leg. "C-c-c-can I f-f-feel y-y-y-you?"

"What?"

The prisoner sputtered helplessly as he tried to say something, but Brute couldn't make any sense of it. Finally, Gray swore again, twice—"Fuck! Fuck!"—and then mimed running his fingertips over his face. Brute understood.

"You want to see—to feel my face."

Gray sighed a bit and nodded twice.

"It's not a nice face." But even as he said it, Brute wondered if a man could tell with his fingers that Brute was ugly. Would he *feel* ugly too?

"P-p-please," Gray whispered. "W-w-w-want t-t-to know y-y-you. H-h-help m-m-me remember. L-l-l-later."

"When I'm gone, you mean."

Gray nodded again and turned his head away.

Maybe Brute should have refused. But nobody had ever wanted to remember him before, and people certainly weren't clamoring to touch him. His skin felt hungry for it, like his stomach when he'd missed a few meals. So he collapsed onto the floor, sitting cross-legged next to Gray, so close that his knees brushed against Gray's blanket-covered leg. "Okay."

Brute had given up trying to guess the prisoner's age, but when Gray smiled at him now, Brute realized that the other man was younger than he'd expected, although well past his youth. Midthirties, maybe. Just a few years older than Brute. How many of those years had he spent chained in this cell?

Gray shifted himself around so that his knees pressed against Brute's. His chains clanked as he moved. He lifted his right hand and reached forward, then seemed surprised when his fingers touched Brute's lower neck instead of his face. "Tall!" he exclaimed, stammer-free.

Brute laughed. "I am." He wondered what mental image Gray had of him, and how close it was to the truth. Then he stopped wondering anything and nearly held his breath as questing fingers ghosted over his closely shorn scalp, over his heavy brow and crooked nose, over his evening-stubbled cheeks, over his scars. Even over his smooth, dry lips—which caused an involuntary shiver.

But then Gray continued to touch him, sliding his fingertips gently down Brute's neck. When he reached the notch between collarbones, he raised his other hand as well and glided his palms to both of Brute's shoulders. "B-b-b-big," he said, sounding impressed.

The knot in Brute's throat was too thick for him to reply, even as Gray's hands moved slowly down his biceps. This man was a witch, Warin had said. Maybe this was some kind of spell, a continuation of Gray's supposedly nefarious deeds. The sensations matched what he suspected magic would feel like—everywhere Gray touched tingled slightly, as a sleeping limb did when it was in the process of waking up.

But Brute remained still, and Gray traced the heavy muscles of his forearms. And then Gray's left hand continued past Brute's wrist and down to the heavy knuckles, while his right hand—well, it ran out of things to feel. Gray gasped. "B-b-b-brute?"

"Accident."

Gray took a deep breath. Brute expected he might be disgusted, but he didn't seem to be. He delicately felt the contours of the rounded stump before pulling away completely. "Y-you're st-st-still strong."

Honestly, Brute was feeling a little weak in the knees. But he climbed to his feet and left the cell, bolting it carefully behind him. He pulled off his trousers and breechclout, and he climbed into his comfortable bed and went to sleep.

If either of them dreamed that night, the images weren't enough to wake them.

 # CHAPTER *Eight*

"YOU seem to want to make a habit of being a hero," said Lord Maudit.

Brute swallowed uncomfortably and looked around the room for a moment before answering. "I'm not, Your Excellency. It was only a drunken ass—a drunken lout, someone who didn't know better than to raise his hand to a child."

Maudit pursed his lips and stood, then walked out from behind his desk. His office had a large window with a view of the sea. It almost hurt Brute's eyes to look out at the sunlight sparkling on water, but Maudit didn't seem bothered. He stood at the window for so long Brute wondered if the interview was complete.

But then Maudit spun around and narrowed his sharp eyes as he assessed Brute. "You haven't run off yet like the others did. But I understand the prisoner has had three... nightmares under your charge."

Brute nodded. The third had been two nights earlier, when he had been awakened by unearthly moans. Some man dying of an abscess in his jaw, apparently. Brute had relayed the message as obediently as the others. "Did the child, the one with the fever...."

"His family brought a healer to him in time. He's fine. Gigo Blackwater perished in a fire a few days ago, however. But what of you? You aren't frightened?" Lord Maudit's next question was blunt. "Aren't you afraid he'll murder you with his visions?"

"I.... He might."

"Then why haven't you run yet?"

"Because…." Brute ran his fingers through his bristly hair. "I'm not a coward, sir."

Maudit waved a hand in his direction. "All those muscles won't protect you from death, you know."

"I do know. I nearly died already, milord."

"Do you *want* to die?"

"No!" Brute was surprised at the vehemence of his own response. Not very long ago his thoughts had been quite different on the matter.

"Then I'll ask you again. Why are you still here?"

"It's my job, milord. My responsibility."

"Responsibility! You feed the man and you clean up his shit."

It seemed to Brute as if he did a bit more than that, although he didn't say so. "I know it's not like… like running a country. But it's…. Until recently I was a laborer. I hauled rocks and timbers and carts."

"Work any mule could do."

"Mostly, yes, milord. But it was my job then and I did it. Now I've been told to look after the prisoner and I do that."

Lord Maudit sneered. "Do you do everything you're told to?"

"Not always." Brute squared his shoulders. "I do when I think it's right."

The lord was silent a moment, although his jaw worked. Finally he sighed very loudly and walked across the room to an ornate wooden armoire. The piece of furniture was huge, taller even than Brute, and it towered over the tiny nobleman. He pulled at a handle on its side and a door swung open; then he reached in and produced a blown-glass cup of blue and gold and a crystal decanter three-quarters full of amber liquid. He poured until the cup was nearly full. Every one of his movements was quick and exact, as if he woke up in the morning and planned out what each muscle would do for the day. When he swallowed his drink, even his throat worked precisely.

He drank the entire contents of the glass, gazing steadily at Brute the whole time. Then he replaced the glass and decanter in the cupboard and closed the door with a tiny *thunk*. He marched over to

Brute, and although Brute was a good two and a half feet taller, somehow it seemed as if Lord Maudit were looking down at him. "What if I offered you thirty gold pieces to leave your employment at the palace?"

Brute's jaw dropped with an audible click. "Thirty...." He'd never even glimpsed a gold piece, not once in his life.

"Thirty gold pieces. I'm sure you cannot do the sums, but that would be enough for you to purchase a home for yourself. Nothing elaborate, but a large step up from whatever hovel you previously inhabited. It would keep even you in food and ale for the rest of your life. Provide enough for a few small luxuries, if you managed your finances with care. You'd be sufficiently well off that you might attract a wife. Some woman who would be willing to overlook your obvious... limitations in exchange for a life of secure comfort."

"Wh-wh-why...." He seemed to have caught Gray's stutter. "Why would you offer me such a thing?"

Lord Maudit's eyes narrowed. "My reasons are no concern of yours. What is your answer, Brute?"

Brute didn't know whether this was some sort of test, and if so, what the proper response was supposed to be. For a moment he pictured himself living in his own home, never having to worry about whether he could afford his next meal. And then he pictured Gray Leynham alone in his miserable cell, with even the small comforts of quilt and scraps of decent food gone. "I'll stay here," he replied firmly.

The lord shook his head. "Dammit, Friddy," he mumbled. Then he sighed again. "Young Warin's family has a long history here."

"Yes, Your Excellency." Brute was taken aback by the conversation's sudden change in direction.

"Not simply as cooks, although I imagine you might appreciate that function the best. Warin's grandfather fought with King Aldhelm at the Battle of Two Rivers, and his great-grandmother was a midwife who attended the royal births. They're good people, Warin's family. Loyal and hardworking. The kind of men and women we rely on to keep the kingdom functioning well."

"Warin and Alys have been very kind to me."

"The boy thinks you ought to be declared a national hero, and his sister isn't far behind in her views."

Brute shifted his feet uncomfortably. "It was a very small thing, milord, and I don't think—"

"What you think is immaterial." Lord Maudit pinched the bridge of his nose. "I've been asked to grant you a boon."

"A… what, sir?"

"A bonus or a favor. A reward of sorts. So. What is it you wish to have?"

Taken aback once more, Brute could only stand there with his mouth open.

The lord rolled his eyes and huffed. "I do have other matters to attend to today. What shall it be? A silver ring, perhaps? A dozen bottles of the king's finest wine? Use of a horse and carriage for a week? A title, maybe? A plot of land—"

"Lessons," Brute blurted out.

"Pardon me?" Lord Maudit's thin eyebrows rose and disappeared under his forelock.

"I want to learn to read. Warin said he used to attend lessons."

"Why would someone like you need to read?"

Brute didn't have an answer to that. He hadn't needed reading to work for Darius, and he didn't need it to care for Gray. It wasn't as if he had delusions of becoming a scholar someday, or of being respected for anything but his size. "I want to… to know things," he finally mumbled.

Lord Maudit snorted, but then he shrugged. "Very well. You shall have your lessons."

IF BRUTE hadn't been simultaneously excited and nervous, he would have been embarrassed. He sat cross-legged on a polished marble floor in a large, mostly unadorned room. A dozen boys and girls—ranging in age from about six to ten—sat in front of him. They kept twisting around to stare at him, erupting into uncontrollable giggles.

The schoolmaster was an ancient man who used a staff to walk—and to poke at the shoulders of children who became too boisterous. Master Sighard looked as if he would have preferred to see a donkey join his class rather than Brute, but clearly he'd been given orders on the matter. That didn't stop him from glaring darkly at Brute from under his fantastically bushy eyebrows.

"We shall now begin our sums," Master Sighard intoned, and several of the children groaned. "I don't suppose you know your numbers either." He pointed the end of his staff at Brute.

"No, sir," Brute admitted.

"Quoen, help him."

Quoen was a tiny girl with messy brown hair and a smudge of breakfast on her chin. Earlier in the morning she'd been chosen to sit beside Brute and show him how she wrote her letters on a piece of slate. She'd taken the job very seriously, quizzing him as she went, and now she scrambled across the floor and plopped herself down at his side. While the Master took charge of the rest of the class, Quoen quietly coached her new partner.

"This is a one," she said, showing him a single straight line. "See? Like one finger. You try."

It was difficult for him to grasp the bit of chalk in his fingers, but he did as told. After he made six attempts to copy her mark, she was finally satisfied. She took the slate back and wrote another figure. "A two. It has a line too, plus a squiggle." His attempts met with considerable disapproval, and it took quite a while before his diminutive teacher was satisfied.

By the time lessons ended at lunchtime, Brute felt helplessly stupid. He stood and stretched his cramped legs—his hips were complaining a little too—and craned his neck down to look at Quoen, who was giving him a gap-toothed smile. "Here," she said, handing her slate up to him. "I wrote the letters on it so's you can practice. I'm gonna see what you remember tomorrow."

"Thank you, Mistress Quoen," he said, which made her giggle before she ran away.

As soon as the children were all gone and before Brute could make his escape, Master Sighard clomped his way over. He must have been a tall man before age had bent his back. His sparse gray hair trailed past his shoulders. "Who put the idea in your head that you should be here?" he demanded. "Is this meant as some kind of joke?"

"It's not a joke, sir. I never had the chance when I was a boy, and I was hoping I could try now."

"Waste of time."

Brute didn't bother to point out that he had plenty of time. His official duties only took a few minutes each morning, and then he had little to do except wander the palace. "I'll do my best," he said.

Master Sighard humphed and hobbled away without another word.

That evening, after he and Gray had eaten, Brute sat at his table with a flickering candle, laboriously copying and recopying Quoen's letters. He didn't know the names of all of them yet, although she'd taught him a rhyming song to help him remember. He hummed the tune to himself as he worked.

"Wh-wh-what are you d-d-d-doing?" Gray's chains wouldn't quite allow him to reach the cell bars, but he shifted forward as far as he could, as if wishing to join Brute.

"I'm... practicing letters. Trying to. I'm not very good at it."

"Wh-wh-why?"

"Because I'm clumsy and stupid and—"

"No! Wh-wh-why l-l-l-learn?"

"Everybody keeps asking me that. The other day I went for a walk, and I saw a bookshop. Hundreds—no, thousands of books. And it was like each one had a secret. I guess I'd like to see some of those secrets." He set the chalk down and rubbed his hand across the smooth tabletop. "I bet you know how to write."

Gray shook his head. "C-c-can't. I l-l-l-lost the w-w-w-words. T-t-t-tongue's c-c-clumsy, a-a-a-and fingers t-t-too. Fuck." He rubbed the heels of his hands over his eyelids. "D-d-don't know if I-I-I-I c-c-can r-r-r-r-read."

It was often a bit of a challenge to decipher the full meaning of Gray's stammered words. Brute pondered a few moments before saying, "You mean you used to speak without a stutter?"

Gray nodded.

"But now you can't, and you can't write either. Why?"

The reply was especially quiet. "The p-p-price." And although Brute might have liked to learn more—because that answer was intriguingly cryptic—Gray turned his back on Brute and scooted into the far corner of his cell, where he leaned his face against the wall.

GRAY had a nightmare nearly every night for the next week, which left Brute feeling haggard and drawn in the morning. But still he showed up promptly for his lessons and set his mind on pleasing Quoen, who was sometimes as harsh a taskmaster as Darius.

"No!" she corrected him for the twentieth time that morning. "That's a *d*. It makes a sound like in *dog*. The *b* is this one, like in your name. See?"

"Buh," he sounded out. "Like Brute."

She nodded magisterially at him. "That's right. Now, what sound does this one make?"

He squinted at the bit of chalk mark. "Um… guh?"

"Very good!" She beamed and patted his big hand with her tiny one. "And this one?"

Before he could answer, Master Sighard hit the tip of his staff twice against the floor. "That is all for today. I've an appointment. Make sure you practice. Wini, I expect you to have those verses memorized for next time." Wini grumbled as the rest of the children cheered, and soon Brute was alone in the room.

The morning was only half gone and it was far too early for lunch, but with nothing else to do with himself, he made his way to the kitchens. He found Alys there in a rare moment of near-repose, sitting on a stool in the yard close to the ovens and shelling peas. She smiled up at him. "Beautiful morning, isn't it? I'm trying to enjoy as much as I can before the heat settles on us."

"Can I join you?"

"Of course!" She waved at the low stone wall behind her, and when he sat down, she turned her stool and baskets around so she was facing him.

"Sorry I can't help you," he said. "I don't think I can manage it one-handed."

"You'd get chalk all over the peas anyway. How are the lessons coming?"

"Slowly. Those children learn so much faster than I do!"

She shrugged. "That's because their heads are empty. Yours is filled with other things. Your past, your duties...." She let her voice trail away as she cocked her head at him. "Do you have a girl waiting for you back in your village, Brute?"

For a moment he thought she was teasing him, but her face was serious, and she'd never yet said anything cruel to him. "No," he said.

"Have you thought about settling down with someone? Most men your age already have, and there are plenty of eligible women around here." She smiled coquettishly and batted her eyelashes.

Brute nearly choked on his own tongue. "You—you're really nice and, and b-beautiful, Alys, and, and any man would be lucky to have you, but, but—"

She burst out laughing, and he wanted to die of mortification. He had been remembering Lord Maudit's words about a girl being willing to overlook Brute's shortcomings in order to gain security, and he knew already that Alys was fond of him so... so he'd momentarily forgotten what a monster he was. "Sorry," he mumbled, his head hanging low to hide his blush, and he scrambled off the wall and began to walk away.

But she stood too, scattering peas in the process, and hurried after him, grabbing at his arm to stop him. "Brute! Wait!"

He couldn't meet her eyes. "I'm an idiot. I'm sorry. I'll just—"

"You'll just sit down again and talk to me!" She let go of his arm to put her hands on her hips. She was giving him very much the same look she gave Warin when the boy was recalcitrant in his duties. So, like a chastened child, Brute resumed his seat on the wall while she picked up her baskets and sat to shell her peas. "I'm sorry," she said. "I didn't mean to laugh."

"I was being stupid. I know nobody like you could ever… ever want me."

"Oh, Brute." She shook her head. "It's not that I couldn't want you. I was laughing at myself, for putting things so badly. I have a… well, a betrothed, I suppose. Cearl. He used to deliver vegetables to the palace, and he's kind of shy, and… and we fell in love. But he said he wouldn't marry me unless his prospects were better. He went off to sea, to earn enough money to buy a fleet of carts and donkeys so he can have his own delivery business. He's been gone nearly a year now."

Brute sighed and tried to get past his humiliation. "You must miss him."

"I do. But Brute, you're a fine man too. That's all I was trying to say. And you look… well, sometimes you look a little lonely. Would you like me to introduce you to some girls? Dreota, for example. Do you know her?" She didn't wait for an answer. "She's a laundress and very sweet, but she's also a little shy. And she's tall! Taller than most men, actually, and for some reason men *do* hate having to crane their necks to look up at their wife's face—makes them feel less manly or some sort of nonsense like that, I guess—so nobody's courted her, and I think the two of you—"

"I like boys." He really did bite his tongue after that awkward blurt—hard enough that he tasted blood—and wished he were capable of shrinking himself down to an insect's size and scurrying away. But instead he remained on the wall, huge and foolish. He cleared his throat. "I mean… I'm attracted to men, not women."

He'd never actually said those words aloud. Back in the village, it was immaterial whom he was attracted to because nobody of either gender would ever reciprocate. There were a few men with the same proclivity, and while most of the other villagers didn't exactly approve, the men weren't ostracized. But, of course, none of those men would have anything to do with Brute. One of them was even a Gedding, one of the boys who had made Brute's life miserable when he was a child. The only time Brute's sexual tastes were at all relevant to anyone but himself was when he made his annual visit to the bawdy house. And then announcing how he felt was hardly necessary: he just paid his coppers and went off with the whore who'd pulled the short straw.

Alys blinked at him a few times and then shrugged. "So do you have a man waiting for you back home?"

"I…. No."

She nodded decisively. "Then I'll introduce you to someone. Let's see…. There's Wuscfrea the cooper, and he's very handsome but always so grouchy. You'd think he had to pay a gold coin apiece for every smile. Now, Huguelin the brewer, he smiles all the time, but I think that's because he's sampling a little too much of his own wares, and besides, he's too old for you. Hmm. Lapurd, maybe. He's one of the guards. He's a little irresponsible, but maybe with a steady partner—"

"You don't mind?" Brute interrupted.

"Mind what? Playing matchmaker? It might be fun, and if it could make you happy—"

"No, I mean mind that I prefer men."

She grinned. "I don't blame you. I prefer them myself. Look, some people might say nasty things, but they're… old-fashioned. Most people here don't care. Why, even one of the princes has male lovers— he took Lord Arnout to the last ball, and of course I wasn't there, but I heard they looked very dashing together. Danced all night with one another, and the king seemed happy enough about it, so who's to criticize?"

"Which prince?" Brute asked, although he already had an inkling of the answer.

"Aldfrid." She frowned. "You haven't set your heart on him, have you? You may have saved his life, but you're still… well, we're not like them, are we? The king would never allow the prince to take a lover who was… so far beneath his station. But there are plenty of more suitable men around, like Nali the baker. He's never actually said he likes boys, but I've seen the way he watches the cartmen when they're carrying bags of flour and—"

"I am not in love with the prince. Even I'm not that stupid. And I appreciate your offer, Alys, but no thank you." He stood.

"Why not?"

He was getting slightly annoyed with her blind persistence. "Because nobody will have me."

That made her set her baskets down again and stand in front of him. "Why not? Your hand? You do just fine without it, and—"

"My hand. My ugly face. My ogreish body. Alys, my mother was a whore and my father was a thief. I'm nobody, nothing."

"Don't you dare say that!" Her green eyes flashed. "Don't you dare! You are a good man, Brute, and a kind one. You're patient with Warin and you're working hard to better yourself and you... you *save* people! All those other things, they don't matter, not to anyone with sense." She reached up to poke him firmly in the chest with a small finger. "Some man is going to find you, Brute, and he's going to sweep you off your great big feet, and then he's gonna spend the rest of his days realizing how damned lucky he is!"

Alys's voice had risen, and several members of the kitchen staff stood there, smiling. But although Brute was embarrassed and couldn't stop another blush, he didn't see anything unkind in their faces—just good-natured amusement at the way the small woman was bullying the enormous man. On impulse, Brute bent down and placed a quick kiss on top of her kerchief-covered head. "Thank you," he said.

He walked away with a song on his lips and an unaccustomed lightness in his heart. Not because he believed her, but because for the first time in his life, he knew that somebody believed in him.

 # CHAPTER
Nine

DESPITE the Brown Tower's thick stone walls, the heat was oppressive enough to keep Brute pinned against his mattress, naked and unmoving. Just the thought of putting on his fine clothes—freshly washed, perhaps by Dreota, the tall laundress—was almost too much to bear. Gray was naked as well, although years' worth of filth caked his skin. The quilt, instead of being wrapped around his shoulders, acted as slight padding under his spread-eagled form.

"I should go get us breakfast," said Brute without enthusiasm.

"N-not h-h-hungry."

"I'm supposed to feed you," Brute said, but didn't actually make any effort to move. The truth was, due to the extra tidbits Brute had been giving him over the past weeks, Gray was noticeably less gaunt. He was thin, but his bones now looked as if they had a bit of padding, and his cheeks were less sunken beneath his matted beard. "Maybe I can find us something light. Fruit."

"Mmm."

Brute had already discovered that Gray was especially fond of fruit. Not surprising, considering he hadn't eaten any for years. When Brute shared the berries Alys gave him, Gray always ended up with red or purple stains adding to the mess on his face and hands, but with a wide and grateful smile. Brute had been sharing a lot of berries lately.

With a supreme effort, he managed to lever himself upright. He used the chamber pot and rinsed his hand and face in the washbasin he'd recently acquired. The basin had an intricate pattern of blue dragons and stylized flowers, and had obviously been made for someone much wealthier than him, but a chip on the rim had caused its original owner to discard it. Brute had bought it for three coppers during one of his infrequent excursions outside the palace walls.

He poured some water into a tin cup, carried it over to the cell, and slid the bolt open with his left elbow. As he did so, Gray climbed to his feet and stood waiting for him. "Here," Brute said, pressing the cup into the other man's hand. "It's sort of warm. I'll get you some cooler water from the well after I'm dressed."

"D-dressed?"

Brute found himself inexplicably embarrassed over their mutual nudity. It wasn't as if Gray could see him, and Brute had touched Gray's bare body many times when comforting him during his nightmares. But still he blushed. "Drink it," he said gruffly, and for some reason that made Gray laugh. Gray's laughter was a wonderful sound, giving no hint of his tongue's usual troubles. It was a warm laugh, deep and slightly intimate. Brute used to hear laughter like that sometimes when he sat in the White Dragon or while he worked. It was the sound a man made among friends.

Gray was still chuckling after Brute took the cup away.

"S-s-swimming."

"What?" Brute had been pulling his shirt over his head when Gray spoke, and he wasn't sure he had heard correctly.

"Y-you should g-g-go swimming. I-i-in the s-sea. It's l-lovely and c-c-c-cold. I used t-to go wh-wh-when the heat g-g-got b-b-b-bad."

"I can't swim," Brute said. What he was thinking as he pulled on his trousers, however, was how nice it must have felt for Gray to play freely in the waves, and what a terrible contrast that was with his current life. For much of the time over the past weeks, Brute had managed to put aside his knowledge that Gray Leynham was a prisoner—and that he was a witch and a traitor—and instead think of him as the quiet companion who shared his chamber. That was a pleasant fantasy, but a false one.

Brute emptied the waste bucket and filled the water jug, then returned to Gray. When he handed over the cup of cool water, the man laughed again and upended it over his own head. The streamlets of water made streaks in the dirt on his face and chest. He grasped Brute's forearm with his hand and smiled up at him. "L-lovely. Thank you."

Everyone at the palace was moving very slowly, as if they were slogging through deep mud. Even the birds seemed to droop where they perched in little patches of shade, and the resident cats and dogs were sprawled on squares of marble paving, looking more like rugs than living animals. The ovens behind the kitchen were not lit, nor were any of the stoves inside. The heat had killed everyone's appetite, it seemed, so the kitchen staff had been given a slight reprieve. Alys was nowhere to be found, but one of the potboys handed Brute a bowl of red berries. "Alys says I'm s'posed to make something for the witch," the boy said. He ran a hand across his sweaty forehead. "I ain't sure I know how, though. Can I give him yesterday's bread in water?"

"Don't bother," Brute said. "He can skip breakfast today."

The boy looked grateful.

Brute left the berries with Gray—along with more water—but didn't stay. He was glad he didn't have any lessons this morning, because although the chamber where they met might be a little cooler than outside, it would still be far too warm to pay attention. The children would be groggy and sticky and restless, Master Sighard would be more ill-tempered than usual, and Brute would have a difficult time concentrating. Especially seeing as his thoughts kept wandering to Gray, and what he would look like with waves playing about his hips and droplets glistening on his skin.

Tired of tromping about in circles and unsuccessfully chasing inappropriate images from his head, Brute went off in search of the guards.

The guards trained daily, and sometimes he'd stand and watch. Nobody seemed to think that strange. In fact, it wasn't unusual for a variety of people to watch. Children sometimes paused for a while on their way between chores; workers would take a few minutes respite from their labors; sometimes even the lords and ladies stood under the shade of a portico and chattered with one another, their eyes on the straining bodies. A good many of the onlookers, like Brute, no doubt admired the sight of young men in fine form and with little in the way of clothing, but others just viewed it as entertainment. When the guards sparred with one another, onlookers would occasionally place small bets on the outcomes.

So Brute often passed the time watching the guards. And about three weeks earlier, when the men were practicing wrestling maneuvers, their captain had walked over to him. "Want to join us?" he asked.

Brute had blinked at him. "I can't fight."

"Don't have to. Just be big—you can do that all right." The captain grinned, revealing two broken front teeth. "Boys might kick you around a little, but you're welcome to kick right back."

Brute had glanced at the guards, who were shouting jeers and encouragement at one another, and then looked back at the captain. "Sounds like fun."

He practiced with them nearly every day after that. He ended up with bruises each time, but it *was* fun, and the soldiers treated him almost like one of their own. Besides, he'd been feeling much too sedentary and was even slightly missing the physical challenge of his old job—plus he was eating far too well. It was good to see the bit of fat he'd accumulated around his belly melt away and his muscles become once again well-defined. The bit of soreness he faced in the evenings was almost welcome.

The close proximity of other men didn't hurt either.

The guards were practicing again today despite the heat. They wore nothing but breechclouts, their torsos and limbs slick with sweat, and they were taking turns flinging axes at targets. Brute couldn't join in with that activity and didn't really want to, so he found the shadiest spot available—up against a wall and under a balcony—and crouched down. Heavy muscles worked and skin glistened, and after a while Brute realized that the heat pooling in his belly had nothing to do with the blinding sun.

For a moment he actually considered Gray's suggestion. Brute had seen the sea, both from the palace windows and as he walked around Tellomer. But he'd never been close enough to touch it, and he wondered what salt water might feel like. He didn't relish the types of stares he'd attract at the beach—everyone in the palace was used to him by now and nobody stared. And he'd feel guilty, out there enjoying the surf while Gray could only remember it.

Fine then. But maybe he could find a different watery way to cool himself off.

The usual bath attendant was on duty, looking wilted and bored. "Could I have a bath, please?" Brute said to her.

"In this weather?"

"I was thinking maybe you could fill the tub with cool water instead."

She considered this for a moment and then shrugged. "Wait here."

It didn't take her as long as usual to prepare. When she returned several minutes later, she wordlessly handed him a stack of clean towels, then bent over her ledger to record his visit. Eventually, she would report to the exchequer, and three coppers would be deducted from his account.

He shed his clothes as soon as he was alone in the little bathing room, then lowered himself into the tub. As he'd hoped, the water was plenty cold—cold enough to make him sigh in relief. He crouched down to submerge himself completely, imagining that steam was rising above him as his heated body met the chilly liquid.

He remained in the tub for a very long time. He didn't scrub, although he did break off a bit of the nicely scented soap to take back to his chambers and use in the morning. It was a small theft, but he thought it might be justified, seeing as he'd paid the full three coppers and hadn't even needed the water warmed. When he finally emerged, his skin was slightly wrinkled and he felt considerably refreshed.

Until he walked back out and into the sunshine. Then he felt like a loaf of bread in an oven. Which reminded him that he had missed lunch. He still wasn't very hungry—he could wait until dinner—but it occurred to him that Gray might need more drinking water. He walked slowly back to the Brown Tower, mumbled a greeting to the guard at the door, and went inside.

It wasn't until he entered his chamber that the smell hit him. He'd become used to the building's constant odor of damp and age, and of course he tried to empty his chamber pot and Gray's bucket as often as possible. But this was simply the reek of filth, and it took him a moment to realize it was coming from the prisoner. Of course. Years without being allowed to wash, and now with the heat: Gray was stewing in his sweat and grime. It might not have been so noticeable if Brute hadn't just bathed, but as it was, the stink was almost unbearable.

Gray stood and smiled when Brute brought him a cup of water. "D-d-did you s-s-swim?"

"I told you. I don't know how."

"Sh-sh-shame. M-my father t-taught me. He was a s-sailor."

Although Gray had grown slightly more talkative of late—and either he was stuttering less or Brute was noticing less—he'd never before mentioned his family. Brute was intrigued even though he knew he shouldn't be. "Was he from Tellomer?"

"Y-yes. Came b-b-back with amazing tales. A-and my mother. She w-w-was from R-r-racinas."

Brute had heard mention of Racinas once or twice, but had no idea where it might be and had never met anyone from there. He'd never even met anyone who was related to someone from there. "Did you ever go there?"

Gray's face tightened. "O-o-o-once."

Because this was obviously a painful subject, Brute went back to the topic of swimming. "What does it feel like, to swim in the sea?"

"W-w-wet," Gray said, a slight smile replacing his frown. "C-cold. I-i-i-it moves about y-you, the s-sea does. Always ch-changing. Lifts y-you up or knocks you d-d-d-down. D-doesn't care who you a-a-aren't."

That was a strange sentiment, Brute thought, but an oddly comforting one. Especially for someone like him, who wasn't so many things and who was so few. But then the entire conversation was odd. It had never before occurred to him that a witch would have family—although of course he must come from somewhere!—or that his father would be someone as ordinary as a sailor, a man who probably loved his son and taught him to swim. "My father was just a thief," he said, and wished he'd learn to stop blurting things out.

"A g-g-good one?"

Brute thought of the little hut he'd lived in as a child. It had seemed comfortable enough to him then, especially in comparison to the dirt-floored place under the house where his great-uncle usually made him sleep, or the stables, or his room at the White Dragon. But in truth, that hut had been small and run-down, and aside from the bed and a few trinkets of his mother's, it had contained very few possessions. "No. He was a poor one. They hanged him when I was a boy."

Gray placed his warm hand on Brute's arm and gave it a quick squeeze. "S-sometimes a d-d-desperate man makes b-b-bad choices."

It was too hot in the cell. Brute stepped away and bolted the door, and then he stood there in the middle of his chamber, his mind whirling in a turmoil he couldn't explain. "I'm going," he said gruffly. And unnecessarily. He took the washbasin and jug with him when he left.

The guard watched with mild curiosity as Brute filled the containers at the well. It was slightly difficult for him to carry them back. He tucked the basin into the crook of his left arm and held the jug in his hand, and he tried not to slosh too much water as he walked. When he got to the door, the guard squinted at Brute's hair, which was still damp from his bath. "You're going to be very clean," the guard observed with unusual garrulousness. Usually they just grunted.

Brute gave him an awkward little shrug and entered the tower.

Gray seemed surprised that Brute had reappeared so soon, even more so when Brute used his free elbow to open the bars. "S-s-something wrong?"

"Not exactly. Hang on." He set the containers on the floor beside Gray and then ducked back into the main chamber to grab his single towel. After a short pause, he opened the bottom drawer and took out his old shirt as well. It was hardly more than a rag, but it could still serve a use.

"Wh-wh-wh-what is it?" Gray asked when Brute was back in the cell.

"Here." Brute pressed the cloths into one of Gray's hands, fished in his pocket to retrieve the bit of soap, and placed it in Gray's other hand. "There's water in the basin at your feet."

"F-f-for what?"

"Washing, of course. I can't take you to the sea or even the baths, but…." His voice trailed away uncomfortably.

Gray licked his lips and then chewed on the lower one. "I-I-I d-d-d-don't—"

"It's hot and you stink. I thought you might want to clean up a little."

"Is… is it p-p-p-p— Fuck! P-permitted?"

Brute gave the same answer he'd told himself about improving the prisoner's meals and giving him a quilt. "Nobody said I couldn't."

Gray laughed. He crouched down and shoved his blankets out of the way, then felt around until he found the washbasin. "M-m-might get a b-b-bit of me clean, anyway."

"Do you want… I could cut your hair. Shave you."

"W-w-would you? P-please?"

"I'm not much of a barber, but I can try."

When Gray nodded enthusiastically, Brute fetched his knife and razor. It couldn't have been comfortable for Gray as Brute hacked away at the matted mess on his head, but Gray didn't complain. Eventually he was left with uneven stubble on top of his skull, clean-shaven cheeks and neck, and an enormous grin. "Good gods, th-that feels better!"

He was handsome, dammit to all hells, with finely sculpted cheekbones and a full bottom lip. His neck looked slightly delicate— almost calling out to be stroked—but the effect was marred by the iron collar, a dark abomination. "I feel l-like a new m-m-man."

Brute mumbled some sort of reply, which was abruptly cut off as Gray began rubbing the soap over his dirty arms and chest. "T-tell me if I'm m-m-missing spots," Gray ordered, which meant that Brute *had* to watch. Not that he could have torn his eyes away even if he tried. He watched as the dirt was gradually scrubbed away, revealing moon-pale skin with a dusting of dark blond hairs and a pair of flat pink nipples. Which was bad enough, but next Gray washed his flat belly, his balls and soft sex and the curls that surrounded them, his thin legs. Brute tasted blood and realized he'd bitten his tongue.

"B-better?" Gray asked, holding his arms out.

"Um, yes."

Gray spun around. "D-do my back?"

The answer should have been no. Brute knew that. But Gray was standing there, right in front of him, and his back really was filthy. And it wasn't as if Brute had never touched him before. At least those were the rationalizations he made as he dumped the dirty water into the slop pail and poured fresh from the ewer. He took the soap and began moving it across the other man's shoulders. This close, and with the dirt gone, he could see that Gray's skin was rubbed raw at the edges of his collar and manacles, and no doubt on his ankles around the cuffs as well. At least the bruises and scrapes Brute had spied when he'd first arrived had faded away, leaving him to wonder if the wounds had been caused by something more than Gray being forced to sleep on the hard floor.

"Wh-what's wrong?"

Brute realized he'd been growling slightly. "Nothing. Sorry." He scrubbed a little harder at Gray's shoulder blades.

When Brute reached Gray's lower back, Gray shifted his stance to spread his legs a little and Brute froze. "Umm…."

"Y-you don't have to. I c-c-can—"

"It's fine," Brute said firmly. He was a grown man. He could manage to scrub a dirty prisoner without acting like an idiot. Even if that prisoner had a surprisingly pleasant ass.

By the time Brute reached the prisoner's feet, Gray was considerably cleaner and fresher smelling, and Brute was uncomfortably hard. He was just feeling thankful that Gray couldn't see the way the fabric of his trousers was straining when Gray made a strangled sort of sound and half turned back to him. Gray was erect too, and his shaved face was colored by a blush. "S-s-sorry," he said with an embarrassed smile. "D-d-didn't think the damn thing even w-w-worked anymore. It…." He made an accurate grab for Brute's soapy hand and ran his long fingers over Brute's wide ones. "C-calloused. F-f-felt good."

Brute didn't pull away, and for several minutes they simply stood there, hand in hand, their breathing sounding very loud against the walls of the cell. Brute wasn't even especially surprised when Gray bent his head and, avoiding the soapy hand, pressed his lips to Brute's thick forearm. "Th-thank you, Brute."

"It's not my name." He clearly was no master of his own tongue.

But Gray only tilted his head. "What?"

"Brute. It's what they call me. What everyone calls me, ever since… since I was a boy. But it's not my name." Sometimes he almost forgot that. He thought of himself as Brute, in fact, and the last person to call him by his given name was his mother, right before she died. She'd hugged him and kissed his hair and called him a good boy, and then she'd poisoned herself from her flask.

"Wh-what is your name?" Gray's voice was soft.

"Aric. I'm Aric."

Gray smiled. "Hello, Aric."

Somehow after that, the newly rechristened Aric extricated himself from Gray's gentle grip. He used the remaining wash water to rinse the floor a bit and replaced the soiled quilt with a fresh one from his shelf. He fetched dinner for himself and Gray and they ate in silence, and then Aric bolted the cell. Everything around him seemed sort of fuzzy and unreal, the edges of everything as soft as his prisoner's name. He opened the top dresser drawer and pulled out the little fabric purse containing a small hoard of coppers, the remnants of a sweets spending spree he and Warin had enjoyed a few days earlier. He tucked the purse in his pocket and walked out of the chamber, out of the tower, out of the palace. His feet knew where to go: to the dingy little corner of Tellomer where the molly houses and brothels were tucked away.

 **CHAPTER**
Ten

ARIC had heard stories about Tellomer's brothels since he was a young boy. He heard rumors that his mother had once worked in them. After Aric's parents died, on the rare occasions when drink put his great-uncle in a good mood instead of an evil one, the old man babbled on about the whores he'd had in Tellomer, and how he impressed the ladies with his size and skills. Even at a tender age, Aric doubted that.

When he grew older, Aric heard men at the White Dragon talking to each other about the bawdy houses, teasing or bragging or offering advice. It was those overheard conversations that taught him that boys could be found for sale, and that gave him hope that, given enough coins, someone might be willing to temporarily overlook Aric's brutish body and repulsive face.

It had taken him a long time to save enough—enough coppers, enough courage—but finally Aric made his first journey into Tellomer during the Festival of the Harvest Moon. His heart hammered in his chest for the entire journey, and when he arrived at the city walls, he was overwhelmed at the sheer size of the place and hadn't any idea which way to go. There weren't any signs pointing to Tellomer's seediest corner—and if there had been, he couldn't have read them—and he was too embarrassed to ask any of the few people on the street. So he wandered aimlessly for a long time, instinctively veering away from the posher parts of town, until he stumbled upon a narrow street that looked somehow both furtive and inviting. The crudely painted signs hanging on the houses at the end of that street had been made with illiterate men like him in mind, and they left no doubt about what sort of business was transacted inside the houses.

Aric had wandered up and down the street uncertainly, half fearing that even with his purse full of coins he'd be turned away. And then he saw a man exiting the most run-down of the houses, pausing to steal a kiss from a jaded-looking young man before scurrying furtively away. The man had been ugly—although not as ugly as Aric—and fat, and he'd had gouty nodules on his ears.

Aric had taken several calming breaths and knocked on the door of that house.

The house was kept by a blocky man with a badly scarred face and thin tufts of dark gray hair. He stood in the open door, looking Aric up and down with deep skepticism. "What?" the man demanded.

"I, um…." Aric swallowed. "I want… um… sex."

The man's eyes narrowed. "Girl or boy?"

"Boy. Or, um, man." Because, although any contact would have been good, what he really craved was a big, strong body against his. Someone he wouldn't have to worry about breaking.

The man gave him another long look. "Forty coppers."

Aric fought back despair. He didn't have that much. "It's supposed to be fifteen." At least so said the men at the White Dragon, when they were laughing together over their exploits.

"Fifteen's what we charge men. Not ogres." The man spat into the street. "Thirty. And if you hurt my boy, I'll have you hung by morning."

"I won't hurt anyone," said Aric, who possessed exactly thirty-three coppers.

The man—who Aric later learned was called Redwald—waited impatiently for Aric to count out three coins and hand over the rest, then led him into a dingy, dirty room that was crowded with ancient furniture. A few young men wearing very little were lounging around the room, playing cards or drinking, and they looked at Aric with varying mixtures of amusement and alarm. Aric wasn't sure how this bit was supposed to go. Did he choose the one who appealed to him most, or did the whores have some sort of turn-taking schedule?

Redwald solved Aric's dilemma by pointing at a sullen-looking man who might once have been pretty but now looked... used up. "Odo. This one's yours."

"No!" Odo cried. "I already had three today."

"Well, this will make four, won't it? Now get off your ass and get to work, before I pound that ass myself."

Aric had put out his hand. "Wait! I don't want... don't want you to force anyone."

Redwald snarled at him. "Do you fucking want a slut, or what?"

Aric stood there without answering until Odo rolled his eyes and heaved himself to his feet. "I'll take him," he said to Redwald in a flat tone. "But I want the rest of the fucking night off."

The blocky man shrugged, which Odo must have taken for agreement because he stomped toward the stairs. "Well? Follow me," he ordered without looking back.

The room he took Aric to was tiny and dark and smelled like sex. Still not bothering to glance Aric's way, Odo loosened his trousers and climbed onto the narrow, blanketless bed. He propped himself on elbows and knees so that his backside was hanging nearly off the edge of the bed, and said, "Get on with it."

His ass was bony, and he was offering it with the same tenderness that Cecil showed when slopping food onto Aric's plate at the White Dragon, but excitement still pooled low in Aric's belly. Tentatively, he reached out and touched one pale cheek.

Odo looked over his shoulder and sighed. "I'm not a fucking maiden you have to seduce. Just fucking ram it in and get it over with."

Aric had some vague ideas of how sex between two men was supposed to go, ideas he'd mainly gleaned from the more drunken conversations in the tavern. "Don't I have to.... I don't want to hurt you."

"I've been fucked by three other men this afternoon. I'm ready."

So Aric had dropped his own trousers and taken a step closer to the bed. But Odo's eyes widened. "Holy fuck! That's not a dick—it's a damned tree trunk."

A strange mixture of pride, embarrassment, and disappointment had washed through Aric. "I don't…. Sorry." He expected to be turned away.

Instead, though, Odo grabbed a small bottle from the floor next to the bed and poured some of the contents onto his fingers before handing the bottle to Aric. "Put some of this on that monster of yours," he ordered, then lay down on his back and stuck his own oily fingers inside himself. Astonished to be witnessing such a thing, Aric simply stood there with the bottle in hand until Odo huffed at him. "Hey! You're supposed to be slicking up, remember?"

"Oh. Sorry." Feeling stupid for apologizing again, Aric followed orders. And then Odo was back on all fours, waiting.

The feeling of being inside another man had been astonishing, but it was hard to ignore Odo's little grunts of pain, or the way his hands were fisted on the mattress. Odo's cock was soft and uninterested in the proceedings. "Am I…. Does it hurt?" Aric asked.

"Of course it fucking hurts. You try ramming a tree trunk up your ass and see if it hurts. Look, just fucking move and get it over with, okay?"

To the relief of them both, it took Aric very little time to climax. When he was through, Odo scrambled away, wiped quickly at himself with a rag, yanked up his trousers, and stalked out of the room without another word.

Later that day, as he trudged home in the darkness, Aric swore to himself that he wouldn't return to Tellomer. But the months passed and his loneliness grew heavy on his shoulders—heavier than any of the burdens he carried for Darius—and when the next festival arrived, he found himself again on the road to Tellomer with thirty coppers in his purse.

HE HAD been nothing but an overgrown boy when he first visited the brothel. Now he was a man, dressed in good-quality clothing and wearing fine boots, and he knew exactly how to get to the hidden little street. He strode confidently through the city, hardly glancing at the people who moved around sluggishly or drooped in wilted heaps wherever they could find a bit of shade. He ignored the way sweat ran down his face and neck, the way it made his shirt stick to his back. He even ignored the busy vendor who was selling fruit juices from the back of a cart.

The city smelled. Not as bad as Gray had, perhaps, but this stink was more variable. Sewage and animal waste and fish and sweat and rotting food. It was almost enough to make him wish for his old job. Hauling loads would be miserable on a day like this, and if anything the heat would be worse away from the sea, but at least the air would smell fresher. Here in Tellomer, the odor only grew worse as he passed the crowded shacks and the miserable beggars. Two very young naked children played desultorily with cornhusk dolls. A scraggly dog scratched at fleas. A wizened old woman whose back was bent nearly in two made a sign in Aric's direction to ward off evil.

Somehow the bright sun didn't quite seem to reach the narrow street that was his destination. The shadows didn't make the air any cooler, however. It was as if the entire neighborhood were permanently shrouded under heavy wool. There were more people on this particular street than he was used to seeing, but that was because he had always come here during the festival. He supposed that in the evenings and through the night this district probably became very lively indeed. Today, though, there were men of various social stations slowly walking down the cobbles, while boys and girls and men and women leaned out of windows or lounged in open doorways, most of them looking more cranky and bored than seductive.

A bosomy woman with improbably colored hair called out to him from a doorstep. "Ho! Giant! Need a little woman to chase away some of the heat?"

He couldn't help but smile. "How much?"

"Twenty-five. And that's with a discount, because you really ought to pay at least two men's worth."

"That's very generous of you. But I'm afraid you don't have what I'm looking for."

"Oh?" she said, her eyebrows arched. Then she rucked up the front of her yellow dress, revealing a pair of slightly bowed legs and a fairly impressive dick below a pot belly. "Are you sure?"

Aric barked a surprised laugh. "Maybe another time."

She let her dress fall back into place. "I can't guarantee the special offer will still stand."

Nobody was visible outside his usual brothel, and he would have wagered a silver coin that the windows of that building hadn't been opened in years. Aric knocked three times before Redwald opened it. The man never seemed to change from year to year. Even his clothing appeared to be the same, perhaps slightly dirtier and more threadbare each year. He looked surprised to see Aric, especially after taking in Aric's new attire. "Come up in the world, have we?" Redwald said.

"A bit."

"And got maimed in the process."

Aric shrugged.

Redwald held out his hand. "Thirty coppers."

"I'll give you twenty."

"What's this? Now that you have more coins jingling in your pockets you think you should pay less?" Redwald coughed out something that might have been intended as a laugh.

But Aric simply shrugged. "I'll give you twenty. Or I can go somewhere else. I think there are other houses on this street that would be glad for my coppers."

The brothel master glared but stepped aside, and when Aric handed him twenty coppers, Redwald counted them twice and then tucked them away in a purse. His boys had been watching the interchange with mild interest and ill-hidden amusement. As usual, most of the faces were new to Aric, but he thought he recognized two or three from previous years. Redwald surveyed the room and seemed about to say something, but Aric stopped him by pointing at a young man who was sprawled in an overstuffed chair. "Him, please," Aric said.

Maybe Redwald would have objected, but the man rose from the chair gracefully and gave a half grin. "This looks like a challenge."

"Watch out, Petrus," said a small redhead on the other side of the room. "He's hung like a stallion."

Petrus's grin didn't falter. "I always did like to ride."

Amidst the guffaws and catcalls, Petrus and Aric made their way upstairs and down the hall. Petrus walked in front, giving Aric a good opportunity to look at his tall, wiry body and butterscotch-colored hair. Then Petrus swung open one of the identical doors that lined the corridor. "Welcome to my castle," he said with a small flourish.

The room was the same as all the others Aric had visited upstairs: tiny, sparely furnished, musty-smelling. It was almost unbearably hot as well. But he didn't take much time to catalog his surroundings, because without hesitation or even a hint of shame, Petrus pulled off his ragged shirt and stepped out of his trousers, leaving himself entirely bare and available for inspection. "You like what you bought?" he asked.

"You're very… very handsome," Aric replied honestly.

"I know. Which is lucky, because I'm not really any good at much of anything except fucking." Petrus seemed cheerful enough about his admission, his mouth still quirked at the corners. "Everyone has a talent, I guess."

"So why are you here?"

"Instead of one of the better houses, you mean? I used to work at some fancy places, but I'm getting kind of old for it. I figured here at least I can still earn for a while, put away a few more coins before I'm done."

It hadn't occurred to Aric that whores might plan for the future. "And then what?"

"Then I'm going to go home to Racinas and build myself a house. Maybe find a wife and have a few kids. Farm a little plot of land."

"I know someone whose family's from Racinas."

Petrus shrugged. "It's not such a wonderful place. Boring. Tellomer's a lot more exciting. All Racinas has to boast about is fertile land, a lot of sheep, and the Vale of the Gods. But it's my home."

"The what?"

"Vale of the Gods. Sacred place with very fancy magics, blah, blah, blah. It's a sort of tourist attraction for the mystically inclined. Now me, I've always been more about the pleasures of the flesh." He winked and then wiggled his hips slightly. "C'mon, stallion. Let's see what you've got."

Aric snorted a laugh and unfastened his trouser button. He'd become very adept at it despite his lost hand. He let his trousers fall to his knees and then pushed his breechclout down as well. Petrus whistled. "Good gods. The rumor was no exaggeration."

"Um, yeah." Aric looked down at the floorboards. "I'll be careful, I promise." But when he glanced up, he saw that Petrus's smile had only widened, and that the boy's own interest was obvious.

"As long as you don't put me out of commission for too long, you don't have to be *too* careful," Petrus said with a happy leer. Then he closed the space between them and reached forward to begin reverently stroking Aric. His hands were small and soft, his fingers very nimble. He leaned his head up against Aric's chest, which was far more intimacy than Aric had expected. More intimacy than he had ever had with another man—except Gray.

He immediately pushed that thought out of his mind and very tentatively slid his fingers through Petrus's soft hair. He expected an angry response, but the lad only tilted his head a bit, giving Aric better access. "You're very clean," Petrus observed.

"I bathed today."

Petrus chuckled. "For me?"

"Well, not exactly, but—"

"It's all right. I was only teasing." And then he dropped gracefully to his knees and slid his mouth over the head of Aric's cock. Aric had thought that the air in the room was hot, but it was cold as well water compared to the moist furnace that surrounded him now. He watched with fascination as the smaller man's head bobbed at his groin. Petrus couldn't take all of him in, but he was clearly doing his best. And either he enjoyed the task or he was a very good actor.

Aric steadied himself with a hand on Petrus's smooth shoulder, and he closed his eyes. But when he did, he saw Gray standing in his cell, naked except for his chains, skin an almost glowing sort of pale. Erect and blushing, a shy smile on his face.

With a defeated groan, Aric pushed Petrus away. Gently, but still Petrus looked up at him with wet lips and wide eyes. "Something's wrong?"

"I… I have to go." Aric took a step back and began awkwardly fumbling at his trousers, trying to pull them back up.

Petrus stood. "Did I do something wrong? You sure seemed to be enjoying."

"I… I was, but…." That twice-damned button!

"You've been here before, so I don't think you're uncomfortable about fucking a man. Is it me? Did you want my ass instead?" He turned around and bent slightly, showing off a slightly rounded and very attractive backside.

"I can't."

Petrus turned around and squinted quizzically at him. Then he gestured at Aric's crotch, where his erection was evident even under the trousers. "You can."

"No, I mean…." Aric sighed heavily and pulled out his purse. "I'm sorry. You're very handsome, and you've been really nice to me. I just can't." He pressed the purse into Petrus's hand. It contained nearly twenty coppers. Not a fortune by any means, but considerably more than the one or two coins whores usually expected as tips.

Petrus weighed the purse in his hand and seemed pleased, but still he said, "Are you sure? We can take it more slowly if you like. That bastard Redwald has plenty of other boys for the other customers tonight." He smiled. "You could even take me out for a drink or two."

"I'm sorry," said Aric, who genuinely was. Petrus was fun, sex aside. His company would almost certainly prove diverting. But Aric gave his shoulder a last squeeze and walked to the door. "I have to go. Someone's waiting for me."

 **CHAPTER**
Eleven

DESPITE the words he'd said to Petrus, Aric didn't return to the palace. Instead, he walked the darkening streets, his head down and his shoulders hunched, ignoring the inevitable stares and even occasional catcalls. Sweat made his shirt and trousers stick to his body, and it ran in stinging rivulets down his face. Shortly after the sun set, the skies began to rumble, and it felt as if the hairs on Aric's arms were standing on end. Lightning flashed. The streets became nearly deserted as everyone rushed to get shop goods, children, and themselves inside. They dragged in their hanging laundry, and shutters clacked closed up and down the streets.

Before he felt a single drop, he heard the rain coming; it was like a thousand footsteps running down the cobbles. And then it was upon him all at once, and he was instantly soaked. Between the dark and the downpour, he could barely see where he was going. His feet splashed through the puddles that appeared out of nowhere. If his mind hadn't been stormier than the weather, he would have worried about his boots.

He walked until his legs were sore and he was shivering with cold, and even when the rain softened to drizzle and then died out altogether, his head remained in turmoil.

Eventually he found himself by the docks. He stood and watched the fishermen ready their boats and sail away, and only when the sky turned from black to purple and the stars began to fade did he turn around and head back to the palace.

"TH-THOUGHT you might not c-c-c-come back." The voice was very soft. In the feeble light of the cell, Aric could make out only the outline of Gray's form, hunched in the corner with his knees drawn against his chest.

"I'm sorry. You must be very hungry. It's too early to get anything much from the kitchens, but I brought some bread and fruit." Aric hadn't eaten anything at all. His stomach was tied in knots and his head ached.

Gray didn't respond, so Aric spent a few minutes fussing at his table. He had peaches, which he sliced and placed in a bowl. Then he washed the sticky mess off his fingers and set the bread in the bowl as well, before filling the tin cup with fresh water. He was well practiced now at juggling things while unbarring the cell, so he didn't spill so much as a drop. He set the food and water on the floor next to Gray.

"I-I'm sorry," Gray said. His head was so bowed that his words were muffled.

"Sorry? For what?"

"Y-y-you were being so k-kind, and... it's b-b-b-been so long since anyone.... Y-you don't have to t-t-t-touch m-me anymore."

Aric shook his head, even though the other man couldn't see it. He didn't understand Gray's distress. Gray had done nothing wrong. He must have been starving for comfort, and he didn't know what his jailer looked like. It was Aric who'd been aroused inappropriately, so why was Gray apologizing? Aric crouched down and set his hand on Gray's shoulder. "It's all right. Eat a little bit. You'll feel better. Or I can fetch you a basin of water and you can wash your face."

But Gray only drew into a tighter ball. "Y-y-you're a good man, Aric. You n-need to g-g-g-go."

Aric squinted in confusion. He'd just been gone for hours. "You... you want some more time to yourself? I can walk around the palace for a while."

"N-no. I mean... *g-go*. Leave T-t-tellomer." He moved so suddenly that Aric startled and fell backward, sprawling on his ass.

Gray was right there on top of him, grabbing Aric's arms. "Go before I dream your d-d-death. Please!"

Aric had no names for the emotions that flooded him. "I'm not afraid," he said, jerking himself away from Gray's grip and scrambling to his feet.

"Y-you should be."

"Everyone says I'm stupid."

Gray knelt on the floor for a moment and then reached for his blanket, which he'd lost when he lurched forward. He gathered the blanket around his shoulders and hunched in the corner again. "I-I don't d-d-deserve your kindness," he said quietly.

Aric wasn't certain that kindness was the right word for what he'd done. Yes, he'd made the prisoner's life slightly more comfortable, but at little cost to himself. And Gray remained chained in a cell. "Is it true then?" Aric asked. "Are you a witch and a traitor?"

To Aric's surprise, Gray laughed bitterly. "Is th-that what they say? No. I suppose th-th-there's a grain of truth to it, though. B-b-but I'm nothing so g-g-grand. I'm a f-f-fool and a weakling, that's all. S-s-selfish and cruel."

Gray's words made little sense to Aric. Why would the crown go to such extremes to keep Gray so miserable if he wasn't a dangerous man who'd done something terrible? Why would the crown bother to keep him at all, in fact? Aric buried his face in his hand. He was just a simple laborer, nothing more, and he was so tired.

As suddenly as the storm had hit the city, sobs rose into Aric's throat, and he had no chance to swallow them. He was instantly overcome, all his strength gone, and he collapsed to his knees and wept.

He hadn't cried since he was very young, since some small thing had disappointed him shortly before his father was hung. He hadn't cried when he witnessed his father's execution or his mother's suicide, not when the sheriff dragged him, unwilling, to the home of his sullen great-uncle. He hadn't cried even once when the village children taunted him or beat him, nor when he was bone-weary from work and his belly was empty, nor when his great-uncle punched and kicked him. He hadn't cried when he'd grown up and was reduced to nothing more than a beast of burden, toiling under Darius's harsh words. Nor when he'd returned home to his lumpy, short bed in his tiny, noisome room, all alone, always all alone. He hadn't cried when he lost his hand and nearly lost his life.

Maybe the tears he shed now were for all of those things. He didn't know. All he knew was that they tore his throat and his chest, and they mortified him. But he couldn't stop them, couldn't stop them at all.

He was so lost in his own grief that it took a long time before he noticed the hand on his shoulder or the other stroking his short hair. And then he felt warm breaths puffing on his face, and his sobs subsided to miserable snuffles. He would have retreated from the cell, but the gentle pressure of the hands seemed to pin him in place.

"M-move a little c-c-closer. The chains w-w-w-won't reach any farther."

Without really intending to, and without opening his swollen eyes, Aric shuffled forward on his knees. As soon as he did, he was enfolded in thin, bare arms. He'd held Gray many times, comforting him during nightmares, but never when Gray was awake. And Gray had never been the one to hold him. In fact, nobody had held Aric since his mother died, and that thought sent him into a fresh and humiliating round of bawling. Gray continued to hold him—although his knees must have been hurting from the hard floor—and he petted Aric's back and hummed a tune that Aric dimly recognized as one of the lullabies he often sang to Gray in the midst of his terrible dreams.

ARIC began groaning before he was fully awake. His back hurt, his muscles ached, and his head pounded. His nose was so stuffy he could barely breathe. And there was a heavy weight across a good part of his body, pinning him down.

Then the weight shifted and chuckled softly, and Aric realized where he was.

"S-silly to sleep on the f-f-floor when you've that nice big b-b-bed. Quite c-comfortable for me, though."

Aric cautiously peeled his eyelids open, but his vision was still blurry and he had to blink several times. "Oh."

Gray laughed again. "Y-your stomach's growling."

"I don't think I ate yesterday," Aric answered, somewhat absently. He was still trying to gather his wooly thoughts, scattered like a wayward flock of sheep.

The weight moved off him completely, taking with it the quilt that had been draped over them both. Aric shivered a little in the chill morning air, and then was grateful for the coolness. "F-f-fetch us breakfast?" Gray suggested. "I spilled my d-d-d-dinner on the floor."

Aric moaned and managed to struggle to a seated position. Gray was hunkered down a few feet away with a small smile on his face. Peach slices were smashed into the dirty floor, replacing the cell's usual odor with that of overripe fruit, and the bowl was overturned. "I'm sorry," said Aric. He rose unsteadily to his feet, wincing as his limbs and back straightened. The floor was even less comfortable than his old bed at the White Dragon. And Gray had been sleeping on that floor for years, with bones considerably less well-padded than Aric's.

"I haven't d-d-done anything useful for… f-for a long t-t-t-time. Nothing except the fucking d-d-d-d-dreams. H-holding you, I felt useful. Strong. Th-thank you."

There was no sensible way to respond to these statements, so Aric only grunted. He could understand the need to feel helpful or valuable in at least a small way—it wasn't only the necessity of earning his room and board that had led him to drag boulders up hills. But he was still deeply embarrassed to have broken down as he did. What right did he have to turn to Gray for comfort? Gray was the one with his eyes missing, the one in chains. Even more troubling, Aric didn't understand why he had fallen apart so terribly. "I'll get breakfast," he said gruffly.

He'd slept with his boots on, but was relieved to discover that the boots themselves weren't ruined. Apparently the shoemaker had waterproofed them somehow. Aric's clothing, however, was a wrinkled and muddy mess. He stripped, washed his face, shaved, and dressed in fresh clothes.

Alys looked slightly relieved to see him. "Sleepyhead," she said, shoving his food buckets into his hand. "Master Sighard will be very unhappy with you for being so late to your lessons."

"I think I'll have to miss the lessons today. My head hurts."

She frowned with concern and stood on tiptoes so she could reach his forehead. Like a mother with a young child, she laid the back of her hand against his skin. "You don't feel as if you have a fever."

"I don't. I think... maybe the storm last night."

"Oh." She nodded knowingly. "Warin's still afraid of thunderstorms. Don't tell him I told you so! But he spent last night shivering in front of a candle and clutching this horribly dirty little wooden horse our father made when Warin was still a baby."

Aric gave her a weak smile before turning back to the Brown Tower. The hall inside the tower seemed especially empty this morning. A few days of exploration some weeks earlier had showed him that he and Gray were the building's only residents. There were four floors of rooms, but most of them were empty, and the rest held nothing but rotting furniture or odd bits and broken pieces of various things, as if someone had intended to fix them someday but never got around to it. On the fourth floor, every room was a barred cell, but none of those had a room adjacent to it like Aric's on the ground floor. He wondered sometimes if his chamber had been purpose-built for Gray's keeper.

When he entered the room, Gray was pacing the cell as much as his chains permitted. Gray stopped to listen as Aric shuffled the breakfast things. "Smells g-g-g-good," Gray finally said.

"Bacon today. And those sweet rolls you like."

Aric brought his own meal into the cell as well, and ate standing up. He noticed that Gray had made some attempts to clean up the cell floor, gathering the pulped fruit and dumping it in his waste bucket. But that left Gray himself sticky and grimy again. "Would you like to wash up?" Aric asked him.

"G-g-gods, yes. Feels so good to be c-c-clean!"

So Aric brought the basin of water—and somehow found himself cleansing the other man's arms and hands. The sliver of soap he'd stolen the day before was all gone, but the water alone did the trick. Gray seemed to enjoy the attention. He stood very still with his arms out, his mouth turned up into a smile. The full extent of his enjoyment became clear when the bath was finished. Gray was erect again—and so was Aric.

"Y-you're comfortable touching another m-m-man," Gray said thoughtfully.

"Yes," Aric replied, although comfortable wasn't how he'd describe his feelings just then.

"D-d-do you desire other men?"

Aric swallowed. "Yes."

"Do you d-d-d-desire *me*?"

This time, Aric took a step backward. "I… I can't…."

"If you want to, you c-can. It's been so l-l-l-long, Aric. So long."

Gray was beautiful. Enough sunlight snuck in at this time of day to illuminate him. He reminded Aric of an illustration in one of the schoolmaster's books he had reverently leafed through the previous week. Although Aric had cut his hair very badly and Gray was still too thin, he was beautiful: his face lifted up and with an expression the nearest to hope that Aric had seen since his arrival. And Gray seemed as eager for contact as he claimed, his breaths coming in short pants.

"I'm ugly," Aric rasped. "Not just a little ugly. Hideous."

"And I'm blind." Gray shook his head slightly. "I know what your f-f-face feels like, b-but to me… you're n-not ugly, Aric. Have you seen those s-statues f-flanking the river's mouth?"

Aric had seen them several times now. They were Lorad and Lokad, the giants who moved the course of the great river, thereby defeating an enormous sea monster and founding Tellomer, many hundreds of years in the past. The statues were as tall as the Brown Tower, hewn of gray stone, and the giants had broad shoulders and proud, handsome faces. They were heroes.

"Th-that's what you look like to m-me," Gray said.

When Aric didn't move, didn't say anything, Gray seemed to shrink into himself a bit. "I d-d-disgust you."

"Gods no!"

"I disgust m-me." Gray turned around and knelt, searching by feel for his quilt.

Aric's head pounded. He left the cell—bolted it shut—and curled in a ball on his big, soft bed.

CHAPTER
Twelve

By NOW, the middle-of-the-night screaming had become familiar, and Aric no longer hesitated in his response. As the first shriek echoed on the stone walls, he was out of bed, heading purposefully to the iron bars. He slid the bolt open in one smooth action and hurried to the shaking figure on the floor, then scooped the wailing man into his arms like a parent might do with a child.

Gray clung to Aric's neck. "It hurts! Oh gods, oh gods, it hurts! Make it stop!" It wasn't his voice, but a thinner one, higher pitched.

Aric soothed him as he always did and thought about all the horrible ways to die. Were there no good ways? Did anyone actually slip peacefully into death, or even welcome it gratefully? If so, Gray never dreamed of them.

"It hurts," Gray sobbed against Aric's shoulder. "It wasn't supposed to. Please. I changed my mind. Make it stop." Aric couldn't make it stop, of course. He could only stroke the uneven stubble on Gray's head as he hummed and waited for the dream to end.

After what felt like a long time but might have been only minutes, Gray's cries became whimpers and then died out altogether. When he slumped in Aric's arms, Aric laid him gently on the floor and covered him with the quilt. Gray was still for only a brief period before stirring and sighing and finally sitting up. He rubbed at his face wearily. "L-lady Torctgud. She's going to drink p-p-poison."

Aric's heart lurched. "Poison? Is that what…." His memories of his mother's death were fragmentary, which he'd always thought was odd. He should have recalled their last moments together with clarity.

But what he remembered was that she caressed him and called him a good boy, and then she was drinking from a small flask, and then she was sprawled on the ground, unmoving and cold, with froth drying around her mouth. Had she suffered as in Gray's nightmare? If so, had her son tried to help her, had he given her some dregs of comfort during her final agonies? Or had he cowered uselessly in the corner?

"Aric? Wh-what's wrong?"

"Nothing." He left the room to report the dream to the guard. Usually when he returned, Gray would have already fallen back into an exhausted sleep. But this time he was still standing, as close to the bars as his chains permitted, his fine brows drawn together in a frown.

"N-n-none of the others lasted this l-long. Th-they couldn't bear it. And none of them h-h-held me when I dreamed."

Aric was slightly embarrassed to realize that Gray knew that he'd been stroking him, singing to him. Up until this point, Aric hadn't known whether Gray was aware of what happened to him during the nightmares. "How well do you remember your dreams after you wake up?"

"I remember every fucking detail." Gray's voice was flat, and he didn't stutter. "I *live* those deaths, Aric. Every one of them."

Aric sat on the edge of his bed. He was glad the room was too dark to see Gray's face. "How have you stayed sane?"

"I tried to go m-m-mad. Thought it might ease my b-b-b-burden. B-but I couldn't. I couldn't." His voice broke slightly, and Aric could hear his harsh breathing. "Part of the p-p-p-price, I suppose."

The price for what? Aric wondered but didn't ask. He simply sat on his bed, looking down at his lap, where his single hand was bunched in a tight fist and his missing hand felt as if it were doing the same. The nonexistent joints of his left hand ached, and his ghostly fingernails dug into invisible skin. For the first time, he wondered what had happened to his severed left hand. Had someone buried it as if it were a body, or was it just thrown away with the rubbish? He felt absurdly guilty for not mourning it properly. After all, it had served him well for a long time. It didn't deserve to be discarded and forgotten.

"My mother took poison," he said, surprising himself.

"H-h-how old were you?"

"I don't know. Six or seven, I think."

"W-was your f-f-father still alive?"

"They'd hung him that morning."

"Ah," Gray sighed. "B-both at once, and you so young."

"I survived. I did fine."

Gray didn't answer right away, but his chains clanked softly. When he did speak, his voice was soft as well. "H-hanging is an easy death. F-f-fast. Painless. Some p-poisons are... g-g-gentle." He spoke with an air of authority, as well he might.

Aric found himself slightly consoled. Maybe his mother's poison had been a gentle one. "It was a long time ago," he said.

"I b-betrayed someone I l-l-loved. A long time ago. But I can still s-s-see the look on his f-f-f-face, j-just as if it were y-yesterday."

"My mother... that wasn't the same thing." Only it was, at least a little bit. Because a part of Aric had always believed that he had betrayed her—and betrayed his father as well—by surviving. He should have drunk the poison too. Everybody in his village thought so. His great-uncle used to tell him that all the time, and not only when he was drunk. Aric should have taken the flask from his mother's hand and finished the last drops, and he should have died that day along with his parents. But he had lived, making his parents' legacy a laughingstock, a target, an ugly simpleton with no more value than a mule.

He was *not* going to cry again.

And just to make sure he didn't, he leapt off the bed and yanked the blanket free, gathering it into his arms. He stalked to the shelves, where he grabbed the other spare blankets—three or four of them, all smelling sweetly of lavender water. He unbolted the cell and entered, threw the quilts onto the floor, and knelt to arrange them in a hasty pile. Then he lay down on them.

After a long hesitation, chains clattered and Gray lay beside him, not quite touching but close enough for Aric to feel his body's warmth. Gray was naked, of course, but Aric wore the trousers he'd hastily pulled on before telling the guard about Lady Torctgud. "Wh-what are you d-doing?" Gray asked.

"This floor is too damned hard."

Gray laughed and then scooted closer. There was a certain amount of shuffling, and Aric swore under his breath at the chains, but eventually they settled on their sides, Gray's back to Aric's front. Their lower bodies didn't quite touch, but Aric's right arm was wrapped around Gray's belly, Gray's forearm was nested over his, and Aric's nose was almost tickled by Gray's short, soft hair.

AS WAS often the case the morning after Gray's nightmare, Aric woke up tired and slightly out of sorts. But he didn't want to miss his lesson—today Master Sighard was going to meet them in the library—so he hurried through his morning routine, not sparing Alys more than a quick smile and a thank you before he rushed to bring breakfast to the tower. He ate quickly, finishing well before Gray did, and then paced the room restlessly.

"G-go," Gray laughed. "I c-c-can eat on my own."

Aric sped away.

Despite Warin's tales about his lessons in the library, this would be Aric's first one. Most meetings with the schoolmaster took place in that large, bare room with the marble floors. Fewer distractions, he said. Even the windows were set too high to view more than the sky. But today they were to receive a lesson on geography and history, and that required maps. These charts, Master Sighard had informed them, were kept in special cases in the library, where they were all to be very quiet and not disturb anyone else who might be in there. And under no circumstances were they permitted to touch the maps—he had focused his glare specifically on Aric while he said that last bit, as if he expected the brute to shred one of those precious documents purely for entertainment.

The library was housed in a building by itself, very close to the West Tower where the royal chambers were and where royalty and nobility conducted most of their important business. Aric had been in the West Tower only twice: on the day he'd first arrived at the palace and then again when Lord Maudit had summoned him and granted his boon. Aric had never been in the library at all.

Quoen met him at the entrance. Her skirts were stained with whatever she'd eaten for breakfast, and she had a smudge of dirt on one cheek. Aric had a sense that Quoen's mother sent her out into the world every morning clean and presentable, but that the tiny girl never stayed that way for long. Today she was as uncowed as ever by Aric's size, and she stood with her hands balled on her hips. "Hurry up! What if Master Sighard bonks you on the head with his stick for being late?"

The schoolmaster hadn't yet used his stick on his oversized student, and Aric wasn't especially worried about it. But he let Quoen wrap her hand around one of his fingers and drag him through the tall door and into the building.

Aric's breath left him in a whoosh. The room was enormous—bigger than a ballroom and with two levels of galleries along the sides. There was a dome in the ceiling and elaborate frescoes. Statues and ceramic vases and paintings were tucked into alcoves throughout. There were vast wooden tables and countless chairs of either carved wood or upholstery. The ornately patterned tile floor was cushioned with carpets larger than any he'd ever seen—deep jewel tones of red and blue and yellow and green. Stoves with decoratively painted tiles were set here and there, although it was not yet the season for them to be lit, and the entire room was bathed in a warm golden light that poured in through high windows. But it was the books that left him paralyzed in wonder. More books by far than any of the shops in Tellomer—perhaps more books than all the shops put together. More books than a hundred men could read in their lifetimes. More books than he'd imagined existed. And there were also heavy wooden cases, some of them partially open so he could see the documents and scrolls stored inside. There were piles of dusty papers here and there, some of them bound with ribbon or string, and folded stacks of parchment and thin sheets of leather.

Quoen gave a hard tug to his arm. "Hurry!" she repeated.

Master Sighard was waiting for them at the far end of the room. He stood next to a long, low case, and his students sat on the floor in front of him, most of them wiggling with boredom. He was scowling. Aric hurried and then sat cross-legged behind all the children. The schoolmaster tapped the tip of his walking stick on the floor twice; the sound echoed loudly. "Today we shall discuss the historical importance of the Great River to our kingdom. I will expect you to be capable of drawing a rough map of the kingdom, as well as being able to recite—in order—the major developments that the river has brought."

He leaned his stick against the cabinet and then, moving with great care, picked up a rolled document that was nearly as tall as he was. He painstakingly unfastened the ribbons that held it shut and then held the document in front of him, his arms stretched so that he was gripping the document's top corners. "This is a map of the kingdom," he intoned. While some of the children looked bored, Aric leaned forward so he could get a better look. The map was done in various colors and contained symbols he couldn't decipher. He did understand, however, that the blue part at the right—which was enhanced by several multicolored sea serpents—must be the sea. At the top there was a lot of green. The great forests, he guessed. A wide band of blue snaked through the entire landmass, beginning near the bottom left of the map and not ending until it met the sea.

The schoolmaster pointed his nose at the oldest boy amongst his students—except for Aric, of course. "Falardo, show the location of Tellomer on the map."

Falardo unfolded himself—he was all elbows and knees and long, bony legs—and hovered his finger over the spot where the river met the sea. "Correct. And Harfaire?" Falardo peered at the map for several long moments before making a small triumphant sound and indicating a spot quite a bit lower than Tellomer and well to the left. Harfaire was not on the river, and a small range of mountains lay between it and the capital city. Currently, travelers from Tellomer had to cross the mountains, which was dangerous during the winter and the rainy season, or go by boat down the river to Porinar and then double back by land to their destination. The nearly completed bridge would give them a third option, which would reduce the length of their journey as well as save them the bother of transferring goods from boat to wagon. Aric's village didn't have a name because it had never needed one, but he supposed it might acquire one soon, and then it would be on maps as well.

While Aric had been pondering these things, Master Sighard had continued to quiz Falardo. Aric didn't see the need to learn these places since he'd never go anywhere. But then the schoolmaster asked his student to locate Racinas, and Aric suddenly focused his attention. Falardo hemmed and hawed for a long time, until Master Sighard huffed and said, "North, idiot. Look to the north," and Falardo pointed at a spot near the sea but far above Tellomer, up amongst the forests.

Aric listened as Master Sighard droned on about the importance of Racinas, which could be reached only by sea. It was an important source of income for the more southerly parts of the kingdom, from which it imported food and fabrics and many crafted goods. But it also exported the finest wool and dried fish of a sort that was especially popular amongst the Tellomerese nobility. There was gold up there too. And, it was said, Racinans were the most beautiful inhabitants of this kingdom or any other. Aric thought about Gray Leynham and Petrus the whore, and he was inclined to agree.

"Racinas was founded even earlier than Tellomer," the schoolmaster was saying. "It was once an independent kingdom, before King Trichtheo conquered it four hundred years ago. But it was very small then, truly hardly more than a village full of priests and acolytes who served the Vale of the Gods."

Without really meaning to, Aric raised his hand. "What is the Vale of the Gods?"

Master Sighard frowned, then evidently decided that the answer would make a legitimate addition to the lesson. "It's one of our most ancient and holy sites. Only pilgrims who purify themselves properly are permitted to enter." With every *p* sound, the schoolmaster sprayed spittle on the unfortunate children who were seated in the front. "There is a sacred pool in the Vale. It is the pool in which Ismundo bathed his wife, the goddess Ebra, after she was wounded in battle with demons. You *have* heard this story, have you not?"

Aric nodded. His great-uncle hadn't bothered to send him to the little village temple, and the priests hadn't exactly invited him in either; but when he was very young, his father used to tell him some of the tales of the gods and goddesses.

The schoolmaster sniffed. "Ismundo bathed Ebra there and she was healed, and because the pool still contains her blood, pilgrims who drink the water may ask for a blessing. If the gods are in a good mood, the pilgrims will be granted that blessing. But because Ebra suffered, so must they: they must always make a great sacrifice in return."

"The price?" Aric whispered to himself.

"Pardon me?"

"Um, I'm sorry, sir. I was just thinking."

"Please stick to tasks of which you're capable," Master Sighard replied tersely as he began rolling up the map.

The lesson ended soon after that. Quoen and the other children scampered away as soon as they were dismissed, but Aric approached the schoolmaster with his head bent. "Master? May I... I'd like to remain here in the library for a while, if I can. I won't break anything!" he added hastily.

"You must remain quiet. And don't disturb anyone." Master Sighard waved his arm to indicate the library at large, where only four or five other people were leafing through papers or searching the shelves.

"Yes, sir."

The schoolmaster gave him a final warning glare before hobbling out of the building.

Aric simply stood there for a very long time, so overwhelmed that he couldn't imagine where to begin. Then he began to wander. He didn't touch anything—he hadn't yet worked up the courage—but he walked slowly, holding his head sideways so he could see the titles. He was pleased to discover that he could read many of them passably well. Some words he couldn't puzzle out, but he'd been concentrating very hard on reading over the past weeks, and now as long as a word wasn't too long or too esoteric, he could usually read it. An odd feeling gathered in his chest, and after a bit of examination he realized it was pride. Here he was, an ignorant, mutilated monster, but he could read. It was as if the entire rest of the world had a wonderful secret that had finally been shared with him.

He wasn't certain how the books in the library were organized, but it didn't especially matter because he wasn't looking for anything in particular. He was astounded at the range of books he found: history, sciences of all kinds, religion, magic, animal husbandry, farming, warfare, sailing. Some were ancient and some looked brand new. And there were books full of stories. It was one of those that finally captured his attention, mostly because of the golden dragon that was embossed on its brown leather spine. He checked his hand to make sure it was clean, wiped it on his trousers to get rid of the sweat, and pulled out the volume. A quick perusal showed him that the book was full of bright pictures as well as words. With a broad smile, he took the book to the nearest chair and sat down to read.

"Brute!"

Aric looked up from a story about pirates and a princess, then gasped and scrambled awkwardly to his feet. "Your Highness! I'm... Lord Maudit said I can have lessons and Master Sighard brought us here today and then—"

Prince Aldfrid put up a hand. "It's fine," he said with a grin. "I was just pleasantly surprised to see you. You look good."

"Um, thank you."

The prince wore riding clothes and, truth be told, smelled slightly of horses. His long yellow hair looked windblown and tangled. And he had a thick book tucked under one arm. "I was just in your village the other day, inspecting the bridge. You'll be happy to know that I stayed suitably far from the edge this time. They haven't any giants left to rescue me."

Aric hid his own grin by ducking his head. "I'm glad you stayed safe, Your Highness."

"Yes, well, I'm sure I'll do some other damned foolish thing soon and end up swallowed by a sea monster or cursed by a witch or something. But how are you getting on, Brute? Lord Maudit told me you'd asked for lessons."

"Yes, sir. I'm very grateful for them."

The prince pointed at the book that was still in Aric's hand. "And putting them to good use, I see. That's good. I was never much of a reader myself—no patience for it—but one of my brothers, Clithe, he nearly lives in this room. He'd be here right now if father hadn't sent him off to negotiate a treaty with the Gernushians. I'm not trusted with such matters myself. Too foolhardy."

"Oh, sir, I'm sure you're—"

"Every bit as foolhardy as they say." The prince shrugged happily. "Also headstrong and impatient. But how are you getting along, Brute? Apart from the lessons, I mean."

"Very well, sir. Everyone is very kind to me and I'm very comfortable."

"And the prisoner?"

Aric tried not to shift from foot to foot. "He's... he's very little trouble, Your Highness. I'm fulfilling all my duties."

"I'm sure you are." Prince Aldfrid's eyes were sharp, even though his tone remained easy. "You're not bothered by the nightmares?"

"They're... they're unpleasant. But more so for him than for me." Damning himself silently for revealing too much, Aric bit his tongue.

The prince gave him a long look before nodding. "How is he?"

Aric had no idea how to answer that question. He didn't know what Aldfrid wanted to hear. So he settled on the truth. "He's suffering, sir. He... I think he tries not to fall into despair, but his life is so miserable. And I think some of the other... keepers abused him." There. Now he was going to be thrown out of the palace and Gray would be alone again. For the hundredth time, Aric wished he were capable of the happy little webs of mistruth that others seemed to spin so easily.

But Prince Aldfrid didn't look angry. Only sad and thoughtful. He stroked his mustache a few times and then said, "Would you like to borrow a book, Brute? Take it back to your room to read at your leisure, I mean."

"I...." Aric shook his head slightly, trying to clear it enough to make sense of the conversation. "I'd like that very much. Thank you, sir."

With another nod, this one brisk, the prince gave a small smile as well. "Excellent. Follow me. I have just the book in mind."

Aric wasn't certain what to do with the dragon book, so he ended up leaving it on the chair. Even with his long legs, he had to walk quickly to catch up with the prince, who had turned down one of the room's short corridors of bookcases. "Hmm, let me see. Should be around here someplace.... Ah!" The prince tugged a slim green volume from the shelf and held it out. "Here you are. Can you remember where to return it when you're finished with it?"

Aric looked around carefully so as to memorize the exact location. "Yes, sir."

"Excellent. After you return it, you may borrow another if you like. But I've a meeting to attend." He patted the book that was still tucked under his arm. "We need to improve the road between here and the bridge, and somehow I seem to have acquired that responsibility. It's the most boring thing imaginable. Almost makes me wish I'd simply plunged off that damned cliff."

The prince gave Aric's arm two hearty pats and then hurried away.

Aric stood there, still more than slightly confused. And then his stomach gave a loud, embarrassing rumble, reminding him that it was lunch time. He wanted to practice with the guards that afternoon too, so he needed to hurry. He detoured by the chair to replace the dragon book onto the shelves and then rushed out of the library and to the tower. He'd drop off the green book there before grabbing lunch and joining the guards.

CAPTAIN JAUN was of the opinion that a well-prepared guardsman ought to do more than practice his weaponry and horsemanship. A guard ought also to be capable of climbing the defensive walls without losing his breath, and carrying sacks and boxes of supplies without collapsing under their weight. If he was stripped of his armor and arrows and blades, he still ought to be able to defeat an enemy through the strength of his hands and legs. The guards grumbled about it under their breath, but Aric was thankful. He wouldn't have been able to join the guards in their training if all they did was shoot arrows or swing swords, and he'd never been on horseback in his life. But he could run with them and lift heavy chunks of iron with them, and even one-handed he could wrestle with them. He liked to do these things not only because they passed the time and kept him fit, not only because they lent him an easy sense of male camaraderie, but also because while he trained his mind was too occupied to dwell on other things.

Today the sky was overcast, and the air was chill enough that most members of the palace staff wore sweaters or cloaks. But after two hours of running around and leaping over obstacles, Aric and the guards were shirtless and drenched in sweat. When Captain Jaun told them they could have a brief break, the men clustered around a cistern, drinking deeply and splashing one another with the cold water. Aric took a metal scoopful and simply dumped it over his head, which made the others laugh.

A barrel-chested man with a face as badly scarred as Aric's clapped him on the shoulder. "Y'oughta give up that cushy position and join the guard instead."

Aric held up the stump of his left arm. "A one-handed guard?"

"So we won't make you an archer. You could just stand at the front and point that ugly face of yours at intruders and they'd scamper away like mice."

The men laughed again, and so did Aric. Comments like that were nothing like the tormenting he'd endured as a boy. In fact, these sorts of comments only made him feel more accepted, because the guards teased one another all the time: this one because he was too fat, another because he was too thin; this one because his wife was pregnant with their tenth child, that one because he was a newlywed. They gave each other nicknames like Big Ears or Rabbit (for prominent front teeth and a distinctly twitchy little nose), and nobody took offense. They were like an especially large and unruly group of brothers, and at times Aric ached to join them. Now, just knowing that they would allow him to do so was enough to bring him joy.

"Enough with the tea party, girls!" shouted Captain Jaun. "I want to see you running up those stairs as if all the demons of hell were nipping at your heels!"

Most of the men groaned, but Aric smiled and loped away. He was the first one to reach the stairs.

The sun set early this time of year, and it was already dark by the time Aric went to fetch his dinner. Alys wasn't anywhere in sight at the kitchens, though, which worried him until an older woman with long gray braids gave him a bright smile. "Her man's just returned this afternoon, thin as a broomstick and with his eyes all moony over her. We won't be seeing either of them for a day or two at least." The cooks and scullery maids and pot boys all laughed uproariously, and Aric understood that the kitchen staff was a family as well.

He carried the dinner buckets back to the tower, where, as usual after dark, the guard at the door lit a candle for him from a nearby torch. That was easier on Aric than trying, one-handed, to light a candle with flint. Nobody except Aric had entered his chamber since the first days after he'd arrived, which was generally a good thing, because it meant nobody saw that Gray was clean and shaved and decently fed.

"Y-you must have had a g-g-good day," Gray said as Aric lit the candles in his room.

Aric turned to their dinners and, as always, began to transfer some of his own fish stew to Gray's bowl. "How can you tell?"

"You were h-h-humming."

"Oh. Sorry."

"D-don't be. It's nice."

Aric smiled shyly and tore off a hunk of his soft bread. Gray had looped and tucked a quilt around himself in some elaborate fashion. He held out his hands as Aric unbolted the cell and stepped inside. "Th-thank you," Gray said when Aric gave him the food. "D-d-did you enjoy the library?"

Although Gray's question reminded him of the strange conversation with the prince, Aric grinned. "It was wonderful. Amazing. Like something from a story."

"There's a ch-chair in the northwest corner—I s-suppose it's still there, likely been there for d-decades—that's especially n-nice. In the afternoon, the s-s-sun shines through those panes of colored g-glass, and if you sit in that chair, it's l-like you're under water."

Aric wondered how the son of a sailor came to know the royal library so intimately, but didn't ask. Instead, he watched the other man slurp his dinner and then use the bread to mop up the last of the sauce. "I saw the prince in the library today," Aric said.

Gray froze in the middle of handing his empty bowl back. "A-Aldfrid?"

"Yes. He… he asked after you."

Gray's expression—always a bit difficult to read anyway—became very guarded. "Oh?"

Aric took the bowl but didn't walk away with it. He hadn't eaten yet himself and was very hungry, but something told him this discussion was important. To whom it was important and why, he couldn't have said. "I think… he seemed distressed about you."

"D-d-d-d-d—Fuck! D-distressed I'm s-s-still alive."

"I don't think so. I think… he cares about you, doesn't he?"

Gray's jaw worked for a moment. "H-he did once." Then he folded himself into a ball in the corner of the cell, and Aric decided it was time to steer the conversation in a slightly different direction.

"He let me borrow a book from the library. He said I could read it here, and when I'm finished with it, I can exchange it for another."

Gray didn't answer, although Aric could tell by the set of his shoulders that he was listening.

"I'm going to have my dinner now," Aric said, "and then I'm going to read. If you want, I can try to read out loud. I'm… I'm still not very good at it, but—"

"I'd like that," Gray interrupted with a soft voice. "I m-miss reading. I miss so damned *much*!" Aric pretended he didn't hear the sounds as Gray worked hard to suppress sobs. Sometimes a man wanted comfort, but sometimes there was greater dignity in being left alone.

The fish stew was good. It filled his belly comfortably, along with the rest of the bread and two small, crisp apples. When the food was gone and his usual tankard of ale empty, Aric washed up at his basin and removed his boots. The green book was sitting on the mattress, which was still bare of blankets. He grabbed the book, tucked it under his arm, and then took the largest of his candles off the shelf. He returned to the cell, which he hadn't bothered to bolt.

In the warm, flickering light, Gray looked very young. He gave Aric a weak smile as the larger man settled beside him, and then Gray scooted a little closer so that their shoulders just barely touched. "Wh-what's the book?"

Aric hadn't even looked, and now that he did, he saw that the cover and spine contained no title, only the embossed and gilded drawing of a boat. He opened the book. The pages inside were thick and yellowed, and the printing looked a little smeary and old-fashioned. There weren't any illustrations. "There are a lot of words here," he said uncertainly.

"B-but you only have to read them one at a t-t-time."

Well, put like that, the challenge did seem slightly less daunting. Aric squinted at the first sentence, not yet having the courage to say it aloud. But when he deciphered its meaning, he couldn't help a startled little gasp.

"Wh-what's wrong?"

"Nothing. It's only that I think this book is about those giants—Lorad and Lokad."

Gray's laughter was warm and hearty, and it loosened something tight in Aric's heart. "I g-guess I'm not the only one who s-s-sees you that way."

"Prince Aldfrid was making a joke."

"M-maybe. H-he liked to tease. He wasn't cruel, though." Gray sighed. "N-never cruel. Come on, Aric. Read to me."

Aric did. Haltingly, and with many mistakes. Sometimes he couldn't figure out a word at all, and then he had to spell it to Gray, who would tell him what those confusing letters meant. But Gray was patient—urging Aric to continue whenever he got frustrated enough to want to give up—and Aric found that after a few pages the task came a little more easily to him. He read about Lorad and Lokad, who were fathered by lightning and birthed from a crevasse in one of the mountains to the west, and who suckled on tree sap and dew. When they were grown, they took pity on the humans, who were suffering from a crop-killing drought. First the giants tried to shake water from the clouds, but then the clouds dried up and blew away. Then they tried to water the earth with their own tears, but their tears were too salty. Finally, an eagle told them of a place to the east where the soil was fertile and the rain plentiful and where, even in drought years, people could feed themselves from the sea. But there was a problem: a terrible monster lurked near the shore, and it would prey on any people who came too close.

So Lorad and Lokad made their way to the land and they found the monster. They fought it, but although they were strong, it drew strength from the water, and they couldn't drag it to shore. They withdrew to treat their wounds and strategize. It began to rain, and they saw how the monster hissed and moaned when the fresh water hit its scales. The brothers were heartened by their discovery, but disappointed when the monster simply sank beneath the waves.

"If we had more fresh water, we could defeat the monster," Lorad said.

"Rain will not be enough. We need a river," said his twin.

The giants set out in search of a river, and they found one: the Great River. Although it would surely have plenty of water for their needs, the Great River looped and twisted like a snake swallowing its own tail.

The giants used all their great strength to reshape the earth, in an attempt to coax the river along the necessary course. When the river still wouldn't budge, they wrapped their great arms around it and wrestled it until it flowed where they wanted, straight into the sea. The sudden influx of fresh water killed the sea monster, and the people cheered.

But Lorad and Lokad had expended too much of themselves. Even as the humans prepared to settle in their new land, the giants collapsed into the Great River and were drowned. When the giant corpses were pulled from the mouth of the river, the people cried and begged the gods to return their heroes to them. The gods wouldn't do that much—gods tended to be rather final in their decisions about death—but they did turn the bodies to stone so that the giants could stand forever at the mouth of the Great River, guarding Tellomer from dangers from the sea.

Aric's voice was hoarse by the time he ended the tale, but he didn't want to go to sleep. There was something so wonderfully intimate about sitting with another person like this, sharing a story, the candlelight flickering in the darkness. It was as if the rest of the world disappeared as long as the storytelling continued.

"Y-you read very well," said Gray. "You m-m-must learn quickly."

"I made a lot of mistakes."

"Everyone does." Gray rested his head on Aric's shoulder. "D-do you see why Friddy chose that book for you? You're a hero too."

Aric snorted. "I'm not."

"When y-you saved Friddy, is that when y-you lost your hand?"

"Yes."

"D-d-did you almost die?"

"Maybe."

Gray rested his hand on Aric's knee. "Sacrificed yourself, j-just like the giants."

"But I didn't mean to! It's only... the prince fell over the cliff, and I didn't think at all, I just moved. I was the tallest and the strongest. I don't think anyone else could have reached him in time. He was injured pretty badly. But I wasn't a hero. I saw something that needed to be done, and I did it."

With a low chuckle, Gray squeezed his knee. "Th-that's what heroes do, Aric."

"But I'm not—"

"You s-saved me."

Aric shook his head and then gave a little tug on the chain that attached Gray's collar to the floor. "You're still a prisoner."

"You *saved* me," Gray repeated firmly to Aric. And then he kissed him.

At first, Aric was too startled to do anything except freeze. He was so focused on the feel of Gray's warm lips against his that he barely noticed when Gray plucked the book out of his hand and then, presumably, set it aside. Aric parted his lips and, for the first time in his life, tasted another man—fish stew and something new, something he guessed was just Gray's own flavor.

Gray wriggled out of the quilt and clambered onto Aric's lap so that his naked chest was pressed against Aric's shirt and his knees straddled Aric's hips. He kissed Aric again, longer and more deeply. Aric's hand hovered in midair; he had no idea where to put it.

Gray moved away, but only enough to drag his lips across Aric's jaw and to just below his ear. "D-do you want this?" he whispered.

"I... I...." Aric was now the one with the stutter. "I-I can't...."

"It doesn't have to m-mean anything. J-just c-comfort given, comfort shared. Or it can mean everything."

Aric's lungs were refusing to work properly, and his hand stopped obeying him, settling on Gray's back, just above the swell of his buttocks. "I've never done this," he admitted.

"You're a v-virgin?"

"No. There are—there were boys during the Harvest Moon Festival. I paid them double." He realized that his words probably made little sense, but he just couldn't be coherent with Gray pressed up against him, breathing against his neck.

"Whores? That's all?"

"Yes."

"N-not the same then. Not the same as when someone w-wants you. And gods, Aric, I want you."

If Aric hadn't been hard already, the throatiness of Gray's declaration would have done the trick. As it was, he let his head fall back—hard enough for it to knock against the stone wall—and he moaned as Gray mouthed at his neck and ground their groins together. Gray was hard as well, but his skin was very soft under Aric's hand, and the muscle of his ass was nicely pliant when Aric allowed his hand to drop a bit farther down.

Aric was much larger and heavier than Gray, yet somehow Gray managed to maneuver them both so that Aric was lying flat on his back on the quilts. Then Gray made Aric's trousers disappear—maybe he truly was a witch—and *then* Gray was stretched out full length on top of him, like a wonderfully living blanket. A wonderfully *moving* blanket, actually, as Gray traced his mouth and fingers over Aric's face, over his neck and collarbones and chest. Gray sucked and nibbled at Aric's nipples, which made Aric gasp and grab the other man's hair, just for something to hold on to.

"G-gods," Gray panted against Aric's chest. "I'm afraid I'm n-not going to last long."

And for some reason, that struck Aric as funny, and he began to laugh. Gray wiggled back up his body, and he laughed too. The sound of their voices mingling was as good as the feeling of their bodies pressed together. "I'd l-like to dream of this tonight," said Gray. "Dream of us. So g-good, isn't it?"

"Yes," answered Aric, who'd never even fantasized something like this. A beautiful man wanting him, valuing him, wrapping Aric's body in pleasure instead of pain. It was more than anyone like him deserved, but he wouldn't say so, not tonight, not when Gray was kissing him again and rubbing his hands on the points of Aric's hips.

"Good gods!" Gray exclaimed.

"I'm sorry?" replied Aric, not sure whether that was the right response and not able to craft anything more clever. Gray's fingers felt so strange around his shaft, warm and strong and soft, but not as soft as Petrus's.

"A d-delightful challenge," Gray said with a chuckle. Then he did something truly unexpected: he lined his cock up against Aric's and held them together. "C-can't quite handle them b-both," he said with something suspiciously like a giggle.

If Gray's hand had felt strange, his cock felt even stranger, although certainly not unpleasant. Aric wanted to touch it, to explore it with his fingers, but he only had one hand, and that hand—occupied with squeezing Gray's ass—didn't want to let go of its prize.

Soon it didn't matter anyway. Gray stroked and rocked his hips, Aric arched his own hips upward, and they were both gasping out their climaxes as their combined spend flowed hot and sticky across their bellies.

Gray collapsed bonelessly atop him. "Fuck," he said succinctly.

Aric was still too light-headed to do more than nod his agreement.

 # CHAPTER
Thirteen

HE WAS merely being kind, Aric told himself. The weather had turned very cold, and even with the stove lit, his chambers in the Brown Tower were freezing at night. He would have been comfortable enough in his bed, which was close to the stove, but Gray shivered and coughed on the cold stone floor of the cell, even with all Aric's quilts. So Aric forsook the bed entirely and slept every night in the cell with Gray. They spooned together with some blankets below them and the rest above, and Aric's big body kept Gray nice and warm. Of course, they made love—Gray's term for it—almost every night, so their blood moved briskly right before sleep, and neither of them felt the least bit chilled.

Besides, with Gray already in his arms, Aric could do his job more efficiently. No more stumbling across the room, half asleep. Now, as soon as Gray began to stir, whether he cried or screamed or simply breathed raggedly, Aric was already holding him, immediately humming and stroking and murmuring words of comfort. And when Gray awakened soon afterward, he had only to whisper the particulars of his dream into Aric's ear, and Aric would rush to tell the guard.

On an especially miserable night, when the rain outside had turned to sleet that clattered noisily against the cobblestones, Gray awakened Aric by moaning and twitching. "Shh," Aric crooned as he always did. "It's all right. Everything's all right."

"So cold." This time Gray's voice was deep and mournful, like the wind when it rushed across the plains near Aric's village.

Aric held him more tightly. "I'll keep you warm."

"No one. No one to hold my hand and ease my way."

"I'm here," said Aric. Gray had told him that, even though he couldn't respond to Aric during his nightmares, he could feel him and hear him, and that he was grateful for it. It was as if he were possessed, he said. Possessed by the spirit of someone not yet dead. "I'm here and you'll wake up soon and I'll make some tea to warm you up."

"Please. Just a thin blanket and a kind word, someone to remember my name." Then Gray's voice devolved to incoherent mumbles, and Aric just held him because he could do nothing else.

Gray shuddered and awoke a few minutes later. He moved backward, pressing himself more firmly against Aric's body. "Itan. He's g-going to die from cold and hunger and... and emptiness, I th-think."

"Gods."

"D-don't bother t-telling the guard."

"Why? Is it too late already?"

"Itan's j-just a beggar. Th-they won't do anything for him."

"But he's going to die!"

Gray squirmed around until he was facing Aric, getting himself slightly tangled in his chains as he did so. Gods, Aric hated those fucking chains. "P-people die every day, Aric. Wh-when I dream of someone important, or s-someone who's in the p-p-palace, they'll try to stop it. But when it's n-nobody, only a beggar... n-n-not worth the effort, I guess."

"I'm nobody," Aric said.

"You're n-not." Gray's breaths puffed against Aric's shoulder, and then he planted a quick kiss on Aric's cheek. "G-g-go tell the guard if it will ease your conscience."

Aric pulled on his clothes and his cloak, and he told the guard, but his conscience wasn't eased one bit.

MASTER SIGHARD'S mood was as gray as this morning's sky. The weather bothered his arthritis, making him hobble more painfully than usual and causing him to wield his stick against wayward students even more freely. Quoen didn't get hit, but her distraction earned a tongue-lashing that made her cry, and then it was Aric's turn to glare at the schoolmaster instead of the other way around.

Everyone was relieved when the day's lessons adjourned early.

Over in the kitchens, even Alys was missing her usual sunny mood. She'd been beaming ever since her man, Cearl, returned from the sea. He'd brought back enough money to start his own carting business, and Alys had made sure he was awarded a contract to deliver to the palace. They were planning a spring wedding, and lately her conversation had been full of talk about the house Cearl had bought not far from the palace itself, and how they were going to fix it up, and how if you stood on the balcony and angled your head just right, you could view the sea. But today she was dour as she handed Aric his lunch. "It's never going to be spring," she said. "It's going to be winter forever and ever, and my feet will always be cold."

He bent down and kissed the top of her head. "Spring will come. The sun will return and the flowers will bloom and you'll have a lovely wedding."

She tried to frown and smile at the same time before she pushed him away. "Go. You wouldn't want to miss slogging through the mud with the guards." She'd decided several weeks earlier that he must have cast his eye on one of the guards, which in her mind explained why he liked working himself half to death with them no matter the weather. She'd been pestering him to name the man and was getting very frustrated by his refusals.

In any case, he didn't join the guards today. Instead, he trudged through the drizzle to the West Tower. The guards on duty at the entrance knew him well by now, and although they raised their eyebrows slightly at his intention to enter this particular building, they didn't stop him.

Without anyone to guide him, he got lost twice and had to ask directions. Eventually, however, he was standing outside Lord Maudit's rooms, trying to convince the round man who was there that he should be permitted inside.

"His Excellency has not summoned you, and you do not have an appointment," the man said, not bothering to look up from his ledger.

"But I need to see him."

"You may make an appointment."

"Great! When?"

A chubby finger ran down the page. "Three weeks from tomorrow. Seven o'clock in the morning."

Aric didn't know how much advance notice Gray's dreams provided, but three weeks was almost certainly too long. "I can't wait. I have to see him today."

"That is not possible."

A few deep breaths helped Aric maintain his calm. Barely. "But it's about Gr—about the prisoner's dream."

That was finally enough to make the man's head snap up, so quickly that his double chin quivered. "Have you informed the guard on duty?"

"Yes. But I need to talk to Lord Maudit too. Please."

The man looked down at his ledger, as if it might have the answer, and wrinkled his nose. "Very well. Wait here." He disappeared through a door so tiny that he had to duck. Aric had a momentary vision of the pudgy man getting stuck halfway through, and he had to swallow a slightly hysterical giggle.

When the man returned a few moments later, he didn't look happy. "His Excellency will see you. Make it quick."

Aric was afraid he was going to be forced to squeeze through the tiny door too, and was relieved when the functionary instead opened the large door a few feet away.

Lord Maudit stood behind his desk, which was piled high with papers, crumb-scattered plates, and half-empty cups of tea. He had ink smudges on his fingers. "What?" he demanded without glancing up from his papers.

"The prisoner had a dream last night, sir."

"I know. The guards informed me."

"Can you tell me… is Itan all right?"

"Who?"

"Itan. The man in the dream."

Lord Maudit managed to look furious and resigned at the same time, although Aric had a sense the anger wasn't directed at him. "Why is it your concern, Brute?"

"I'm there every time he dreams, sir. I hear what he says when… when he's dying. It's awful. I'd like to know if he's been saved."

"We save some of them. More than half. That boy who was to die the other day by tumbling off the wall—one of Lord Sohier's ill-behaved brats—he was caught in time."

Aric was relieved to learn that, but still he persevered. "And what about Itan?"

Lord Maudit picked up a cup, sipped at it, made a face, and put it back down. "Itan will almost certainly die."

"Because nobody's going to help him."

"That beggar could be anywhere in the city, Brute."

"And there are dozens of guardsmen. Send them out to the poorer parts of Tellomer and they'll find him."

"And do what with him?"

"Feed him!" With an effort, Aric lowered his voice. "Get him warm. Take him to a healer."

"And then? Chances are he's unable or unwilling to work. So we house him somewhere until he wastes away from old age. And what of all the other beggars here in the city? Or the people starving in their villages? All the people throughout the kingdom who die because they haven't the money for food or shelter or healers? Shall we house them too?"

"But you have so much." Aric was aware that his voice had shrunk. "Everyone here at the palace has so much. Even me."

Lord Maudit looked longingly at the enormous chest that housed his liquor, but he didn't leave his desk. "Everyone here is well provided for. And each person is free to give away whatever he or she wishes. But if we take it away from them to give to the poor, they will resist. Revolutions have been fought over less. I'll not risk rebellion for the sake of one beggar." He picked up a sheaf of papers. "Now go. I've work to do."

Aric's heart was heavy as he left Lord Maudit's chambers. The round man looked smug. Aric brushed past him and stalked down the corridor, but once he was out of sight, he ducked into a small alcove and leaned against the wall to think. He could speak with Captain Jaun, but Aric knew that the captain would never deploy his guards throughout the city without orders to do so. That left Aric with only one potential ally.

He didn't know where in the West Tower the royal chambers were, and when he asked a girl who was rushing by, she looked at him aghast and kept on moving. So he resorted to skulking around, avoiding other people whenever possible. The tower had a lot of nooks and crannies, and endless hallways with endless doors, and funny little stairways that seemed to lead to nowhere at all. He was starting to despair when he noticed that the hanging tapestries were becoming more sumptuous, the statuary and other décor more covered in gilt. He was finally stopped by a pair of guards who wore the royal scarlet and cream, but their uniforms were considerably fancier than any he'd seen before. He didn't recognize these men.

"Idiot!" the older one hissed at him. "You don't belong here. Go away."

"But… I need to speak with Prince Aldfrid."

The guards laughed. "You want to have a little chat with His Highness, do you? Just fancy dropping on in and sitting down over tea?"

"It's about Gray Leynham. The prisoner," he added, probably unnecessarily.

The guards' eyes narrowed. "His Highness has nothing to do with the traitor. Now go before you end up in irons as well."

Aric went. And although he spent more time stalking the hallways, he couldn't think of any other plans. Shortly before dinnertime, he gave up. He tried to hide his anxiety from Gray that night, but it was hard. The sky was spitting sleet again; even the sound of it made Aric shiver. He read aloud—from a book about brewing ale that he'd grabbed rather randomly from the library the day before—until his eyes felt gritty and his throat hurt. Then they lay down together, huddled for warmth, and swiftly fell asleep.

THE weather hadn't improved by morning. Aric wore his warmest trousers, a sweater Alys had given him, and his thick wool cloak, but he was still thoroughly chilled by the time he fetched their breakfast and brought it back. "Are you warm enough?" he asked Gray. "I've added more coal to the stove, but it's so far away from you."

Gray was huddled under a big pile of quilts. "I'm f-fine. I've endured worse w-with only my old b-blanket."

"How?" Aric demanded. "How have you survived so much with so little?"

"What else c-c-can I do? I endure or I die. You f-forget, Aric. I earned this."

Aric didn't think anything should have earned Gray's bleak existence.

Before he walked back into the biting cold, Aric made his lover— his lover! Wasn't that an odd thought?—a cup of scalding tea. He intended to go to his lessons, which, due to the weather, were being held in a small storeroom near the kitchens, kept cozy by the heat of the cooking fires. It was a location of last resort, used only in the most dire of circumstances—when Master Sighard was almost crippled from his arthritis—because the tiny space was crowded and noisy from the activities of the kitchen staff.

But Aric didn't turn toward the kitchens. Instead he crossed the palace grounds via the most direct route possible and exited through the front gates. His head was down against the rain, and he wasn't paying much attention to his surroundings. He knew that what he sought wouldn't be found so near the palace, where the houses were large and sumptuous and the shops sold expensive goods that the inhabitants of those houses were apt to purchase. He was several minutes outside the gates when someone tugged on his cloak. He spun, fist curled defensively. But it was only Warin, with wet hair, a dripping red nose, and a cheery grin.

"You walk *fast*!" Warin said. He was slightly out of breath.

"What are you doing here?"

"Coming with you."

"No you're not. Go home."

Warin crossed his arms stubbornly. "Can't make me. C'mon, Brute. I been stuck inside the palace forever, and Alys is being really cranky. Please?" He batted his eyelashes as well as any coquette.

"I'm not out for candy today, Warin, and you should be inside where it's warm and dry."

Ignoring the second part of Aric's statement, Warin asked, "What are you out for?"

Aric sighed. "I'm looking for a beggar named Itan."

"I'll help!"

Aric stood with rain dripping down his neck and considered his options. He could drag the boy back to the castle, but unless Warin were somehow physically restrained, he'd just end up following at Aric's heels again. And Aric didn't have time to waste on games like that. He dampened a momentary image of Warin in chains and Gray free to move about. Not that he wanted Warin imprisoned, of course, but Aric's life would certainly be simpler at the moment if he were. "Your sister will have my hide over this," he said and resumed walking.

Warin trotted at his side like an eager puppy. "Alys is too busy being mad at Cearl. She caught him talking to some of his sailor friends the other day, and then they had a great big fight, with all this screaming and crying. Cearl says he's thinking of going back to sea so's they can have a fancier house and more carts and stuff, and Alys says she doesn't care about all that and she just wants him. Then she threw a dish at the wall."

"I'm sorry they're having problems."

"Yeah." Warin hopped into a puddle, splashing cold water all over Aric's trousers. Eventually the wetness would soak through, chilling him even more. "I figure that's what they get for being in love. I'm never gonna do that. People in love are stupid."

Another image of Gray came to Aric's mind. This time Gray was fast asleep in Aric's arms on the floor of the cell, his soft hair tickling Aric's nose. "Oh gods, no!"

"What's the matter, Brute?"

"I... nothing." Just realized he'd fallen in love, that was all. He hurried his pace.

It seemed to Aric that the more modest a neighborhood, the narrower and more haphazardly platted were its streets. Near the palace, the streets were wide and straight and orderly and, in the warmer months, lined with pots of colorful flowers. Here, though, buildings seemed to loom crookedly overhead, while streets ran off at odd angles, sometimes looping back, sometimes abruptly stopping altogether. The only thing that lined the streets here was refuse. There were very few people outside, but he could feel eyes following him from behind shutters or from the shadowed depths of the ancient buildings' doorways. He spied a narrow close with an arched stone roof, and he dragged Warin into it. The close smelled strongly of piss, and several blanket-draped figures were hunched along its walls. "Stay here," he hissed at Warin, who shrugged and then kicked idly at a small pile of sodden fabric.

"Is Itan here?" Aric said loudly. He was met with silence, so he said, "Is one of you Itan? Do you know where I can find him?"

A woman's voice, cracked and ragged, replied. "I'll be Itan for two coppers, my dear." The other people in the close hacked with laughter.

The woman's jibe aside, it occurred to Aric that he should have brought some coins with him. But he rarely carried them—they weren't needed inside the palace, where his few expenses were recorded in ledgers—and he hadn't exactly planned this excursion ahead of time. "Please," he said. "I need to find Itan."

"Did you look in your ass?" More coughing laughter.

Aric shook his head, grabbed Warin's arm, and went back into the rain.

There were dozens of closes like that one, each packed with humanity's wretched dregs, and tiny alleys where people sought what shelter they could under sagging balconies and half-collapsed houses where rotting timbers provided a bit of respite from the rain. None of the miserable people in these places admitted to knowing someone named Itan, although they were quick to make crude jokes at Aric's expense, or to wheedle him for money. One boy barely older than

Warin, with a pockmarked face and a clubfoot, offered his own body in exchange for Aric's cloak. Wordlessly, Aric removed the cloak and handed it to the boy, then walked away.

"You're going to be cold!" Warin protested, still running to keep up. "And wet."

Aric coughed. "I was cold and wet anyway."

"But your cloak, it's really expensive. The crown won't pay for another one for you this year."

"Then I'll pay for it myself."

"You can't save everyone, Brute," said Warin, sounding wise far beyond his years.

"I know. But I can help that boy sleep a little more comfortably tonight."

In the next close, they encountered a mother huddled with two toddlers and a newborn. Aric wasn't sure the newborn was still alive. He wished he still had his cloak to give away. Instead, he unbuttoned his sweater and handed it to the speechless woman.

"Brute!" Warin squawked. "If you end up dead from the cold, Alys will whip me bloody."

"I'm not your responsibility."

Warin bunched his fists on his hips. "Yeah? If not mine, then whose are you?"

"I'm responsible for myself," Aric replied, even as he asked himself if that was true. Hadn't he simply allowed circumstances to buffet him from place to place? He hadn't really made many true decisions in his life, and those that he did—going out in terrible weather and then stripping himself half naked, for example—were often questionable.

He bent almost double to search for Itan under a raised chicken coop, squeezed sideways through a narrow space between two splintery wooden buildings, and yanked at the door to a seemingly abandoned shed. By the time he'd done all that, and explored more alleys and closes besides, he was feeling oddly warm and light-headed, and he had to lean against a stone wall to rest.

"It's almost dark," said Warin, worry making his voice higher than usual. "We won't be able to see anything at all around here once the sun sets."

"A few more minutes," Aric said, and coughed painfully.

"I think you're sick. You don't look good."

"I never look good."

"Brute!"

Aric shook his head. "Just one more street."

That street turned out to be even more miserable than the last. Even in the rain, and even through his snotty nose, Aric could tell that it reeked of garbage and sewage. He supposed maybe people actually lived in the tilting, nearly windowless structures, but they seemed dark and abandoned. Something that sounded like bones rattled in the wind, and the cobbles gave way to slimy mud, so strewn with offal that Aric was actually thankful for poor visibility. "There's nobody here," Warin said, already edging back in the direction from which they'd come.

Aric was inclined to agree. Shivering, with shoulders slumped, he turned away. And then he heard a whimper. At first he thought it might be the wind, but when he peered carefully at a bundle of sticks and rags that was scrunched up against one wall, the bundle moved. Just a little.

Aric hunched down and put out a tentative hand. The bundle jerked slightly and moaned. Not sticks and rags at all, he now saw, but a man. Possibly a young man, although it was hard to tell in the gloom and with the man's face covered in filth. His eyes stared sightlessly ahead, opaque and white. "Itan?" Aric rasped.

The man groaned and tried to turn his head a bit more, but didn't seem to have the strength. He was hardly more than a skin-bound skeleton, and when Aric touched his forehead, it was as cold as the rain. "Yes," said the man in a barely audible whisper.

"Gods. I'm... I'm going to take you someplace safe, all right? Somewhere warm. I'll find a healer." As he spoke, he slid his arms under Itan and picked him up as gently as possible. Itan weighed almost nothing at all and should have been easy to carry, but Aric felt weak as a child and staggered a bit as he tried to walk. "It's all right. It's all right, Itan."

Warin had dashed back to Aric's side. "How can I help?"

"Where can I find a healer?"

"I… I don't know. There's one at the palace, but…."

Aric shook his head. He'd never make it that far. But he kept putting one foot in front of the other because there was nothing else he could do. It was a difficult task. His legs were numb, and it felt as if someone had lifted the top of his skull and poured it full of mud.

He was in a neighborhood full of boarded up carts, still far from the palace, when his legs gave out and he fell to his knees. He managed to keep hold of Itan as he fell, but just barely. He remained like that for a long time, his head bowed, trying to regain enough strength to stand.

"Brute! Brute, you have to get up!" It sounded as if Warin might be crying.

Aric looked down at Itan and saw that it didn't matter. None of it mattered. Itan's eyes were still open, but his breathing had stopped. Aric hadn't even noticed when the beggar had died.

Hot tears mingled with the cold rain dripping down his face.

"Brute?"

He managed to get to his feet again. He staggered to the side of the street and laid Itan out on the cobbles. He spent a few moments rearranging the thin limbs: legs straight and together, arms crossed over the narrow chest. He used his palm to close the eyelids. And then, because he had nothing else to give, he tugged his fine linen shirt over his head and placed it over Itan's face like a shroud. "I'm sorry, Itan," he whispered. "I promise I'll remember your name."

Bare-chested, too feverish to care, and with Warin doing his best to keep him moving, Aric somehow made his way back to the palace.

 # CHAPTER
Fourteen

"Y-YOU were right. You really are v-very stupid."

Aric peeled one eye open, but that didn't help much. He still saw nothing but blackness. He could smell, though. The citrusy soap he stole from the bathhouse, coal smoke from the tile stove, damp stone, and a waste bucket that needed emptying. He could feel as well. Soft quilts beneath him and over his legs and stomach, and familiar long fingers kneading at his chest.

"Why w-were you out in a s-storm half naked and sick? Is this some strange v-village ritual?" Gray's voice was soft and soothing despite the rebuke of the words.

"Itan," Aric said with a sigh.

The hands stopped their movement. "And?"

"Too late. He died in my arms."

"Oh, Aric." Gray stroked Aric's face. "H-he didn't die alone."

Aric supposed he should have drawn some comfort from that, but his heart felt hard and his mouth tasted bitter. "He could have been saved if someone had helped him earlier. And there are so many others, Gray!"

"I kn-know. Now shush a m-minute. I'm almost d-done." He started pressing at Aric's chest again, brief little digs with his fingertips. He was muttering something unintelligible as he worked, and little sparks of heat were traveling from each finger across Aric's body, warming him and clearing his head.

"You're a witch!" Aric exclaimed, sitting up so abruptly his head spun.

"H-hardly." Gray pushed him back down onto the blanket. "A h-healer. N-not a very good one, b-but I can manage a fever. If you'll stay still."

"I'm… how did I get here?"

"N-no idea. You came lumbering in, wheezing like a b-bellows, and collapsed at my feet."

"Oh." Aric didn't remember that part. Didn't remember much of anything after abandoning Itan's body, actually. He hoped Warin had gotten back home safely, and that he hadn't caught a fever as well.

Gray must have finished his healing, because he began running fingers through Aric's tangled hair instead. "D-do you want to light a candle?"

Aric considered the question. "No," he finally answered. The darkness felt safe, for some reason. Certainly the dark didn't matter to Gray, who lay down beside him and pulled the quilts up to their shoulders. It was only when Gray was snuggled against him that Aric remembered. "I didn't bring you dinner."

Gray snorted. "I c-can miss a meal. It's late and you n-need to rest. I'm not letting you b-back outside tonight."

That made Aric chuckle, because it wasn't as if Gray could do anything to stop him. Anyway, he was very tired, and it was nice to be fussed over a little, and Gray was very warm in his arms. He yawned.

"S-sleep, giant. I've a tale for you t-tomorrow."

ALYS frowned at him. "Warin said you were sick. What on earth were you thinking, Brute?"

He took the food pails from her hands. "I'm fine. I just needed some sleep."

"But your cloak! And the sweater I made you!"

He hung his head. "I'm sorry, Alys. It's only—"

"I know," she said gently, while giving him a punch on the arm. "Your heart's as big as the rest of you. It's fine. I'll knit you another."

"You don't have to."

This time she tugged his head down for a quick buss to his cheek. "I want to. Now go! I'll send Warin to tell the schoolmaster you're too ill for lessons today. I've packed enough here for your lunch as well. I don't want you getting out of bed until dinner."

His fever was gone, but her commands sounded pretty appealing anyway.

He and Gray ate a big breakfast while sitting on the quilts, and Aric set the rest of the food on the table for later. He added more coal to the stove while he was there, and then rejoined Gray in the cell. Gray managed to maneuver him around again so that Aric lay on his back with his head in Gray's lap—a new thing for them, and rather nice. Aric closed his eyes and quietly hummed with pleasure when Gray began working on his tangles.

"Maybe I should have the barber shave my head again."

"D-don't. I like the feel of your c-curls."

That was possibly the most ridiculous thing anyone had ever said to Aric. But then his was turning out to be a ridiculous life, wasn't it? He remembered his epiphany from the previous afternoon: love. He was in love with Gray Leynham: prisoner, supposed witch, and traitor.

"You said you had a tale for me," Aric said.

"Hmm. It's a s-sordid tale. You might not like it."

"Is it about you?"

Gray made an affirmative grunt.

"Then I want to hear it. You know all my secrets, but I know barely anything about you. Why are you here, Gray? Why these?" He reached over to rattle a chain.

"M-my father was a sailor. You knew that. Mother was a seamstress. Very beautiful."

"Like you."

Gray snorted and tugged at a lock of Aric's hair. "I h-had an older sister, but she died when I was young. And not much later, w-we learned that I had a gift. I healed a sick p-puppy."

Aric tried to picture Gray as a boy, running free and getting into mischief and mending animals. But all he could see were stone walls and chains.

"M-my parents brought me here to the p-palace. The crown would educate ch-children with healing skills, would train them. My p-parents thought my future would be brighter here."

"They just left you?"

"No." Gray worked at an especially stubborn knot. "They lived nearby. I g-got to visit them sometimes. And I was busy here. I l-liked my lessons. It turned out my gift was weak, b-but I was allowed to stay. They thought they'd make a clerk of me. I was h-happy with that." Apparently satisfied with the condition of Aric's hair, Gray traced his fingertips over the scars on his face instead.

"Did you become a clerk?" Aric asked, trying to imagine Gray rushing around the West Tower with stacks of paper.

"N-no. I met Friddy."

"Prince Aldfrid."

"We were of an age. And h-he was s-so dashing! I f-fell head over heels the first time I saw him. Is he s-still handsome, Aric?"

Aric sighed. "Very."

"We were hardly m-more than boys. We became lovers. It was v-very exciting, you know. S-secret assignations in d-dark corners, lots of sneaking here and there. I think we liked the intrigue as m-much as the romance. Until we were f-found out, of course."

"What happened?"

"N-nothing so horrible. We were young, and p-people understood. Nobody even minded that Friddy was fucking a boy. He h-has older brothers to produce heirs. They only minded that it was me. Not me p-personally. Just… I was far beneath his station. C-can't have the nobility screwing commoners—not openly, anyhow. Th-the gods know they do it in secret often enough."

Feeling indignant on Gray's behalf, Aric frowned until Gray smoothed his brow. "But you're really smart," Aric said. "And beautiful. And you can heal—even if it's only a little bit, that's more than most people. You're special, Gray."

Gray smiled. "Thank you. But I'm still no blue blood. I was allowed to stay, but Friddy was t-told he must never see me again. I was c-crushed. I thought I was in love."

Someday—maybe someday soon—Aric would be separated from Gray, and then he would be crushed. He'd never dared to love anyone before, and he was pretty certain he'd never manage it again. Although he'd resigned himself to being alone long ago, perhaps even on the day his parents died, now it would hurt so badly, like an old wound freshly reopened.

"I'm sorry," he said.

"So am I. B-but not for that. Really, they were right. What future could a prince have with me? I sh-should have seen that. Soon enough I'd have found someone else. H-he wasn't my one true love, like in a story. But I was a d-damned fool. I decided to m-make myself worthy, to prove my value."

"What did you do?"

After a long pause, Gray answered. "I went to R-racinas."

Although the fever was gone, Aric felt suddenly ill. He twisted out of Gray's lap and stood, then padded into the main chamber. Alys had given him an old pot a couple months earlier, a badly dented one with the end of its handle broken off. But it was good enough for heating water. He poured some water into the pot from the jug, then set the pot on top of the coal stove. Although it wasn't really intended for cooking, the tiles got hot enough to suffice, and within a few minutes the water was steaming. He transferred it into the teapot—chipped in several places and also a gift from Alys. Then he sprinkled in a few pinches of tea bought at a place not far from Warin's favorite candy shop. It hadn't been very expensive, since it was mostly local herbs rather than imported leaves, but he liked the taste and the way it warmed his belly.

As he waited for the tea to steep, he listened to the coal fire roar and the rain splatter outside. Cozy sounds when you were snug indoors.

Aric's hand was big enough that he could carry both pottery cups at once. He brought them into the cell, where Gray smiled at him as he took his. Aric sat down, and Gray wrapped his hands around the cup, breathing in the aroma of the steam. "R-rose hips, mint, and lemon b-balm? Should have drunk this when y-you were becoming ill. You m-might not have needed me."

I need you. But Aric said instead, "You healed me just fine."

They sat in silence, sipping at their tea until Gray's story resumed.

"I w-went to the Vale of the Gods," he said at last. "I knew there w-would be a price, so I brought every c-coin I owned. F-f-fool. What use have the gods for coppers?"

"What did you ask for?"

"P-power. Give me magic, I said. Not this paltry healing gift. M-magic the crown can use." He laughed humorlessly. "The gods g-gave me what I asked for. I could feel it in me. Still can. It's l-like… like holding a hot coal in your hand. B-but it's in here." He tapped his head.

Aric tried to imagine that and couldn't. "Does it hurt?"

"Yes. No. It's a g-good pain, like when you enter my b-body."

It was silly for Aric to blush about something like that, but he did. And somehow Gray could tell, because he chuckled and stroked Aric's face. "Such a sweet g-giant," he said, which only made Aric's cheeks burn hotter. But at least he understood what Gray meant, because sometimes Gray entered him. And while Gray wasn't as big as Aric and always took care to prepare him well, there was always a little bit of burning at first, an odd sort of feeling of being stretched and filled. Not that Aric minded. In fact, sometimes he and Gray got into good-natured arguments as to whose turn it was to bottom—a dispute that neither of them really lost, no matter how it turned out.

"I was pleased with the f-feeling. Less so when I l-learned I c-could hardly speak. Fucking stutter. Couldn't write anymore either. But I th-thought it was a fair enough price." Gray stopped and frowned. "Why has my stutter nearly g-gone of late?"

"Maybe you've paid enough," Aric said.

Gray shook his head. "I didn't realize wh-what I could do for several days. I w-was staying at an inn near Racinas, and I dreamt that another g-guest died from apoplexy. The next day, he d-did. It was… horrible. I was devastated, but too naïve to know it was only the first of many. I h-had more dreams on the journey home. A s-sailor caught in a rope and d-dragged overboard. Another dying from an infected wwound. I was a wreck by the time I returned to Tellomer. B-but, I thought, at least I c-can have Friddy."

Aric pressed up against his shoulder. "What happened?"

"I sh-showed them my gift. Not Friddy—I wasn't allowed to see him. Lord Maudit and h-his cronies. And they were fucking thankful f-for my dreams. Offered m-me a good salary, fancy apartments in the p-palace, everything I wanted. Except Friddy. I still wasn't g-good enough for him."

"That's not right!" Aric said indignantly. "You were good enough for him to begin with, and then after you'd gone to such lengths to be...."

"Useful. I w-was useful but not noble. I should have known b-better, but I told you, I was a fool." Gray ran his palm over his hair, smoothing it back, and then gently banged his head against the wall three times. "I was heartbroken, and the d-dreams, they got less bearable every n-night. M-my only consolation was that maybe I was helping people. Saving a f-few lives. I even saved P-prince Cadell's son once, from a f-fall from a horse. And j-just a few nights later, I dreamed of another child. An infant, d-daughter of a beggar. She would die because h-her mother hadn't enough milk and c-couldn't afford a wet nurse."

Aric felt ill again. He knew where this tale was heading. "Gods, Gray."

"G-gods didn't help her either. L-like you and Itan, I found her too late. D-damned hard to search when I could barely speak."

Aric squeezed his arm, but Gray wrenched himself free and sprang to his feet. He paced the few strides his chains permitted him, reminding Aric of a caged bear he'd seen when he was a boy. The bear's claws and teeth had been pulled, and it walked back and forth, back and forth, roaring its anger and despair.

"I was fucking f-furious. I fled from the palace to the city. I stayed first with my parents, but I couldn't bear the sorrow in their eyes, so then I s-simply hid. I h-had silver and gold, and I m-moved from one inn to another. T-told nobody of my dreams." Gray's breaths were coming fast and heavy, as if he were still fleeing. It must have been hell for him to be alone like that, Aric thought, unable to communicate and with nobody to soothe him.

Gray abruptly stopped his frantic movements and collapsed onto his knees on the blankets. "I dreamed Queen Lentia's death."

Aric couldn't help but gasp. He remembered when the queen had died. Aric's great-uncle had died a year or two earlier, and Aric was still nowhere near his full size. A dozen years ago, perhaps. The queen had been walking in the palace gardens and was stung by a wasp—normally an event of little import, but her face had swelled and she had collapsed, unable to breathe. She was dead within minutes. The entire kingdom was in mourning for months, and it was rumored that the king never truly recovered from the loss. And now it occurred to Aric that she was not only the queen, but also Prince Aldfrid's mother. The mother of the man Gray loved.

"It was s-spite," Gray said quietly. "Nothing but petty v-vengeance. I said nothing, and f-four days later she was gone. I could... I could have lived with m-myself after that, I think. Convinced myself that her d-death was a price the crown owed. B-but vengeance is empty if your victim is unaware. I r-returned to the palace and told Lord Maudit. D-don't know what I expected them to d-do to me. Hang m-me, perhaps."

"Did you want to be hung?" Aric asked in a small voice.

"M-maybe. The dreams.... But they d-didn't show me that mercy." He rattled the chains that connected to his wrists. "They put me here, so I c-could continue to dream for them. I saw Friddy f-for one moment, just before they dragged me into this building. I thought he'd b-be enraged at me, b-but he only looked betrayed."

Gray sank to the floor and folded his legs in front of him. One palm covered his useless eyes, as if he were still trying to block out the sight of his former lover's face. Aric didn't touch him, didn't say anything, didn't even move. Outside, the wind gusted, making the rain rattle against the wall. Aric closed his eyes and ran a finger around the rim of his empty cup. It wasn't quite smooth; there was a small bump in one spot, and he rubbed and rubbed at it until the cup cracked under the pressure. The length of his finger was sliced open on the shard, but he didn't cry out. Instead, he put the finger in his mouth and sucked at the coppery taste until the bleeding stopped. Gray could probably heal it, he thought. But Aric didn't say anything.

When the minutes dragged by and Gray remained silent and unmoving, Aric scooped up the pottery shards and Gray's undamaged cup. He walked back to the main chamber, where he tossed the broken pieces into his chamber pot and set Gray's cup on the table. Then he put the teapot on top of the stove for a few moments, just enough to reheat the tea. He refilled Gray's cup, returned to the cell, and pushed the cup into Gray's hand. Gray took it silently but dipped his face and inhaled the steam. "D-do you hate me now?" he said after a brief pause. "Now that you kn-know."

"No," Aric replied, because a simple answer seemed best. A simple answer from a simple man.

Gray exhaled shakily and sipped at his tea.

"I guess I understand why they've treated you so badly," Aric said after a while. "I don't think you deserved it, but I can see why they'd lock you up, why they'd... keep you like this. It's horrible, and you should have been forgiven long ago. You were young and they'd hurt you. But why did they take your eyes as well?"

"They didn't."

Only two words, but they sent a chill through Aric's heart that was far worse than the cold he'd felt the night before. "Oh no," he whispered. "What did you do?"

"I thought... if I'm b-blind I can't have the Sight anymore. You see how w-well that worked." He made a sound somewhere between a laugh and a sob.

Aric couldn't bear it anymore. He crouched in front of Gray and gathered him in his arms, heedless of the warm tea that spilled between them. Gray was stiff at first, but only for a moment, and then he sighed and returned the embrace, tucking his face into the crook of Aric's neck. "I'm a f-fool," he said.

Not as much as me, Aric thought, because he was already formulating a plan.

 # CHAPTER
Fifteen

ARIC may have been stupid, but he wasn't a complete idiot. He decided that he wouldn't say a word to Gray until it was too late. He'd never before had a secret—except his love for Gray—or anyone to keep a secret from. It felt a bit strange, like having a bird trapped in his chest and trying to get out.

Or maybe his new secret was more like a seed, planted inside himself and slowly growing. Now it was only a tender shoot, but as he coaxed it and fed it, it would get a bit bigger every day, sending tendrils upward and outward. He hoped someday soon it would flower and bear fruit.

Stop, he told himself sternly, deciding he made a much better mule than a poet.

"Do you find the Yganfrian War amusing, Brute?"

Aric snapped back to the here and now. "Sorry," he mumbled.

Master Sighard cracked his stick on the floor, clearly wishing he could crack it over Aric's skull instead. "Why don't you explain the factors that led to the war," said the schoolmaster as the children snickered.

"Um… there was a famine, and the barons were delinquent in collecting taxes, so the king—"

"*Which* king?"

Aric wracked his brain. "Uh… Bolbec?"

"Bolbec the Third, you mean."

"Right. King Bolbec the Third was trying to increase his naval forces because he was fearing an invasion from… the south. But he didn't have the funds without the taxes, and—"

"Yes, yes, yes. That bit is obvious. What were the names of the barons who sided with the king?"

Aric hadn't any idea. He stared at the ceiling high above, as if it might provide the answer, and when it didn't, he looked at Quoen instead. She only shrugged. He was going to start blurting names at random when the door slammed open, startling them all. Warin came running across the polished floor at top speed. "Brute! Lord Maudit wants to see you."

Aric stood. "Excuse me, sir."

The schoolmaster glowered, but he couldn't very well prohibit his student from responding to Lord Maudit's summons. "Tomorrow I shall expect a full report from you on the causes and consequences of the Yganfrian War."

"Yes, sir," said Aric. He was already halfway to the door.

Warin bounced along at his side as they made their way to the West Tower. The sky was bright blue streaked with a few white clouds, and the trees in the palace gardens were covered in white and pink blossoms. A few noblewomen were out in bright-colored dresses, their shoulders covered only by light shawls and their hair done up in impossibly intricate knots. They laughed to one another as Aric passed, but he was used to that and paid very little attention. He was too busy worrying about why Lord Maudit wanted to see him. Had someone finally entered Aric's chambers in the Brown Tower and discovered the relatively comfortable way in which he'd been keeping Gray? Had someone decided to relieve Aric of his duties, perhaps send him away altogether? Had Lord Maudit somehow sussed out what was going on in Aric's head?

He was a nervous wreck by the time they reached the West Tower. Warin was clearly willing—in fact, eager—to follow him inside, but a guard shooed the boy away, and Aric was left on his own.

The round man frowned at him but ushered him into the office, where Lord Maudit was deep in conversation with a pair of men in embroidered waistcoats. He looked up when Aric entered, motioned impatiently for him to wait near the door, and continued talking. The men had thick accents that were hard to understand, but they seemed to be discussing something to do with the security of trade routes and bandits. Aric decided it was nothing to do with him and went back to fretting. Sweat was dripping down his back and making him itch, but he tried his best not to fidget. He wished he was back under Master Sighard's disapproving gaze.

After an eternity or two, Lord Maudit and his guests seemed to reach some sort of agreement. They shook hands and exchanged papers, and the men in waistcoats spared Aric quick, derisive looks before they sailed out of the office. Lord Maudit made a beeline for his desk, where a half-empty glass of amber liquid was sitting somewhat precariously atop an uneven pile of books. He threw back the remaining liquor in one long swallow before gesturing for Aric to approach.

"You've been here nearly a year," Lord Maudit said without preamble.

"Yes, Your Excellency."

"Nobody else has ever lasted a year. Not even close."

Aric wasn't sure how to respond to that, so he said nothing.

"Why haven't you left, Brute?"

"I have nowhere else to go."

Lord Maudit narrowed his eyes. "Do you know why he's kept like he is?"

"I… I heard, sir."

"And what do you think of that?"

Aric couldn't lie about this. He met the lord's eyes. "It's horrible, Your Excellency. He's been miserable for so long."

"He betrayed his queen and his kingdom. He betrayed his supposed friend."

"He was young, sir."

Lord Maudit shook his head. "When you were younger, did you betray your friends like that?"

"I had no friends, sir." And then, because he might never have another chance, he added, "Please, Your Excellency. Hasn't it been enough? Can't he be let go now? Or at least given a bit more freedom? I could... I could escort him around the palace now and then, or maybe—"

"No." With a heavy sigh, Lord Maudit looked into the bottom of his empty glass. "Gray Leynham's sentence was pronounced by the king himself, and it is final. More than a decade later, and the king still mourns his wife."

They were difficult words to hear, every one of them like the tightening of a chain around Aric's heart. But they also strengthened his resolve to see his plans through—assuming he wasn't ejected from the palace forthwith.

Lord Maudit set his glass down on the desk again, this time on a bit of bare wood that hadn't yet been covered by papers. "Prince Aldfrid has asked me to convey to you his appreciation for your dedication to duty. He understands that your task is a... taxing one. I have ordered that your salary be doubled. Two silver coins each month and two extra for the festival."

Aric gasped. He had barely any need of coins as it was, so he had a healthy balance on the ledgers. He couldn't imagine what he'd do with twice as much. Oh, but yes he could. He could give it away, couldn't he? He could live here at the palace in comfort, spend a few coppers now and then on this or that, and have most of his pay left over. How many beggars could be fed on two silver coins each month? How many blankets could he buy to hand out when it got cold? How many times could he pay a healer to stop a fever, mend a twisted limb?

"You may go now," Lord Maudit said, and after a brief pause, Aric hurried away.

He didn't hurry all that far, however. Once he was outside the West Tower, he found a sunny bench that was tucked away near the laundry, where the sweet smell of lavender and soap drifted by his nose and a flock of sparrows argued over some crumbs scattered on the cobbles.

Life had never been so complicated when all he had to do was haul rocks up a hill. He'd never been responsible for anyone's fate then—barely even his own—and he'd had no decisions to make. Now he felt again as if he had a great weight on his shoulders, but it wasn't one he could simply remove and drop to the ground. And no matter what he did, he was going to do harm to someone.

He'd never had much use for prayers. He'd always figured that the gods had more important people to listen to. But now he bowed his head and closed his eyes. "Please," he murmured. "Please guide me. Just this once."

Not surprisingly, no celestial being appeared in front of him to tell him what to do.

When his butt grew sore from sitting on the stone bench, he stood and made his way to the kitchens. Lunch, at least, would be dependable and uncomplicated. He found Alys right away and helped her carry a huge bag of carrots inside.

She blew a stray wisp of hair out of her face and looked at him from the corner of her eye. "Warin tells me Lord Maudit wanted to see you."

"Hmm." He leaned up against a wall—as much out of the way as possible—and crossed his arms.

"Is something wrong?"

"No. He just wanted to pass on the prince's thanks for staying so long."

"Oh." She dumped an armful of carrots into a wooden tub, picked up a knife, and began to peel. "Why have you stayed so long, Brute? Doesn't it get to you, the screaming in the night?"

"Of course it does. It's terrible." He didn't tell her that it was even worse when the screaming man was in your arms, trembling and crying.

"But you haven't run away."

"I guess I'm too stupid to know better."

She snorted. "Come on by tonight after dinner. We want to discuss the wedding with you."

He didn't know what that was about, but he said okay and picked up his lunch pail from one of the broad, scarred tables and carried it back to the Brown Tower.

Gray was standing in the corner of the cell, humming something under his breath. He looked up with a broad smile as soon as Aric entered the room. "I was h-hoping you'd come by." His stutter had disappeared almost entirely in recent weeks, although it still reappeared when he woke up after one of his nightmares.

Aric felt an immediate twinge of guilt for all the time he'd sat on the bench. "I'm sorry. You must get so bored."

"I'm used to bored. Nowadays I think of the books you've read me. Or I just think of you." His smile didn't go away, but it faded a little, became wistful. "Those thoughts will do me well when you're gone."

"Gone?" For the second time in a few hours, Aric's heart thumped with fear. "Who says I'm going anywhere?"

"You've been here for ages. You c-can't... can't last forever. You shouldn't. N-now that you can read, you could be a clerk, a scribe. Maybe they'd find work for you in the l-library."

"Maybe, but I'm not going anywhere."

Aric had stopped bolting the cell several weeks earlier. There wasn't much point in it, given the chains that still kept the prisoner affixed to the floor. If anyone came to check on Gray, they were going to find plenty of things to make them angry: Gray's clean hair and body, his shaved face, his pile of quilts, the thin layer of fat he'd accumulated between skin and bones. And it was easier for Aric to enter with his hand full if he didn't have to fuss with the lock every time. So now he just walked in through the open door and handed Gray a hunk of still-warm bread. "Here. Eat."

Gray took a bite and chewed at it thoughtfully. "Wh-why are you staying?"

"*Why* is everyone asking me that today?" Aric cried.

"Who else asked?"

"Lord Maudit."

"Speak to him d-daily, do you?"

Aric huffed with exasperation. "He summoned me today. He said the prince was grateful that I've stuck around, and then His Excellency doubled my pay."

"So that's why you're still here? The pay?"

"I'm here because I love you!" Aric yelled, and then bit his tongue. Gods, that was *not* something he'd intended to say out loud.

Gray had gone very still. "Wh-wh-what?"

"Nothing."

Gray closed the few feet between them and poked him in the chest with a single long finger. "That was not n-nothing."

If Aric were the one afflicted with a stutter, it might have saved him many times over. Instead, he suffered from the opposite problem: a tongue that was much faster than his brain. "Pretend I didn't say it," he begged.

"I damned well will n-not!"

"It doesn't…. You don't…. I know you could never…."

"Never what?" Gray said. He'd moved even closer, so that his chest was almost touching Aric's. If Aric were a foot and a half shorter, they would be nose to nose. As it was, Gray had his neck tilted back, and even though he had no eyes, he seemed to be seeing Aric, to be looking right through him.

"Please don't do this," whispered Aric.

"Don't what?" Gray reached up and cupped his cheek in one hand. "Don't t-tell you my heart beats for you? Don't tell you my s-soul sings for you? Don't tell you that you're hope to me, l-life to me, the c-center of my fucking universe?"

Aric tried to get a response out, but his treacherous tongue now refused to work at all.

"I love you, idiot," Gray said.

"But… I'm—"

"Don't you d-dare say you're ugly or stupid or w-worthless. Don't you dare! Y-you're a giant because an ordinary man's body is t-too small for what you are."

Aric had somehow been backed up against the wall. Now he slid slowly down, the stone scratching his back. He ended up on his ass with Gray crouching in front of him. "But you love Prince—" Aric began.

"I th-thought I did, very long ago. He was pretty, Aric, and w-we had fun. Maybe I r-really did love him. I don't know anymore. But I know what I feel n-now."

"I'm your jailer!"

"N-nobody can remove these chains. B-but you've freed my heart."

Aric wasn't sure whether to laugh or cry. Maybe he could do both at once. He'd never imagined anyone declaring love for him, least of all in a dank cell inside the royal palace. He'd never imagined anyone waxing poetic over him. But gods, none of this made his life any easier, did it? Was this how the gods answered his prayers for a sign? If so, they truly possessed a wicked sense of humor.

"What if I could?" Aric asked very quietly, deciding that it was time to share his secret. "What if I could remove those chains?"

Gray lurched to his feet and backed away. "No. N-n-no! Wh-wh-wh— Fuck! Whatever you're th-thinking, no."

"I can't leave you here. I just can't."

"C-can't take me either. Y-y-you'll get yourself killed. And for what? I c-can—we can be happy here. H-happy enough."

So tempting. But Aric sighed. "Those chains…. We lie together, and they're *there*. Besides, I'm here at the whim of others. The prince could sack me. Someone could come in here and see you… see that you're not completely miserable. I risked my life to save a prince I didn't even know. Don't you think I'd do the same for you?"

Gray allowed himself to collapse to the floor. He massaged his temples as if he had a headache and then rubbed at his eyelids. "Of c-course you would," he said wearily. "But, Aric, th-they'll search for us. And I'll still b-be blind, still with the fucking Sight."

"I can lead you. I bet I'll be good at it—I'm easy to find. And… I have an idea about the other thing."

Gray lifted his eyebrows questioningly.

"We're going to go to Racinas and give your gift back."

For a moment, Gray simply sat there with his mouth hanging open. Then he barked out a laugh and scooted across the floor until he was sitting next to Aric, their arms touching. "Y-you're an idiot and I'm a fool," he said. "And gods, I love you."

 # CHAPTER *Sixteen*

WHILE some of the palace staff lived in the city of Tellomer, many lived on the palace grounds in a series of orderly buildings protected by the southeast corner of the outer wall. The buildings—made of timber and plaster, with red-tiled roofs—stood four stories tall. Alys's flat was on the ground floor and had a miniscule garden in the back, with the first shoots of greenery just peeking through the soil of a few earthen pots.

Aric had never been inside her home. Had never, in fact, been inside anyone's house, aside from Hilma Gedding, the village healer. But Alys smiled broadly when he appeared at the door, and she ushered him in. He had to duck to get through the entrance, and he had little headroom once inside.

The flat was simply two rooms. One contained two beds and a chest of drawers, while the other had a third bed up against a wall, as well as a slightly crooked table, mismatched chairs, several shelves full of miscellaneous household items, and a slightly oversized fireplace. The flat felt crowded, and must have been even more so when Alys and Warin's parents were alive and the entire large family lived crammed inside. But it was a cheery place as well, with bits of colored fabric hung on the walls and chipped pottery, seashells, rocks, and little wooden toys arranged here and there.

"Sit down, sit down," Alys fussed, pushing him back against a chair. He sat and smiled at Cearl, who had a bowl of soup in his hands. Aric had met Cearl a few times before and liked him. He was a very quiet man with prominent ears and crooked teeth, the sort who tended to fade into the background, but he gazed at Alys with complete adoration, and his face lit up whenever she glanced his way.

"Have some tea," said Alys, plunking a cup down in front of Aric.

"Thank you. Where's Warin?"

"Oh, off somewhere. Tired of hearing about the wedding, I'm sure." She looked around until she found a pair of Warin's trousers folded over a chair back. She took a needle and thread from a shelf, then sat down to mend a tear in the knee. Aric smiled. He never saw her idle, not for one moment.

"What will Warin do when you've moved to your new house? Will he go with?" They had several other siblings who lived in the palace; perhaps the boy would remain with one of them.

"We haven't quite worked that out yet. He's excited at the thought of having the run of the city, but I'm not sure that's such a great idea. And he wants to work for Cearl, to be a carter, but if he stays here he can maybe become a clerk." She smiled fondly. "He knows his way around the West Tower better than anyone."

"I guess being a clerk doesn't sound very exciting to a boy his age."

"No. I'm just lucky Cearl's been able to talk him out of a life at sea."

Cearl chuckled into his soup bowl. "Can see him now, climbing the rigging like a monkey."

Alys pointed her needle at her betrothed. "Warin is *not* becoming a sailor."

"Of course not, dear."

Aric had to sip at his tea to hide a smile. It was too hot and burnt his tongue. But even as he sat there, a terrible idea concerning Gray's freedom came into his head, and he nearly dropped the cup.

"Are you all right, Brute?" Alys asked with concern.

"Oh. Sorry. I just… sorry." He decided a change of subject would be good. "Are you all ready for the wedding, then?" The date was coming up—they'd be married on the first day of spring, only two weeks away.

"Well, that's why I asked you to come by. We've arranged almost everything. I've been given permission to hold the ceremony in that little garden near the library. Won't that be pretty? I hope the trees are still blooming. It'll be in the evening, after dinner's done. And the chief assistant acolyte from the palace temple will recite the blessings. It's quite an honor."

Aric remembered what Lord Maudit once told him. "Your family's well thought of here."

She blushed. "Thank you. We'll have some lovely little cakes and flowers, and Cearl's brother can play the lute!"

Cearl nodded sagely. "He always was the talented one."

"It sounds beautiful," Aric said honestly.

"It will be," she said firmly. "And I'd like you to strew the seeds for us."

He gaped. It was an ancient ritual, both an offering to the gods and a symbol of fertility: seeds were tossed onto the ground, and a short blessing was recited. The person who performed these acts couldn't be a blood relative of either the bride or groom, but was usually a close family friend. "Oh, Alys, you must have someone else—"

"I might, but Warin insisted. I'd like it too." She reached over and placed her hand over his. "You've been a good friend."

He was going to die, and that was all. He was just going to collapse and die. The day had been too much for him, far too much. Maybe he was dreaming the entire thing.

"Thank you," he said hoarsely.

Alys seemed satisfied. She tied off a knot in her sewing and broke the thread, then began searching for more holes. "I'm going to have to let these hems out soon," she said. "He's growing so fast. The other day he asked me if maybe he'll grow as tall as you."

"I hope not!" Aric said, flattered but horrified.

"'S not so great being short either," said Cearl, who was a couple of inches shorter than Alys. "Handy on a ship, though. Don't take up much space."

"I've never been on one," Aric said. And then added carefully, "It might be interesting. How much would passage be to, say, Racinas?"

"Two silver coins," Cearl answered promptly, and was glared at by his wife-to-be.

"You're not thinking of leaving, are you?" asked Alys. She looked genuinely worried. And then her frown smoothed. "You're lonely. I told you, I'll introduce you to Lapurd the guard. I'm sure you've seen him. He has those black curls, and he always looks like he hasn't shaved yet that day. I saw him just yesterday, lounging around the kitchens and hoping for a few extra scraps. If he comes by tomorrow—"

"I'm not lonely," Aric interrupted.

Cearl snickered. "Al, not everyone moons around, looking for their beloved all day."

"You should be very glad I mooned for you, Cearl Oken."

"Every minute of my life," he responded with a smile. "Maybe Brute here prefers a solitary life. Quieter."

"He does not. Nobody wants to be alone. Am I right?" she demanded of Aric.

"I'm not alone," he answered, very quietly.

"Well, of course not. You have us. But someone to keep you warm at night?"

"I'm not alone," he repeated.

She frowned in confusion, and then her green eyes went very wide. "Oh! Oh!"

Aric sank down in his chair a little. Gray was right. He was an idiot.

Cearl seemed confused, and stared at Alys as if he were afraid she was having some sort of fit. And she did seem to be: her mouth was opening and closing like a fish, and her face had gone very pale. "Brute! He's a witch! And a—"

"A traitor. I know the stories, Alys. And I know the truth. He's just a man who made a terrible mistake. But I think... I'm pretty sure he's a *good* man."

Alys remained silent for a very long time, chewing on her lip and staring at Aric. Aric tried not to fidget. And Cearl just sat there, slurping at the remains of his soup. Finally, Alys put her sewing aside and stood.

She walked around the table to where Aric was sitting and kissed the top of his head, just as he'd seen her do to Warin. "Be careful, Brute," she said.

"I've b-been thinking about your idea," Gray said. He was pacing his cell when Aric returned from Alys's house, and he continued to pace while Aric washed up and got undressed. But as soon as Aric entered the cell and lay down on the quilts, Gray joined him, his warm, lean body pressed against Aric's. "It w-won't work," Gray said.

"Which part of it?"

"Any p-part of it! You can't get me out of here. If y-you somehow did, you can't get me to Racinas. They'll be right on our tails, and I d-doubt the giant and the b-blind man who screams in his sleep can travel unnoticed. And if we somehow magically made it to the V-vale, I can't simply return their gift, j-just like that."

"That's... a lot of problems," Aric admitted. He didn't add the other obstacles weighing on his mind: giving up his friends and the closest thing to home and acceptance he'd had since he was small. Betraying the trust that had been given to him by the prince and Lord Maudit. Abandoning the small world he knew for the vast unknown.

"S-so you'll give it up then?" Gray stroked his fingertips on the tender bit of skin under Aric's ear. He knew that a touch there drove Aric wild. They knew everything about one another's bodies by now, and that was a heady realization for Aric. "We'll stay," Gray continued. "B-be as happy as we can for as long as we can. It's m-more than I ever expected."

It was more than Aric had ever expected too, but somehow it wasn't enough. He smoothed his palm over Gray's hip and traced the little crease just beneath it. He liked to lick at that spot, even nibble gently, until Gray would arch his hips upward and tug at Aric's hair and beg for *more*.

"I'm going to try," Aric said.

"All th-those tales of Lorad and Lokad have turned your head. You think y-you're an epic hero. But you can't m-move rivers, Aric."

"I don't need to move a river. I just need to move one skinny man."

Gray made a sound against Aric's chest that was somewhere between a sigh and a laugh. And then they didn't speak at all for a while, unless moans and half-swallowed words of encouragement counted. Aric loved the way Gray felt now, still thin but so much stronger than before. Aric no longer feared that his lover might break if he forgot to be slow and gentle. In fact, Gray urged him to be a little rougher, a little harder. "N-not made of china," he gasped into Aric's ear. "Want to feel you. Let g-go a little, Ar. For me." And Aric did let go just a bit, like setting down a burden for just a moment, and Gray cried out and marked Aric's skin with his teeth.

Afterward they lay bathed in sweat, hearts still hammering in their chests. Gray reached over to play idly with Aric's hair, and Aric wondered if things felt different to a blind man. Certainly he'd never thought his own hair was all that interesting, but Gray seemed to like it. Gray liked Aric's eyebrows too, and the curve of his ears, and even the little divot in Aric's jutting chin.

"What color were your eyes?" Aric asked, for no particular reason.

"Blue. Y-yours?"

"Mixed. One's hazel and the other brown."

"You truly are unique, aren't you?"

"I suppose so."

"And you're all m-mine." Gray flopped over onto his belly, stretching his leg and arm across Aric's body. Aric could feel the chains, heavy and cold, and it was as if they were fastened to him as well.

 # CHAPTER
Seventeen

THE exchequer's office was in the West Tower, and that made Aric nervous. What if someone—Lord Maudit even—saw him and wondered why he was there? Of course, the exchequer might be regularly reporting Aric's expenditures anyway, in which case alarm bells were sure to go off. Nonetheless, Aric squared his shoulders and marched confidently down the long corridor that bustled with activity. He was pleased with himself for being able to read the signs now, and had no trouble identifying the office he wanted. It lay through an arched doorway with the heavy door propped open. Inside, men bent over ledgers, and hundreds of oversized books lined the walls. The room smelled of dust and ink.

"Yes?" demanded a man about Aric's age. He was dressed all in brown, from the cap on his head to his ridiculous pointed shoes.

"I'd like to have the coins I've earned. Please."

The man raised an eyebrow. "And who are you?"

"I'm... called Brute." He wouldn't say that was his name, not anymore, but only Gray knew him as Aric.

"Of course you are. And what have you done for the crown to earn your coins?"

"I... I watch Gray Leynham."

Now the man's eyes widened. "The prisoner who dreams! A terrible thing, just terrible. How do you stand it?"

"How do you stand spending all day with ink stains on your fingers?"

The man looked at his hands as if he'd never noticed, then shrugged. "Comes with the job."

"So do the dreams."

"Fine then. Wait here."

Aric watched as the man crossed the room and stood looking at a particular shelf, running his finger down the spines of the books. He quickly found the one he was looking for, brought it over, and set it on the tall table near Aric. "Let's see. Brute." He leafed through the pages for several moments. "Ah! Well, that's an impressive account. Jailers are paid better than clerks, it seems. How much do you want?"

"All of it."

"All— That's a lot of money! What on earth do you plan to do with it?"

"Is that part of your job as well?" Aric asked, maybe a little rudely. "Poking your nose into other men's business?"

Surprisingly, the clerk didn't seem offended. In fact, his tone was slightly cheery when he replied. "No, not really. Does make things more interesting, though. It's not often I get giants in here wanting a small fortune."

"Can I have my coins please?"

"Wait here," the man said again.

This time he disappeared through a small doorway at the far end of the room. The door was heavily reinforced with iron bands and sported three impressive-looking locks. Naturally, that made Aric curious about what lay behind it, and as he waited, he considered all the treasures and surprises that the palace must hold. Even though he'd lived in the palace for a year, he'd really seen only a small portion of it. Most of it was closed off to someone like him. On the other hand, he knew very well where the palace's greatest treasure was held: in Aric's own chambers, behind the bars of a cell door.

The clerk seemed to take a very long time, and the other people in the room kept giving Aric long and skeptical looks. But finally the clerk reappeared with a small copper bowl in his hands. When he set the bowl on the table next to the ledger, Aric saw that it was filled with shiny silver coins and a handful of copper ones as well. The clerk

painstakingly counted them out—eleven silver and thirteen copper—
and then counted them twice more. When he was satisfied that he was
correct, he picked up a quill, dipped it in a pot of ink, and wrote some
numbers in his ledger. "That's every bit of it," he said.

Two days earlier, Aric had bought a small leather purse. Now he
placed the coins in the purse, carefully so as not to drop any, and tucked
the purse away in his clothes. "Thank you."

"Really. What will you do with it all?"

Brute just smiled enigmatically and walked out the door.
Withdrawing his money was only a very minor step and, by far, the
easiest of the goals he must accomplish in order to set Gray free. But
with the very real weight of the coins in his pocket, he felt as if Gray's
escape was truly underway.

"WHY can't I go with you?" Warin whined. "You let me go when we
were looking for Itan—"

"I had no choice," Aric interrupted gruffly, although he was
secretly pleased that the boy remembered the dead beggar's name.
Perhaps it brought Itan some peace, knowing he wasn't forgotten.

"But I'm bored! And Alys keeps sending me on wedding errands,
double-checking stuff that's already set."

"I think she's a little nervous about it."

"Why? She's already spending every spare minute with darling
Cearl. All she has to do now is mumble a few words."

Aric ruffled the boy's red hair. "She's still going to love you just
as much, you know."

"She's going to leave the palace. It's our home, Brute!" Warin
kicked at a stone, sending it skittering across the courtyard.

"Have you settled what's going to happen to you?"

"No." Warin scowled, and then brightened. "Can I live with you?
I'll be good! I'll—"

Aric put his hand on the boy's shoulder. "No, Warin. You can't.
I'm not fit to be responsible for you."

"I can be responsible for myself. I'm not a little kid!"

"No, you're not. But you can't stay with me. The prisoner has nightmares, remember?"

Warin nodded slightly and looked up at him. "Are they really, really bad? Do they scare you?"

Aric hunched down so he could look the boy in the eyes. "They terrify me," he answered honestly. Then he stood up straight and mussed Warin's hair again. "Go find something to do. I'll be back in a few hours."

Warin pouted and muttered, and then he stomped away.

It was a fine day for a walk in any case. Aric wore the cloak he'd bought after giving his first one to the beggar, but by the time he'd left the palace gates and descended the gentle hill to the piers, he felt warm and thirsty. He was considering removing the cloak and tucking it under his arm, but its royal colors lent him at least a bit of respectability. People still stared, and some even jeered, but most only tilted their heads and, most likely, wondered on what business the ugly giant served the crown. As he passed the statue of Lokad, he gave its base a friendly little pat, and he looked across the mouth of the river at the matching statue of Lorad. Both stone giants looked more resolute than ever.

Aric had come down to the docks with Warin five or six times in the past. The boy loved to watch all the activity: the sailors in their exotic clothes and with their strange languages, the boxes and bags of cargo being carried on or hauled off the great ships. There were taverns nearby as well, rough places for rough men, and male and female whores often strutted around. Aric steered well clear of them when he was with Warin, but today he entered a tavern that seemed maybe slightly more reputable than the others.

It was midafternoon, but the place was already crowded. The smell reminded him of the White Dragon—sour ale and bad food—and the faces weren't any friendlier. But Aric had found confidence somewhere in the past year, and he didn't slink to the back, hiding like a shameful secret. Instead he sat at a sticky table in the middle and caught the landlord's eye. "A pint," Aric said.

The landlord grunted something back and retreated behind the bar. He returned a few moments later with a tankard, the suds sloshing over the rim. "Half," he said as he slammed the cup onto the table.

Aric had a copper ready for him. He put it in the landlord's outstretched hand. "Bring me another when this one's gone."

He'd become spoiled, drinking the palace ale. This stuff was watery and bitter. Just like Cecil Gedding's, Aric thought with a smile.

"What's so funny?"

Compared to anyone but Aric, the man who'd lumbered over to confront him would be huge. He had wild, greasy hair, a dark beard that didn't look especially clean, and a scar—more impressive than any of Aric's—bisecting his right cheek. His shirt was half-unbuttoned, revealing tufts of dark hair on his chest. His trousers were oddly shaped and were cinched around his waist with a length of rope. He looked like he might eat small children for breakfast.

Aric gave him an easy grin. "Just an old memory."

"Shouldn't be smiling at yourself. Folks'll think you're touched in the head." The man narrowed his eyes. "Maybe you *are* touched in the head. You don't look too bright. Where'd you steal that cloak?"

"The cloak is mine. I'm not a thief. I'm not a lunatic either."

"What are you then?"

Aric lifted his tankard. "Just thirsty."

"I'm thirsty too."

"Then why don't you join me and I'll buy you a pint?"

The man's frown gave way to a snaggletoothed grin, and he plopped into the chair opposite Aric. "I don't see many as are bigger'n me. Bet I could take you in a fight."

"Wouldn't be a fair fight," Aric replied, waving his stump. "And I'm here to drink, not to brawl."

"'M just sayin'."

Aric waved at the landlord, pointed to his new companion, and held up a single finger. When the landlord brought another tankard to the table, the bearded man chortled happily. "Ran out of coins afore I ran out of shore leave. 'S a damned shame." He took a large swig and then belched.

"You're a sailor then?"

"Course I'm a fucking sailor. Why else would I be in this rathole? Ship out tomorrow morning. 'S all right. I fucked all the good whores here already. And some of the bad ones." He guffawed at his own joke and took another swallow.

"Where will you sail to?"

The man scratched his head thoughtfully. "Dunno. Cap'n owns the ship outright, takes her wherever he wants. He was talking 'bout heading east, off to Neritinia. The women are ugly as shit—almost as ugly as you—but they got some mighty fine liquor. Drink that stuff and you won't stand steady for a week. Won't care what the women look like, neither. You ever been?"

"I've never been anywhere."

"Don't know how you can stand it, glued to one place like a fucking barnacle on a rock. Me, I been everywhere, and I never stay nowhere for long. When I die they can throw my fucking carcass overboard and I'll keep on traveling in the fishes' bellies." More hearty laughter and another long drink. His tankard was almost empty already.

Aric waved another copper at the landlord. "Have you ever been to Racinas?" he asked as nonchalantly as possible.

"Course I been to Racinas. 'Bout a hundred goddamn times." He turned his head and spat on the floor. "Nothing to see up there 'cept for lots of fucking trees and sheep. Oh, but them girls are pretty enough."

"How long does it take to get there from here?"

The sailor shrugged. "Five, six days. Depends on the winds and currents. You just hug the coastline the whole way. I like the deep water routes better myself."

The landlord brought two fresh tankards and took the copper. Aric had drunk very little of his first cup of ale, so he just kept one of the new ones in front of him and pushed the other across the table. His new friend took it with a jaunty little salute.

"Are there a lot of boats that go from Tellomer to Racinas?" asked Aric.

"Yeah, sure. 'S one almost every day." The sailor waved in the general direction of the door and the piers. "Jus' take a look at berths twelve and thirteen. Always a squat little tub anchored at one or both of 'em, offloading all that fucking wool and then filling up with all the shit they need up north." He snorted. "You ask me, you can keep your gods-damned wool and your stupid trees. Kayindo is where I like to go. Always warm there, and the girls go around half nekid. They got beaches with sand like fine sugar."

"That sounds nice."

"Bet your fucking ass it's nice. If I was to stick anywhere, Kayindo'd be it." With that pronouncement, the man gulped his second pint of ale.

Aric figured he'd heard enough by then, but the sailor had turned garrulous. Even without the inducement of more drink, he remained at Aric's table for another hour or so, spinning unlikely yarns about women he'd fucked in places Aric had never heard of. The man didn't seem to expect Aric to contribute more than a nod to the conversation now and then, so Aric sipped at his ale and nodded, and reminded himself: *berths twelve and thirteen.*

ARIC hadn't actually eaten anything at the dockside tavern, and although it was too early for dinner, he found himself hungry when he left the sailor's company. He wandered back in the general direction of the palace, stopping to buy grilled meat on a stick from a vendor's cart. The meat was good, even if he couldn't quite identify what sort of animal it had been—and wasn't sure he really wanted to know.

Stomach momentarily satisfied, he found himself on a street lined with modest shops that sold clothing and fabric and household goods. New goods, but nothing fancy. They were the sort of wares that servants might buy, or simple businessmen like Cearl. Aric hoped to find something nice to give to Cearl and Alys as a gift, but he'd never bought anyone a gift before and had no idea where to begin. Should he get them something practical for their new home, like a pot—or something decorative and a little frivolous, like baskets dyed fantastic colors? He meandered up and down the street for a while, perusing the goods, ignoring the shopkeepers' distrustful stares.

He somehow found himself in a store that sold men's clothing. There would be nothing for the bride and groom there, and Aric didn't need anything for himself. Even if he did, it was unlikely that he'd find anything to fit him. But then his eyes fell on a shirt of woven red and blue cotton, and he knew exactly who that shirt would fit. Those trousers as well—the soft-looking ones in light brown. And the lightweight coat with the oversized hood, which would be good for late-season chills or spring downpours. Or in case the sea winds blew.

Aric ended up buying two shirts, the trousers, the coat, two breechclouts, and two pairs of woolen socks.

The parcel felt ridiculous tucked under his arm. He was an idiot to be purchasing such things. His plans would never succeed, and Gray would never wear them. And yet the solidity of the items felt good, just like the weight of the silver he'd gotten from the exchequer three days earlier. Something real, not just idle daydreams.

He turned up the street in the direction of the palace but didn't get very far before he passed a middle-aged man and woman selling items from the back of a wagon. Most of their inventory consisted of brightly embroidered curtains, probably crafted by the woman herself. Even now she was sitting on a stool and stitching cheery blue flowers. Aric paused to consider the curtains, thinking that they might make a suitable gift. But then he saw what was tucked up against one side of the wagon, near where the man was standing and chewing on a twig. A group of small stone figures.

"Carve 'em myself," the man said.

"What are they for?"

The man made a face, and then, speaking slowly as if to a stupid child, he said, "They're gods and goddesses and such. They protect folks' homes."

Two of the statues were taller than the others and almost identical to each other. Aric recognized them and smiled. "How much for Lorad and Lokad?"

"Like those two, do you? Figures." The man chuckled and chewed on his stick as he thought. "Thirty coppers for the pair."

It was a lot of money, but Aric handed over the coins without complaint, then waited while the man wrapped them in some rough sacking. "It's always good to have a giant or two looking after you," the man said as he handed over the heavy parcel.

Aric hurried back to the palace. It was nearly dinnertime, and he'd need to drop his purchases off at the Brown Tower before fetching his and Gray's meals. Not only didn't he want Alys getting nosy about the contents, but juggling the parcels plus the dinner pails would be a bit too much for his single hand.

The guard at the tower door was a mousy little man with a bald head. Aric didn't know his name. Because the guards feared standing so close to the prisoner for very long—a superstitious dread that nobody seemed to question—they were kept on duty for only a few weeks at a time. Aric supposed the task must have been exceptionally boring as well, save for the rush of adrenaline that came with a new dream message.

"What's that?" the guard asked, narrowing his eyes at the items in Aric's arms.

"Mine. What do you care?"

"Don't. Just being friendly. Oh, and you got new clothes."

Aric froze. "What?"

"New clothes. King gives 'em to all the guards and staff every spring. 'T's not fair, really—yours take twice as much fabric as anyone else's." He shrugged. "They were delivered this afternoon."

Aric's heart began to beat so fast that he was sure the guard must see it hammering away in his chest, and the blood roaring in his ears was nearly loud enough to deafen him. He tried to keep his voice even. "Someone... someone brought clothes to my chambers?"

The guard laughed. "Nah. Too scared to go near the witch, she was. I put 'em right inside the door here. You'll see 'em when you go in."

With the rush of relief, Aric's legs nearly gave out. "Uh, thanks," he managed to mumble, then squeezed inside before the guard had the door fully open. Sure enough, a pile of fabric was folded on top of a large wooden chest. With some difficulty, he managed to scoop up the new clothes before proceeding down the corridor.

"You've been out in the c-city," Gray said with a smile as soon as Aric entered the room. "Where did you go?" He liked to hear about

Aric's mundane daily adventures. Not much of a surprise, given his very limited life.

"I picked up a few things. Gifts." He didn't mention that some of the gifts were for Gray; that information could wait. "And I guess new clothes were brought for me today." He set everything down on the bed, which he hadn't slept in for months.

"The king is g-generous," said Gray emotionlessly.

Aric could only sigh. "Yes, to a fortunate few." Gray's clothing was still wrapped and tied in a neat bundle, and Aric decided to keep it that way for now. He tucked the bundle into a dresser drawer. Then he examined the clothes he'd been brought: four new shirts and two pairs of trousers, in addition to breechclouts and socks and handkerchiefs. All as finely made as usual, and obviously sewn just for him. He thought of how he must have looked when he first appeared at the palace, with his monstrous face and oversized body and shabby clothes and bare feet. His face and body remained the same, but now at least he could cover himself well, and he was almost in love with his wonderful boots. Yes, the royal family had been very generous to him indeed.

He put his new trousers away. But as he went to do the same with the shirts, something tumbled to the floor, landing on the stone with a *clink*. He bent curiously to pick it up.

It was a small iron key.

 # CHAPTER
Eighteen

PLAIN and black and insignificant, it weighed very little and looked tiny, cradled in his enormous palm.

"Aric? Aric, is something wr-wrong?"

Aric didn't answer his lover. His throat wouldn't work. Instead he walked slowly into the cell and stood very near to Gray, who reached for him at once. "G-gods, Aric, what is it?"

"Can I… can I see your arm? Please?" His voice sounded odd to his own ears. A little strangled and too high-pitched.

It was a mark of Gray's trust in him that, although Gray's face was drawn in a frown, he immediately held out his right arm. Aric just looked at it for a moment. Although Gray's arm was steady, Aric was trembling. So it was with some difficulty that he positioned the key properly between thumb and forefinger, slipped the end of it into the tiny hole in the manacle, and twisted.

The lock opened with a click.

"A-a-a-aric?" Now Gray's hand was shaking too. "Wh-wh-wh-wh— Fuck!"

"A key. There was a key." He couldn't stop staring at Gray's wrist, where the metal cuff had opened, revealing a strip of extremely pale skin. It was odd, really. He'd become so intimate with the other man's body, and yet there were a few small parts of it he'd not yet seen. He wanted to press his lips to that tiny span of flesh.

But Gray was stroking that strip of skin with his own fingertips, and then—ever so carefully—touching the key, which still protruded from the lock. He began to breathe very hard, noisy in the close confines of the cell. "How?" he managed to rasp without a stutter.

"I have no idea. It just…. I was putting my new clothing away, and it fell. Someone must have put it there."

Someone. But who? Surely not the mousy little guard. The tailor wouldn't have had access to the key, nor any reason to hand it over. Perhaps it was the person who had delivered the clothing, or maybe…. Aric's head was whirling too much for him to think straight. He hadn't any idea where the key came from. And he didn't know what its appearance signified.

He was interrupted in his thoughts by the decisive snap of metal. Gray had pushed the manacle closed again and turned the key, and now was holding it out. "T-take this and throw it d-down the well," he commanded, although his voice wavered.

"No! Gray, it's the key!"

"It's d-disaster waiting to happen."

"But now we can get the chains off," Aric protested, stating the obvious. He'd been thinking for weeks about how he was going to accomplish that. He'd envisioned all sorts of wild scenarios in which he took Captain Jaun hostage and demanded the key, or through casual conversation learned where the key was kept so he could sneak in and steal it. Even in his imagination, those scenarios had seemed more than unlikely, and he hadn't come up with anything better. But now he didn't have to.

"And then wh-what, Aric? It's still impossible. We'd only g-get caught and then… gods, if I l-lost you…."

"But someone gave us this key. There must be a reason. Someone must—"

"A trap."

Maybe. But Aric wouldn't throw the key in the well. He would hide it instead, tucking it into that little pile of handkerchiefs left behind by a previous resident and now lying in the bottom drawer of Aric's dresser. But gods, it pained him so much to see that narrow strip of skin obscured by iron again, to see the chains trailing from Gray's neck and limbs as solidly as always.

Gray sat down in his corner and drew his knees to his chest. He rested his cheek on his knees and rocked himself very slightly.

"I'll go fetch dinner," Aric said softly. "But Gray? It's not impossible."

ALYS smiled at him as she handed him dinner. "Are you all right, Brute? You look a little… worried."

"I think I just have a lot on my mind."

Her smile disappeared, and her gaze strayed in the direction of the Brown Tower. "Is he…. Is there a problem? Brute, I told you to be careful."

"I am careful and there's no problem." He tried to look untroubled. "I got my new clothes today."

She blinked at him a few times before nodding. "Oh! Yes, I guess it's that time of year again, isn't it? Now, you won't get anything else until next year, so don't give them away." She gave no sign that there was anything special about this particular delivery of clothing, or that the subject held any special meaning to her.

"It was a surprise," he replied carefully. "They were waiting for me at the tower today."

"I should have mentioned it to you, but didn't think of it. I got mine last week." She smoothed at her skirt, which he supposed might have been a new one. He never paid much attention to what she wore. "It's nice that they included me, even though they know I'll be leaving soon. Or maybe they just forgot that part!" She giggled.

"So… this happens every year? The tailor makes new clothes, and he brings them right to me?"

Alys shrugged. "I think his daughters actually do the delivery. I've never seen him outside his workshop, actually. Almost any time of day or night you can see him there, sewing away. His daughters bring him his meals as well, and they tell me they have to force him to eat. He enjoys his work, I guess."

Aric exchanged a few small pleasantries with her and then left the kitchens. He detoured past the tailor, and as Alys had said, the open windows revealed the man bent over lengths of fabric. Three girls who looked very much alike sat at a table, eating and chatting with one another. Aric had seen them about the palace now and then, but hadn't realized who they were, and he'd never exchanged so much as a word with any of them. Surely none of them could be responsible for bringing him the key.

And that still left the question of who did, but it seemed as if it was a mystery that would remain unsolved for now. He didn't want to arouse suspicion by asking too many questions.

Gray didn't want to eat. Didn't want to do anything, in fact, but huddle in his corner with his face buried in his arms. Aric poked and prodded at him, trying to persuade him to at least down some of his mush, until finally Gray snapped his head up and growled, "L-leave me alone!"

Aric took the words literally. He finished his meal at the table and then left the chamber. But he didn't leave the tower itself. Instead, fat candle in hand, he continued the exploration he'd begun before in fits and starts. Really, there wasn't much to see inside the tower. The few things that were stored there clearly hadn't been touched in generations and were more thoroughly forgotten than Gray Leynham. Aric wondered whether the tower had been abandoned before Gray was incarcerated there, and if so, why. Space wasn't exactly tight within the palace grounds, but it wasn't generally wasted either. As far as he had seen, everything in the palace had some purpose, even if that purpose was only to amuse the nobles. The Brown Tower seemed to be nothing except a prison for a single man—and home for his keeper.

On the ground floor of the tower, a narrow hallway branched off the main one. He'd been down it once before but found nothing of interest—just a few empty, doorless chambers, a stack of moldering cloth that was almost as tall as he was, and a lot of mouse droppings. But there was also a small window, down at the very end. It was an odd window, placed only a few inches from the floor and covered with thin metal bars. Wooden shutters shielded the window as well, and were bolted on the inside. Perhaps the opening had originally been intended for deliveries into the building, or perhaps the ground floor had once been lower than it was now. Certainly the window seemed as old as the tower itself, and that was very, very old.

Which meant the iron bars were ancient as well, and rusted due to the constant damp.

Aric carefully set the candle on the floor, wrapped his hand around one of the bars, and gave an experimental tug. The metal crumbled almost as easily as if it were a twig.

Humming thoughtfully to himself, Aric picked up the candle again and retraced his steps to his chamber.

CHAPTER
Nineteen

BY THE afternoon of her wedding, Alys had worked herself into a nervous frenzy. Aric was pretty sure it wasn't the wedding itself that was making her so anxious, but rather her impending departure from the palace. She'd lived her entire life inside the palace walls, venturing out into Tellomer itself only rarely. Her parents had lived at the palace, and theirs before them. Her new home wasn't too far away, and she'd doubtless be visiting the palace often, but still, the change must be feeling monumental to her. She'd no longer be the girl who worked in the palace kitchens. Instead, she would be the wife of Cearl Oken, mistress of a house of her own, and co-proprietor of a carting enterprise.

Therefore, she could be forgiven for snapping at Warin and Aric and Cearl and everyone else who came within range. But wisely, the men in her life did the best they could to stay as far from her as possible all day. It was Cearl who had the brilliant idea that he, Aric, and Warin could spend the afternoon carrying her belongings from the palace to their new home. Her things could have easily fit on one of his larger wagons, but he claimed that those wagons were all in use, and that the only conveyance available was a single wheelbarrow. He also said that the wheelbarrow had a bad axel and could carry only light loads. The axel felt fine to Aric, but he didn't say so, because it provided the perfect excuse for the three men to make numerous trips—keeping them far away from Alys and her sharp tongue.

But as much as they tried to stretch the task out, eventually every single item Alys owned had been carried over, and Aric, Cearl, and Warin stood mournfully around the empty barrow in the palace courtyard. "Maybe we could sneak some of her stuff back and then take it away again?" Warin said hopefully, but Cearl shook his head.

"I'm fairly sure she'd notice."

"Maybe you guys have more presents somewhere?" As was the custom, friends had been giving the couple gifts all week. The gifts remained wrapped in burlap or paper, or tucked into baskets and jars, all to be opened on the wedding night. Aric hoped they liked the statues of the giants. Now that he'd seen the new house, he could picture the giants flanking the front door, guarding the new family faithfully. But the giants and all the other gifts had already been taken to the new house. They were arranged on Alys and Cearl's bed, because that was part of the fun of it: the newlyweds would have to wade through all their new belongings before their marriage could be consummated.

Cearl smiled ruefully. "Nope. All the presents are there already. All we have left to take back is the barrow itself."

Aric swallowed thickly. "Um… could I borrow it? I'll return it tomorrow."

Cearl gave him a very long look. The man was so quiet that Aric had never noticed how sharp his eyes were, how perceptive his gaze. Aric tried not to fidget.

"Why do you need it, Brute?" asked Warin. "You got something to carry? I'll help!"

Aric bit his lip, not wanting to lie but unsure how to answer. To his surprise, Cearl gave the boy a friendly cuff to the shoulder. "Let him be, Warin. He doesn't need you in his business all the time."

"But—"

"Come on. The flowers need arranging for tonight."

Warin grumbled and rolled his eyes, then loped in the direction of the garden where the ceremony would be held.

Cearl turned a serious face Aric's way. "You're welcome to it, Brute. Just… be careful. The boy and Alys, they really care about you."

Aric dipped his head. "Thank you."

After Cearl walked away, Aric pushed the cart toward the Brown Tower. It was a bit of an awkward task for him due to the missing hand, but he'd already learned that he could sort of prop the left handle on his stump and steer with the right handle. The system worked tolerably well, although he wasn't sure how successful he'd be with a heavy load. Now, in any case, he had little trouble trundling the barrow over the cobbles and behind the tower, into the narrow passageway that ran between the tower and the back of the bulky armory. His covert observations had already told him that few people ventured into the little alley, which seemed to be a favorite place for the palace cats to hunt for rats. Even if someone did come across the wheelbarrow, they'd probably think little of it. Carts and wagons of all shapes and sizes could be found on the palace grounds any time of day.

The morning had been Alys's last hours in the kitchen, since she'd been granted the afternoon and evening off to prepare for her wedding. Most likely because the chief cook couldn't stand her irritable presence one moment longer. When Aric had fetched breakfast, Alys had been teary. But now it was dinnertime and she was gone, and an older woman with frizzy brown hair gave him his buckets instead.

"Dinner smells good tonight," Aric announced when he returned to his chambers.

Gray grunted a reply. He'd been unusually quiet since the discovery of the key days earlier, but when Aric joined him beneath the quilts every night, Gray had clung to him desperately, repeatedly touching every part of Aric's body as if he meant to memorize it, as if he feared he might never touch it again. Their lovemaking had been unusually raw each night; it carried a sense of urgency that had never been there before.

Aric sat beside Gray, and they ate without speaking to one another. When they were finished, Aric handed him a candy he'd saved from his last visit to the sweet shop with Warin. Gray sucked on the candy for a while and then slowly toppled to his side so that his head and body rested against Aric. "Y-you're so strong. But you can't do miracles."

"I know," Aric sighed. "I can't do much, really. But I try."

"D-don't. Just... stay. Please."

"I won't leave you," Aric vowed. "But tonight I've a wedding to attend."

That made Gray smile a little in the darkness. "When I w-was fifteen, I went to a wedding. My f-father's cousin. Everyone drank too much wine, including me. I ended up under some bushes, having sex with a p-pretty boy. My first time."

"Prince Aldfrid wasn't your first?"

Gray chuckled. "N-no. I was very experienced by the time he had me. I'd had sex three and a h-half times by then."

"Half?"

"S-silly story. Go to your wedding. I'll tell you when you c-come back."

So Aric made himself as presentable as possible, washing and shaving and combing his hair. He'd become almost used to his reflection in the mirror by now, so seeing himself so plainly was no longer such an unpleasant shock. Now he looked himself over, straightened his clothing, and set off for the celebration.

He'd never attended a wedding before; he wasn't exactly at the top of most people's invitation lists. But when he was a boy, he'd slunk through the darkness and spied on a couple of them from afar. They hadn't really seemed that interesting to him, although the food had looked good. But tonight was different because it was Alys getting married, and she was his friend.

The little garden was strewn with yellow blossoms. Alys stood in the center, looking beautiful. Her red hair was loose, hanging halfway to her waist, and she wore a circlet of flowers around her head. More flowers were strung around her neck like a gaudy necklace. Her feet were bare, and her smile was radiant. Cearl wore flowers too, both in his hair and around his neck, and he stared at his bride as if dumbfounded over his good luck.

There were about two dozen guests, and Warin and their other siblings, and the chief acolyte in his purple robes. Aric took his place at the back, in part so as not to obscure anyone's view. Several people turned to look at him, but they didn't frown or chase him away. A few even smiled at him, making him feel welcome. He *was* welcome here, he realized. He could stay, and this could be his home. He would have good friends. He would belong in a way he'd never dreamed of.

But Gray would remain in chains.

The acolyte intoned his prayers and passed several small bowls to the couple. Alys and Cearl dipped a finger in each bowl and pressed their fingers together, then gave the bowls to Warin, who looked very serious about his task of lining them back up again on the ground. There was water, both sweet and salty, and earth. There was honey, and there were ashes. There was blood, and there was wine. Then Alys and Cearl recited their promise to one another: "To thee I give myself, body, heart, and soul. I take thee into myself, body, heart, and soul. I will have no others, and you will always be mine."

Aric wished he could say those words to Gray, could laugh a little while an acolyte drizzled oil on their heads, could join with friends and family in a blessing to Bercthun and Breguswid, god and goddess of love and loyalty. He wished he could simply stand under a starlit sky and hold Gray's hand.

The acolyte said a few more words, and then everyone was looking expectantly at Aric. He startled a little and then, slightly embarrassed to be the center of attention, took a small bowl of seeds from Alys's hand. He had to balance the bowl inside his left elbow. Then he took a pinch of the seeds in his fingers and said the blessing he'd been practicing obsessively for the past week: "Bercthun and Breguswid, let Cearl and Alys Oken be fruitful, let their children be as grasses in the plain and trees in the forest, let their love grow in bounty and joy." He tossed the seeds onto the ground as he'd been instructed, then recited the prayer again and again, each time scattering another pinch of seeds, until the bowl was empty. When he was through, Alys gave him a warm smile.

Warin took the bowl from him, and the acolyte filled it with sweet wine. Cearl held it for Alys while she took a few sips, and then she reciprocated. The acolyte flicked some scented water at them with his fingertips, and everyone cheered, even Aric. The newlyweds held hands and bowed, both of them beaming.

A table had been set up to one side. It was piled with fruit and little cakes and the phallic biscuits—complete with strategically placed walnuts—that were traditional for weddings. Wine and ale were poured as well. With only one hand, Aric couldn't eat and drink at the same time, and in any case he wanted a clear head, so he bypassed the alcohol and ate several cakes instead. On a whim, he snuck one of the biscuits into a pocket. Gray wouldn't be able to see its shape, but he could feel it, and Aric thought it might bring a chuckle.

It was quite late when someone shouted that it was time for the newlyweds to leave. Everyone crowded around the new couple to wish them well. Everyone but Aric, who hung back awkwardly. But Alys and Cearl came to him. Cearl gave him a steady look and an almost imperceptible nod before shaking his hand. Alys threw her arms around Aric and squeezed hard. He kissed the top of her head. "Happiness to both of you," he whispered through a thick throat.

And then Alys and Cearl left—accompanied by good-natured jeers and lewd catcalls—and Aric went back to the Brown Tower.

Gray was still awake when Aric got back, but just barely. "How was the w-wedding?" he asked sleepily.

"Nice. Look, I brought you something." Aric handed him the biscuit. Gray laughed when he realized what it was and waggled his eyebrows as he nibbled on the biscuit's tip. Aric undressed, and they lay down together in the cell, and they petted and rubbed against one another until Gray cried out his completion against Aric's neck and Aric shuddered his climax a moment later. Gray fell asleep almost immediately, encircled in Aric's arms. But Aric remained wide awake.

Somewhere in the still, cold hours before dawn, Gray began to whimper. Aric held him tight and crooned nonsense and waited, and then Gray's whimpers turned to moans. "Don't let me die," he said in a high-pitched tone. "Is my baby all right? I want to see him grow up. Please!" Aric kissed away Gray's tears, knowing the comfort was appreciated even though his lover was not conscious.

Gray woke up a few minutes later with a long, exhausted sigh. "Eaba Limsey will die in childbirth," he said.

Aric kissed his cheek. "No she won't. I'll go pass your message on." He stood and dressed. But instead of simply pulling on a pair of trousers, which was usually enough for his purposes this time of night, he put on a breechclout first. He also tugged a shirt over his head and struggled with his socks—always a challenge for him—and boots. Finally, he shrugged on his cloak.

The mousy guard seemed a bit agitated over this particular dream, but then they often were. Aric didn't wait around to find out why.

Gray was asleep again, snoring softly. But he woke up when Aric slid open the creaky drawer in order to get at the key. "Aric?" Gray asked.

"I'll be right there." Before entering the cell, Aric retrieved the set of clothes he'd prepared earlier in the day. Nearly everything else he owned was wrapped in a bundle and tucked into a satchel he'd bought a few weeks earlier. His belongings didn't amount to much, but they were more numerous than when he first arrived at the palace. And of course there was also the purse full of coins, which he tucked carefully into his clothes.

"Wh-what are you doing?" Gray asked warily.

Aric didn't answer him. Instead, he entered the cell and stood over Gray and the pile of quilts. "Stand up, please," he said after a moment.

"Aric?"

"I can haul you to your feet, but I'd rather you cooperate."

Gray stood. "Aric, d-don't— G-g-g-gods, what do you think—" But he stopped completely when Aric unlocked the iron collar. The collar fell open, revealing an indentation with slightly reddish lines along the edges. "Ar...." Gray moaned. He was shivering, and not from the cold.

Aric felt almost heartless as he bent to release the cuffs around Gray's ankles, then straightened to unlock the manacles as well. Gray looked so *naked* without the chains on him, so vulnerable, and scared.

At least Aric could do something about the naked part. "Here," he said, shoving a pair of trousers against Gray's chest.

"I-I-I c-c-c-c— Fuck! C-c-can't."

Aric tried to put every bit of strength he possessed into his voice, and to suppress every hint of fear. "You can."

Gray's hands were shaking wildly, but he took the trousers. And then a bit of a farce followed, as a one-handed man attempted to help a blind man who hadn't worn clothes in over a decade get dressed. Much muttered swearing ensued, along with a bit of slightly hysterical laughter. But eventually Gray was dressed. He held his body strangely, obviously unused to the feeling of fabric on his skin, and he shook his head. "H-hope you know what you're doing."

"I don't," Aric answered cheerfully. "Grab a couple of the quilts, please. My hand is full."

"W-we're both mad," Gray muttered, but he did as he was told. Then he took a deep breath, put a hand on Aric's shoulder, and followed him out of the cell. They shuffled out of Aric's chamber and down the corridor. It was very dark, but Aric knew the way, and the lack of light didn't matter to Gray. Their ragged breaths seemed to echo off the walls.

They turned down the narrow hallway and made their way to the end. "This part is a little tricky," Aric said. "Hang on."

"F-for dear life."

Aric set his satchel down, knelt, and began to tug at the iron bars that covered the low window. He made more noise than he would have liked, but hoped that it didn't matter. Few people would be awake this time of night, and he was fairly certain that none of them would be anywhere nearby. Even the guard at the tower door was probably still off somewhere, conveying Gray's most recent dream.

The bars gave easily, and the shutters opened with nothing worse than a protesting squeal. Aric turned and put his hand on Gray's shoulder. "You have to trust me on this, okay?"

"I d-do."

Even in their desperate situation, Aric's heart swelled. Gray trusted him. He bent to place a quick kiss on his lover's cheek. "I can't fit out this window, but you can. Climb out, and I'll hand you the quilts and my bag. There's a wheelbarrow easily within reach. Climb on in and cover yourself and the bag with the quilts." He puffed out a lungful of air. "And then you're going to have to wait. As soon as the sun rises, I'll come fetch you."

"I'll—" Gray's voice broke, and he swallowed before beginning again. "I'll b-be alone?"

"Not for long. It's nearly dawn already, and then I'll come for you. Nobody's going to find you, Gray."

Gray nodded quickly, and Aric couldn't help but lean down to press their foreheads together. "This is a shock, I know. You've been in that damned cell for so long. But you survived... gods, Gray. You survived so much. You can manage this."

"M-maybe the gods don't hate me so much after all."

"If the gods hate you, the gods are bigger idiots than me," Aric replied, feeling suddenly foolhardy and a little giddy. He was having an adventure. He was *doing* something. He was fucking well going to save the man he loved.

Gray laughed and cuffed him lightly on the head. Then he felt around until he found the satchel, which he hoisted over one shoulder. Clutching the quilts under one arm, he managed to squirm through the window. "G-good thing you didn't fatten me up any more," he panted, and then he was through. Aric couldn't see him due to the darkness and the thickness of the wall, but he heard a soft thunk and a muffled oath, probably as Gray walked into the barrow. Wood creaked. And that was it.

Aric pulled the shutters closed and bolted them. He found the pile of rotted fabric that someone long dead had left in the hallway, and he moved it in front of the little window. A careful search would eventually reveal Gray's means of escape, but at least for a while, his exit would remain a mystery—all the better if the palace feared the disappearance was due to a witch's dire magic—and Aric figured the bit of subterfuge could only help their chances of getting away.

He returned to his chambers for the last time. They seemed very empty without Gray. For no particular reason, he closed and bolted the cell door, and then he tidied the room as best as he could in the dark. The people of the palace had been good to him, and although he might betray them, he didn't need to leave a mess behind as well.

He paced, glancing at the window every few minutes, trying not to think of how Gray was doing, what Gray was thinking, whether Gray was terrified, huddled blind and alone under the quilts.

When the soft gray light of morning stole through the chamber's single window, Aric washed. He couldn't shave because his razor was in the satchel with Gray. He took one last look at the ugly face in the mirror and gave himself a twisted smile. Then he left for the final time.

The guard at the door was bony and cross-eyed. Evidently the mousy one was off duty. It didn't matter. This one grunted a morning greeting and watched disinterestedly as Aric emptied the waste pail. Aric left the pail near the door, as he sometimes did when he was in a hurry. He walked toward the kitchens, but as soon as he was out of sight of the guard, he turned and doubled back, trying to look as innocent as possible, approaching the Brown Tower from the back. The only things of interest in the alley between the tower and the armory were a sleepy orange cat and a nondescript wheelbarrow.

It's hard for a seven-and-a-half-foot tall man to make himself invisible, but Aric did his best as he turned down the alley. He stopped when he got to the barrow and whispered, "It's me." The quilts twitched the tiniest bit in answer.

Now Aric had to push the cart up the alley, across a courtyard, and around several buildings. He could smell the kitchens not too far away and remembered that neither he nor Gray had eaten, but he wasn't sure he could have managed breakfast anyway. His stomach felt tied up in knots.

Nobody paid him much attention, although a few people he knew gave him waves or smiles. The palace staff was well used to him by now, and even the fact that he was pushing a wheelbarrow wasn't remarkable. He'd run errands for Alys on occasion before.

The morning crowds were just beginning to pass in and out through the palace gates: delivery men with their carts, errand boys, citizens of the kingdom who had business with the crown, noblewomen and their servants on their way to the shops, couriers with arms full of bundled papers. The guards barely glanced at Aric and his wheelbarrow as he exited.

Aric's hope was that it would take a long time before anyone noticed that he and Gray were missing. He was going to be absent from lessons that morning, but Master Sighard would very likely chalk that up to the aftermath of the wedding the night before. He certainly wouldn't complain to anyone that Aric wasn't there. If Alys still worked in the kitchens, she would notice that he didn't appear to collect his meals, but since she was gone and nobody else had been put specifically in charge of him, there was nobody to remark on his failure to appear. Sometimes Warin came looking for him, but Warin was staying with a brother outside the palace for a few days and then moving in with Alys. And maybe the guards would notice that Aric didn't train with them in the afternoon, but he didn't train with them every day anyway. In fact, this week they had been practicing archery, which would clearly hold little interest for him.

The wheelbarrow wobbled and bounced over the cobblestones. He hoped Gray wasn't too uncomfortable. It would be difficult to remain motionless and cramped for so long.

Within minutes, Aric was approaching Alys's new house, a tall, narrow building with a red roof and flower boxes in every window. He couldn't stop a broad smile when he caught sight of the statues that now flanked the front door: Lorad and Lokad looking fierce and protective, and each of them with a flower garland around the neck. But Aric didn't stop at the front door. He wheeled the cart around the back, where there was a long, thin yard. Chickens clucked inside a henhouse, and a cat—this one a fat tabby—stared at him from atop a small shed. He smelled a stable nearby. Aric found a shrub that would screen the view from the house, and that's where he parked the barrow.

With a quick glance around, he peeled back the quilts.

Gray was curled tightly around the satchel. Aric put a gentle hand on Gray's shoulder and whispered, "We're out of the palace now. You can get out."

Very slowly, Gray uncurled himself. He kept a hand on the edge of the cart for balance and climbed out. He had to stretch to get circulation going in his cramped limbs, and then he turned to Aric and smiled a little. For the first time, Aric had a good look at Gray Leynham in the sunshine. His hair was thick and golden, the color of a fresh-baked loaf of bread. His skin was white as parchment. He had marks on his neck and wrists where the irons had been for so long, and he was still too thin. But he stood straight and tall, and his full lips were curled in a brave grin. "All right, my giant," he said. "Where w-will you take me now?"

 # CHAPTER
Twenty

PEOPLE stared as Aric led the way to the docks. But then people always stared at him, even when an eyeless man wasn't hanging onto his left elbow. If the passersby noticed how closely Gray was pressing against Aric, they doubtless thought it was only the natural hesitancy of a man who couldn't see. They wouldn't have seen how tense the blind man's body was, how often he was wracked with fine but uncontrollable trembling.

Aric pitched his voice very low. "I'm sorry, Gray. I know this has to be overwhelming. I wish we had more time."

"B-but we don't. I know. D-d-do I look horrible? Are people g-gaping?"

"They can hardly see you past me," Aric answered honestly. "And you look fine."

"My f-f-face. My eyes...."

Aric realized that Gray had probably been a little vain once upon a time, as beautiful boys are wont to be. "You're a little thin and too pale. People probably think you've been ill lately." Which gave Aric an idea, actually, one he filed away for later. He gave Gray a brief pat on the shoulder. "Believe me, I am an expert on monsters, and you're not even close."

Gray snorted slightly, which Aric thought was promising. Then Gray took a few deep breaths in an obvious effort to maintain calm. "I remember these smells. G-gods, I remember. And the sounds! T-t-tellomer hasn't changed, has she?"

"I don't think Tellomer has changed much in centuries."

"Where are we now, Aric? What are we p-passing?"

"Ateliers. Painters and sculptors and people like that. Warin told me the nobles and rich folks hire these artists to make their houses pretty." It wasn't the most direct route from Alys's house to the docks, but it was the quietest. It allowed them to avoid the markets that would be packed with shoppers this time of day and also the neighborhoods where the working poor lived in cramped little flats.

"I used t-to be able to draw," Gray said quietly. "Not well enough t-t-to make a living from it, but I enjoyed it. I drew Friddy."

Another loss he had suffered, Aric thought. One Aric hadn't even guessed at. How many ragged little holes were hidden in his lover's heart? "Are your feet hurting?" he asked. Unsure of Gray's size, he hadn't bothered to buy him shoes. He knew from his own experience that poorly fitting footwear could be worse than none at all. Besides, the stone floor of the cell was as hard and rough as the cobbles on which they were walking.

"They're f-fine."

After a few more blocks, they turned downhill, and Gray sniffed. "F-f-fish."

"The fish market's not far from here."

"And the d-docks."

"And the docks," Aric agreed.

Gray came to a sudden halt, breaking his contact with Aric, so Aric stopped too. "What is it?" Aric asked with concern.

"L-leave me. You've set m-me free and now you can go. They'll ch-chase me, not you."

"Gods, Gray! No!"

"If they f-find me, I'll say I b-b-bewitched you."

Not caring what sort of spectacle they might be making, Aric grabbed Gray's arm. "I'm not leaving you. If I have to swing you over my shoulder and carry you, I'll do it, but I'm not going anywhere without you."

After a brief pause, Gray nodded and gave a small, shaky smile. "I g-guess walking has more dignity." He disentangled himself from Aric's grip and grasped Aric's elbow again.

As always, there was considerable activity at the piers. Aric had to weave his way through the crowds, and twice Gray was wrenched away, but both times they were quickly able to reunite. Luckily, the berths Aric sought were relatively close by, and he was relieved to discover that ships were tied at both of them. He and Gray pulled away from the crowds and stood up against a building, Aric spending a few minutes watching the ships over people's heads. It seemed to him that most of the work going on at berth thirteen involved unloading cargo, whereas at berth twelve men were dragging full sacks and crates onto the ship. He had to use his considerable bulk to work them closer to the gangway at berth twelve.

The ship was called the *Ouragan,* and to Aric's admittedly unpracticed eyes, it seemed to be nothing special. It wasn't sleek and deadly-looking like the warships that flew the royal crest. It was big and blocky, and the goddess at the prow was crudely carved and in need of repainting. *All right*, he thought. An ugly ship, but serviceable. A brute of a boat, perhaps.

He hovered uncertainly until he spied a middle-aged man standing at the edge of the gangplank with a sheaf of papers in one hand and a quill in the other. He had a bottle of ink in the chest pocket of his coat, and splotches and splatters of blue-black were all over the coat's front and lapels.

Aric waited until there was a momentary lull in the loading of cargo and approached the man. "Excuse me?" Aric said.

The man didn't even look surprised at the sight of the ugly giant and the blind man. Just irritated. "Whattaya want?"

"This ship is going to Racinas?"

The man huffed. "She always goes to Racinas. Twice a month she goes to Racinas and twice a month she comes back. Prob'ly since before you were born."

"And when does it—um, she leave?"

"Tonight, if you get your ass out of the way so's we can load 'er up."

Still clutching Aric's arm, Gray may have snickered slightly.

"Could we book passage?" Aric asked.

This time the man rolled his eyes. "Unless you can squeeze yourselves into boxes, I ain't the one to ask. You wanna talk to Mr. Noft. He's the first mate."

"All right. Where can we find him?"

"On the ship, of course."

Gray stumbled slightly as they climbed the gangway, but Aric caught him and kept him from falling. "Th-thanks," Gray mumbled.

"Watch your step now. There's a little drop down to the ship's deck."

The sailors aboard the ship were too busy with ropes and sails and things to spare the newcomers more than a glance. Aric and Gray stood uncertainly until a small girl wearing trousers and a boy's shirt, her long hair in wild snarls, came over and looked up at them. "What do you want?" she demanded imperiously.

"We're looking for Mr. Noft."

"He's over there with my papa." She pointed toward the bow. "My papa is the captain of the *Ouragan*, and he doesn't want any ogres on his ship."

To Aric's surprise, Gray took a half step forward. "My friend's not an ogre, m-miss. He's a giant, and that's much b-better. Great-great-grandson of Lokad himself."

She wrinkled her nose thoughtfully. "What happened to your eyes?"

"I f-found some golden raven's eggs and tried to steal one, and sh-she pecked out my eyes. Then she flew me high in the air, higher than the mountaintops, and she dropped me. B-but my giant caught me. See? I broke off his h-hand. But I was saved."

The little girl's brown eyes had gone very wide, and her mouth had dropped open. She turned and ran toward the bow, yelling at the top of her lungs: "Papa! Papa! I found a giant!"

Aric followed her with Gray in tow. Aric had a vision of Gray as a very young man, cocky smile in place and eyes flashing with mischief, charming everyone who came within reach. "A golden raven?"

"Th-they're rare and very strong. You d-don't want to cross them. But you caught me."

Two men were leaning against the railing. The older one was listening to the little girl as she waved her arms and babbled about birds and ogres. The younger one had skin the color of a storm cloud and hair and eyes as black as iron. Aric had seen men who looked like him a few times during his walks around Tellomer. Warin said they came from some exotic kingdom far to the west, a place where housecats grew as big as horses and where the gods made the earth itself tremble when they grew angry.

"See? See?" cried the girl. "I told you, Papa!"

The captain and the first mate gave Aric and Gray long, level looks. "How can I help you?" the captain asked, more cordially than Aric expected.

"We'd like to secure passage to Racinas, sir. The man by the gangway said to speak with Mr. Noft."

"Why do you want to go to Racinas?" asked the man Aric assumed was Mr. Noft. He had a strange accent, a bit musical in its intonations.

"My friend's been sick, and the healer said a change of air would do him well. He has family from Racinas, so we thought we'd try there."

"And you are willing to accompany your friend on this rather urgent journey?"

Aric lifted his chin. "I am."

"They can't be thieves, Mr. Noft," said the captain. "The giant's far too big for it, and the pretty one's far too blind."

"We're not thieves," Aric confirmed. He'd never stolen anything but Gray Leynham. He'd even returned the wheelbarrow to Cearl, and inside it were the quilts they'd taken from the palace.

"It is not their... honesty that concerns me now, Captain," said Mr. Noft. Then he turned back to Gray and Aric. "What are you to one another?"

Aric hesitated for a moment, unsure how to respond, and Gray jumped in. "I love him," he said simply but a little fiercely.

Mr. Noft's bushy eyebrows rose. "You love... *that*? It is because you are blind and do not know how he is, perhaps."

Aric blushed with anger and shame and gritted his teeth. He'd become used to the easy acceptance by the palace staff and had almost forgotten the sting of casual derision. But Gray frowned and stepped closer to the first mate, his hands fisted at his sides. "I know *exactly* how he is, asshole, and that's why I love him."

Aric expected them both to be thrown off the ship at once. But instead, Mr. Noft and the captain burst into laughter. When he calmed a bit, Mr. Noft gave a courtly little bow. "I apologize. There are those who have heard that my captain prefers his lovers to be male and a bit... unusual, and at times these people seek to make sport of it."

Gray shook his head. "I don't c-care who you or the captain f— um, prefer." He turned slightly red, probably remembering the presence of the captain's daughter. "We just want to g-get to Racinas."

"Very well. The *Ouragan* is a cargo ship, not a passenger transport. We have no cabin for you, and the crew's quarters and hold will be full. But you may sleep on the deck so long as you remain out of the way. The weather should be fine for this journey, and we will provide meals and blankets. Three silver coins." Mr. Noft smiled a little. "One for you and two for your large friend, who I presume eats twice as much."

It was Aric who answered. "All right." He fumbled with his purse—always a bit awkward with the missing hand—and withdrew the coins, which Mr. Noft took with another little bow. Meanwhile, the captain's daughter was bouncing up and down and clapping her hands, apparently pleased with the new passengers.

Mr. Noft ended up summoning a scrawny sailor, who showed Gray and Aric a bit of the deck they could call their own. It was a tiny spot just barely big enough for the two of them, wedged between the curved railing and the forecastle. The sailor ran off and then returned a moment later with a pile of thin blankets, explaining how the blankets and Aric's satchel could be secured against the inside of the hull by ropes when not in use. "Bell rings five times fast when it's time for meals," the sailor said. "Just follow the crowds down to the galley to get yours. Grub's usually not bad heading north this time of year, and everyone gets two pints of ale a day. Cap'n doesn't much like drunks."

Aric and Gray thanked the sailor, and he hurried away. Gray's legs seemed to suddenly give out, and he collapsed to the deck. He scooted until his back rested against the hull. Aric sat down next to him and sighed with relief. "I'm going to be hungry by the time we set sail."

"M-me too. Last thing I ate was that b-biscuit you brought me."

"I should have bought us something as we were walking here."

"Your m-mind was on other things. It's okay. We won't s-starve."

Aric suddenly yawned so hugely that his jaw popped. "Do you think the captain and Mr. Noft are lovers?"

"Maybe," Gray said through a yawn of his own. He slumped against Aric's side.

Men were still rushing back and forth across the deck, cargo was thumping into place in the hold, and sailors were yelling out to each other as they climbed the masts and set things in place. The sounds from shore were still loud as well: vendors calling, carters shouting for people to clear their way, wagon wheels rattling against the cobbles. The fugitives weren't free of Tellomer yet, and they were far from safe. But Gray had slept very little the night before and Aric not at all, so exhaustion and nerves soon caught up with them both. Long before the *Ouragan* raised anchor, they were both fast asleep.

"I'M GOING to die," Aric groaned. "I *want* to die." He wasn't exaggerating. Someone could have run him through with a sword and tossed him overboard and he'd have sunk happily—gratefully—to the bottom of the sea, pleased to have the roiling in his stomach finally stop.

Gray only chuckled. "You'll be fine. D-don't know what the problem is, really. The seas are calm. The first time I sailed to R-racinas it was winter and a storm hit, and the ship p-pitched and heaved—"

"Uh!" Aric scrambled to the railing and did some heaving of his own, much to the amusement of several bored sailors nearby. If he'd been capable of making the effort, he might have thrown himself right over the rail. They were only one day into their journey, which meant they had another four or five days remaining. *Might as well have been four or five centuries*, Aric thought, and sank back down to the deck, wiping his mouth with the back of his hand.

Gray nudged him. "H-here. Drink this." He held a tin cup to Aric's mouth and helped him drink, just as Aric had helped him during Aric's first few nights in the Brown Tower. Gray had begged the cup and a jar of fresh water from a sailor and had kept it at hand. Aric wouldn't starve if he missed a few meals, but Gray said he didn't want him to become dehydrated.

"Sorry," Aric said miserably, after swallowing a few mouthfuls. "I'm supposed to be helping you."

"You're d-doing fine. You brought me here, and the f-fresh air is lovely. I can f-feel the sun on my skin. Do I have a b-bit of a burn?"

Aric tried to focus. "You're a little pink."

Gray laughed delightedly. "Wonderful! And I've been finding my way around quite well. Even a b-blind man can't get too lost on a ship, and Delly's b-been enjoying leading me about."

Delly was the captain's rather wild young daughter, and she had apparently fallen in love with Gray. She stuck close to him whenever she could escape her chores. Aric could understand her adoration, because Gray had a seemingly endless collection of tales for her— mostly ones in which Gray got himself in some fantastical mishap and Aric ended up saving him. "The Saga of the Seasick Giant," Gray was calling his stories, which made Delly giggle and Aric groan.

Now, Aric curled into a ball on his side, squeezed his eyes shut, and tried to pretend he was on solid ground. It took him a few minutes to realize that Gray was humming quietly, one of the songs Aric used to soothe Gray after his nightmares. One of the songs Aric's mother had crooned to him long ago. Gray's long fingers stroked the hair away from Aric's brow very lightly, as if he wasn't sure his touch would be welcomed. "I-I don't mind helping you for a change," he said. "It's nice to f-feel useful. I'm sorry I can't h-heal this."

"Mmm," said Aric, because if he opened his mouth he might vomit again. But he smiled a little when Gray laid a damp folded cloth across his brow. As miserable as he was, it was almost worth it just to be taken care of.

"CAN you see the city yet?"

Aric squinted at the horizon. "No. Just trees. Lots of trees."

"Oh." Gray leaned against him, and Aric put his arm around Gray's shoulders. Over the past few days, his stomach had settled into a constant but light queasiness. At Gray's insistence, he'd been able to manage a little soup and dry bread three times a day. But he was still very much looking forward to solid land, and fervently hoping that he never again had to travel by sea.

"How far is it from the harbor to the Vale of the Gods?" he asked. He and Gray hadn't yet discussed their plans for when they reached the city. One obstacle at a time seemed to be enough, really.

"It's almost a day's walk. W-we should stay at an inn tonight and g-go tomorrow."

"All right." An inn sounded good. Hopefully they could find one nicer than the White Dragon, but Aric would have gladly slept in a pigsty rather than spend another night on the *Ouragan*.

After a while, Gray bumped up against Aric's side. Aric had noticed that his lover liked to touch him often. Not just sexually—there had been none of that since they left the palace—and not just for comfort or to help Gray find his way. It was as if Gray wanted to confirm the reality of Aric's presence often, like he needed to reassure himself that Aric was real. As for Aric, he couldn't get enough of looking at the other man, of seeing him standing under an open sky, clothed and free of chains. He liked to watch Gray interact with Delly as well, or even with the sailors, because then Aric could get glimpses of the man Gray had once been: vibrant and spirited, a natural flirt and entertainer. No wonder he had caught a prince's eye.

"We d-don't have to go to the Vale," said Gray, interrupting Aric's thoughts.

"No, we don't. But if you don't get rid of the dreams, and we don't have the guards to warn the people you dream about... can you live with that?"

Gray turned his head away. "N-no."

"Then we'll go to the Vale."

"And what w-will it cost me to give the gift back? What d-damned price must I pay this time?"

"I don't know," Aric said out loud. But to himself, he added, *None at all. It's my price this time.*

Gray didn't have to know that, not yet.

 # CHAPTER
Twenty-One

RACINAS had a small natural harbor, holding only three large ships, a scattering of medium-sized fishing boats, and a flotilla of small craft. There was no palace on a hill—only a gray stone fort near the harbor's mouth. After the captain and Mr. Noft and Delly and several of the sailors had wished Gray and Aric well, Aric shouldered his satchel and led Gray to land.

Racinas might have seemed overwhelming to Aric when he was fresh from a small village, but after a year in Tellomer, this far-flung city felt quiet and sedate. The buildings were made of wood rather than brick or stone, and none were more than three stories tall. Taverns were clustered close to the port, just as in Tellomer, but there were fewer of them, and they seemed sleepier, as if the sailors here would rather eat and drink instead of gamble and fight. Even the whores—male and female—seemed a little lazy. They did nothing more than call out cheerful obscenities from in front of tavern doors.

The captain of the *Ouragan* had recommended an inn and given them directions. Aric found their way with only a few missteps and was very pleased to see that the Four Wolves appeared clean and well kept. The landlady was a tall, heavy woman with a shrewd eye. She quickly appraised the quality of Aric and Gray's clothing and gave a satisfied nod. Aric had learned in Tellomer that his expensive-looking clothes helped business people overlook his size and face. "I've a room for you. It's a large one, and the mattress is almost new. Ten coppers for the both of you with dinner and breakfast."

"Do you have a bath?" Aric asked. He'd become used to the palace baths and was missing them already.

"Another two coppers if you don't mind sharing. Want me to have my girl get it ready now?"

"Gray?" Aric asked.

Gray looked very eager. "A b-bath would be *lovely*."

The landlady summoned a teenaged girl who was obviously her daughter, and while the girl ran off to prepare the bath, the landlady took her guests to their room on the second floor. The room was an enormous improvement over Aric's old place at the White Dragon. It was spacious, as the proprietress had promised, and had a large window facing the harbor. The bed was made up with a bright, cheery bedspread; two low, overstuffed chairs were arranged in front of a clean-swept fireplace. The floor was white-painted planks with small rugs scattered here and there. Everything was spotlessly clean, and a bouquet of fresh flowers sat on the mantel.

"Dinner's in two hours. We'll lay a fire for you while you eat."

Aric glanced at Gray, who looked a little tense. "Would it be possible for us to eat up here?"

The landlady shrugged one big shoulder. "I'll have my girl bring it up when it's ready."

"Thank you." Aric paid her twelve coppers and waited for her to close the door. Then he turned and touched Gray's shoulder. "Are you all right?"

"I think so. D-dinner in our room is a good idea."

"I thought the fewer people who see us, the better."

"D-does it feel good to be on land again?"

"It does," Aric answered, although in truth he still felt as if the floor were rocking beneath his feet.

After a few minutes of resting and settling in, Aric took clean clothes from his satchel for himself and for Gray. He was missing the palace laundries and couldn't help but laugh at how spoiled he'd become over the past months.

The bath was located in a low-ceilinged room attached to the back of the inn. The girl had just finished getting it ready as they arrived, so she simply smiled, pointed at the towels and soap, then left. Aric bolted the door behind her and took a happy look around. The bathtub was much more ornate than he'd expected—sunk into the floor, decoratively tiled, and able to fit two men with no problem, even if one of them was a giant. The tiles were set in an abstract pattern that suggested waves and fishes, and vapor rose gently from the water into the cool air. The room had no windows, but a half dozen fat candles were set on shelves throughout, and a tidy fire roared in a tiled stove. A bench had been set in front of the stove, inviting bathers to relax in comfort as they dried.

"It's g-good?" Gray asked.

"Take off your clothes and find out." Aric was already pulling his shirt over his head. It took him a very short time to remove everything else and set it aside, and by the time he did, Gray was naked as well. Aric's breath caught at the sight of him. He'd seen Gray unclothed every day for the past year—except on the ship, of course—but this was different. The chains were gone, and the Brown Tower was far, far away.

Perhaps Gray's thoughts were running along the same lines, because he had a wicked grin and his cock was half-filled. "Will you scrub my b-back?" he asked with a slight purr.

"I'll scrub anything you want."

Aric took Gray's hand and helped him into the water. A seat was built into the edges of the tub, and Gray squeezed himself in beside Aric. For several minutes they simply sat there, inhaling the slightly spiced air and relaxing. But when Aric reached across Gray to grab the soap, Gray took hold of his arm and began kissing it, beginning at the wrist and working his way up to the shoulder. When he got to Aric's neck, he repositioned himself so that he was straddling Aric's hips. Their cocks ground together under the water while Gray gnawed and licked at Aric's neck, and Aric stroked the smooth skin at the small of the other man's back. Aric let his head fall back and his eyes drift closed as Gray nibbled his way across a collarbone and then down to a hard, sensitive nipple. Aric clenched his teeth so as not to cry out. He didn't know who might be listening and what reaction there might be to two men's amorous activities in the bath.

Gray turned his attention to the other nipple, and Aric moved his hand so that he was cupping Gray's ass. There was more meat on that ass than there used to be, and it felt solid and firm under his palm. He began to tease a little, trailing a fingertip just barely into the crease between Gray's cheeks and then forward, to that wonderfully sensitive bit of skin just behind Gray's balls. Aric's skin felt too tight, the sensations almost too much, and all that he could think of was how damned good it was not to have the chains in the way. In fact, that thought inspired him to push Gray away from his chest and then pull him up close again so that Aric could kiss at the raised ridge of skin where the collar had been.

Gray made a needy little sound and then froze. Aric stilled as well, not sure what was wrong.

"Aric?" Gray said in a small voice. "Wh-what did you do with the k-k-k-key?"

It took several seconds for Aric to figure out what he was talking about, and then another few to remember the answer. "I… I think it's in the satchel. I didn't want to just leave it. I wasn't sure if it would get someone in trouble if it was discovered. Why? I can throw it away if you want. I'd forgotten about it."

"Th-there are probably m-m-m-more. And i-i-if there aren't, th-th-they could j-j-j-just make m-m-more ch-chains."

Gray's stutter hadn't been this bad in months, and Aric didn't understand what was bothering him. "It doesn't matter, Gray. You're not going back to the Brown Tower. Not ever."

Gray began to shake, and he buried his face in his hands, making it harder for Aric to understand what he was saying. "B-b-b-but I w-w-was s-safe there, you s-s-s-see? It w-w-w-w-was always th-th-the fucking s-same, b-but I kn-kn-kn-knew it. Knew e-e-every fucking s-s-s-stone. I d-d-d-deserved to b-be l-l-l-l— Fuck! L-locked away a-and I w-was and n-n-n-now everything's new a-a-a-a-and so fucking b-b-b-b-big and I-i-i-i d-don't kn-kn-kn-kn-know h-h-h-h…." His voice cracked and broke completely, and all he seemed to be able to do was howl into his palms and tremble. And then he was crying, and Aric realized it was the first time he'd seen Gray really cry outside of a nightmare.

Aric wrapped his arms around Gray and held him tight.

He thought of a bird, a sparrow his mother had kept in a cage. It had been a gift from Aric's father, a little brown thing that would hop from one perch to another and peck at seeds from Aric's baby-sized fingers and sing in cheery little bursts. His mother would whistle back at it, which always made Aric laugh. And then came that dawn when the sheriff burst into their little home and took Aric's father away—the sheriff and some of the other Geddings had dragged him right out of that comfortable bed wearing only his trousers and with his hair all morning-wild. Aric's mother had yelled at Aric to *Stay here!* and she'd run after the sheriff and her husband. Aric had crouched in the corner, frightened and confused.

His mother came back a while later. Her face was still as stone, and her eyes were dry. She'd gathered Aric into her lap and held him— much like he was now holding Gray—and she'd sung him one of her songs.

When the song was over, she set Aric gently on the ground. She walked across the room and took the birdcage off its little table, then walked to the open door. She opened the little latch on the cage, and after a brief pause, the sparrow flew away.

It didn't go far, though. In fact, it flew back into the hut, and his mother had to shoo it out with a broom, after which she closed the door. But Aric could still hear it on the tree nearby, on the roof, on the little ledge outside the window, chirping and chirping away.

"Why, Mother?" Aric had asked, mystified why the bird didn't simply fly away.

"He doesn't know how to be free." And she'd collapsed to the floor, her face hidden in her hands.

Three days later, the sparrow was still nearby when the sheriff came again—more quietly this time—and led Aric's mother to the village square, her son close at her heels. Aric's father had been brought into the square, and for a brief moment, Aric had been thrilled to see him—until he noticed the rope around his father's hands, the fear on his father's face. Aric stood and watched his father die.

The sparrow was there outside the hut when his mother took him home again. It sang as the Geddings came and took almost everything the family had owned. He could hear it singing—much more frantically now—as his mother drank from a silver flask. It only stopped singing that night, when Aric cowered in the hut, his mother's corpse a few feet from him on the floor. The sheriff came one last time in the morning, maybe to see if there was anything he'd missed the afternoon before, and he discovered the body. He took Aric away, and as they walked down the path that led to the village, Aric looked in vain but couldn't find the sparrow.

He liked to think it had finally learned to be free and had flown away. Maybe it had found some new sparrow friends. But even when he was very young, he had known that in all likelihood, the bird had starved or fallen to a predator.

"You're not the sparrow," Aric said.

The sheer nonsense of that statement was enough to halt Gray's sobs and make him raise his head. "Wh-what?"

"This has... it's all been a lot for you. It's been a lot for *me*. I never expected to travel any farther than Tellomer, and I never thought I'd be a fugitive. I'm scared too."

Aric hadn't really meant to admit his fear—he was supposed to be the strong one now, the protector—but his words made Gray sigh and melt back against him, his head on Aric's shoulder and his arms around his body. "G-good," he mumbled. Which didn't make any sense to Aric, but then Aric's own comment about the stupid sparrow certainly made no more sense to Gray.

Gray was kissing him again. More softly now. His movements spoke less of hunger than of the need to touch and the desire to unite. He didn't use his teeth anymore, just lips and fingertips and flicks of his tongue, and he began to arch and rock on Aric's lap so that soon their cocks—which had softened while Gray cried—filled again. Gray's movements were slow. If Aric tried to do more than tender stroking of Gray's back, his lover tsked at him and slowed even more, so that soon Aric was floating in sweet torment as deep as the bath water. Deeper. As deep as the sea itself. And still Gray took his time and hummed and nuzzled and ran his fingers through Aric's hair.

Gray kissed him squarely on the mouth. Aric could barely breathe anymore and didn't care—what did he need with all that air anyway? He had everything he wanted, everything he needed, right in his lap and up against him, warm and pliant and firm, demanding and yielding, smelling of sea salt and spices and ale.

Aric's climax took him by surprise, and Gray swallowed his moans like candy.

Eventually they did get clean. Aric soaped Gray, just as he'd promised, and then Gray soaped him, joking as he did that the landlady should charge a giant double for soap. They rinsed. Aric helped Gray out of the bath, and they stood in front of the stove to dry themselves with clean, lemon-scented towels. Then they dressed and headed back up to their borrowed room.

They had just settled in when a knock sounded at their door. Aric smelled their dinner even before he opened the door. The landlady's daughter was there with a tray and a shy smile.

Dinner turned out to be a rich mutton stew with crusty rolls and some sort of tart green fruit Aric didn't recognize. He was famished and the food was good, but not as good as what he'd had from the palace kitchens. That thought reminded him of Alys. He wondered if she was happy, and he fervently hoped she'd faced no trouble because of Gray's disappearance.

Although it was still quite early when dinner was done, both of them were exhausted. Besides, they intended to set out again as soon as the sun rose. They stripped and climbed into the bed. It was plenty big enough for the two of them, and as the landlady had promised, the mattress felt new. But Aric's missing hand was clenched tight. He'd barely noticed the ache over the past several months—it was only an occasional, passing nuisance—but now it hurt as much as when he'd awoken in Hilma Gedding's bed and discovered that he was facing an abrupt change in his life. He tried to ignore the pain, or to imagine the ghostly hand slowly relaxing, but neither strategy worked. And Gray was next to him, tossing and turning restlessly.

"Is something wrong?" Aric finally whispered to him.

"I c-can't...." Gray sighed. "The fucking bed is too soft."

So Aric cuffed him gently on the shoulder and kissed his hair, then pushed him out of bed so he could drag the blankets down to the floor. Aric wrapped himself around Gray, then wrapped a blanket around both of them. Gray made a happy little sound and fell immediately to sleep, and Aric was not far behind him.

ARIC had become skilled at waking up when Gray's dream had barely begun. Maybe even in his sleep he could sense the tension in his lover's body. Aric was already smoothing Gray's skin and crooning in Gray's ear when the moaning began. Sometimes Gray would flail and kick during his nightmares, but now he was very, very still except for the rapid movements of his chest. Aric could feel Gray's heart beating frantically, like a bird in a cage.

"No," Gray breathed in a deep, hoarse voice. "Not yet."

"Shh," Aric said, although he knew it would do no good.

"Please keep him safe for me."

Aric's own heart tightened, and his stomach clenched.

"Please! Keep him free and happy." Gray uttered a terrible groan, like the sound of a timber giving under too much weight. Then he shuddered, and although Aric couldn't see him in the dark room, he could feel the tears that dampened Gray's stubbled cheeks. The tears wet Aric's face as he pressed their cheeks together.

"Ssh," Aric said again. He was proud of himself for keeping his voice soft and steady. "It's only a dream. I'm here holding you now, and I'm real."

Gray didn't say anything else. He shuddered again, this time so violently Aric almost lost his grip, and his throat made an awful clicking sound. Then he went completely still.

Usually Gray woke up within minutes after a dream. Tonight was no exception—Aric could hear the slight change in his breathing and could feel the subtle shift in his muscles. But Gray didn't move and didn't say anything; he simply lay quietly in Aric's arms.

It was Aric who spoke first, his voice deep and hoarse in the darkened room. "It was only a dream."

"Y-you never told me your missing h-hand aches."

"Gray—"

"Your hand aches, and you h-have a little t-twinge in your hips. Did you hurt them once?"

"When I fell, rescuing the prince. The healer took care of it."

"N-not completely. If I were more skilled, I c-could make the pain go away."

Aric squeezed him. "You do. All the time."

"B-but I can't...." Gray took a deep breath and let it out. "Aric, y-you're going to—"

"No!" Aric surprised even himself, his voice was so loud. More quietly but just as urgently he said, "No. Don't say it."

"F-fine."

Aric didn't want to know how he died. Who would want that sort of information hanging over his head? He'd seen what a man looked like when he faced the end, had seen the fear and resignation and despair on his father's face. If he had a day left, or a week or a month, he didn't want that knowledge weighing him down. But what Gray had said during the dream—what *Aric* had said during the dream. It was too early in their escape, and Gray wasn't yet safe. Aric had to know so he could make sure he got Gray to safety. "How?" he asked into Gray's soft hair.

"I'm s-sorry. If I could take it b-back, undream it somehow...."

"I know. Tell me, Gray. Please."

Gray paused for a long time, slowly rubbing his own collarbone, and when he spoke, his voice was oddly strained. "The w-water. You're going to drown." Quick as a fish, Gray twisted in Aric's arms so that they were facing one another. He spoke quickly, urgently, without a stammer. "Forget the fucking Vale. We'll go inland, far from the sea."

"And far from rivers?"

"Of course!"

"How about lakes? And ponds? And inns with bathtubs? How about horse troughs and wells and buckets? Gray, I can't escape water forever."

Gray made an inarticulate and frustrated sound. "But you c-can't just keep holding your course."

"Why not? Maybe we head deep into the forest and I drown in a mud puddle." He surprised both of them by laughing. "I almost drowned once before, but I survived. Maybe the gods had something in mind for me. Maybe they wanted me to set you free. Or maybe—I don't know. Maybe it's all one big joke, and this is how the gods stay entertained. I'm not nearly smart enough to second-guess them. I'm just going to have to do what I think is best and hope it turns out."

"And if it doesn't? If y-you die tomorrow?"

"Then I'll consider myself lucky to have had the last year. I made friends, Gray. Real friends. And I felt... welcomed. I had adventures! And gods, I met you." Aric bumped their foreheads together hard enough to hurt. "I met you."

"Stubborn b-bastard!"

"I am," Aric said almost happily. He was more than a strong back—he had a resolute mind. That was another change the past year had wrought.

And Gray couldn't very well argue with that, so he didn't try. Instead, he surprised Aric with more of his soft kisses. They made love for the second time that evening, then fell asleep, and this time, neither of them dreamed.

 # CHAPTER
Twenty-Two

THE morning light was still soft and tentative when they went downstairs, but the landlady was already awake. Aric could smell bread baking, and his mouth watered hopefully.

"Were you comfortable?" she asked them. "Was the bed good enough?"

Aric smiled. "It was perfect." He'd dismantled their nest on the floor and replaced the blankets on the mattress before they left. He didn't want to worry the proprietress of the Four Wolves, making her question the comfort of her accommodations.

She nodded. "Breakfast will be ready in an hour. We've ham steaks this morning and thick porridge, and—"

"We can't stay. Is there something we could take with us now?"

She sniffed in evident disapproval of people who didn't sit down to proper meals, but then she bustled away into the kitchen. She returned a few minutes later with a fabric-wrapped parcel. "It's yesterday's bread. Today's is still in the oven. And some cheese and dried currants. I hope that will do."

"Thank you," Aric said, and Gray gave one of those bows that would have looked stupid if Aric attempted it, but managed to look graceful and elegant for Gray. Then they set out into a city that was just waking up.

The streets of Racinas were packed dirt rather than cobbles. Aric nudged his companion's shoulder. "Are your feet all right? I imagine there won't be any pavement between here and the Vale."

"No, there w-won't, but I'm fine. Feels good, actually."

Aric had to take him at his word because it was too early to find a shoemaker. The air was a bit chilly, but that wasn't why Aric kept his cloak wrapped tightly about him. He did it because the cloak felt like a sort of armor. He knew there was no logic to that notion—armor wouldn't help him if he was going to drown—but it helped settle his mind. In fact, he found himself surprisingly undisturbed by the news of his impending death. For a year now, he'd been expecting Gray to dream about him, and he meant what he'd said to Gray the previous night. It had a very good year, far better than he'd ever have dreamed possible. The only painful part had been Gray's captivity, and now that was over. Aric's only remaining worry was ridding Gray of his dreams and ensuring that he stayed free and secure.

And it was those goals that Aric considered as he led Gray through Racinas. He was also considering a change of plan. His original idea had been to visit the Vale and then see if he could arrange transport to the west. He'd read in a library book that there was a road through the forest—rough but passable, except in winter—that skirted the northern edge of the kingdom and eventually led to Freanas, the small and fairly isolated kingdom to the northwest. He had some silver left, which would probably last them a while if he was careful. And after that... well, he'd hoped that he'd be able to find some way to support them both.

Of course, that idea had been based on the assumption that Gray would want to stay with him once the nightmares were gone and the crown was no longer in pursuit. But maybe Gray would have had enough of Aric by then. If that was the case, Aric's heart would break, but he'd understand. And before he left he'd make sure Gray had someplace comfortable to live and some way to bring bread to the table, because until he managed those things, Gray was still his charge.

But now there was the dream, which threw everything into question. If Aric did change course as Gray had suggested, would that avert his death? Or would the new course be the route that led him to disaster? It was too confusing to think about, and as they neared the outskirts of town, Aric decided to just let it be. He would do his best and accept whatever fate the gods gave him.

And then a wicked thought struck him. If he was meant to die anyway, why not take advantage of that fact?

"S-slow down! I can't keep up with your long l-legs."

Aric hadn't realized he'd hurried his pace; he made the effort to ease up. "Sorry. I was distracted."

"Wh-what are we passing now? It sounds quieter."

Aric hadn't really been paying much attention to their surroundings, and now he took a look around. "We're still on the main street. That's the right way, isn't it?"

"Yes. Straight from the h-harbor and through the c-city. The locals say Ebra herself m-made the road, after her husband Ismundo cured her in the Vale. She l-led him to the sea and to a sh-ship made of ice, and they sailed together to the heavens."

"I'd forgotten that part of the story."

Gray smiled. "There's m-more. The other gods wouldn't let Ismundo in because he was only human. So Ebra g-gave him half her immortality."

"What would someone do with half immortality?"

"L-live a very, v-very long time," Gray answered with a chuckle.

"But if Ebra gave him half, does that mean she'd die someday? Gods aren't supposed to die."

"I suppose she decided it's b-better to live a shorter time with someone you love than l-live forever without him."

"Oh," Aric said. He could understand that. He pulled his left arm just slightly closer to his body, so that more of Gray was touching him. "There are mostly just houses here. Wood houses with painted trim and little gardens in front. They're pretty."

"I remember. It's a p-pretty town. I w-wanted more excitement when I was a boy, but afterward I th-thought it would have been a nice place to live."

For a brief moment, Aric entertained a happy vision of sharing one of the neat little houses with Gray—maybe that one over there, with the fancy red scrollwork under the windows and the little grape arbor off to the side. Gray would get used to sleeping on a mattress again, and Aric would have a bath installed somewhere. Aric would find some way to make a living; his missing hand would be less of a handicap now that he could read. Gray could spend every day out of doors, charming the neighbors, learning his way around Racinas as well as he'd once known his cell. And Gray would sleep every night through, his only dreams sweet ones.

It seemed like so little to want.

"Do you think the king's men are far behind us?" Aric asked, even though he didn't want to.

"D-don't know. People will have seen us walking to the docks and boarding the *Ouragan*."

Aric sighed. "I wish I was a little less conspicuous."

"Nothing to be done about it. When they learned we were on the *Ouragan* they'll have kn-known we were bound for Racinas. They'll likely have f-followed in one of the royal caravels."

"Is that bad?" Aric had been too sick to pick up any nautical knowledge during the journey from Tellomer.

"They're f-faster than the *Ouragan*."

Aric tried to comfort himself with the thought that he and Gray had probably had many hours' head start—the *Ouragan* had sailed before noon, and Gray's absence likely hadn't been noticed until well after dinner. And even then, it might have taken the guards some time to trace the escape route. But he couldn't help glance behind them, half expecting to see men in scarlet-and-cream uniforms running up the street.

But no pursuers appeared, at least not yet. The houses gradually became more widely scattered, with the gardens around them looking more like small farms. People were digging at the soil, pulling up weeds, and planting seeds. They gave Aric and Gray mildly curious glances, but nothing more. Doubtless they were accustomed to desperate-looking types on the way to beg favors at the Vale. Aric noticed that the rumors he'd heard seemed to be true: the residents of Racinas were very attractive, with the same broad, sharp cheekbones and sunshine-colored hair as Gray and Petrus the whore. He wondered where Gray's mother had lived and what her family had been like. Were some of Gray's relatives still in the city?

The road began to rise, gently but surely, and the farms looked more like grassy meadows. Sheep grazed on the spring grass, and lambs gamboled amongst the ewes. If he had been born a sheep, Aric thought that this would be a good place for it.

But then the fields began to disappear, replaced by fir trees—first small and scattered, but as the road continued to ascend, the trunks grew thicker and taller and closer together. Finally the sun reached the travelers in only isolated splotches. Gray inhaled deeply. "Smells lovely, d-doesn't it?"

It did. No coal smoke, no animal or human waste, no rubbish or sweat. The sounds were different too. None of Tellomer's raucous chaos, and not even the constant, busy babble of Aric's home village. The air seemed hushed, so that the sounds of their footsteps and breathing and the twittering of birds up above echoed much more loudly than usual. Aric wondered if the logs he'd wrestled with back in his village, the timbers being used to build the bridge, came from this place.

"C-could we rest?" Gray asked after a while. "Sorry. It's b-been a long time since I've moved so much."

Aric immediately felt guilty and led him to a fallen tree a few feet from the road. "Sit here. Gods, Gray, I'm sorry. I wasn't thinking. We haven't even eaten and—"

"It's fine, Ar. Y-you can't think of everything all the time. You sit too, and let's have a l-late breakfast."

They shared the cheese and currants and the bread—still good, even if a day old—and drank ale from a tin flask. It wasn't a fancy breakfast, but it was enough to fill their bellies. After a few more minutes of sitting, they resumed their walking with renewed energy.

"I've never seen a forest before," Aric said. "I didn't realize trees were so big. Even I feel tiny next to them. I bet we could hide out here and nobody would ever find us."

"And y-you're an expert at hunting? Because I'm guessing my aim w-would be a little off." Gray sounded amused at the idea.

"I've never killed anything in my life."

"My g-gentle giant," Gray laughed, pulling Aric to a halt on the path and tugging his head down by the hair, giving him a long and thorough kiss.

THEY stopped briefly twice more, and Gray continued to seem in high spirits. But then Aric's stomach began to rumble demandingly, and he noticed that Gray was slightly favoring his right foot. Aric was feeling caught between the urge to pick up the pace and the desire to protect his lover from harm when they came to a small clearing.

Aric halted. "There's a funny sort of building here."

"G-good! It was built long ago for pilgrims. There may even be food. The priests at the V-vale tend to it now and then."

The rough-hewn log building was about eight feet square, and the entry was simply a low, uncovered opening that forced Aric to duck to get inside. There were no windows, but spaces between the logs allowed dusty filtered light into the structure. Furnishings consisted of a wonky table, two wobbly benches that could serve as narrow beds, and a shelf containing some wax-sealed clay jars. Aric opened a few and assessed the contents: dried meat, some sort of biscuit the consistency of thin bricks, and mushy fruit floating in fermented juice.

"Not much of a meal, but I guess it'll do," he said, handing Gray a chunk of meat.

"There's a little stream v-very close, if you want to fetch us some water."

"All right. I'll try not to drown in it."

Gray made a very strange face and then nodded.

Aric took the tin flask with him. He cocked his head when he stepped out of the hut and then followed the sound of muted trickling, away from the road and behind some bushes. It was a very shallow creek. He probably couldn't have drowned in it if he'd tried. But it was enough to slake his thirst and fill the container for Gray.

"Do they get a lot of pilgrims this way?" he asked when he reentered the hut.

Gray took a gulp of water. "I'm not sure. I think quite a f-few people visit just to see the Vale and pay their respect to the gods. Most don't ask for a g-gift. They don't want to pay the p-price. Only the foolish ones d-do that."

"You're no fool. You were in love."

Gray's smile was slow and warm, and he reached over to touch Aric's arm. "I had no fucking idea what real love is."

"And you do now?" Aric knew it was stupid, but he was greedy for just a little reassurance.

"Gods, yes! Ismundo didn't love Ebra any m-more than I love you."

Aric snorted. "First I was a statue of a giant who moved rivers, and now I'm a goddess?"

"N-not exactly." Gray's hand moved down to pat Aric's groin.

Aric had another of those quick visions. This one involved tearing every shred of clothing off Gray, dragging him out into the soft greenery and fallen needles outside the hut's entrance, and rutting until Aric was as blind as Gray was. It was a very tempting idea. It was also impossible. The king's men could show up any moment, and in any case, Aric wanted to reach the Vale before sunset.

Gray was still limping a little when they set off again, but he refused to talk about it or allow Aric to take a look at his foot. "It's n-nothing. Just a little sore."

The trees continued endlessly until it seemed to Aric as if they'd been in the forest forever. There were no real landmarks, and if they had come upon even a single crossroad or alternate pathway, he would have suspected that they were wandering in circles. But then they came to another clearing, this one much larger, with a two-story building that was considerably more elaborate than the hut where they'd lunched. It was decrepit, however, the front door hanging unevenly and the roof sagging under years of moss and leaves and branches.

"What's this place?" Aric asked.

"It was an inn. Closed n-not long before I was here last. Too little trade, I guess."

Aric grunted in response. But what he was actually thinking was how the place looked like it had been abandoned a very long time ago. And for all those years that it had been accumulating debris and falling apart, Gray had been chained in a tiny cell, naked and cold and starved.

Maybe these thoughts occurred to Gray as well, even though he couldn't see the structure, because he had an uneasy look on his face and was tugging Aric along. "Come on. It's g-getting late, isn't it? I can feel the air cooling."

He was right, and Aric led them on.

Only a short time later, he realized that the road had begun to slope downward. It was a very gentle slope and the trees were still thick, so he couldn't see what lay ahead of them, but he suspected they were approaching the Vale, and he hastened their pace. Gray had to make a bit of an effort to keep up, but he didn't complain and Aric didn't slow. The road rose again, very briefly, and then dropped quite steeply out of the trees—and finally Aric could see the Vale.

It was actually a long, broad valley, with more wooded hills rising up on the other side. The valley itself was green but bare of trees, except for those ringing a small blue lake. It was shaped a little like a fish, he thought: fat and round on one end and tapering to a sort of tail on the other. This was the place he had been thinking about for months, the place that had ruined Gray and, indirectly, changed Aric's life forever. It didn't look impressive enough to cause such transformations.

The sun was beginning to sink low on the horizon, so he continued to walk quickly downhill, almost dragging Gray alongside. A few low buildings were scattered not far from the pond, and it was to those that the road seemed to lead. It didn't take long to reach them, and as Aric and Gray approached, three priests in faded purple robes came out to meet them. The oldest was quite ancient and wizened, and he gave Gray a slightly startled look that made Aric wonder if the priest recognized him. The other two were younger, one of them short and plump and the second of about average height and very handsome.

"Greetings," said the oldest priest. "I hope your journey to the Vale was a pleasant one."

Gray surprised Aric by giving the priest one of his bows. "Th-thank you. We've come a long way."

"Please, follow us and join us for our evening meal. Then we will prepare some beds for you for tonight. Our quarters here are simple, but most pilgrims find them pleasant."

"No," Aric said. "Um, I mean, no thank you. Not yet anyway. We'd like… we have a request for the gods."

The younger priests' polite smiles disappeared, and their faces became grave. The oldest one just looked sad. "You understand there is a price, and it is always a dear one."

It was Gray who answered. "I know."

"Perhaps you would wait until morning, then. Consider your decision just a bit longer."

"We've d-decided, sir. And we haven't t-time to spare."

The priests exchanged glances, and then the oldest one shrugged. "Very well. A purification ritual must be performed before you may approach the pool. Kashta will attend to you."

As it turned out, Kashta was the handsome priest, a man in his early twenties with unruly brown hair and warm brown eyes. He took them to one of the little buildings, a structure not much more complicated than the hut in which they'd rested earlier in the day. But long sticks of incense burned in this place, as did several huge candles. There was a washstand that held a silver pitcher and an ornately decorated basin. Several shelves hung on the wall; some were bare and some contained little pots and jars.

"Please," Kashta said when they were inside. "Remove your clothing." He had a strange accent with a sort of liquidity that Aric found soothing. He watched as the priest closed a panel of bright fabric over the doorway, and then Aric turned to Gray. "Do you need help?"

"I think I c-can manage to strip by myself, thank you," Gray replied with a smile. He began to unfasten the buttons of his shirt, but Aric could see that his hands were trembling slightly. In fact, Aric's own hand was none too steady as he worked at the large button on his trousers. But eventually he and Gray stood bare on the wood floor of the hut, waiting. The scars from the shackles seemed very clear on Gray's body, but at least his bones were no longer prominent, and he stood very straight. As for Aric, it was the absence of the cloak that made him feel especially naked, which he knew was silly.

Without comment, Kashta took their clothing, folded it carefully, and set it on a shelf. He put Aric's satchel there as well. Then he padded over to the washstand and poured some water into the basin. "Please cleanse your face and hands."

Aric led Gray to the basin, but Gray lifted the corner of his mouth. "Let me wash you, Aric. P-please." It was a strangely intimate act to be performing in front of a stranger, but the priest didn't seem surprised or upset. He simply waited while Gray dabbed water over Aric's cheeks and brow, then took Aric's hand in both of his and dipped it in the basin.

"It's half the work with me," Aric joked.

"Is the m-missing hand still hurting?"

"No." It was a lie; it had been aching all day.

Gray probably sensed the untruth, because he made a face. But he didn't pursue the matter, instead tending to his own washing.

Then Kashta came forward with one of the little clay pots. He dipped his fingers inside, and they came out smeared with a greenish, leafy-smelling ointment. He mumbled some sort of blessing under his breath as he smeared the ointment on Aric's forehead, chest, belly, and—embarrassingly—his soft penis. Then the priest did the same to Gray, bringing a slight stab of jealousy to Aric at the sight of someone else touching his lover.

After the ointment, there were herbs to be sprinkled on their heads—Aric had to crouch for that part—then droplets of oil on their feet, and finally a nauseating-looking paste applied to their wrists. The two of them smelled, Aric thought, like an over-spiced dinner.

Kashta seemed satisfied, but he didn't return their clothing. Instead he took lengths of red silk and tied them around Aric's and Gray's loins like breechclouts. Aric had never worn silk before, and he liked the feeling of it against his skin. But that thought made him blush a little, and then blush even more when the handsome priest gave him a knowing wink.

"Follow me, please," said Kashta, leading them out of the hut and toward the ring of trees. The other priests weren't in sight, and when Aric took a nervous glance in the direction of the road, there were no hordes of soldiers either.

Kashta stopped just outside the trees. "I will not go any further. But the rest is simple. The supplicant must merely kneel before the pool and offer up his request to the gods, and then fill his hands with water for a drink. Only one handful," he added sternly, as if the visitors might be considering draining the entire pool.

Aric took Gray's hand in his and began the walk through the trees. His heart was fluttering in his chest and Gray's breathing sounded a bit labored, and the trees themselves grew more thickly than Aric had anticipated.

Which was perfect for what he had to do next.

Aric squeezed Gray's hand, mumbled a single word—"Sorry"— and let go. Then he began to run to the pool.

 # CHAPTER
Twenty-Three

"ARIC! *Aric!* Damn you, you idiot, get the fuck back here!"

As Aric dodged around trees and raced for the pool, he was hoping most vehemently that the gods wouldn't mind Gray's outburst in their sacred Vale. Really, the gods shouldn't fault Gray for it, Aric thought. Of course Gray was upset. Aric had deliberately abandoned him amongst the maze of vegetation, leaving the blind man to stumble around as he helplessly tried to feel his way to the water.

Naturally, Aric got there first.

He remembered Gray's dream about drowning, but such a fate seemed pretty unlikely at the moment, and he didn't have the luxury of caring. He threw himself onto his knees at the grassy edge of the pool, and, ignoring the continued swearing and increasingly incensed shouting coming from the trees, he lifted his eyes to the heavens. He didn't have the pretty words Gray would have; Gray probably would have made a poem out of his plea. Aric just had to hope the gods didn't mind his plain language.

"Please. Gray Leynham, he made a mistake all those years ago. He was really only a boy. And he's suffered so much for it. Please, please take your gift back. Take away his Sight. I'll pay whatever price you want. Take my other hand, take my life, take…. I give you everything I have. Just please do this for Gray."

Gray was still swearing furiously, and with Aric's voice as a guide, he was coming closer.

With only one hand, Aric couldn't make a very good cup to hold the water from the pool. But his hand was a big one, and he was able to scoop a mouthful of liquid into his palm. The water tasted oddly salty and metallic—like blood, in fact. And although it was cool inside his mouth, it burned like fire as it traveled down his throat. Perhaps it was only his imagination, but he thought he could feel it filling his body and running through his veins. He didn't hear a godly voice, yet there was a sort of echo, as if someone had just spoken. Deep in his heart, Aric knew to a certainty that his plea had been granted.

And then Gray was falling against him, sending them both tumbling to the ground. Gray ended up straddled across Aric's torso, hitting him with open hands. It hurt, and Aric could easily have dislodged him, but he didn't even try.

"You *bastard*!" Gray yelled. Tears of rage ran down his face, which had gone an alarming red. "You lying, sneaking bastard! How dare you! That was my fucking problem to fix, not yours. Gods, Aric, not yours. You're a damned hero, not... not an asshole who ruins his life." He continued on in that vein for some time, until his blows grew weaker and his angry words faded away. Then he simply sat on Aric's stomach with his head bowed and hands curled into fists.

Aric didn't move. He was probably a little bruised. Anyway, he didn't really mind lying there: the ground was as soft as any mattress, and the silk of Gray's breechclout felt nice against his skin. Who knew how much longer he would have before the gods took their payment. He'd offered them everything, and he was still willing to give it. "You're not stuttering," he observed quietly.

Gray's answer was equally soft. "I felt it go. My gift, I mean. It was like... like a candle being blown out." He suddenly collapsed forward so that he was draped across Aric's sore chest. "Have you been planning this all along?"

"More or less."

"*Why*, Aric? You've seen what begging from the gods did to me. Why would you bring something like that on yourself?"

The answer was simple. "Because I love you."

When Gray sighed, his breath tickled the hairs on Aric's chest. "Idiot. I don't deserve that kind of love. What have I ever done for you?"

"You made me feel like someone cared about me," Aric answered, and then felt a little ashamed. He truly was an idiot. "Look, you don't have to…. You don't owe me anything. We'll get you somewhere safe and find a way for you to live, and if you don't want me, that's fine, I'll—"

"It's damned well *not* fine! I have you, Aric, and I'd fight the gods themselves before I'd give you up."

Aric was somewhat glad that Gray couldn't see the goofy grin that spread across his face. But then Gray was nuzzling at his neck, and Aric was suddenly acutely aware of the fact that they were both nearly naked. "Um… I'm not sure if a sacred pool is the right place for this."

"Probably not." Gray scrambled off him and waited as Aric rose to his feet with a slight moan. "I'm not sorry I hit you. I haven't forgiven you yet."

Aric decided he could bear Gray's anger under the circumstances. "Let's go. The sun's setting, and we need to find someplace to sleep."

Gray took Aric's arm. "The priests will let us stay here for the night."

"But if the king's men come—"

"Aric, there's nothing for miles and miles but trees. Do you want to try traveling through the forest in the dark?"

Aric didn't. It was bad enough one of them couldn't see. So in the thickening twilight he took Gray back through the ring of trees, to where Kashta was waiting with his arms crossed on his chest. "It sounded like you were killing one another! Have you any idea how that would desecrate this holy place?"

"We're both alive," Gray answered. "But my giant is an idiot. A *sneaky* idiot."

Kashta raised an eyebrow, and Aric thought he saw the corner of the priest's mouth twitch. "Oh. Well, I take it you have completed your supplication."

"Yes. Could we sleep here tonight?"

"Of course. We have a meal for you as well." He took them back toward the cluster of little buildings. There was still no sign of the other priests, but Aric could see smoke rising from two of the buildings and into the purple sky. The building they entered wasn't the one where they'd been purified, but it was roughly the same size. It contained nothing but two blanketed mats on opposite sides of the floor, three sconces with flickering candles, and a washstand with basin, jug, and towels.

"You may push the mats together if you prefer," Kashta said. His face definitely had the hint of a mischievous smile that time. "It is not luxurious, but I hope it will do."

Aric nodded at him. "It's fine. Thank you." It was certainly nicer than Gray's cell, and it was doubtless less vermin-infested than his old room at the White Dragon.

"Excellent. There is a latrine in back. Wait here, please, and I'll fetch your dinner."

Relieved that they wouldn't have to eat with the priests—Aric had no idea how to make conversation with them—he sat on one of the mats. Gray folded himself down beside him, just close enough that their knees touched. "I feel like I could sleep for a week," he said with a yawn. "I haven't really slept soundly since... well, since the last time I was here."

"Now you can."

Gray nudged him hard. "Except now I'll be worrying about you."

"I can take care of myself." He always had.

"At least the gods didn't take your voice. I can't imagine how we'd communicate if you had my stammer."

"We'd find some way, I suppose."

They were still mulling that over—or perhaps thinking about what the gods would take instead—when Kashta reentered the hut, a bit overladen. He had a big covered bowl in his hands, Aric's and Gray's clothing tucked under one arm, Aric's boots shoved under the other arm, and the satchel hanging a little precariously from one shoulder. "I thought maybe you might like to get dressed again eventually," he said with a grin. Somehow he managed to set down the bowl in front of them and put their belongings neatly in one corner, all without spilling or dropping a thing.

Whatever was in the bowl smelled wonderful, and Aric's stomach growled loud enough to make both of the others chuckle. Gray reached out, trying to find the lid, but Aric's conscience prickled and he grabbed Gray's wrist.

"Um," Aric began, looking up at the smiling priest. "You've been very kind to us."

Kashta shrugged. "This is why I am here."

"But… I think I have to tell you something."

"I am a priest. You may admit anything to me."

Gray pulled his wrist away and set his palm on Aric's thigh. "It's not that kind of confession."

Kashta still didn't look alarmed, although he did have his head cocked slightly with interest.

Aric took a deep breath. "There might be—there probably is someone chasing us. The king's soldiers. We're fugitives, I guess."

"Did you do something so terrible?"

"No. I… I stole Gray. He was a prisoner."

"Ah." The priest's handsome face remained serene. "And today you did not ask the gods to do something awful to the men who are chasing you, so that you might get away?"

Aric was shocked at the very thought. "Of course not! We don't want to hurt them. I'm sure they think they're doing the right thing."

Kashta nodded. "I see. The Vale is a sanctuary. No person who has entered this place may be lawfully harmed or taken by force, not even by the king's men. At least, not so long as the person remains within the Vale."

Warm relief washed through Aric's body. "But won't you get in trouble for letting us stay?"

"No. Our calling and function is to welcome pilgrims and to assist them in their visit. It is not our place to choose who may enter. After all, some come to the Vale to ask the gods forgiveness or to atone for their wrongs. We cannot turn away anyone who wishes to come here, and the king is well aware of this." He gave a very slight bow. "But I thank you for your concern. Now, eat before your food is cold, and then sleep. In the morning we can discuss your options."

Aric liked that, the idea of having options. It seemed as if he'd had very few before. But even as he relaxed his shoulders, he was hit by a sudden insight, and he knew what he had to do. He winced a little, which made Kashta frown. "Are you well, sir?"

"Just tired. And a little sore."

"Very well. Enjoy your meal. Good night." The priest left, allowing the fabric over the hut's opening to fall closed behind him.

The bowl proved to contain a very generous helping of something that looked a little like Gray's mush but tasted much, much better. Two spoons had been provided, but Gray seemed to be amused by feeding Aric himself. His aim wasn't perfect, and some of the food ended up on Aric's chin or cheeks instead, but Gray licked it off. By the time their meal was finished, both men had erections visible through the thin silk fabric of their breechclouts.

"Is it disrespectful to have sex here, do you think?" Aric asked as he cleared the bowl away.

"If it were, I don't think the priest would have given permission to push the mats together. I'm pretty certain he knows what we are to one another."

"Good." But getting ready for bed seemed to take forever. Aric led them to the latrine and then back to the hut. He moved the mats and, almost reverently, untwisted the silk from around Gray's hips. He wasn't sure what to do with the length of fabric, so he ended up folding it and setting it aside. Then he pushed Gray gently into a sitting position on the nearer mat and used a dampened bit of one of the worn, soft towels to clean him: his face and hands first and then his feet, which looked a little red and slightly blistered, but not too bad overall. He took his comb out of the satchel and untangled Gray's hair. He considered shaving him as well, but Gray was beginning to slump with exhaustion, so he skipped it. His own ablutions went much more quickly. When his strip of silk was folded as well, he maneuvered Gray into place on the mats and lay down beside him.

Before Aric met Gray, he had known only one kind of sex: the fast and businesslike kind with the boy whores of Tellomer. Over the past several months, however, he'd learned that there were as many flavors to the physical act as there were spices in the royal kitchens—a thousand ways two bodies could fit together, with movements urgent or sleepy, playful or demanding, rough as splintered wood or soft as silk. It was a revelation to him still.

Tonight's lovemaking was bittersweet, Gray's earlier anger still putting an edge to things, but their mutual awareness of a price to be paid making them savor every moment as if it were the last. Their completions came in long sighs rather than shouts, and when it was over, Aric found himself feeling empty and full at the same time.

They kissed tenderly, lazily, and stroked at sensitized flesh until they finally fell still in one another's arms.

A SOFT rain had begun to fall while they slept. It was hardly more than a mist, but Aric was still grateful for his boots and cloak. He looked back from the doorway of the little hut, just barely able to make out the shape of his lover sleeping under the woolen blanket. He wished he had paper and ink so that he could write Gray a letter. Surely one of the priests would be able to read it to him. *Stay here*, the letter would say. *Stay safe. The priests will give you sanctuary and find you work to do, and the Vale will be a pleasant place to live. I love you, Gray Leynham. Be well.*

But there was no paper and ink. So Aric left all he had: his satchel with his extra clothes, the leather purse that still contained silver coins, and his lover in a deep and dreamless sleep.

 # CHAPTER
Twenty-Four

NO MOON was visible to light Aric's way, but he found the road with only a little difficulty, and from there it was only a matter of keeping his feet on the hard-packed dirt and climbing back up the slope. Soon the forest had closed around him again. He'd never been in such complete darkness before, never been so entirely alone. He drew the cloak around himself and began to hum, but the sound of it only seemed to emphasize the misty silence, and he soon stopped.

He chided himself for feeling lonely. He'd spent well over two decades without companionship, and he should have been familiar with the feeling. But over the past months, he'd become accustomed to Gray's presence. Even early on, when Gray was mostly silent and they very rarely touched, Aric had known that Gray was there, listening in the darkness. Now he felt as if a piece of himself had been torn away, something important that would slowly kill him by its loss. Or not so slowly, perhaps.

He didn't have a particular destination in mind. He just figured he'd walk until he met up with the king's men—and if he didn't find them by the time he got back to Racinas, he'd just wait for them at the harbor. They should reward him for saving them part of the journey, he thought wryly.

But the drizzle became a shower, and the shower became a pelting rain, and even the thick branches overhead didn't give him much protection from the downpour. His joke to Gray about drowning in a puddle suddenly seemed less impossible. To make matters worse, he'd begun the long descent back toward the sea—thunder rumbling over the din of the rain—and his footing grew treacherous on the slick mud of the roadway. So when he came to the clearing with the decrepit former inn, he decided that he'd try to wait out the weather with a roof over his head.

It wasn't until he entered the building that he realized how little roof there really was, the holes illuminated by occasional flashes of lightning. The forest had been eager to reclaim its territory, and the structure was barely holding together. Standing in what once must have been the inn's public room, he could look up through gaping holes in the ceiling and catch glimpses of the rooms above. The amount of rain that was falling onto his head told him that those rooms had little in the way of intact ceilings either. Fallen timbers and pieces of broken furniture lay littered about, and everything was strewn with broken boughs, moldering leaves, and birds' nests. The entire building looked as if it might fall down with one good gust of wind. It was a forlorn place where ghosts seemed to hover just out of sight, and if it hadn't been raining so very hard he would have turned around and gone back outside.

Aric moved as carefully as possible, seeking a relatively dry and clean spot to lie down. He didn't want his clumsy, oversized body to knock against one of the rotted support pillars that were barely keeping the structure upright. He found a place in one corner where part of the upper floor had completely collapsed, forming a sort of cave of rubble. Spider webs clung to his face, and he just barely fit inside. It wasn't until he'd crawled in with the cloak hunched around him that he caught a pungent animal smell and realized that other creatures might have sought shelter here as well. Luckily, nothing came growling out of the night to contest its den.

He wrapped the cloak around himself as tightly as possible and lay down. Although he'd grown used to sleeping on floors, he wasn't remotely comfortable. Maybe it was because this was the first time in many months that he was sleeping with empty arms.

The rain stopped, and exhaustion caught up with him. He drifted into a restless sleep, hearing the wind whenever he came near wakefulness, but too tired to care.

SUNLIGHT, pouring through the building's holes, awakened him. He crawled out of his makeshift den, stretched unhappily, and scratched at his stubbled cheeks. His muscles—sore from Gray's pummeling as well as the hard floor—protested every movement, and as usual, his stomach was quick to remind him that it was empty.

But the morning was warm and breezy, and birds were singing. He wondered what Gray was doing just then. Had one of the priests helped him find his way to the latrine and given him breakfast? Was he still raging over his abandonment, or had he realized already that Aric's departure was the best choice? Even now, was he considering flirting with Kashta, who Aric was pretty certain would not be averse to the idea?

Aric glowered, first at the idea of Gray finding another lover, and then at himself for being so petty. He wanted Gray to be happy, and he wanted someone to look after him. Whatever claims Aric had tentatively had on Gray Leynham were now null and void.

"Stop it!" he said out loud, as fiercely as he could. He should have known better these past months—a brute like him had no happy endings ahead of him, no life filled with love. He never should have even dreamed of it.

Brute left the building and stood in the clearing. The sky was cloudless, and the sun was high. The gentle wind moved the hem of his cloak and made a soft sound through the trees. He'd slept much later than he'd intended, but he took time to wander around to the back of the building. Weeds and saplings had taken over a courtyard, and a stable was completely in ruins, but there was a cistern with a tin cup attached to a rusty chain. He filled the cup and drank it down three times, hoping to placate his hunger a little bit. Then he emptied his bladder against a tree, drank some more water, and returned to the front of the building.

He decided he wouldn't walk to Racinas that day. Despite his late awakening, he was weary. He found himself an almost dry spot on the inn's sagging porch, then sat up against the wall and tried not to think at all. It was a surprisingly difficult task for a stupid man like him, and in the end, he sang to himself instead. Not his mother's lullabies, but the bawdy songs he'd heard at the White Dragon, the boastful chants the palace guards liked to bellow, the sprightly tunes that the sailors on the *Ouragan* had sung. His voice boomed across the clearing, as hoarse and off-key as always.

So it was that he didn't hear the men until they were nearly upon him. In fact, he barely had time to scramble to his feet when an arrow came flying at him and shot into his left shoulder. He shouted with pain and surprise and yanked the arrow out. Another came at him, missing him by inches and thudding into the wooden wall.

"Stop!" bellowed a voice. "Dammit, stop shooting him!"

Brute growled at the approaching soldiers but didn't move. The soldiers wore light armor with ornaments in scarlet and cream. There were eight of them, six still on their horses and two already dismounted. One of those was the archer, who held his bow at the ready but didn't let loose another arrow. Brute didn't recognize the soldiers. They looked more hardened than the guards he'd known at the palace, and they stared at him with disgust.

But Brute did recognize two of the mounted men. One of them was very small, his clothing meticulously neat despite his travels. And the other was tall, with yellow hair and a matching beard.

"Your Highness," Brute said through teeth gritted against the pain. "Lord Maudit."

It was Prince Aldfrid who spoke, and his voice was softer than Brute expected. "Where is he? What have you done with the prisoner?"

Brute shook his head. "He's safe. But I'm here. Take me. Punish me in his place."

Lord Maudit started to say something, but the prince held up a hand to silence him. "It doesn't work like that, Brute. You can't pay for what he did." He enunciated every word very slowly and carefully, as if speaking to a small child.

"He's paid enough. He's suffered for years, and nothing you do to him will change the past. His misery won't bring back your mother."

Prince Aldfrid flinched and had to look away for a moment. When he looked back, his eyes were full of sorrow. "This wasn't.... I shouldn't have involved you in this. You're a good man, aren't you?"

"I'm a monster. You can see for yourself. Take me back to Tellomer and do what you want with me. I'm sure the crowds will be pleased to see a monster beaten and bloodied. Everyone will think how brave you are, how strong, and nobody will care that a man they've largely forgotten has escaped his chains."

The prince hopped gracefully off his horse and walked toward Brute. "I wish... I wish I could just let him go. I do. I loved him once." He glanced back at Lord Maudit, who was glaring furiously at him. "If it were my choice, he'd have been free long ago. But my father—"

"Did you even try to stand up to your father? You say you loved Gray, but you've gone on with your merry life knowing that he was in torment just a few minutes' walk from your rooms." Brute couldn't believe he was speaking to a prince like this, but his shoulder burned and he was tired and angry, and he had nothing left to lose. "If someone I loved was suffering like that, I'd spend every minute of every day doing whatever I could to free him."

"I did," the prince said in a whisper.

"No. *I* did."

Prince Aldfrid's face crumpled, and for a moment, Brute was certain the man was going to cry. But then his chin firmed. "I am the king's son. I have more obligation than anyone to obey the law. Tell me where he is, Brute. You saved my life once, and I know you meant well with Gray. I'll beg my father to be lenient with you."

"I don't fucking care what you do to me!" Brute roared. The soldiers touched the hilts of their swords nervously, and the archer raised his bow. Brute ignored them all. "I won't let you put him back in that cell!"

The prince stood there staring wordlessly, and for a brief second, Brute entertained the wild hope that he'd order his men to turn around and sail back to Tellomer. But then Lord Maudit hopped down from his horse with an oath. "This has gone on long enough," he spat. "I'll go look for Gray Leynham myself."

The soldiers continued to look uneasy, but nobody stopped the lord as he stomped past the prince and then onto the porch and, without even glancing at Brute, entered the inn. But he came out again in a minute, his face sharp with anger. "Can't see a damned thing in there. Get me a candle!"

It was unclear for whom his order was intended, and the soldiers exchanged looks. Then one of them fumbled in his horse's saddlebag and produced a taper, while another found a flint and tinder. Mindful of the breeze, they didn't try to light the taper immediately. Instead, giving Brute a very wide berth, the men joined Lord Maudit on the porch and, after a few tries, lit the wick.

As soon as Lord Maudit snatched the candle, the men scampered away, and no one followed him back into the building. The soldiers stood with their weapons at hand, Prince Aldfrid stared at Brute with a carefully expressionless face, and Brute tried to ignore the throbbing pain in his shoulder. Blood was soaking through his fine cloak, and he felt irrationally sad about that.

"I'm sorry," the prince finally said. "About the arrow. I think my men were scared of you."

"Of course they were. I'm a monster."

Prince Aldfrid shook his head. "I've known that wasn't true from the moment you climbed down that cliff to save me."

And Brute was struck with a sudden certainty, one that would have occurred to him much earlier if he wasn't so stupid. "You sent the key," he whispered.

After a long pause, the prince gave an almost imperceptible nod. In a voice that wouldn't carry to the soldiers behind him he said, "At first, I only knew that you were a good man. And brave. A man who had nothing much to lose, and who could probably be persuaded to come to the palace, and one who... who'd treat a prisoner well. I think... I think not all of the others have."

Brute remembered the bruises that had marred Gray's emaciated body when Brute had first arrived. "They haven't," he said.

Prince Aldfrid squeezed his eyes shut, as if he were the one in pain. When he opened them, he nodded again. "And I hoped you would stay with him for a while. It was all I could do for him."

Anger flared in Brute's chest. "You could have stood up to your father for him!"

"I did!" More quietly, the prince repeated, "I did. I yelled and argued and begged and.... My father's not a cruel man, but he's hard. Someone like me, one prince of many, I can afford to be soft. But a king can't. And my mother's death very nearly ruined him. My father wouldn't budge at all, and sending you was the most I could do."

Brute snorted. "Wasn't much, was it?"

"But it was. I heard what people said about you around the palace, the way they regarded you so well, and I knew you'd be treating Gray as well as anyone could. Not long after you arrived, I told the exchequer to send word to me if you withdrew all your money. I thought that would mean you intended to abandon your post, and maybe I could get to you first and dissuade you. But you never did."

"Until recently."

"Until recently," Prince Aldfrid confirmed. "I'd forgotten all about my orders to the exchequer by then, actually, but when he sent me a message...." He paused to run his fingers through his hair. "I hoped you were planning maybe something more than simply quitting."

Brute was feeling slightly light-headed, maybe from blood loss or maybe just from exhaustion. "If you helped me then, why are you here now? Why not just let us go?"

"Because the king sent Maud, not me. And I thought maybe if I came along for your capture...."

"Then what?"

The prince shrugged. "I'm not sure. I guess I hoped I could make things a little easier on both of you. Make sure you weren't hurt."

Brute looked down at his bloodstained cloak. "That went well, didn't it?"

"Dammit! You know, nothing much is ever expected of me, and that's what I give. I don't make decisions and plans, I don't think much about the consequences of my actions, and I'm a damned coward. I'm not brave like you."

Somewhat taken aback to hear an admission like that from a prince, Brute was silent for a moment. Then he sighed. "When you gave me the key, did you really expect we'd get away?"

"No. But... it was the ghost of a chance, I guess. And he's had at least a taste of freedom these past days, hasn't he? Isn't that something?" When Brute didn't answer, the prince cocked his head a little. "Why did you do it, Brute? Why risk so much for him?"

"I love him."

To Brute's surprise, Prince Aldfrid wasn't angry. In fact, he gave a sad little smile. "Good. I mean, despite everything, I'm glad he's had that at least. Gods, he was... he was special."

"He still is," Brute responded evenly.

They remained silent a while longer. Brute wished he could sit down for a bit. He was pretty sure the bleeding had stopped, or at least slowed down, but his entire left arm was wracked with pain, all the way from the fresh wound down to the nonexistent hand.

One of the horses snorted impatiently, startling both Brute and Aldfrid out of their thoughts. "Where is he?" Aldfrid asked gently.

"Sanctuary."

The prince frowned and opened his mouth, no doubt intending to demand clarification, but a tremendous crash came from the inn. Brute whirled around in time to see the inn's frame wobble a little, and then there was a second bang, louder than the first. "What the hell?" Aldfrid exclaimed, and as he began to move toward the building, a muffled and incoherent cry sounded from inside. "Maud!" There was a strange intensity in the way Aldfrid called the name.

At that moment, Brute realized several things. First, that something within the fragile structure had collapsed, most likely trapping or injuring Lord Maudit. Second, that the prince and the lord were lovers—another fact that should have been obvious long ago. And third, that the best course for everyone was for Brute to risk his life again.

As the prince ran toward the door, Brute put out his good arm and grabbed him. The soldiers, who were already very ill at ease, surged forward. "Let me," Brute said urgently. "You stay out here."

Prince Aldfrid looked up at him, wild-eyed. And then he gave a short nod and stepped back. "Stand down!" he roared at his men, then turned back to Brute and gave him a pleading look. "Brute...."

"I know. Just stay back."

The prince nodded again, but his head whipped up when he caught a whiff of the odor Brute had scented just a few seconds earlier. "Smoke! Oh gods, the candle!"

Brute didn't wait for more conversation. He ran into the structure, ducking to avoid a ceiling beam that sagged just inside the doorway. The entire interior had shifted, chunks of ceiling fallen to the floor and one of the interior walls toppled completely. Footing was treacherous, but he hurried as quickly as he could, the acrid smell of burning wood already filling the air. Smoke made both breathing and visibility difficult. Like the idiot he was, Brute made straight for the source of the smoke.

It was with considerable dismay that he saw flames licking at the beams overhead. Evidently the night winds and morning breezes had destabilized the building and dried some of the timbers. *Flames overhead.* He realized that Lord Maudit was on the second floor. "Sir?" he called. "Your Excellency?"

He was answered with an urgent groan.

Even before the wind and the fire, Brute would not have chanced going upstairs. He hadn't been at all sure the floor would support his weight. Now, of course, he was fairly certain it wouldn't. But he didn't see any other options, apart from endangering the prince and soldiers or allowing a man to burn to death. Swearing out loud at his own stupidity, Brute backtracked until he found the stairs.

The staircase had certainly been sturdy and well made originally, but time and weather and insects had warped and cracked the wood, splitting the treads and risers and sending the frame out of true. Brute felt them wobble alarmingly with every step he took, yet he rushed upward anyway. The stairway didn't collapse until he was nearly at the top, and he was just barely able to swing his arms forward—yelping at the fresh pain—and haul himself up onto the floor above. Assuming he survived, he'd need to find another way down.

"Lord Maudit?" he yelled.

The answering sound was weaker than the first, and it came from somewhere down the hallway to his left. Taking care to avoid the holes in the floor, and keeping as much as possible to the edges of the hallway where he hoped the structure was strongest, Brute ran. The smoke became so thick that it blinded him almost completely, and every breath became a choking cough. He could feel the heat of the fire even before he turned the corner; the flames roared like a living beast.

Brute climbed over a giant beam and crawled under another one, and that's when he saw a man's head and torso sticking out from beneath a pile of timber and plaster. The man was trying to scream but couldn't seem to fill his lungs properly, and his hands scrabbled uselessly at the floor.

Brute dove forward. He couldn't lift the debris one-handed, so he was forced to put his shoulders underneath and push upward. He dimly felt the arrow wound reopen but didn't register the pain. He was too busy putting all his strength into his task—a strength that had carried boulders and heaved logs, that had pulled wagons and carts, that had rescued a prince and freed a prisoner. It was a giant's strength.

The wreckage shifted. Not much, mere inches. But it was enough to loosen Lord Maudit, and Brute used his foot to shove the man out of the way. As soon as Maudit was free, Brute allowed the load to slip from his back, which made the entire building shudder warningly.

He couldn't tell how badly Lord Maudit was hurt, but the man wasn't making any effort to move. Brute scooped him up and threw him over his wounded shoulder, very glad that Maudit was a small man.

Getting back down the hallway was no small task, with the smoke roiling and fire burning, and his lungs and his left arm protesting every movement. Brute had to avoid the obstacles without causing further damage to himself, Lord Maudit, or the building, and he had to sidestep the holes in the floor, praying everything would hold under their combined weight. He passed the collapsed stairway, which was now nothing more than a hole, and moved as quickly as possible down the opposite hall. He was disappointed but not surprised when he found no additional stairs. But he did stumble into a mostly intact room with a large window, and that was going to have to be enough.

Looking out the window, he discovered the room was at the front of the building. Prince Aldfrid was not far away, pacing frantically, while the soldiers tried to hold the horses, which were whinnying and trying to back away from the fire.

A huge *boom!* shook the building as another piece collapsed. Even over the thundering of the fire, Brute could hear the building creaking ominously. "Hey!" he yelled, and then coughed. "Hey!"

Aldfrid came sprinting closer.

"I'm going to have to hand him down to you. Can you catch him?"

"Yes! But hurry!" A resounding crash punctuated his words.

It was a hell of an awkward thing, and Brute wished more than ever that he still possessed two hands. He had to grip both of Lord Maudit's thin ankles in one fist and—hoping that the lord's legs weren't too badly injured already—dangle him upside down out the window. In the process, Brute leaned so far out and down that he was in danger of falling out himself. Fortunately, the window wasn't too high, and one of the soldiers, perhaps the brightest of the bunch, ran forward to help. The two men were able to catch Maudit and bear him to the ground in a sort of controlled fall. Then the prince took the lord's shoulders and the soldier his feet, and they carried him quickly away, out of range of the fire and the building itself.

Brute was just wondering whether he was ready to risk jumping to the ground when the fire gave a huge, triumphant bellow. The sound was so loud that Brute was deafened by it, and he didn't even hear the deep, sustained rumble as the entire inn collapsed around him.

THUMP thump thump. His heart felt like a hammer in his chest. He was dimly aware that there was pain—a lot of it—but it didn't seem to belong to him. It was very far away. He didn't feel frightened, not even of the fire that was tickling at his boots or of the blood that was pooling around him. Mostly, he was sad, and his tears tickled as they ran down his face. His life was a fair price, one he'd offered to the gods himself, so he couldn't complain. He just wished he could be certain that Gray would stay safe. "Gray," he sighed.

He imagined he felt hands knocking against his shoulders and then slipping under his armpits. He imagined he heard a familiar voice made thick with smoke: "Idiot."

He tried to find the breath to laugh. "You were wrong," he whispered weakly. "It's fire, not water."

"I lied," answered the imaginary voice, just before something gave Brute's body a tremendous tug, and then everything went black.

 # CHAPTER
Twenty-Five

HE RECOGNIZED the tingling warmth of a healer's touch, so he knew he must be alive, but there wasn't much solace in the realization. Assuredly, the entire past year must have been the product of a brain addled by a fall from a cliff. Everything—the adventure, the friends, the love—had been a wishful hallucination, and soon he would open his eyes and look up at Hilma Gedding's ceiling. And then he'd be nothing but an ugly, mutilated freak with nowhere to go.

So he kept his eyes closed for a very long time.

But then the healer began to sing, and the awareness slowly filtered into his mind that the song wasn't what he expected. "That's not a healing chant," he said, all rusty-voiced.

The response was full of good humor. "The lullaby's been working better. So has the Ballad of the Silver-Tongued Rogue. Want me to switch to that instead?"

"You're not Hilma Gedding."

"I most certainly hope not."

Brute finally pried his eyelids open. Gray Leynham was hunched over him, warm palms pressing lightly against Brute's bare chest and a smile playing at the corners of his mouth. Brute blinked a few times, but Gray didn't disappear. Bright relief rushed through him like the sun cutting through clouds—until he realized what must have happened and gloom settled back in. "Oh gods, they took you anyway!" He was suddenly furious—had Kashta lied about sanctuary, or had Prince Aldfrid violated it?

"I'm not taken, and you need to stay still," Gray answered calmly. His hands made little soothing motions, and Brute didn't know whether that was part of the healing or if Gray was just trying to calm him down.

"But you're— I don't...."

"I told you to stay still! You've used up every bit of my healing skill as it is, Aric. I don't want you to reinjure yourself."

With considerable effort, Brute relaxed. "I don't understand," he said, and he sounded pathetic even to his own ears.

"You ended up with a burning inn collapsed on your head, love. Even a giant can't walk away from that unscathed."

Nothing that Gray said after "love" registered. Brute felt a little loopy and a lot confused, and he was beginning to suspect that he really was delusional after all. But when he reached up to grab one of Gray's wrists, that certainly felt real. He could even feel the little ridge of scarring from the manacles Gray had worn for so long. He tried to focus his eyes on his surroundings. "Where is this?"

"The Vale of course. It's fortunate that the Vale is mostly downhill from the inn—I think the horse would have given up if he'd had to drag you uphill."

"Drag?"

"They made a litter for you. And one for Maud too. I wish I could have seen it. We must have looked like quite a parade."

Before Brute could formulate his next question—and really, he had so many he didn't know where to begin—Gray gently pulled his hand away and reached for a small pottery cup. He wormed an arm under Brute's head and raised it a little so he could drink. The tea was lukewarm but tasted bright and tangy, like berries, and it slaked the thirst Brute hadn't realized he had.

When the cup was empty, Gray set Brute's head gently back down on something soft. "How are you feeling?" he asked. "Are you in much pain?"

Brute did a quick self-inventory. He ached from head to toe— with his hips giving a particular twinge. His lungs felt scratchy, and he was weak. But there was nothing that he would call pain. "I'm all right. Did... you fix me up?"

"Turns out I'm a better healer than I thought, at least when someone I love is dying."

There was that word again, the word that made everything else fade in comparison. But then something else that Gray had said finally registered. "You said *we*. When you were talking about the parade from the inn to the Vale, you said *we*. You were at the inn?"

"He's the one who rescued you."

Brute startled to hear another voice—he hadn't noticed that anyone else was in the hut. But Kashta was standing off to one side in his old purple robes, gnawing on a green apple. He gave Brute a little wave. "I am very happy that you have survived," the priest said.

"Um, me too. But what did you mean about Gray rescuing me?" Even as he asked the question, Brute remembered hands seizing him and tugging him away. He turned to glare at Gray, who of course couldn't see, and said, "You lied about your dream!"

Gray didn't look the least bit repentant. "I thought I could keep you away from the pond in the Vale if I told you it was water. I should have known you'd be too big of an idiot to keep clear of your death." Now it was his turn to frown. "I underestimated your idiocy, though. You left me here! What in all hells did you think you were doing?"

"Paying the price," Brute mumbled, then sighed. "I thought that maybe if the king had *me* to punish they'd let you be."

"That was stupid, Aric."

"So was lying to me!" And as Brute's brain continued to slowly roll along, he seized on something else. "Why did you leave the Vale? You were safe here."

"But you weren't safe!" Gray snapped. "I woke up and you were gone and... and at first I thought you'd just abandoned me. But you wouldn't, would you? But there was the fucking dream so I knew where you'd gone. I made Kashta take me."

Kashta added, "We arrived just in time. The building had fallen, and Prince Aldfrid was shouting that you were inside. He and one of the soldiers had tried to find you, but there was too much smoke." He smiled slightly. "It took a man who is accustomed to navigating in darkness to find you."

Brute inhaled sharply and looked at Gray. "You went into the burning ruins?"

"You're not the only one who can be a damned hero!" Gray said angrily before jumping to his feet. "Dammit, Aric! Even Lorad and Lokad had their limits, and I don't want a lover who's a charred corpse or a damn statue. I may be a blind fool who's never done anything worthwhile, but can't you at least understand that I'd risk anything to save you? You're all I fucking want!" With an inarticulate growl, he stomped out of the hut. The fabric at the opening fell closed behind him.

The priest appeared unruffled by the interchange. He took another crunching bite of his apple, chewed, and swallowed. "He was terrified he would lose you. Do you know the story of how the Vale came to be?"

"Ismundo and Ebra."

"Very good," Kashta said, like a pleased schoolmaster. "They are gods who favor men and women who would sacrifice all for those whom they love. They led Gray to you, they gave him the strength to pull you out of that building, and they helped him to heal you." He nodded as if to himself. "Yes. I believe you two are very much favored."

"But why would Gray love me like that? I'm...." Brute flopped his arms a little, at a loss for words. "I'm just...."

"You are the man Gray loves, and you love him, and that is all that is important."

The priest bit his apple again and, still chewing, he left the hut.

WHEN Gray returned an hour or so later, he didn't say anything. He gave Brute a cup of water—Brute was able to drink by himself this time—and then lay next to him on the mat, their bodies resting gently against one another. "Idiot," Gray said quietly, fondly.

It was as good an endearment as any.

BY THE next day, Brute felt recovered enough to stand and even walk. When he wanted to use the latrine instead of a chamber pot, Gray insisted on accompanying him, with Brute's arm across his shoulders in case he should stumble.

"It's a sad day when a giant needs guidance from a blind man so he can take a piss," Gray said, but he didn't sound sad at all. In fact, there was a certain spring in his steps, a confidence Brute hadn't seen before.

"I could go by myself," Brute pointed out.

"Yes, but why, when you don't have to?"

Which was an excellent point. "Did you really heal me with lullabies?" Brute asked.

"I couldn't remember the damned chants very well. They were too long ago. But you used to sing those songs—back when you first came to the tower. They were like a balm on my soul. I thought maybe they'd help you too. And they did." He shook his head in wonder. "A few days ago I thought you were dead, and here you are, up and stomping about."

"I'm not stomping," Brute protested, at which point he finally realized that his feet were bare. "My boots! Where are my boots?"

"Ashes, or very nearly so. Your cloak too. If it wasn't for the fact that your high-quality clothing helped protect you, you'd be ashes too."

"Oh."

Brute managed to use the latrine without incident, but he wasn't ready yet to return to the hut. The warm sun felt good on his face, the air smelled sweet, and the ground was soft underfoot. With his arm around Gray's shoulders, they walked a slow circuit, pausing every now and then for Brute to admire the view of the tree-covered hills on either side of the Vale. But as they rounded the row of huts, Brute caught sight of a horse being tended by a man in scarlet and cream, and he sighed unhappily. "Lord Maudit."

"He's not well enough yet to ride, but Kashta tells me he will be soon. One of the other priests is a healer too."

Brute was pleased that the man had survived, but the subject raised other matters as well. "Are you going to be all right staying here in the Vale? It's better than that cell by far, but it's really just another prison."

"Aric, I'd live in a cave or a dungeon or… on the damned moon if it meant I could be with you. This place is fine. I can probably earn my way by helping with the healing—Kashta says a lot of the pilgrims who come here are ill or injured. And I bet they'll find some work for a giant to do."

"A one-handed giant."

"You've accomplished plenty with that one hand."

Brute had to smile because Gray was right. And it was a comforting thought, that they might stay in the Vale and remain safe and maybe even do some good. But still he worried. What if the king came after them anyway? He was the supreme authority, after all— couldn't he do things like that? Or what if Gray grew tired of living in such isolation, or the priests grew tired of extending their hospitality? Another voice whispered, too, that Brute would miss his friends at the palace.

But Brute didn't voice these concerns. Instead, he allowed Gray to take him back to their hut—and he silently admired how well Gray was getting around a new location without his sight—and then he was tired and had to lie down. But Gray lay down with him, and for the first time since Brute was injured, they made love. A little furtively, a little carefully due to Brute's continuing recovery, but tenderly and sweetly and very, very well.

 # CHAPTER
Twenty-Six

THE priests of the Vale of the Gods did not own a bath. But they had something even better: a natural hot spring feeding a stone pool large enough for several people to soak in comfort. It was tucked among some trees that provided a little privacy. It wasn't used for cleansing—in fact, Brute and Gray were instructed to wash themselves first. Kashta said the hot spring was intended for meditation and purification, but by the merry way his eyes sparkled and the way his mouth curled into a grin, Brute suspected that even the priests enjoyed the warm waters mostly for their wonderfully soothing effects.

By the time Brute and Gray emerged from the pool, pink-skinned and melty-muscled, Brute felt as if they'd finally soaked away the odor of smoke and burnt wood that had clung to them for nearly two weeks. Still a little damp, they laughingly struggled into their clothing and started back toward their hut. Gray had been spending a lot of time in the sun over the past days, and his pale skin had gained some color. His hair had lightened a shade or two, and if it hadn't made Brute feel ridiculous, he would have compared it to spun gold.

"Kashta said he was going to make that fruit soup again tonight," Brute said happily as they walked back along the springy grass.

"Really? I thought you depleted the supply of fruit after the gallons you downed last time."

"You did pretty well yourself, for a little man," replied Brute, poking at his lover's belly. Gray wasn't fat, not by any stretch of the imagination, but with good food and exercise, he'd filled out beautifully, and his muscles were sleek under his smooth skin.

"I am not little," protested Gray.

"Not where it counts, anyway," said Brute, earning himself a surprisingly well-aimed slap on the ass. Gods, as much as he loved seeing Gray able to move about freely and enjoy some of life's comforts, what truly made Brute's heart sing was seeing the other man's playfulness emerge. Gray's sleep was easy now—deep and untroubled—and he woke up smiling, ready to rouse Brute in all senses of the word. He teased and joked and made even the oldest priest laugh, and somehow managed to charm them all without making Brute feel clumsy or excluded. Brute fell a little bit more in love with him every day.

They found Kashta sitting on a felled log not far from the huts. He'd pulled his robes down to his waist, exposing his arms and torso, and was tilting his smiling face up to the sky. He looked back down and opened his eyes as the other men neared, and his face remained full of happiness. "You enjoyed your meditation?" he asked.

"I don't know how to meditate," Brute answered. "We just sat and soaked."

"Ah, but that is the best form of meditation: to live simply in the moment and enjoy it."

Gray flopped down on the grass with his back resting against Kashta's log. When Kashta didn't seem to mind, Brute joined them, lowering himself ungracefully next to Gray. His hips and legs still gave him an uncomfortable pull now and then. He hadn't mentioned it to Gray, but he was fairly certain his beloved knew anyway because he insisted on massaging Brute every night before they slept. Of course, it may have been simply the pleasant aftereffects of the massage that truly motivated Gray, because inevitably the therapeutic touching turned more intimate, until both of them were moaning their pleasure.

Gray interrupted Brute's agreeable reverie with a head-bump to the shoulder, then said to Kashta, "I thought meditation was supposed to be all about thinking how wonderful the gods are and how grateful we are to them."

Kashta was nearly imperturbable, even when Gray's comments became irreverent. Now, the priest only grinned. "There are many ways to meditate. One of them is enjoying the gifts the gods have given us.

That is why they give them, after all. Suppose you had a child and you gave her a doll. What would please you most—her rote appreciation or the hours she spent playing with it? The true thanks is the happiness of the recipient."

Gray nodded thoughtfully, which spurred Kashta to continue. Sometimes Brute thought that the priest would have made a very good schoolmaster, much more patient and pleasant to look at than Sighard. "We meditate when we enjoy the gifts of nature," Kashta said, "such as good food or pretty scenery or pools for soaking. And we meditate when we enjoy our own gifts. My colleague Parvel, for example, is a very fine woodworker. He keeps all the buildings and furniture in good repair, and he even carves pretty ornaments that we sell to pilgrims as souvenirs. It is how we pay for our food. When he is working, the delight is plain on his face, and that is meditation as well."

Brute thought he understood. "So Gray meditates when he heals, doesn't he?"

"Precisely."

"But what about me? I don't do anything well."

Gray poked him hard in the arm, and Kashta rolled his eyes. "You, my friend, carry a burden better than any man I have met."

Brute squinted at him. "But... I haven't hauled loads since I lost my hand."

"Not that sort of burden," the priest said, waving his hand dismissively. "Nearly anyone can carry a rock, although I imagine you carried bigger ones than most could manage. I mean the burden of caring. You care deeply for those around you. Even those who might do you harm." He gestured in the general direction of the hut where Lord Maudit still lay in recovery.

"Oh. But I don't *mean* to do things like that. I don't plan it."

"And Parvel didn't mean to be a woodworker. He just is. He told me once that when he was a very small child his parents would hide their knives from him because they were afraid he would hurt himself, but he was never content until he found those knives and began to whittle away."

Gray nodded in agreement. "Kashta's right. What you did for me... even in the very beginning, when I was filthy and couldn't speak and was probably scaring the hell out of you with those damned dreams... you were reminding me in all these tiny ways that I was human. You talked to me and gave me a quilt and...." He made a choked sound deep in his throat and ducked his head. But when he raised it a moment later he was smiling. He leaned his weight against Brute and sighed. "Mine."

This was a nice enough sentiment that for a long time the three of them sat silently, listening to birds warble and insects chirp, and a muted *thunk-thunk* that Brute realized was probably Parvel hacking away at a chunk of wood. But Kashta's words were still bumping around in Brute's skull, and eventually they bumped into a worry he'd been trying to ignore for days.

"Should I expect to lose something important soon?" he asked quietly.

Although he'd spoken to the priest, it was Gray who answered, voice sharpened with concern. "What do you mean?"

"I owe the gods a price. I thought... when I was buried under the inn, I thought my life was the price, and that was all right with me. I mean, I'd offered myself, and I couldn't really complain that they'd accepted. I was just sad that I'd never see you again, never know if you were really safe." It was his turn to have a thick throat, so he cleared it. "But I *didn't* die, of course, so now I'm wondering what the price will be."

Gray looked concerned and a little angry—he was sometimes impatient with the gods, for pretty good reason, Brute thought—but Kashta stood and then knelt on the grass in front of Brute. He took Brute's big, calloused hand in his own soft ones and squeezed. "You have paid, my friend."

"How have I paid? I'm alive, and I have Gray and a place to live, and... and I have everything. I haven't given the gods a thing."

"I told you. This place is sacred to Ebra and Ismundo. He used all his strength to heal her when she was wounded by demons, and she gave up her immortality to keep him with her as long as possible. You offered everything you had—even your life—for the benefit of the man you love. And because you gave freely and unselfishly out of love, the only price the gods will expect of you is that the two of you continue to cherish one another and care for each other. That is payment enough."

Kashta's words seemed too good to be true, but they sent a deep and abiding peace through Brute, all the way to his core. "Thank you," he said, and even he wasn't sure whether he was thanking the priest or the gods.

PILGRIMS arrived at the Vale almost daily, sometimes even several in one day. They usually gave Gray and Brute curious looks, but most were intent on their own concerns and quickly turned away. For their part, Gray and Brute stayed out of the pilgrims' way. They were content for the time being, just the two of them in their own little universe, with occasional visits from Kashta.

Usually, the pilgrims would arrive late in the day and be shown to one of the huts, where the priests would feed them and help them settle down. And in the mornings, the guests would eat again and then spend their time strolling the Vale or sitting on one of the strategically placed logs. Meditating, Brute supposed. Giving thanks to the gods or praying or simply satisfying themselves with having visited. A very few chose to drink from the pool, and the priests always tried to warn them away first. None of them looked happier or more relieved when they left the pool, which led Brute to wonder whether it was ever a good idea to bargain with the gods. It seemed to him that most people would be happier simply settling for whatever the gods chose to give them, and letting it go at that.

Whether they visited the pool or not, the visitors would spend a second night, and in the morning return to Racinas. Although the priests never asked for money, some of the pilgrims left copper or silver coins. Many of them bought Parvel's carvings of animals or people, which really were wonderfully detailed. And some left other gifts— food or clothing, cookware, baskets, even chickens or ducks. Whatever the priests couldn't use, they traded for food during their infrequent trips to the city.

A few weeks after Gray and Brute arrived, on a balmy evening in which the stars sparkled overhead like jewels, the two of them rested in front of their hut. Brute sat cross-legged with his back against the wall, and Gray lay with his head in Brute's lap, lazily telling a funny story about a crush he'd had on a neighbor girl when he was six or seven years old.

"She was a year or two older than me and the most terrible tyrant," he said with a soft laugh. "I think she only put up with me because I was willing to let her boss me around. Once she even convinced me to climb up on the rooftop with her and toss clods of dirt down at passersby. Then her mother caught sight of us, and she told *my* mother, and I had to do extra chores for a week."

Brute stroked Gray's cheek. "You were a difficult child, weren't you?"

"Impossible," Gray responded with a wide grin.

Brute was just going to suggest they go inside—and explore just how impossible Gray might be—when he spied a figure approaching them from the other huts. As the figure neared, he saw it was Kashta, and that he had something bulky tucked under an arm. "It looks as if you two are about ready to retire and do some meditation," he teased, waggling his eyebrows suggestively.

Brute was glad for the darkness when he blushed.

"Sex is meditation too?" asked Gray.

"Of course! Is it not another gift from the gods?"

"I guess so. My giant here, he's especially gifted."

Kashta laughed, and Brute's cheeks flamed.

"Well," the priest said, "before you get too… grateful, I have a gift to give you. This one is not from the gods."

"Oh?" Gray sat up. As soon as he did, Kashta dropped his burden in Brute's lap.

"Books!" exclaimed Brute. There were half a dozen of them, but he didn't have enough light to read the titles.

"The woman who left today gave them to us. We have a few weeks before we take them on our next journey to Racinas. I thought you might enjoy them in the meantime."

"Yes please!" Brute said with such enthusiasm that the two other men laughed.

"Very well. I shall leave you to your meditation. Good night."

One of the books was a guide for herbalists, which neither Gray nor Brute found especially interesting, although Brute thought the illustrations were pretty. Two of them were history books, one was a cookbook, and one contained philosophical musings on the origins of kindness and evil. Brute set these aside for later perusal. The one that captured the attention of both men was a first-hand account written a generation earlier by a man who had traveled to Freanas, the kingdom to the northwest. He claimed to have traveled even farther as well, although his descriptions of what he saw there were so fantastic and outlandish that both Gray and Brute wondered if the author had made it all up.

"It would be interesting to find out," Gray said a little longingly. "Whether it's true, I mean. Do you suppose there are truly places where magic doesn't work or lands are so dry that rain never falls?"

"Maybe. What about some of those creatures he described? Like the one that is like a lizard but long and without legs, or those tiny fish that strip the flesh off the largest animals."

Gray nodded pensively, and Brute squeezed his shoulder. "Do you wish we could go?" Brute asked. "Because we can if you want. I'd take you anywhere you wish."

"No. Not when the king could chase us. We're safe here."

"Do you really think he'd chase us past the kingdom's borders?"

"I don't know. I don't know, and I won't risk you. I won't make a fugitive of you."

Brute didn't want to be a fugitive either. Didn't want it for either of them. But he couldn't help but wonder how long their contentment would last.

BRUTE and Gray were finishing their lunch—fruit and grilled lamb—when they heard hoofbeats. Brute assumed more pilgrims were arriving, although most of them arrived on foot. He'd asked about that, and Kashta had explained that most people considered the journey itself to be part of the pilgrimage, so even wealthy visitors walked as a way of demonstrating their humility and devotion.

But when Brute and Gray left their hut—to wash the lunch dishes and then maybe take a walk—Brute recognized the new arrival by sight at the same time that Gray did by sound. They both froze. It was Gray who began walking again first, muttering under his breath, "Can't hide inside forever, can we?"

Prince Aldfrid had dismounted and was leading his horse to a tree with good grazing nearby, but he must have caught movement out of the corner of his eye. He turned and looked at Gray and Brute, and then waited for them to approach. Even as they got closer, Brute couldn't read the prince's expression. Kashta and the other priests were there, however, and they didn't look alarmed. Of course, in Brute's experience Kashta *never* looked alarmed.

"You're looking a damn sight better than when I saw you last," Aldfrid said to Brute. "I still can't believe you're not dead."

"Gray is a good healer."

"Apparently so."

A slightly awkward silence descended, but none of them failed to notice that Gray took hold of Brute's arm—not for guidance or comfort, but rather in a possessive sort of way, as if he was claiming his territory. Brute liked it. He was also pleased with the realization that the prince had come alone, which meant his entire party consisted of Lord Maudit, who was still confined to a hut, and the soldier who had been left at the Vale when Aldfrid and the others returned to Tellomer. Not much of a force if the prince intended to recapture the fugitives.

It was the prince who finally broke the silence. "I need to speak with Maud for a while. But when I'm done, I'd like to talk to the two of you, if I might."

"Fine," Gray responded. He spun around, somehow managing to drag Brute with him, and stomped away in the opposite direction.

"I won't let him take you," Brute announced when they were out of the prince's earshot.

"You don't have to keep saving me, you know."

"I do too."

Gray snorted. "Well, in case you haven't noticed, now I get to save you as well. And I won't let him take you either."

That settled, they went for their walk as originally planned. Spring had turned to early summer, so that the hillsides were a lush dark green, and bees and butterflies were everywhere. A hawk circled far overhead, reminding Brute that not all birds cowered in cages. Today the Vale didn't feel confining, but he wondered if they'd feel the same when winter fell, or when the following summer rolled around. Maybe the next time the priests went to Racinas he could give them some silver and ask them to bring more books. That might help.

Gray sang as they walked. His voice was much nicer than Brute's, clear and fine, without Brute's usual hoarseness or tendency to wander off key. Sometimes very late at night when they lay together, limp and sated, Gray would run his fingers through Brute's hair and softly hum lullabies. At those times Brute felt that his heart might burst from joy. But now Gray had chosen ribald tavern tunes. The two of them were on the way back to the hut—Gray was halfway through the song about the tinker and the mule—when he stopped abruptly and brought Brute's hand to his lips for a quick, dry kiss. "I can hear you worrying," he said. "Stop it. I think we'll be fine. Kashta says the gods favor us."

"But your eyes, and all those years in the cell... doesn't sound much to me like the gods favor you."

"But they brought you to me, didn't they?"

Whatever answer Brute may have given was stopped when Gray tugged him down for another kiss, this one lips against lips, tongue dancing with tongue. By the time they pulled apart, they were both panting a little and their faces were flushed. "Let's go," Gray purred suggestively.

An excellent idea, Brute thought. But then he looked up and saw a figure standing by their hut. "Prince Aldfrid's watching us."

"Let him." And to prove his point, he pulled at Brute's hair until Brute leaned down for another scorching kiss despite the audience.

Brute didn't have to lead Gray back. In fact, Gray walked slightly ahead, his chin up and his arms swinging comfortably. It was almost impossible to believe that this confident, handsome man was the same person who'd huddled in chains, mute and filthy, only a little over a year ago.

Prince Aldfrid nodded a greeting to them as they approached, then apparently realizing that Gray couldn't see, gave a soft hello.

Gray grunted a sort of reply.

"Will you sit with me now? I've brought wine from Racinas." The prince held up a bottle of red liquid. "It's the best. They bury it in a clay jar for six months and then age it for another eighteen months in an oak barrel."

With another grunt, Gray pushed past him and settled on a log that he and Brute had recently dragged in front of their hut. He grabbed Brute's hand and pulled him down next to him, which left the prince to shrug philosophically and sit on the slightly damp ground. "Have you glasses?" Aldfrid asked.

"This isn't the palace dining room, Friddy."

After a little struggle, the prince uncorked the bottle. He took a healthy swallow, humming with appreciation. Then he passed the bottle to Brute. The wine was sweet and strong and by far the best he'd ever tasted. He had a second mouthful before handing it to Gray. Gray sniffed it before he drank, and then he gave the bottle back to Aldfrid.

"How's Maud?" Gray asked.

"He's... getting better. He can walk a few steps. The priest says he'll grow stronger with exercise." Aldfrid sighed. "He'll always limp badly. But at least he's alive. Thanks to Brute."

"My giant saves everyone, doesn't he?"

"I suppose he does." The prince frowned. "Why haven't you tried to heal Maud? By the looks of it, you'd do a better job than the priest."

"Because just thinking about that little ass makes me seethe with anger. I couldn't possibly get in the right frame of mind for healing. I'd probably end up killing him if I tried."

Prince Aldfrid looked startled by those words. "He was your friend once."

"That was a very long time ago. He never lifted a finger to help me when I was in the Brown Tower. He was probably thrilled to have me out of the way so he could set his claws more firmly into you."

Gray reached out demandingly until he was handed the bottle again. He had a swig and then rolled the bottle in his palms.

"He didn't… it wasn't like that, Gray. He couldn't go up against my father's decree any better than I could, and it hurt him to see you…." He cleared his throat. "It hurt us both."

Gray frowned and didn't answer.

Prince Aldfrid looked as if he might grab the wine back but then seemed to change his mind. "It's my father I wanted to talk to you about, actually."

"The old bastard clamoring to have me dragged back?"

"He was." The prince scratched at his beard. "He was not at all happy that I returned without you."

"Sorry to disappoint," Gray said with a sneer, then handed the bottle to Brute.

Prince Aldfrid chewed at his lip for a moment and then sat up straighter. "I told him everything—about how you'd been mistreated for years, about how Brute had cared for you. I told him I gave Brute the key."

That last sentence must have surprised Gray. He made a sudden, explosive noise and tilted his head a bit. Brute was surprised as well, and tried to picture the king's reaction to hearing about the criminal exploits of an ugly giant. He decided he needed more wine and drank some, and then was startled to find the bottle nearly empty. He gave it to the prince, who finished it off and set it aside.

"I told him what happened in the woods," Aldfrid said. "How Brute saved Maud and then you saved Brute. How you've lost your gift of Sight. How… how you love each other, as deeply as my father loved my mother. And I told him that I would not be responsible for imprisoning either of you, and I'd stand in the way of anyone who tried."

"Did you, now?" Gray said, sounding more bemused than anything. "And how did His Majesty respond?"

The prince barked a short laugh. "Not well. He had a royal tantrum, actually, and for a while, I thought I'd be the next one locked up in the Brown Tower. But a few hours later he had me fetched back, and he was... a lot calmer. He said he was pleased I'd finally shown some courage. How'd he put it? 'Never thought until today you had balls, son.' I told him I'd been doubting it myself."

For the first time, Brute detected a bit of fondness in the way Gray regarded his former lover. As if to keep Brute from feeling jealous, Gray set a hand on Brute's knee and squeezed. But it was to the prince that he spoke, very softly, "I could have told you that you had it in you. You just never had a chance to notice it."

"No, I guess I didn't," Aldfrid answered with a wry smile. "I don't notice half of what goes on around me. Never have. Anyway, my father has had a change of heart. He issued a new decree, Gray. You've been pardoned. Brute as well. You're both free to leave the Vale and go wherever you wish, and you'll never be locked up again."

The news made Gray go so still that Brute wasn't sure he was breathing. For Brute, the words were like the sudden roar of a fire on a cold winter day, like thick stew in a starving belly, like a storm ending and being replaced with blinding sun.

"Where will we go?" Gray asked very quietly.

Aldfrid answered with a smile. "Anywhere. Stay here, move on. Come back to the palace if you want. We could always use a healer, and Brute's friends are missing him. We'd find you better accommodations this time."

Gray seemed to be considering the options, but to Brute, their destination wasn't important. They were both truly free, and they were together, and that was everything in the world.

Finally, Gray nodded. "We're going to have to think about this, my giant and I. We might want to travel the world. But there's one more thing you have to do."

"Oh?" Aldfrid said.

"Stop calling him Brute. His name is Aric."

Prince Aldfrid's smile grew. He rose gracefully to his feet and gave a deep bow. "My apologies. Aric, I would be very pleased if you would count me as a friend."

Due to the lump in his throat, Aric could only nod.

Gray stood as well and pulled Aric up with him. "Go visit with Maud, Friddy. He's probably half-crazy after weeks in that hut." He smiled wickedly. "Ask Kashta to have a talk with you about meditation."

And without even a nod to the puzzled prince, Gray dragged Aric into the hut and tugged the fabric door closed. Unfastening Aric's shirt, Gray whispered, "Lie down with me, my love, and let's celebrate our freedom. And then"—his face positively glowed with wonder—"we have our lives to plan."

ACKNOWLEDGMENTS

THIS story is one of those that has been churning around in my head for a long time. I'd like to thank some of the people who helped me get it out of my head and into your hands.

I am grateful to my friends Sheree Adams, Jan M. Mike, and Ginny Palmieri for reading drafts of this novel and for reassuring me that other people might love Brute too. Their feedback helped make this a better story. My deepest thanks to Karen Witzke, who polished off the rough edges and made Brute shine. And, as always, my thanks to Dennis, Allison, and Quinn—my cheerleaders, my support staff, and the lights of my life.

KIM FIELDING is very pleased every time someone calls her eclectic. She has migrated back and forth across the western two-thirds of the United States and currently lives in California, where she long ago ran out of bookshelf space. She's a university professor who dreams of being able to travel and write full-time. She also dreams of having two perfectly behaved children, a husband who isn't obsessed with football, and a house that cleans itself. Some dreams are more easily obtained than others.

Kim can be found on her blogs:
http://kfieldingwrites.blogspot.com/
http://www.goodreads.com/author/show/4105707.Kim_Fielding/blog
and on Facebook:
http://www.facebook.com/#!/pages/Kim-Fielding/286938444652579
Her e-mail is dephalqu@yahoo.com.

Also from KIM FIELDING

SPEECHLESS

KIM FIELDING

Also from KIM FIELDING

GOOD
BONES

KIM FIELDING

http://www.dreamspinnerpress.com

Read more from KIM FIELDING in

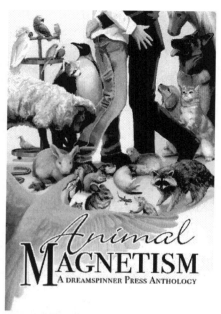

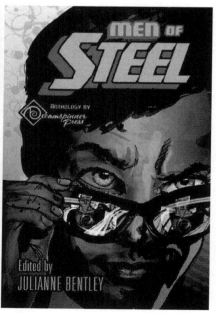

Printed in Great Britain
by Amazon

36104455R00150